About USA Inc.

Created and Compiled by Mar

February 2011

This report looks at the federal government as if it were a business, with the goal of informing the debate about our nation's financial situation and outlook. In it, we examine USA Inc.'s income statement and balance sheet. We aim to interpret the underlying data and facts and illustrate patterns and trends in easy-to-understand ways. We analyze the drivers of federal revenue and the history of expense growth, and we examine basic scenarios for how America might move toward positive cash flow.

Thanks go out to Liang Wu and Fred Miller and former Morgan Stanley colleagues whose contributions to this report were invaluable. In addition, Richard Ravitch, Emil Henry, Laura Tyson, Al Gore, Meg Whitman, John Cogan, Peter Orszag and Chris Liddell provided inspiration and insights as the report developed. It includes a 2-page foreword; a 12-page text summary; and 460 PowerPoint slides containing data-rich observations. There's a lot of material – think of it as a book that happens to be a slide presentation.

We hope the slides in particular provide relevant context for the debate about America's financials. To kick-start the dialogue, we are making the entire slide portion of the report available as a single work for non-commercial distribution (but not for excerpting, or modifying or creating derivatives) under the Creative Commons license. The spirit of connectivity and sharing has become the essence of the Internet, and we encourage interested parties to use the slides to advance the discussion of America's financial present and future. If you would like to add your own data-driven observations, contribute your insights, improve or clarify ours, please contact us to request permission and provide your suggestions. This document is only a starting point for discussion; the information in it will benefit greatly from your thoughtful input.

This report is available online and on iPad at www.kpcb.com/usainc

In addition, print copies are available at www.amazon.com

Foreword

George P. Shultz, Paul Volcker, Michael Bloomberg, Richard Ravitch and John Doerr

February 2011

Our country is in deep financial trouble. Federal, state and local governments are deep in debt yet continue to spend beyond their means, seemingly unable to stop. Our current path is simply unsustainable. What to do?

A lot of people have offered suggestions and proposed solutions. Few follow the four key guideposts to success that we see for setting our country back on the right path:

1) create a deep and widely held perception of the reality of the problem and the stakes involved;

2) reassure citizens that there are practical solutions;

3) develop support in key constituencies; and

4) determine the right timing to deliver the solutions.

USA Inc. uses each of these guideposts, and more; it is full of ideas that can help us build a better future for our children and our country.

First, Mary Meeker and her co-contributors describe America's problems in an imaginative way that should allow anyone to grasp them both intellectually and emotionally. By imagining the federal government as a company, they provide a simple framework for understanding our current situation. They show how deficits are piling up on our income statement as spending outstrips income and how our liabilities far exceed nominal assets on our balance sheet. *USA Inc.* also considers additional assets – hard to value physical assets and our intangible wealth – our creativity and energy and our tradition of an open, competitive society.

Additionally, the report considers important trends, pointing specifically to an intolerable failure to educate many in the K-12 grades, despite our knowledge of how to do so. And all these important emotional arguments help drive a gut reaction to add to data provided to reinforce the intellectual reasons we already have.

Second, *USA Inc.* provides a productive way to think about solving our challenges. Once we have created an emotional and intellectual connection to the problem, we want people to act and drive the solution, not to throw up their hands in frustration. The authors' ingenious indirect approach is to ask what a turnaround expert would do and what questions he or she would ask. The report describes how we first stumbled into this mess, by failing to predict the magnitude of program costs, by creating perverse incentives for excessive behavior, and by missing important trends. By pointing to the impact of individual responsibility, *USA Inc.* gives us reason to believe that a practical solution exists and can be realized.

Third, the report highlights how powerful bipartisan constituencies have emerged in the past to tackle great issues for the betterment of our nation, including tax reform, civil liberties, healthcare, education and national defense. Just as presidents of both parties rose to the occasion to preside over the difficult process of containment during the half-century cold war, we know we can still find leaders who are willing to step up and overcome political or philosophical differences for a good cause, even in these difficult times.

Finally, the report makes an important contribution to the question of timing. Momentum will follow once the process begins to gain support, and *USA Inc.* should help by stimulating broad recognition and understanding of the challenges, by providing ways to think about solutions, and by helping constituencies of action to emerge. As the old saying goes, "If not now, when? If not us, who?"

With this pioneering report, we have a refreshing, business-minded approach to understanding and addressing our nation's future. Read on…you may be surprised by how much you learn. We hope you will be motivated to help solve the problem!

Imagine for a moment that the United States government is a public corporation. Imagine that its management structure, fiscal performance, and budget are all up for review. Now imagine that you're a shareholder in USA Inc. How do you feel about your investment?

Because 45% of us own shares in publicly traded companies, nearly half the country expects quarterly updates on our investments. But although **100%** of us are stakeholders in the United States, very few of us look closely at Washington's financials. If we were long-term investors, how would we evaluate the federal government's business model, strategic plans, and operating efficiency? How would we react to its earnings reports? Nearly two-thirds of all American households pay federal income taxes, but very few of us take the time to dig into the numbers of the entity that, on average, collects 13% of our annual gross income (not counting another 15-30% for payroll and various state and local taxes).

We believe it's especially important to pay closer attention to one of our most important investments.

As American citizens and taxpayers, we care about the future of our country. As investors, we're in an on-going search for data and insights that will help us make more informed investment decisions. It's easier to predict the future if one has a keen understanding of the past, but we found ourselves struggling to find good information about America's financials. So we decided to assemble – in one place and in a user-friendly format – some of the best data about the world's biggest "business." We also provide some historical context for how USA Inc.'s financial model has evolved over decades. And, as investors, we look at trend lines which help us understand the patterns (and often future directions) of key financial drivers like revenue and expenses.

The complexity of USA Inc.'s challenges is well known, and our presentation is just a starting point; it's far from perfect or complete. But we are convinced that citizens – and investors – should understand the business of their government. Thomas Jefferson and Alexis de Tocqueville knew that – armed with the right information – the enlightened citizenry of America would make the right decisions. It is our humble hope that a transparent financial framework can help inform future debates.

In the conviction that every citizen should understand the finances of USA Inc. and the plans of its "management team," we examine USA Inc.'s income statement and balance sheet and present them in a basic, easy-to-use format. We summarize our thoughts in PowerPoint form and in this brief text summary at www.kpcb.com/usainc. We encourage people to take our data and thoughts and study them, critique them, augment them, share them, and make them better. There's a lot of material – think of it as a book that happens to be a slide presentation.

There are two caveats. First, we do not make policy recommendations. We try to help clarify some of the issues in a straightforward, analytical way. We aim to present data, trends, and facts about USA Inc.'s key revenue and expense drivers to provide context for how its financials have reached their present state. Our observations come from publicly available information, and we use the tools of basic financial analysis to interpret it. Forecasts generally come from 3rd-party agencies like the Congressional Budget Office (CBO), the nonpartisan federal agency charged with reviewing the financial impact of legislation. Second, the 'devil is in the details.' For US policy makers, the timing of material changes will be especially difficult, given the current economic environment.

By the standards of any public corporation, USA Inc.'s financials are discouraging.

True, USA Inc. has many fundamental strengths. On an operating basis (excluding Medicare and Medicaid spending and one-time charges), the federal government's profit & loss statement is solid, with a 4% median net margin over the last 15 years. But cash flow is deep in the red (by almost $1.3 trillion last year, or -$11,000 per household), and USA Inc.'s net worth is negative and deteriorating. That net worth figure includes the present value of unfunded entitlement liabilities but not hard-to-value assets such as natural resources, the power to tax or mint currency, or what Treasury calls "heritage" or "stewardship assets" like national parks. Nevertheless, the trends are clear, and critical warning signs are evident in nearly every data point we examine.

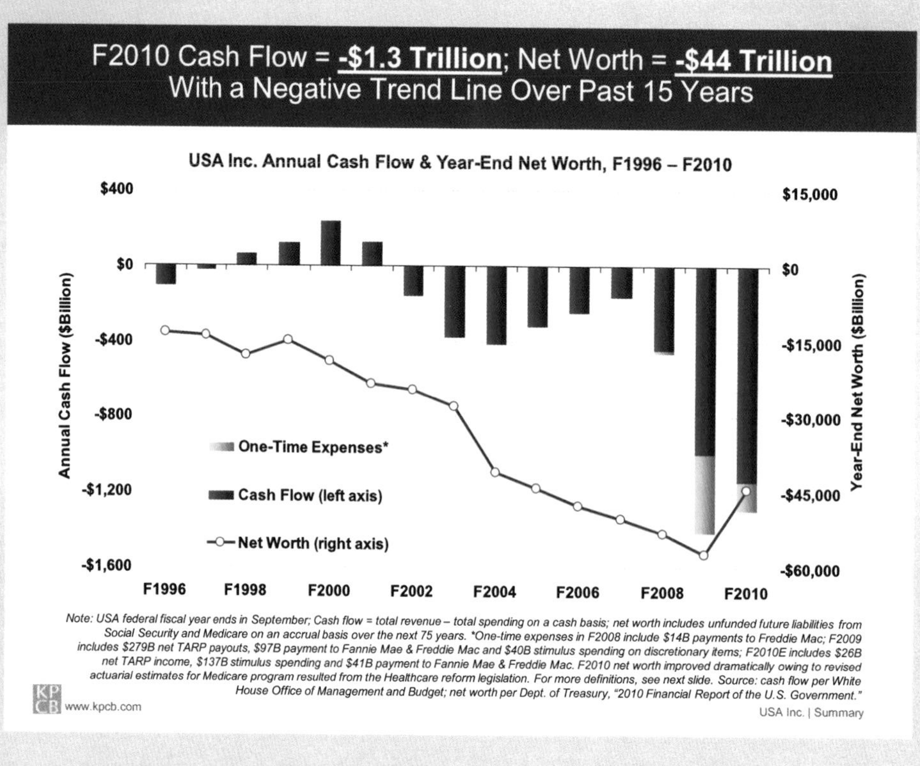

Underfunded entitlements are among the most severe financial burdens USA Inc. faces. And because some of the most underfunded programs are intended to help the nation's poorest, the electorate must understand the full dimensions of the challenges.

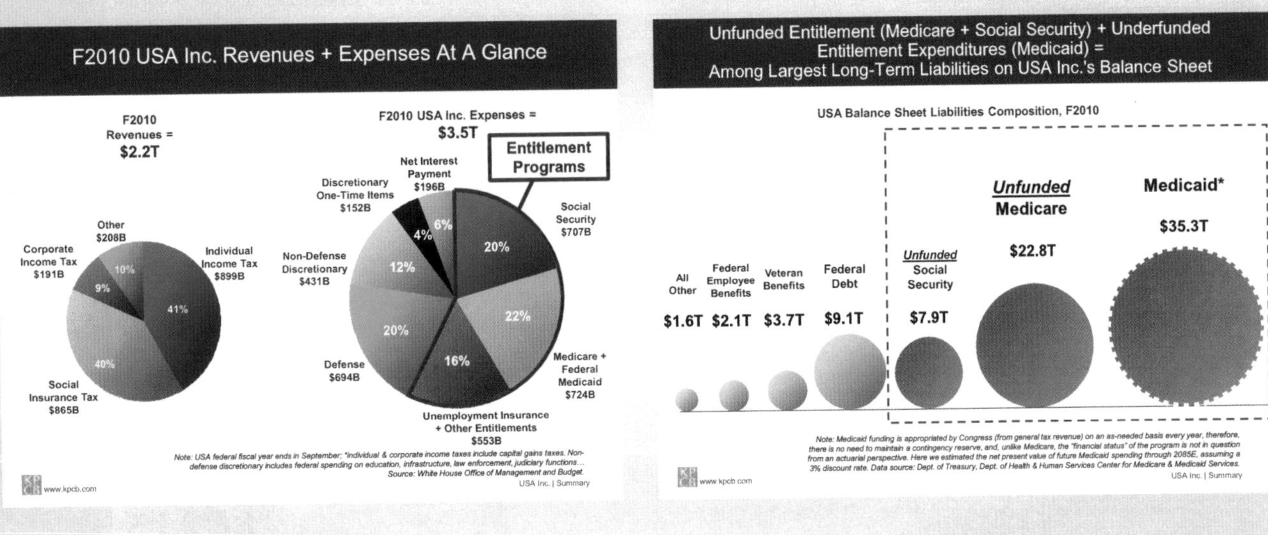

Some consider defense outlays – which have nearly doubled in the last decade, to 5% of GDP – a principal cause of USA Inc.'s financial dilemma. But defense spending is still below its 7% share of GDP from 1948 to 2000; it accounted for 20% of the budget in 2010, compared with 41% of all government spending between 1789 and 1930. The principal challenges lie elsewhere. Since the Great Depression, USA Inc. has steadily added "business lines" and, with the best of intentions, created various entitlement programs. They serve many of the nation's poorest, whose struggles have been made worse by the recent financial crisis. Apart from Social Security and unemployment insurance, however, funding for these programs has been woefully inadequate – and getting worse.

Entitlement expenses amount to $16,000 per household per year, and entitlement spending far outstrips funding, by more than $1 trillion (or $9,000 per household) in 2010. More than 35% of the US population receives entitlement dollars or is on the government payroll, up from ~20% in 1966. Given the high correlation of rising entitlement income with declining savings, do Americans feel less compelled to save if they depend on the government for their future savings? It is interesting to note that in China the household savings rate is ~36%, per our estimates based on CEIC data, in part due to a higher degree of self-reliance – and far fewer established pension plans. In the USA, the personal savings rate (defined as savings as percent of disposable income) was 6% in 2010 and only 3% from 2000 to 2008.

Millions of Americans have come to rely on Medicare and Medicaid – and spending has skyrocketed, to 21% of USA Inc.'s total expenses (or $724B) in F2010, up from 5% forty years ago.

Together, Medicaid and Medicare – the programs providing health insurance to low-income households and the elderly, respectively – now account for 35% of total healthcare spending in the USA. Since their creation in 1965, both programs have expanded markedly. Medicaid now serves 16% of all Americans, compared with 2% at its inception; Medicare now serves 15% of the population, up from 10% in 1966. As more Americans receive benefits and as healthcare costs continue to outstrip GDP growth, total spending for the two entitlement programs is accelerating. Over the last decade alone, Medicaid spending has doubled in real terms, with total program costs running at $273 billion in F2010. Over the last 43 years, real Medicare spending per beneficiary has risen 25 times, driving program costs well (10x) above original projections. In fact, Medicare spending exceeded related revenues by $272 billion last year.

Amid the rancor about government's role in healthcare spending, one fact is undeniable: government spending on healthcare now consumes 8.2% of GDP, compared with just 1.3% fifty years ago.

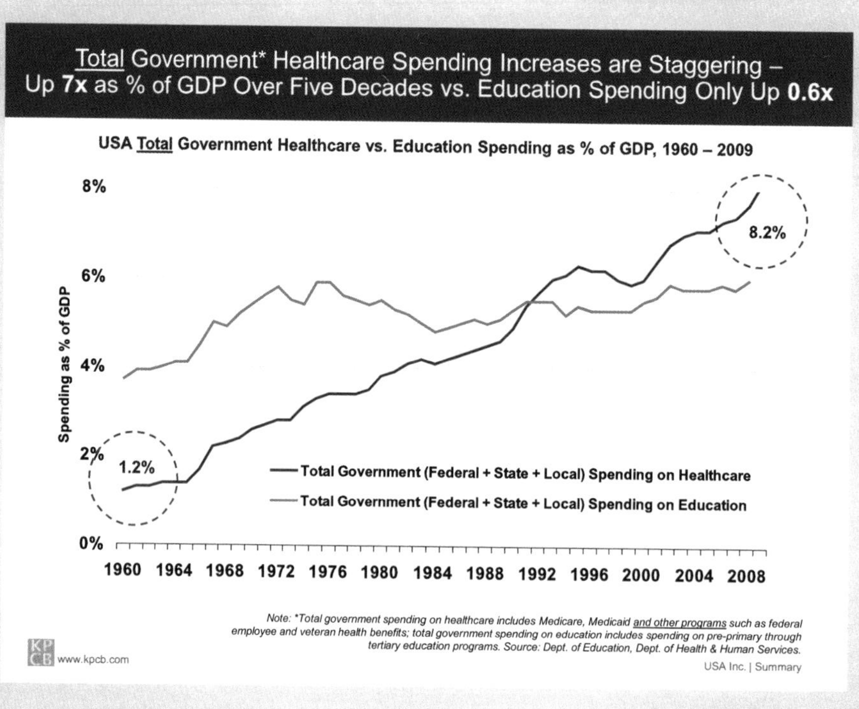

The overall healthcare funding mix in the US is skewed toward private health insurance due to the predominance of employer-sponsored funding (which covers 157MM working Americans and their families, or 58% of the total population in 2008 vs. 64% in 1999). This mixed private-public funding scheme has resulted in implicit cross-subsidies, whereby healthcare providers push costs onto the private market to help subsidize lower payments from public programs. This tends to help drive a cycle of higher private market costs causing higher insurance premiums, leading to the slow erosion of private market coverage and a greater enrollment burden for government programs.

The Patient Protection and Affordable Care Act, enacted in early 2010, includes the biggest changes to healthcare since 1965 and will eventually expand health insurance coverage by ~10%, to 32 million new lives. Increased access likely means higher spending if healthcare costs continue to grow 2 percentage points faster than per capita income (as they have over the past 40 years). The CBO sees a potential $143B reduction in the deficit over the next 10 years, but this assumes that growth in Medicare costs will slow – an assumption the CBO admits is highly uncertain.

Unemployment Insurance and Social Security are adequately funded...for now. Their future, unfortunately, isn't so clear.

Unemployment Insurance is cyclical and, apart from the 2007-09 recession, generally operates with a surplus. Payroll taxes kept Social Security mainly at break-even until 1975-81 when expenses began to exceed revenue. Reforms that cut average benefits by 5%, raised tax rates by 2.3%, and increased the full retirement age by 3% (to 67) restored the system's stability for the next 25 years, but the demographic outlook is poor for its pay-as-you-go funding structure. In 1950, 100 workers supported six beneficiaries; today, 100 workers support 33 beneficiaries. Since Social Security began in 1935, American life expectancy has risen 26% (to 78), but the "retirement age" for full benefits has increased only 3%.

Regardless of the emotional debate about entitlements, fiscal reality can't be ignored – if these programs aren't reformed, one way or another, USA Inc.'s balance sheet will go from bad to worse.

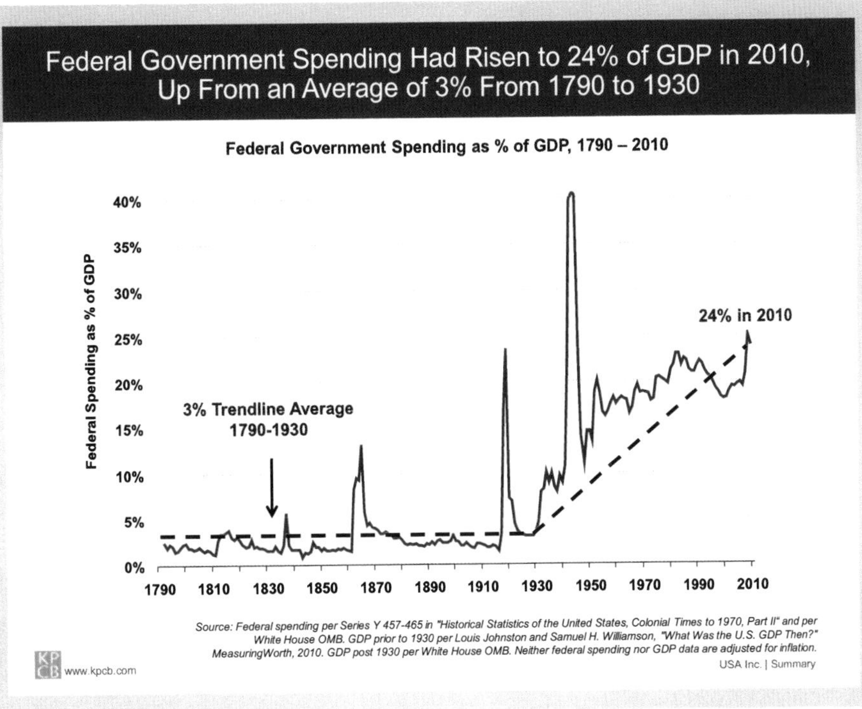

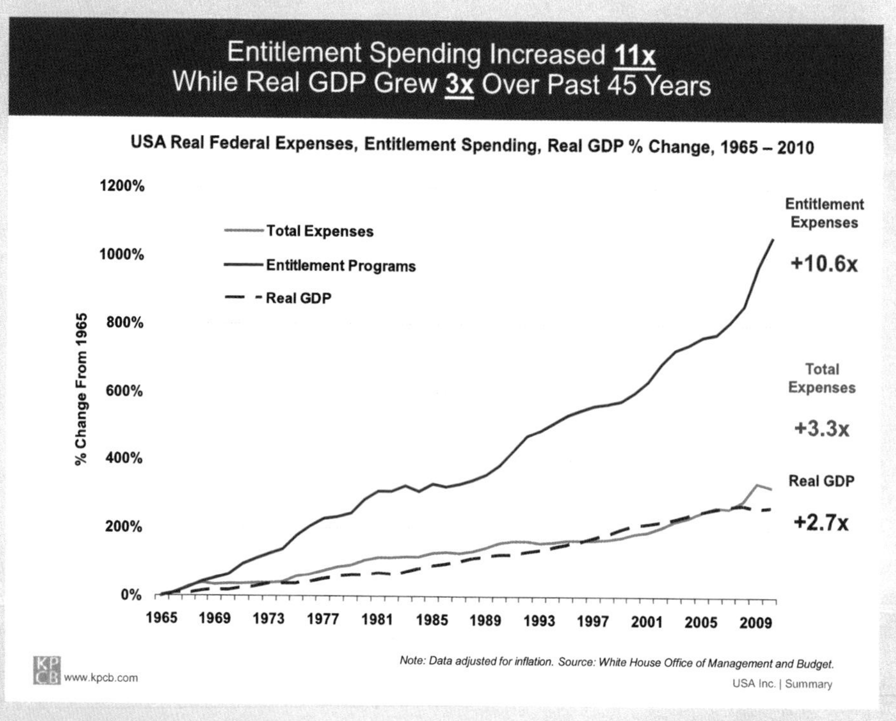

Take a step back, and imagine what the founding fathers would think if they saw how our country's finances have changed. From 1790 to 1930, government spending on average accounted for just 3% of American GDP. Today, government spending absorbs closer to 24% of GDP.

It's likely that they would be even more surprised by the debt we have taken on to pay for this expansion. As a percentage of GDP, the federal government's public debt has doubled over the last 30 years, to 53% of GDP. This figure does not include claims on future resources from underfunded entitlements and potential liabilities from Fannie Mae and Freddie Mac, the Government Sponsored Enterprises (GSEs). If it did include these claims, gross federal debt accounted for 94% of GDP in 2010. The public debt to GDP ratio is likely to triple to 146% over the next 20 years, per CBO. The main reason is entitlement expense. Since 1970, these costs have grown 5.5 times faster than GDP, while revenues have lagged, especially corporate tax revenues. By 2037, cumulative deficits from Social Security could add another $11.6 trillion to the public debt.

The problem gets worse. Even as USA Inc.'s debt has been rising for decades, plunging interest rates have kept the cost of supporting it relatively steady. Last year's interest bill would have been 155% (or $290 billion) higher if rates had been at their 30-year average of 6% (vs. 2% in 2010). As debt levels rise and interest rates normalize, net interest payments could grow 20% or more annually. Below-average debt maturities in recent years have also kept the Treasury's borrowing costs down, but this trend, too, will drive up interest payments once interest rates rise.

Can we afford to wait until the turning point comes? By 2025, entitlements plus net interest payments will absorb all – yes, all – of USA Inc.'s revenue, per CBO.

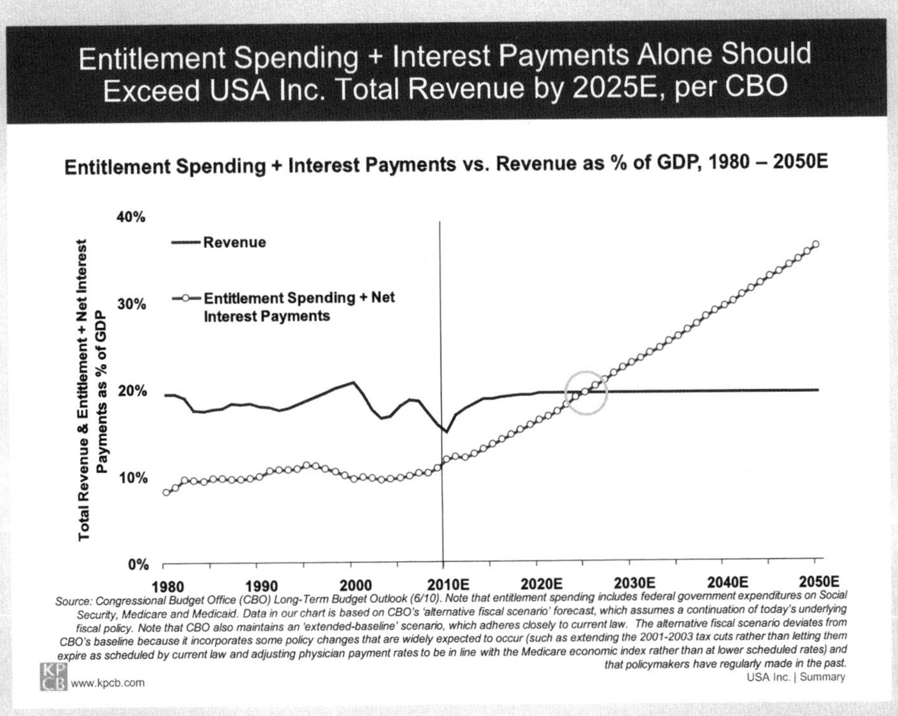

Entitlement Spending + Interest Payments Alone Should Exceed USA Inc. Total Revenue by 2025E, per CBO
Entitlement Spending + Interest Payments vs. Revenue as % of GDP, 1980 – 2050E
Total Revenue & Entitlement + Net Interest Payments as % of GDP
40%
30%
20%
10%
0%
Revenue
Entitlement Spending + Net Interest Payments
1980
1990
2000
2010E
2020E
2030E
2040E
2050E
Source: Congressional Budget Office (CBO) Long-Term Budget Outlook (6/10). Note that entitlement spending includes federal government expenditures on Social Security, Medicare and Medicaid. Data in our chart is based on CBO's 'alternative fiscal scenario' forecast, which assumes a continuation of today's underlying fiscal policy. Note that CBO also maintains an 'extended-baseline' scenario, which adheres closely to current law. The alternative fiscal scenario deviates from CBO's baseline because it incorporates some policy changes that are widely expected to occur (such as extending the 2001-2003 tax cuts rather than letting them expire as scheduled by current law and adjusting physician payment rates to be in line with the Medicare economic index rather than at lower scheduled rates) and that policymakers have regularly made in the past.
KP CB www.kpcb.com
USA Inc. | Summary

Less than 15 years from now, in other words, USA Inc. – based on current forecasts for revenue and expenses - would have nothing left over to spend on defense, education, infrastructure, and R&D, which today account for only 32% of USA Inc. spending, down from 69% forty years ago. This critical juncture is getting ever closer. Just ten years ago, the CBO thought federal revenue would support entitlement spending and interest payments until 2060 – 35 years beyond its current projection. This dramatic forecast change over the past ten years helps illustrate, in our view, how important it is to focus on the here-and-now trend lines and take actions based on those trends.

How would a turnaround expert determine 'normal' revenue and expenses?

The first step would be to examine the main drivers of revenue and expenses. It's not a pretty picture. While revenue – mainly taxes on individual and corporate income – is highly correlated (83%) with GDP growth, expenses – mostly entitlement spending – are less correlated (73%) with GDP. With that as backdrop, our turnaround expert might try to help management and shareholders (citizens) achieve a long-term balance by determining "normal" levels of revenue and expenses:

- From 1965 to 2005 (a period chosen to exclude abnormal trends related to the recent recession), annual revenue growth (3%) has been roughly in line with GDP growth, but corporate income taxes have grown 2% a year. Social insurance taxes grew 5% annually and represented 37% of USA Inc. revenue, compared with 19% in 1965. An expert might ask:
    - What level of social insurance or entitlement taxes can USA Inc. support without reducing job creation?
    - Are low corporate income taxes important to global competitive advantage and stimulating growth?
- Entitlement spending has risen 5% a year on average since 1965, well above average annual GDP growth of 3%, and now absorbs 51% of all expenses, more than twice its share in 1965. Defense and non-defense discretionary spending (including infrastructure, education, and law enforcement) is up just 1-2% annually over that period. Questions for shareholders:
    - Do USA Inc.'s operations run at maximum efficiency? Where are the opportunities for cost savings?
    - Should all expense categories be benchmarked against GDP growth? Should some grow faster or slower than GDP? If so, what are the key determinants?
    - Would greater investment in infrastructure, education, and global competitiveness yield more long-term security for the elderly and disadvantaged?

With expenses outstripping revenues by a large (and growing) margin, a turnaround expert would develop an analytical framework for readjusting USA Inc.'s business model and strategic plans. Prudence would dictate that our expert assume below-trend GDP growth and above-trend unemployment, plus rising interest rates – all of which would make the base case operating scenario fairly gloomy.

This analysis can't ignore our dependence on entitlements. Almost one-third of all Americans have grown up in an environment of lean savings and heavy reliance on government healthcare subsidies. It's not just a question of numbers – it's a question of our responsibilities as citizens...and what kind of society we want to be.

Some 90 million Americans (out of a total population of 307 million) have grown accustomed to support from entitlement programs; so, too, have 14 million workers in the healthcare industry who, directly or indirectly, benefit from government subsidies via Medicare and Medicaid. Low personal savings and high unemployment make radical change difficult. Political will can be difficult to summon, especially during election campaigns.

At the same time, however, these numbers don't lie. With our demographics and our debts, we're on a collision course with the future. The good news: Although time is growing short, we still have the capacity to create positive outcomes.

Even though USA Inc. can print money and raise taxes, USA Inc. cannot sustain its financial imbalance indefinitely – especially as the Baby Boomer generation nears retirement age. Net debt levels are approaching warning levels, and some polls suggest that Americans consider reducing debt a national priority. Change is legally possible. Unlike underfunded pension liabilities that can bankrupt companies, USA Inc.'s underfunded liabilities are not legal contracts. Congress has the authority to change the level and conditions for Social Security and Medicare benefits; the federal government, together with the states, can also alter eligibility and benefit levels for Medicaid.

Options for entitlement reform, operating efficiency, and stronger long-term GDP growth.

As analysts, not public policy experts, we can offer mathematical illustrations as a framework for discussion (not necessarily as actual solutions). We also present policy options from third-party organizations such as the CBO.

Reforming entitlement programs – Social Security.

The underfunding could be addressed through some or all of the following mechanical changes: increasing the full retirement age to as high as 73 (from the current level of 67); and/or reducing average annual social security benefits by up to 12% (from $13,010 to $11,489); and/or increasing the social security tax rate from 12.4% to 14.2%. Options proposed by the CBO include similar measures, as well as adjustments to initial benefits and index levels. Of course, the low personal savings rates of average Americans – 3% of disposable income, compared with a 10% average from 1965 to 1985 – limit flexibility, at least in the early years of any reform.

Reforming entitlement programs – Medicare and Medicaid.

Mathematical illustrations for these programs, the most underfunded, seem draconian: Reducing average Medicare benefits by 53%, to $5,588 per year, or increasing the Medicare tax rate by 3.9 percentage points, to 6.8%, or some combination of these changes would address the underfunding of Medicare. As for Medicaid, the lack of a dedicated funding stream (i.e., a tax similar to the Medicare payroll tax) makes the math even more difficult. But by one measure from the Kaiser Family Foundation, 60% of the Medicaid budget in 2001 was spent on so-called optional recipients (such as mid- to low-income population above poverty level) or on optional services (such as dental services and prescription drug benefits). Reducing or controlling these benefits could help control Medicaid spending – but increase the burden on some poor and disabled groups.

Ultimately, the primary issue facing the US healthcare system is ever-rising costs, historically driven by increases in price and utilization. Beneath sustained medical cost inflation is an entitlement mentality bolted onto a volume-based reimbursement scheme. All else being equal, the outcome is an incentive to spend: Underlying societal, financial, and liability factors combine to fuel an inefficient, expensive healthcare system.

Improving operating efficiency.

With nearly one government civilian worker (federal, state and local) for every six households, efficiency gains seem possible. A 20-year trend line of declining federal civilian headcount was reversed in the late 1990s.

Resuming that trend would imply a 15% potential headcount reduction over five years and save nearly $300 billion over the next ten years. USA Inc. could also focus intensively on local private company outsourcing, where state and local governments are finding real productivity gains.

Improving long-term GDP growth – productivity and employment.

Fundamentally, federal revenues depend on GDP growth and related tax levies on consumers and businesses. Higher GDP growth won't be easy to achieve as households rebuild savings in the aftermath of a recession. To break even without changing expense levels or tax policies, USA Inc. would need real GDP growth of 6-7% in F2012-14 and 4-5% in F2015-20, according to our estimates based on CBO data – highly unlikely, given 40-year average GDP growth of 3%. While USA Inc. could temporarily increase government spending and investment to make up for lower private demand in the near term, the country needs policies that foster productivity and employment gains for sustainable long-term economic growth.

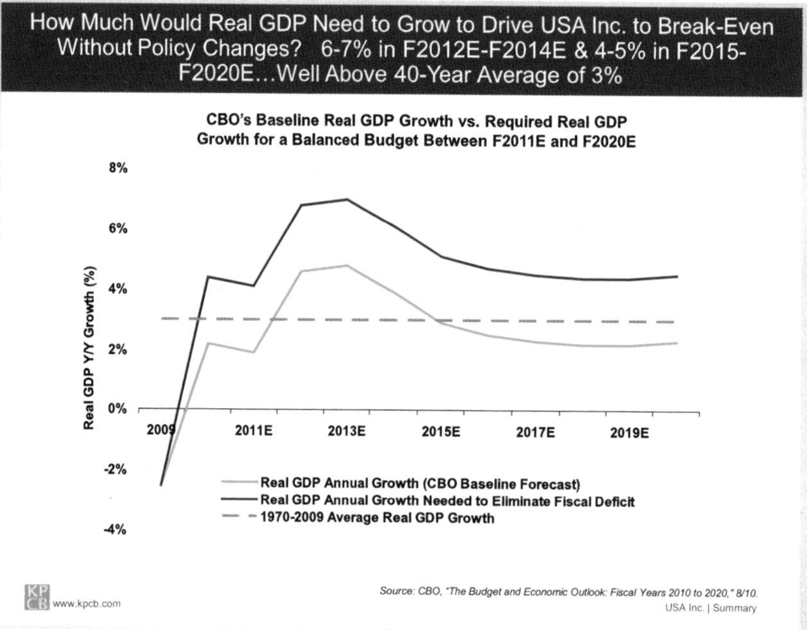

Productivity gains and increased employment each contributed roughly half of the long-term GDP growth between 1970 and 2009, per the National Bureau of Economic Research. Since the 1960s, as more resources have gone to entitlements and interest payments, USA Inc. has scaled back its investment in technology R&D and infrastructure as percentages of GDP. Competitors are making these investments. India plans to double infrastructure spending as a percent of GDP by 2013, and its tertiary (college) educated population will double over the next ten years, according to Morgan Stanley analysts, enabling its GDP growth to accelerate to 9-10% annually by 2015 (China's annual GDP growth is forecast to remain near 8% by 2015). USA Inc. can't match India's demographic advantage, but technology can help.

For employment gains, USA Inc. should minimize tax and regulatory uncertainties and encourage businesses to add workers. While hiring and R&D-related tax credits may add to near-term deficits, over time, they should drive job and GDP growth. Immigration reform could also help: A Federal Reserve study in 2010 shows that immigration does not take jobs from U.S.-born workers but boosts productivity and income per worker.

Changing tax policies.

Using another simple mechanical illustration, covering the 2010 budget deficit (excluding one-time charges) by taxes alone would mean doubling individual income tax rates across the board, to roughly 26-30% of gross income, we estimate. Such major tax increases would ultimately be self-defeating if they reduce private income and consumption. However, reducing tax expenditures and subsidies such as mortgage interest deductions would broaden the tax base and net up to $1.7 trillion in additional revenue over the next decade, per CBO. A tax based on consumption - like a value added tax (VAT) - could also redirect the economy toward savings and investment, though there would be drawbacks.

These issues are undoubtedly complex, and difficult decisions must be made. But inaction may be the greatest risk of all. The time to act is now, and our first responsibility as investors in USA Inc. is to understand the task at hand.

Our review finds serious challenges in USA Inc.'s financials. The 'management team' has created incentives to spend on healthcare, housing, and current consumption. At the margin, investing in productive capital, education, and technology – the very tools needed to compete in the global marketplace – has stagnated.

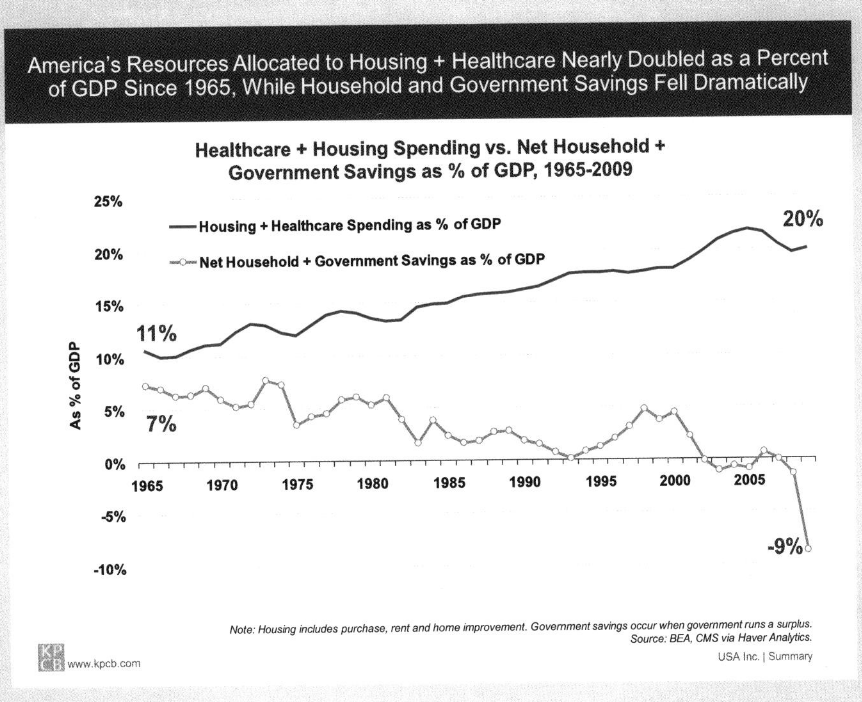

With these trends, USA Inc. will not be immune to the sudden crises that have afflicted others with similar unfunded liabilities, leverage, and productivity trends. The sovereign credit issues in Europe suggest what might lie ahead for USA Inc. shareholders – and our children. In effect, USA Inc. is maxing out its credit card. It has fallen into a pattern of spending more than it earns and is issuing debt at nearly every turn. Common principles for overcoming this kind of burden include the following:

1) *Acknowledge the problem* – some 80% of Americans believe 'dealing with our growing budget deficit and national debt' is a national priority, according to a Peter G. Peterson Foundation survey in 11/09;

2) *Examine past errors* – People need clear descriptions and analysis to understand how the US arrived at its current financial condition – a 'turnaround CEO' would certainly initiate a 'no holds barred' analysis of the purpose, success and operating efficiency of all of USA Inc.'s spending;

3) *Make amends for past errors* – Most Americans today at least acknowledge the problems at personal levels and say they rarely or never spend more than what they can afford (63% according to a 2007 Pew Research study). The average American knows the importance of managing a budget. Perhaps more would be willing to sacrifice for the greater good with an understandable plan to serve the country's long-term best interests;

4) *Develop a new code of behavior* – Policymakers, businesses (including investment firms), and citizens need to share responsibility for past failures and develop a plan for future successes.

Past generations of Americans have responded to major challenges with collective sacrifice and hard work. Will ours also rise to the occasion?

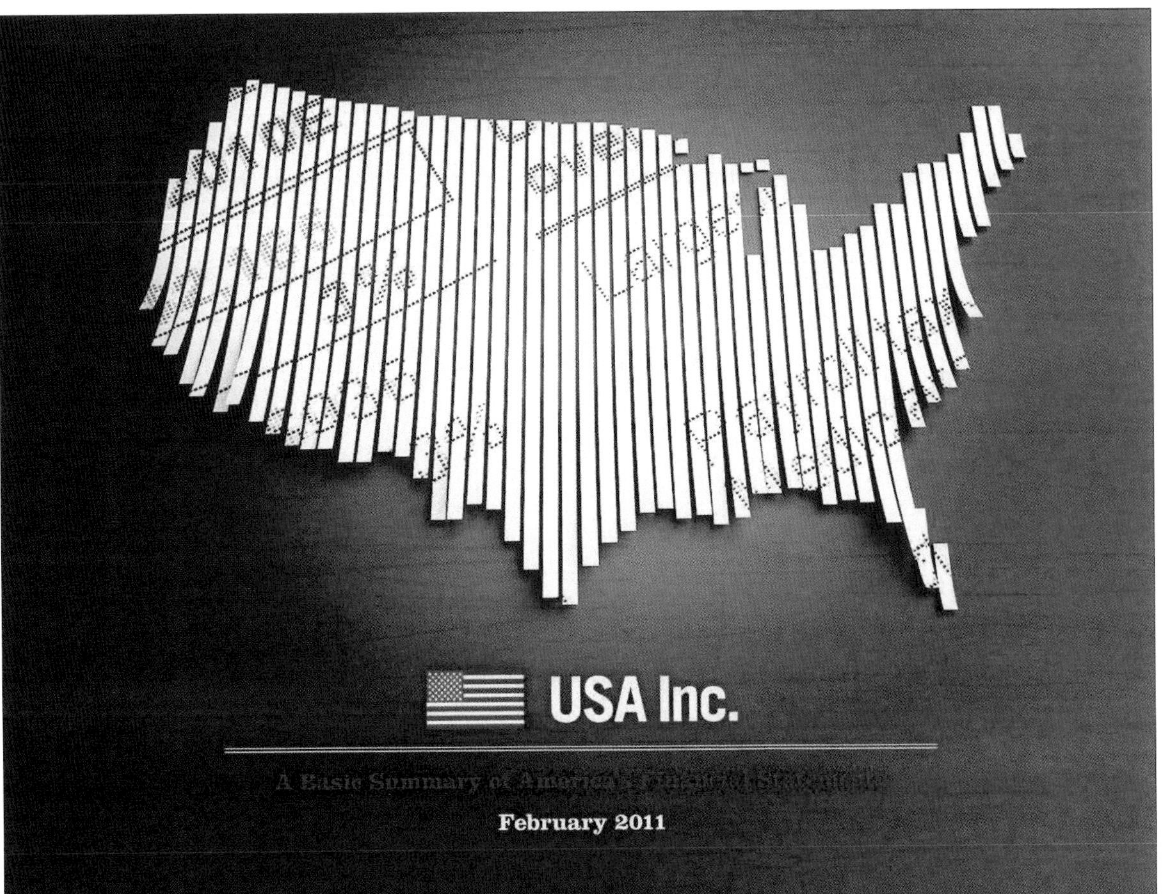

USA Inc. – Outline

1	Introduction
2	High-Level Thoughts on Income Statement/Balance Sheet
3	Income Statement Drilldown
4	Balance Sheet Drilldown
5	What Might a Turnaround Expert – Empowered to Improve USA Inc.'s Financials – Consider?
6	Consequences of Inaction
7	Summary
8	Appendix

This page is intentionally left blank.

Introduction

About This Report

Presentation Premise

For America to remain the great country it has been for the past 235 years, it must determine the best ways to honor the government's fundamental mission derived from the Constitution:

...to form a more perfect union, establish justice, insure domestic tranquility, provide for the common defense, promote the general welfare and secure the blessings of liberty to ourselves and our posterity.

To this end, government should aim to help create a vibrant environment for economic growth and productive employment. It should manage its operations and programs as effectively and efficiently as possible, improve its financial position by driving the federal government's income statement to long-term break-even, and reduce the unsustainable level of debt on its balance sheet.

USA Inc. Concept

Healthy financials and compelling growth prospects are key to success for businesses (and countries). So if the US federal government – which we call USA Inc. – were a business, how would public shareholders view it? How would long-term investors evaluate the federal government's business model, strategic plans, and operating efficiency? How would analysts react to its earnings reports? Although some 45%[1] of American households own shares in publicly traded companies and receive related quarterly financial statements, not many "stakeholders" look closely at Washington's financials. Nearly two-thirds of all American households[2] pay federal income taxes, but very few take the time to dig into the numbers of the entity that, on average, collects 13%[3] of all Americans' annual gross income (not counting another 15-30% for payroll and various state and local taxes).

We drill down on USA Inc.'s past, present, and (in some cases) future financial dynamics and focus on the country's income statement and balance sheet and related trends. We isolate and review key expense and revenue drivers. On the expense side, we examine the major entitlement programs (Medicare, Medicaid and Social Security) as well as defense and other major discretionary programs. On the revenue side, we focus on GDP growth (driven by labor productivity and employment in the long run) and tax policies.

We present basic numbers-driven scenarios for addressing USA Inc.'s financial challenges. In addition, we lay out the type of basic checklists that corporate turnaround experts might use as starting points when looking at some of USA Inc.'s business model challenges.

Source: 1) 2008 ICI (Investment Company Institute) / SIFMA (Securities Industry and Financial Markets Association) Equity and Bond Owners Survey; 2) Number of tax returns with positive tax liability (91MM) divided by total number of returns filed (142MM), per Tax Foundation calculations based on IRS data; 3) Total federal income taxes (ex. payroll taxes) paid divided by total adjusted gross income, per IRS 2007 data.

Why We Wrote This Report

As American citizens / tax payers, we care about the future of our country. As investors, we search for data and insights to help us make better investment decisions. (It's easier to predict the future with a keen understanding of the past.)

We found ourselves searching for better information about the state of America's financials, and we decided to assemble – in one place and in a user-friendly format – some of the best data about the world's biggest "business." In addition, we have attempted to provide some historical context for how USA Inc.'s financial model has evolved over decades.

The complexity of USA Inc.'s challenges is well known, and our presentation is just a starting point; it's far from perfect or complete. But we are convinced that citizens – and investors – should understand the business of their government. Thomas Jefferson and Alexis de Tocqueville knew that – armed with the right information – the enlightened citizenry of America would make the right decisions. It is our humble hope that a transparent financial framework can help inform future debates.

What You'll Find Here…

In the conviction that every citizen should understand the finances of USA Inc. and the plans of its "management team," we examine USA Inc.'s income statement and balance sheet and present them in a basic, easy-to-use format.

In this document, a broad group of people helped us drill into our federal government's basic financial metrics. We summarize our thoughts in PowerPoint form here and also have provided a brief text summary at www.kpcb.com/usainc.

We encourage people to take our data and thoughts and study them, critique them, augment them, share them, and make them better. There's a lot of material – think of it as a book that happens to be a slide presentation.

…And What You Won't

We do not make policy recommendations. We try to help clarify some of the issues in a simple, analytically-based way. We aim to present data, trends, and facts about USA Inc.'s key revenue and expense drivers to provide context for how its financials have reached their present state.

We did not base this analysis on proprietary data. Our observations come from publicly available information, and we use the tools of basic financial analysis to interpret it. Forecasts generally come from 3rd-party agencies like the Congressional Budget Office (CBO). For US policy makers, the timing of material changes will be especially difficult, given the current economic environment.

No doubt, there will be compliments and criticism of things in the presentation (or missing from it). We hope that this report helps advance the discussion and we welcome others to opine with views (backed up by data).

We Focus on Federal, Not State & Local Government Data

- **Federal / State & Local Governments Share Different Responsibilities**
  - Federal government is financially responsible for all or the majority of **Defense, Social Security, Medicare and Interest Payments** on federal debt and coordinates / shares funding for public investment in education / infrastructure.
  - State & local governments are financially responsible for all or the majority of **Education, Transportation** (Road Construction & Maintenance), **Public Safety** (Police / Fire Protection / Law Courts / Prisons) and **Environment & Housing** (Parks & Recreation / Community Development / Sewerage & Waste Management).
  - Federal / state & local governments share financial responsibility in **Medicaid** and **Unemployment Insurance**.
- **We Focus on the Federal Government**
  - State and local governments face many similar long-term financial challenges and may ultimately require federal assistance. To be sure, the size of state & local government budget deficits ($70 billion[1] in aggregate in F2009) and debt-to-GDP ratio (7%[2] on average in F2008) pales by comparison to the federal government's ($1.3 trillion budget deficit, 62% debt-to-GDP ratio in F2010). But these metrics may understate state & local governments' financial challenges by 50% or more[3] because they exclude the long-term cost of public pension and other post employment benefit (OPEB) liabilities.

Note: 1) Per National Conference of State Legislatures, State fiscal years ends in June. $70B aggregate excludes deficits from Puerto Rico ($3B deficits in F2009). 2) Debt-to-GDP ratio per Census Bureau State & Local Government Finance; 3) Calculation based on the claim that $1T of collective short fall in State & local government pension and OPEB funding would be $2.5T using corporate accounting rules, per Orin S. Kramer, "How to Cheat a Retirement Fund," 9/10.

Summary

Highlights from F2010 USA Inc. Financials

- **Summary –** USA Inc. has challenges.
- **Cash Flow –** While recession depressed F2008-F2010 results, cash flow has been negative for 9 consecutive years ($4.8 trillion, cumulative), with no end to losses in sight. Negative cash flow implies that USA Inc. can't afford the services it is providing to 'customers,' many of whom are people with few alternatives.
- **Balance Sheet –** Net worth is negative and deteriorating.
- **Off-Balance Sheet Liabilities –** Off-balance sheet liabilities of at least $31 trillion (primarily unfunded Medicare and Social Security obligations) amount to nearly $3 for every $1 of debt on the books. Just as unfunded corporate pensions and other post-employment benefits (OPEB) weigh on public corporations, unfunded entitlements, over time, may increase USA Inc.'s cost of capital. And today's off-balance sheet liabilities will be tomorrow's on-balance sheet debt.
- **Conclusion –** Publicly traded companies with similar financial trends would be pressed by shareholders to pursue a turnaround. The good news: USA Inc.'s underlying asset base and entrepreneurial culture are strong. The financial trends can shift toward a positive direction, but both 'management' and 'shareholders' will need collective focus, willpower, commitment, and sacrifice.

Note: USA federal fiscal year ends in September; Cash flow = total revenue – total spending on a cash basis; net worth includes unfunded future liabilities from Social Security and Medicare on an accrual basis over the next 75 years. Source: cash flow per White House Office of Management and Budget; net worth per Dept. of Treasury, "2010 Financial Report of the U.S. Government," adjusted to include unfunded liabilities of Social Security and Medicare.

Drilldown on USA Inc. Financials…

- **To analysts looking at USA Inc. as a public corporation, the financials are challenged**
  - Excluding Medicare / Medicaid spending and one-time charges, USA Inc. has supported a 4% average net margin[1] over 15 years, but cash flow is deep in the red by negative $1.3 trillion last year (or -$11,000 per household), and net worth[2] is negative $44 trillion (or -$371,000 per household).
- **The main culprits: entitlement programs, mounting debt, and one-time charges**
  - Since the Great Depression, USA Inc. has steadily added "business lines" and, with the best of intentions, created various entitlement programs. Some of these serve the nation's poorest, whose struggles have been made worse by the financial crisis. Apart from Social Security and unemployment insurance, however, funding for these programs has been woefully inadequate – and getting worse.
  - Entitlement expenses (adjusted for inflation) rose 70% over the last 15 years, and USA Inc. entitlement spending now equals $16,600 per household per year; annual spending exceeds dedicated funding by more than $1 trillion (and rising). Net debt levels are approaching warning levels, and one-time charges only compound the problem.
  - Some consider defense spending a major cause of USA Inc.'s financial dilemma. Re-setting priorities and streamlining could yield savings – $788 billion by 2018, according to one recent study[3] – perhaps without damaging security. But entitlement spending has a bigger impact on USA Inc. financials. Although defense nearly doubled in the last decade, to 5% of GDP, it is still below its 7% share of GDP from 1948 to 2000. It accounted for 20% of the budget in 2010, but 41% of all government spending between 1789 and 1930.

Note: 1) Net margin defined as net income divided by total revenue; 2) net worth defined as assets (ex. stewardship assets like national parks and heritage assets like the Washington Monument) minus liabilities minus the net present value of unfunded entitlements (such as Social Security and Medicare), data per Treasury Dept.'s "2010 Annual Report on the U.S. Government"; 3) Gordon Adams and Matthew Leatherman, "A Leaner and Meaner National Defense," Foreign Affairs, *Jan/Feb 2011)*

…Drilldown on USA Inc. Financials…

- **Medicare and Medicaid, largely underfunded (based on 'dedicated' revenue) and growing rapidly, accounted for 21% (or $724B) of USA Inc.'s total expenses in F2010, up from 5% forty years ago**
  - Together, these two programs represent 35% of all (annual) US healthcare spending; Federal Medicaid spending has doubled in real terms over the last decade, to $273 billion annually.
- **Total government healthcare spending consumes 8.2% of GDP compared with just 1.3% fifty years ago; the new health reform law could increase USA Inc.'s budget deficit**
  - As government healthcare spending expands, USA Inc.'s red ink will get much worse if healthcare costs continue growing 2 percentage points faster than per capita income (as they have for 40 years).
- **Unemployment Insurance and Social Security are adequately funded...for now. The future, not so bright**
  - Demographic trends have exacerbated the funding problems for Medicare and Social Security – of the 102 million increased enrollment between 1965 and 2009, 42 million (or 41%) is due to an aging population. With a 26% longer life expectancy but a 3% increase in retirement age (since Social Security was created in 1935), deficits from Social Security could add $11.6 trillion (or 140%) to the public debt by 2037E, per Congressional Budget Office (CBO).

...Drilldown on USA Inc. Financials

- **If entitlement programs are not reformed, USA Inc.'s balance sheet will go from bad to worse**
  - Public debt has doubled over the last 30 years, to 62% of GDP. This ratio is expected to surpass the 90% threshold* – above which real GDP growth could slow considerably – in 10 years and could near 150% of GDP in 20 years if entitlement expenses continue to soar, per CBO.
  - As government healthcare spending expands, USA Inc.'s red ink will get much worse if healthcare costs continue growing 2 percentage points faster than per capita income (as they have for 40 years).
- **The turning point: Within 15 years (by 2025), entitlements plus net interest expenses will absorb all – yes, all – of USA Inc.'s annual revenue, per CBO**
  - That would require USA Inc. to borrow funds for defense, education, infrastructure, and R&D spending, which today account for 32% of USA Inc. spending (excluding one-time items), down dramatically from 69% forty years ago.
  - It's notable that CBO's projection from 10 years ago (in 1999) showed Federal revenue sufficient to support entitlement spending + interest payments until 2060E – 35 years later than current projection.

*Note: *Carmen Reinhart and Kenneth Rogoff observed from 3,700 historical annual data points from 44 countries that the relationship between government debt and real GDP growth is weak for debt/GDP ratios below a threshold of 90 percent of GDP. Above 90 percent, median growth rates fall by one percent, and average growth falls considerably more. We note that while Reinhart and Rogoff's observations are based on 'gross debt' data, in the U.S., debt held by the public is closer to the European countries' definition of government gross debt. For more information, see Reinhart and Rogoff, "Growth in a Time of Debt," 1/10.*

How Might One Think About Turning Around USA Inc.?...

- **Key focus areas would likely be reducing USA Inc.'s budget deficit and improving / restructuring the 'business model'...**
  - One would likely drill down on USA Inc.'s key revenue and expense drivers, then develop a basic analytical framework for 'normal' revenue / expenses, then compare options.

  Looking at history...
  - Annual growth in revenue of 3% has been roughly in line with GDP for 40 years* while corporate income taxes grew at 2%. Social insurance taxes (for Social Security / Medicare) grew 5% annually and now represent 37% of USA Inc. revenue, compared with 19% in 1965.
  - Annual growth in expenses of 3% has been roughly in line with revenue, but entitlements are up 5% per annum - and now absorb 51% of all USA Inc.'s expense - more than twice their share in 1965; defense and other discretionary spending growth has been just 1-2%.

  One might ask...
  - Should expense and revenue levels be re-thought and re-set so USA Inc. operates near break-even and expense growth (with needed puts and takes) matches GDP growth, thus adopting a 'don't spend more than you earn' approach to managing USA Inc.'s financials?

*Note: *We chose a 40-year period from 1965 to 2005 to examine 'normal' levels of revenue and expenses. We did not choose the most recent 40-year period (1969 to 2009) as USA was in deep recession in 2008 / 2009 and underwent significant tax policy fluctuations in 1968 /1969, so many metrics (like individual income and corporate profit) varied significantly from 'normal' levels.*

…How Might One Think About Turning Around USA Inc.?

One might consider…

- **Options for reducing expenses by focusing on entitlement reform and operating efficiency**
  - Formula changes could help Social Security's underfunding, but look too draconian for Medicare/Medicaid; the underlying healthcare cost dilemma requires business process restructuring and realigned incentives.
  - Resuming the 20-year trend line for lower Federal civilian employment, plus more flexible compensation systems and selective local outsourcing, could help streamline USA Inc.'s operations.
- **Options for increasing revenue by focusing on driving long-term GDP growth and changing tax policies**
  - USA Inc. should examine ways to invest in growth that provides a high return (ROI) via new investment in technology, education, and infrastructure and could stimulate productivity gains and employment growth.
  - Reducing tax subsidies (like exemptions on mortgage interest payments or healthcare benefits) and changing the tax system in other ways could increase USA Inc.'s revenue without raising income taxes to punitive – and self-defeating – levels. Such tax policy changes could help re-balance USA's economy between consumption and savings and re-orient business lines towards investment-led growth, though there are potential risks and drawbacks.
- **History suggests the long-term consequences of inaction could be severe**
  - USA Inc. has many assets, but it must start addressing its spending/debt challenges now.

Sizing Costs Related to USA Inc.'s Key Financial Challenges & Potential AND / OR Solutions

- **To create frameworks for discussion, the next slide summarizes USA Inc.'s various financial challenges and the projected future cost of each main expense driver.**
  - The estimated future cost is calculated as the net present value of expected 'dedicated' future income (such as payroll taxes) minus expected future expenses (such as benefits paid) over the next 75 years.
- **Then we ask the question: 'What can we do to solve these financial challenges?'**
  - The potential solutions include a range of simple *mathematical illustrations* (such as changing program characteristics or increasing tax rates) *and/or program-specific policy solutions* proposed or considered by lawmakers and agencies like the CBO (such as indexing Social Security initial benefits to growth in cost of living).
- **These mathematical illustrations are only a mechanical answer to key financial challenges and not realistic solutions. In reality, a combination of detailed policy changes will likely be required to bridge the future funding gap.**

Overview of USA Inc.'s Key Financial Challenges & Potential *and/or* Solutions

Rank	Financial Challenge	Net Present Cost[1] ($T / % of 2010 GDP)	Mathematical Illustrations *and/or* Potential Policy Solutions[2]
1	Medicaid	$35 Trillion[3] / 239%	• Isolate and address the drivers of medical cost inflation • Improve efficiency / productivity of healthcare system • Reduce coverage for optional benefits & optional enrollees
2	Medicare	$23 Trillion / 156%	• Reduce benefits • Increase Medicare tax rate • Isolate and address the drivers of medical cost inflation • Improve efficiency / productivity of healthcare system
3	Social Security	$8 Trillion / 54%	• Raise retirement age • Reduce benefits • Increase Social Security tax rate • Reduce future initial benefits by indexing to cost of living growth rather than wage growth • Subject benefits to means test to determine eligibility
4	Slow GDP / USA Revenue Growth	--	• Invest in technology / infrastructure / education • Remove tax & regulatory uncertainties to stimulate employment growth • Reduce subsidies and tax expenditures & broaden tax base
5	Government Inefficiencies	--	• Resume the 20-year trend line for lower Federal civilian employment • Implement more flexible compensation systems • Consolidate / selectively local outsource certain functions

Note: 1) Net Present Cost is calculated as the present value of expected future net liabilities (expected revenue minus expected costs) for each program / issue over the next 75 years, Medicare estimate per Dept. of Treasury, "2010 Financial Report of the U.S. Government," Social Security estimate per Social Security Trustees' Report (8/10). 2) For more details on potential solutions, see slides 252-410 or full USA Inc. presentation. 3) Medicaid does not have dedicated revenue source and its $35T net present cost excludes funding from general tax revenue, NPV analysis based on 3% discount rate applied to CBO's projection for annual inflation-adjusted expenses.

The Essence of America's Financial Conundrum & Math Problem?

While a hefty 80% of Americans indicate balancing the budget should be one of the country's top priorities, per a Peter G. Peterson Foundation survey in 11/09…

…only 12% of Americans support cutting spending on Medicare or Social Security, per a Pew Research Center survey, 2/11.

Some might call this 'having your cake and eating it too…'

The Challenge Before Us

Policymakers, businesses and citizens need to share responsibility for past failures and develop a plan for future successes.

Past generations of Americans have responded to major challenges with collective sacrifice and hard work.

Will ours also rise to the occasion?

This page is intentionally left blank.

High-Level Thoughts on Income Statement/Balance Sheet

How Would You Feel if…

…your Cash Flow was NEGATIVE for each of the past 9 years…

…your Net Worth* has been NEGATIVE for as long as you can remember…

… it would take 20 years of your income at the current level to pay off your existing debt – assuming you don't take on any more debt.

*Note: *See slide 30 for net worth qualifier.*

Welcome to the Financial Reality (& Negative Trend) of USA Inc. F2010 Cash Flow = **-$1.3 Trillion**; Net Worth = **-$44 Trillion**

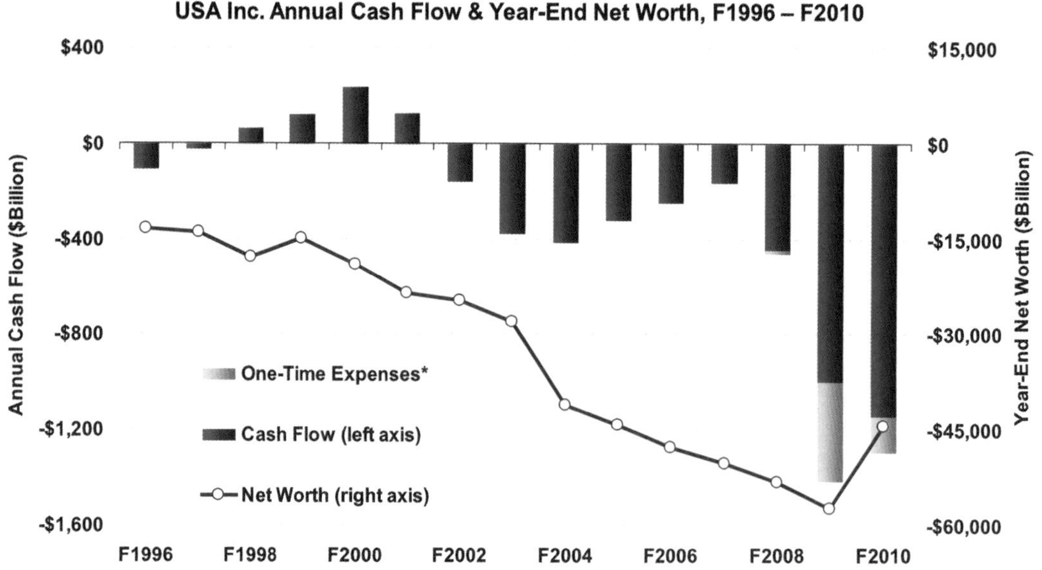

*Note: USA federal fiscal year ends in September; Cash flow = total revenue – total spending on a cash basis; net worth includes unfunded future liabilities from Social Security and Medicare on an accrual basis over the next 75 years. *One-time expenses in F2008 include $14B payments to Freddie Mac; F2009 includes $279B net TARP payouts, $97B payment to Fannie Mae & Freddie Mac and $40B stimulus spending on discretionary items; F2010 includes $26B net TARP income, $137B stimulus spending and $41B payment to Fannie Mae & Freddie Mac. F2010 net worth improved dramatically owing to revised actuarial estimates for Medicare program resulted from the Healthcare reform legislation. For more definitions, see next slide. Source: cash flow per White House Office of Management and Budget; net worth per Dept. of Treasury, "2010 Financial Report of the U.S. Government."*

Think About That…

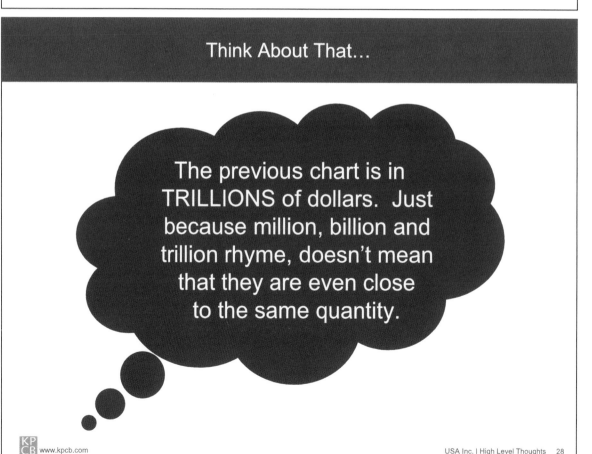

The previous chart is in TRILLIONS of dollars. Just because million, billion and trillion rhyme, doesn't mean that they are even close to the same quantity.

Only Politicians Work in Trillions of Dollars—Here's How Much That Is

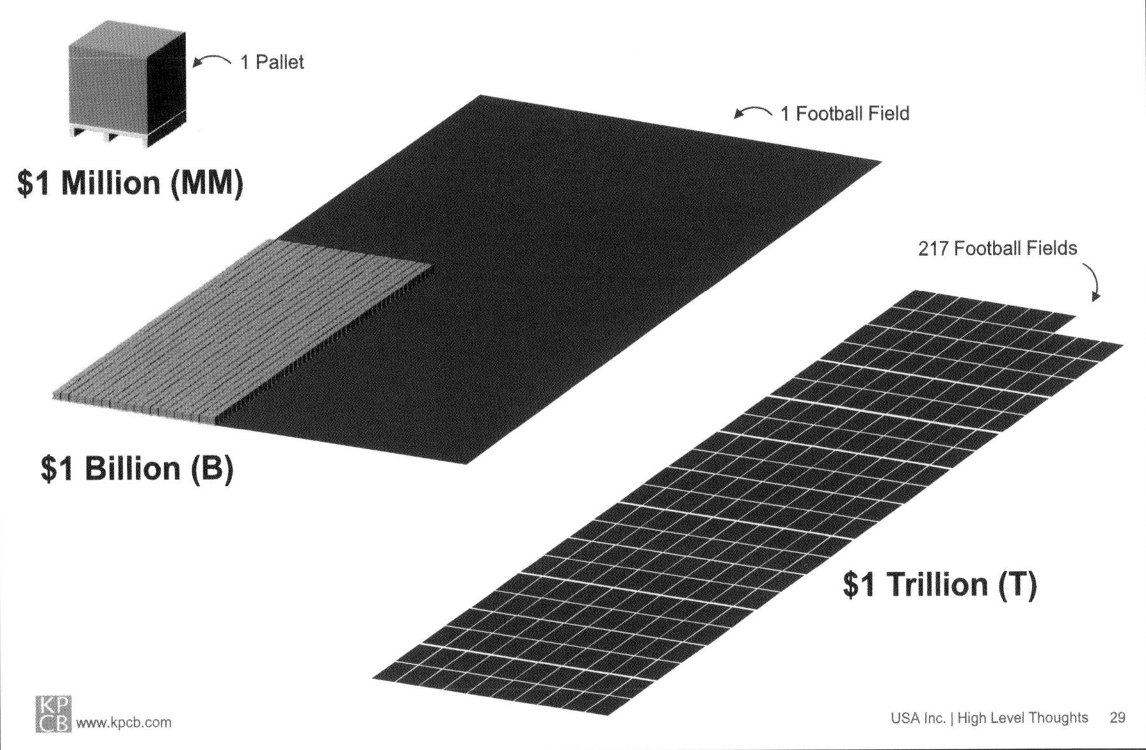

Net Worth Qualifier

- **The balance sheet / net worth calculation does not include the power to tax** – the net present value of the sovereign power to tax and the ability to print the world's reserve currency would clearly bolster USA Inc.'s assets – if they could be accurately calculated.
- **Plant, Property & Equipment (PP&E) on USA Inc.'s balance sheet is valued at $829B[1] (or 29% of USA Inc.'s total stated assets)** – this includes tangible assets such as buildings, internal use software and civilian and military equipment.
- **The PP&E calculation <u>DOES NOT</u> include** the value of USA Inc.'s holdings in the likes of public land (estimated to be worth $408B per OMB)[1], highways, natural gas, oil reserves, mineral rights (estimated to be worth $345B per OMB), forest, air space, radio frequency spectrum, national parks and other heritage and stewardship assets which USA Inc. does not anticipate to use for general government operations. The good news for USA Inc. is that the aggregate value of these heritage and stewardship assets could be significant.

Note: 1) USA Inc.'s holding of land is measured in non-financial units such as acres of land and lakes, and number of National Parks and National Marine Sanctuaries. Land under USA Inc.'s stewardship accounts for 28% of the total U.S. landmass as of 9/10. Dept. of Interior reported 552 national wildlife refuges, 378 park units, 134 geographic management areas, 67 fish hatcheries under their management as of 9/10. Dept. of Defense reported 203,000 acres of public land and 16,140,000 acres withdrawn public land, the USDA's Forest Service managed an estimated 155 national forests, while the Dept. of Commerce had 13 National Marine Sanctuaries, which included near–shore coral reefs and open ocean, as of 9/10. Dept. of Treasury, "2010 Financial Report of the U.S. Government."

A Word of Warning About Comparing Corporate & Government Accounting…

- Government accounting standards do not report the present value of future entitlement payments (such as Social Security or Medicare) as liabilities. Instead, entitlement payments are recognized only when they are paid.
- Our analysis takes a different view: governments create liabilities when they enact entitlements and do not provide for revenues adequate to fund them.
- We measure the entitlement liability as the present value of estimated entitlement payments in excess of expected revenues for citizens of working age based on Social Security and Medicare Trust Funds' actuarial analysis.
- Government accounting standards also do not recognize the value of internally-generated intangible assets (such as the sovereign power to tax). We do not recognize those assets either, as we have no basis to measure them. But the US government has substantial intangible assets that should provide future economic benefits.

Note: For more discussion on alternatives to corporate and official government accounting methods, see Laurence J. Kotlikoff, Alan J. Auerbach, and Jagadeesh Gokhale, "Generational Accounting: A Meaningful Way to Assess Generational Policy," published on 12/94 in The Journal of Economic Perspectives.
Source: Greg Jonas, Morgan Stanley Research.

…and About Government Budgeting

- Federal government budgeting follows arcane practices that are very different from corporate budgeting – and can neglect solutions to structural problems in favor of short-term expediency.
- Federal government does not distinguish capital budget (for long-term investment) from operating budget (for day-to-day operations). As a result, when funding is limited, government may choose to reduce investments for the future to preserve resources for day-to-day operations.
- Budget "scoring" rules give Congress incentives to hide the true costs...and help Congressional committees defend their turf.*

*Note: *For more detail, refer to slide 116 on congressional budget scoring rules related to recent Healthcare reform.*

Metric Definitions & Qualifiers

- **Cash Flow** = 'Cash In' *Minus* 'Cash Out'
  - Calculated on a <u>cash basis</u> (which excludes changes in non-cash accrual of future liabilities) for simplicity.

- **One-Time Expenses** = 'Spending *Minus* Repayments' for Non-Recurring Programs
  - Net costs of programs such as TARP, ARRA, and GSE bailouts.

- **Net Worth** = Assets *Minus* Liabilities *Minus* Unfunded Entitlement Liabilities
  - <u>Assets</u> include cash & investments, taxes receivable, property, plant & equipment (as defined by Department of Treasury).
  - <u>Liabilities</u> include accounts payable, accrued payroll & benefits, federal debt, federal employee & veteran benefits payable…
  - <u>Unfunded Entitlement Liabilities</u> include the present value of future expenditures in excess of dedicated future revenues in Medicare and Social Security over the next 75 years.

Note: USA Inc. accounts do not follow the same GAAP as corporations.

Common Financial Metrics Applied to USA Inc. in F2010

- **Cash Flow Per Share = -$4,171**
  - USA Inc.'s F2010 cash flow -$1.3 trillion, divided by population of ~310 million (assuming each citizen holds one share of USA Inc.).

- **Net Debt to EBITDA Ratio = -8x**
  - USA Inc. net debt held by public ($9.1 trillion) divided by USA Inc. F2010 EBITDA (-$1.1 trillion). It's notable that the ratio compares with S&P500 average of 1.4x in 2010.

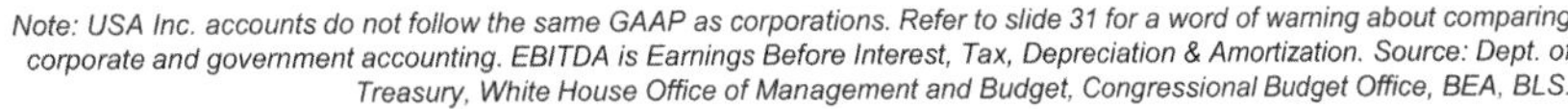
Note: USA Inc. accounts do not follow the same GAAP as corporations. Refer to slide 31 for a word of warning about comparing corporate and government accounting. EBITDA is Earnings Before Interest, Tax, Depreciation & Amortization. Source: Dept. of Treasury, White House Office of Management and Budget, Congressional Budget Office, BEA, BLS.

Even Adjusting For Cyclical Impact of Recessions, USA Inc.'s 2010 Structural Operating Loss = **-$817 Billion** vs. -$78 Billion 15 Years Ago

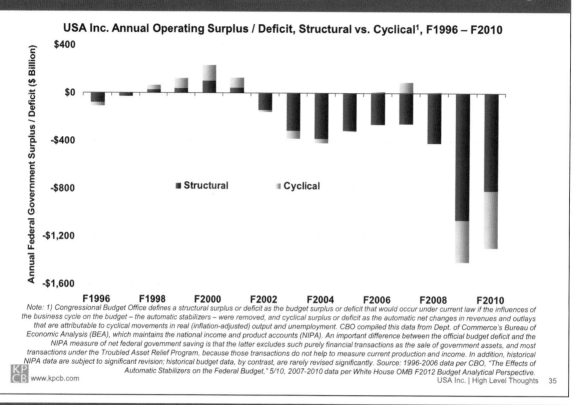

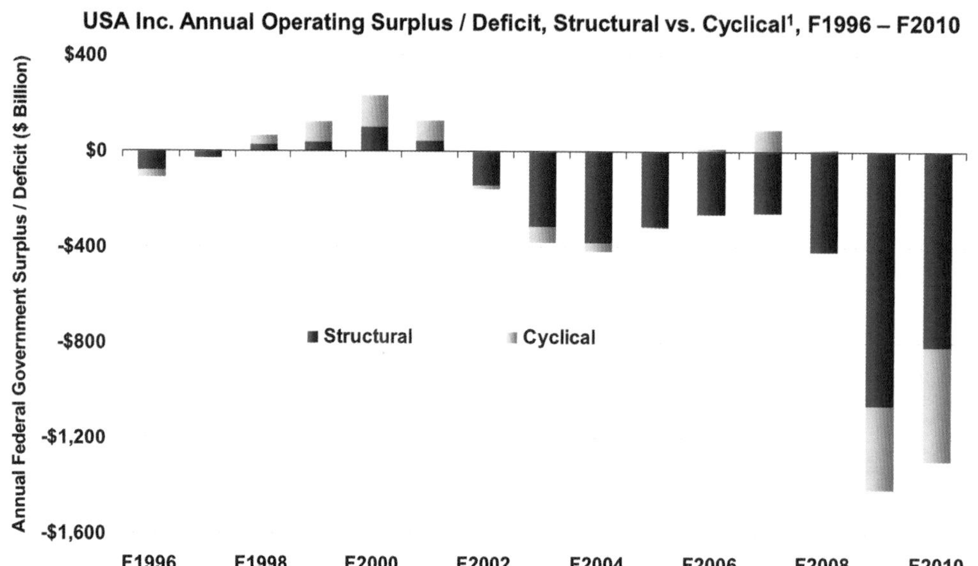

Note: 1) Congressional Budget Office defines a structural surplus or deficit as the budget surplus or deficit that would occur under current law if the influences of the business cycle on the budget – the automatic stabilizers – were removed, and cyclical surplus or deficit as the automatic net changes in revenues and outlays that are attributable to cyclical movements in real (inflation-adjusted) output and unemployment. CBO compiled this data from Dept. of Commerce's Bureau of Economic Analysis (BEA), which maintains the national income and product accounts (NIPA). An important difference between the official budget deficit and the NIPA measure of net federal government saving is that the latter excludes such purely financial transactions as the sale of government assets, and most transactions under the Troubled Asset Relief Program, because those transactions do not help to measure current production and income. In addition, historical NIPA data are subject to significant revision; historical budget data, by contrast, are rarely revised significantly. Source: 1996-2006 data per CBO, "The Effects of Automatic Stabilizers on the Federal Budget," 5/10, 2007-2010 data per White House OMB F2012 Budget Analytical Perspective.

Understanding Differences Between Economist Language vs. Equity Investor Translation

Economist Language	Equity Investor Approximate Translation*
• **Budget Deficit** – The amount by which a government's expenditures exceed its receipts over a particular period of time.	• **Cash Flow** – 'Cash in' minus 'cash out.'
• **Structural Deficit** – The portion of the budget deficit that results from a fundamental imbalance in government receipts and expenditures, as opposed to one based on the business cycle or one-time factors.	• **Cash Flow (ex. One-Time Items)*** – 'Cash in' minus 'cash out' excluding expenditures that are one-time in nature (such as economic stimulus spending).
• **Cyclical Deficit** – The portion of the budget deficit that results from cyclical factors such as economic recessions rather than from underlying fiscal policy.	• **One-Time Expenses*** – TARP / GSE / stimulus spending related to economic recession.
• **Federal Debt Held By the Public** – The accumulation of all previous fiscal years' deficits.	• **Debt** – Cumulative negative cash flow financed by borrowing.

*Note: *We acknowledge that while the concept of 'cash flow ex. one-time items' and 'one-time expenses' is similar to 'structural deficit' and 'cyclical deficit,' respectively, these terms are not interchangeable and have different definitions. Congressional Budget Office defines a structural surplus or deficit as the budget surplus or deficit that would occur under current law if the influences of the business cycle on the budget – the automatic stabilizers – were removed, and cyclical surplus or deficit as the automatic net changes in revenues and outlays that are attributable to cyclical movements in real (inflation-adjusted) output and unemployment.*

How Did USA Inc.'s Financial Reality Get to this Difficult Point?

USA Inc. Has Not Adequately Funded Its Entitlement Programs

Recessions come and go (and affect USA's revenue), but future claims (related to entitlement program commitments) on USA Inc. now meaningfully exceed its projected cash flows.

For the last 40 years, management (the government) has committed more long-term benefits through 'entitlement' programs like Medicaid / Medicare / Social Security…without developing a sound plan to pay for them.

Many of these programs provide important services to low-income, unemployed, and disabled Americans in great need for help. But without proper financing, support may dwindle.

USA Inc. Has Substantially Expanded Its "Business Lines" Over Past 80 Years

From 1789 to 1930, 41%[1] of USA Inc.'s cumulative budget was dedicated to defense spending (compared with 20%[1] in F2010), per the Census Bureau.

This began to change in the 1930s, when the federal government substantially expanded its role (in effect, expanded its "business lines") in response to the Great Depression.

Note: 1) 41% is the cumulative defense spending (excluding veterans' benefits and services) as % of cumulative total federal spending from 1789 to 1930. Including veterans' benefits and services, defense spending would have been 49% of cumulative annual budget from 1789 to 1930 and would have been 22% in F2009. Source: Census Bureau, "Historical Statistics of the United States, Colonial Times to 1970," Data series Y 457-465.

USA Inc. "Business Lines" Have Expanded From Defense to Insurance & Other Areas

USA Inc. Major 'Business Line' Spending as % of GDP, F1800 vs. F1900 vs. F2000

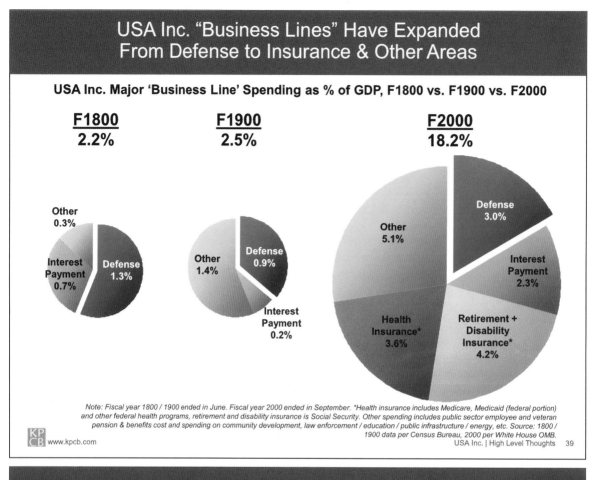

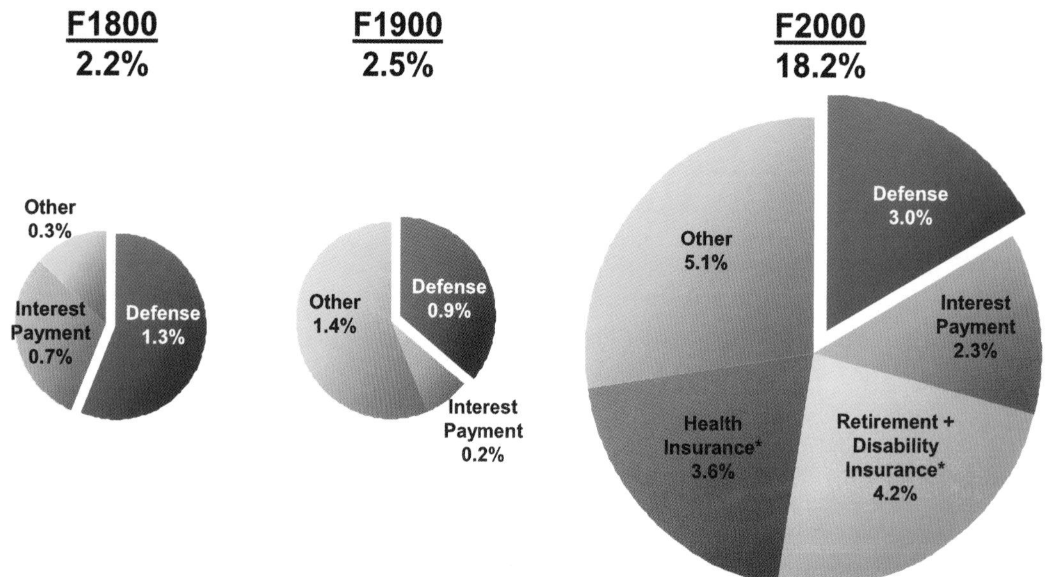

*Note: Fiscal year 1800 / 1900 ended in June. Fiscal year 2000 ended in September. *Health insurance includes Medicare, Medicaid (federal portion) and other federal health programs, retirement and disability insurance is Social Security. Other spending includes public sector employee and veteran pension & benefits cost and spending on community development, law enforcement / education / public infrastructure / energy, etc. Source: 1800 / 1900 data per Census Bureau, 2000 per White House OMB.*

USA Inc. First 155 Years (1776-1930) = Era of Defense
Dept. of Army + Navy = 41%[1] of Cumulative Spending From 1789-1930

USA Inc.'s Budget Outlays For the First 155 Years (1776-1930)[2]

	1789-1791	1800	1850	1900	1930	1789-1930 Cumulative
Total Federal Government Outlays ($MM)	**$4**	**$11**	**$40**	**$521**	**$3,320**	**$98,747**
Defense	**$1**	**$6**	**$17**	**$191**	**$839**	**$40,332**
% of Total Outlays	***15%***	***56%***	***44%***	***37%***	***25%***	***41%***
Dept. of the Army	***$1***	***$3***	***$9***	***$135***	***$465***	***$28,831***
% of Total Outlays	***15%***	***24%***	***24%***	***26%***	***14%***	***29%***
Dept. of the Navy	***$0***	***$3***	***$8***	***$56***	***$374***	***$11,500***
% of Total Outlays	--	***32%***	***20%***	***11%***	***11%***	***12%***
Interest on the Public Debt	**$2**	**$3**	**$4**	**$40**	**$659**	**$13,790**
% of Total Outlays	***55%***	***31%***	***10%***	***8%***	***20%***	***14%***
Other*	**$1**	**$1**	**$18**	**$290**	**$1,822**	**$44,626**
% of Total Outlays	***30%***	***13%***	***47%***	***56%***	***55%***	***45%***
Veteran Compensation and Pensions	***$0***	***$0***	***$2***	***$141***	***$221***	***$8,273***
% of Total Outlays	***4%***	***1%***	***5%***	***27%***	***7%***	***8%***

*Note: Data is rounded and not adjusted for inflation. 1) 41% is the cumulative defense spending (excluding veterans' benefits and services) as % of cumulative total federal spending from 1789 to 1930. Including veterans' benefits and services, defense spending would have been 49% of cumulative annual budget from 1789 to 1930. 2) Data not available from 1776 to 1789. * Other includes various spending on administration, legislation and veteran compensation and pensions. Source: Census Bureau, "Historical Statistics of the United States, Colonial Times to 1970," Data series Y 457-465.*

USA Inc. Next 80 Years (1931-2010) = Era of Expansion

Defense Down to 20% of Spending; Social Security + Healthcare Up to 44% in F2010

USA Inc.'s Budget Outlays For the Next 78 Years (1931-2010)[2]

	1931	... 1940	... 1950	... 1960	... 1970	... 1980	... 1990	... 2000	... 2010
Total Federal Government Outlays ($B)	**$4**	**$9**	**$43**	**$92**	**$196**	**$591**	**$1,253**	**$1,789**	**$3,456**
Defense	**$1**	**$2**	**$14**	**$48**	**$82**	**$134**	**$299**	**$294**	**$694**
% of Total Outlays	***23%***	***20%***	***32%***	***52%***	***42%***	***23%***	***24%***	***16%***	***20%***
Interest on the Public Debt	**$1**	**$1**	**$5**	**$7**	**$14**	**$53**	**$184**	**$223**	**$196**
% of Total Outlays	***17%***	***11%***	***11%***	***8%***	***7%***	***9%***	***15%***	***12%***	***6%***
Retirement & Disability Insurance	**$0**	**$0**	**$1**	**$12**	**$30**	**$119**	**$249**	**$409**	**$707**
% of Total Outlays	***0%***	***0%***	***2%***	***13%***	***15%***	***20%***	***20%***	***23%***	***20%***
Healthcare	**$0**	**$0**	**$0**	**$1**	**$12**	**$55**	**$156**	**$352**	**$821**
% of Total Outlays	***0%***	***1%***	***1%***	***1%***	***6%***	***9%***	***12%***	***20%***	***24%***
Physical Resources (Energy / Housing...)	**$0**	**$2**	**$4**	**$8**	**$16**	**$66**	**$126**	**$85**	**$89**
% of Total Outlays	***5%***	***26%***	***9%***	***9%***	***8%***	***11%***	***10%***	***5%***	***3%***
Other	**$2**	**$4**	**$19**	**$17**	**$42**	**$165**	**$239**	**$426**	**$950**
% of Total Outlays	***55%***	***42%***	***45%***	***18%***	***21%***	***28%***	***19%***	***24%***	***27%***

Note: Data is rounded and not adjusted for inflation. Physical resources include energy, natural resources, commerce & housing credit, transportation infrastructure, community and regional development. Other includes international affairs, agriculture, administration of justice, general government, education and veterans' benefits and services. Source: 1931-1939 data per Census Bureau, "Historical Statistics of the United States, Colonial Times to 1970." 1940-2010 data per White House OMB.

USA Inc. "Business Line" Extensions: 1930 – 2010

1970's · 1960's · 1950's · 1940's · 1930's

"Business Line" Extensions	F2010 Expense ($B)	Agencies / Programs Created (Year)	Goals
Energy Policy	**$12**	Department of Energy (1977)	Establish the Strategic Petroleum Reserve / mandate automobile fuel efficiency standards & temporary oil price control
Community Development	**13**	Community Development Block Grant* (1974)	Provide federal grants to local governments for projects like parking lots / museums / street repairs
Healthcare	**724**	Medicare / Medicaid (1965)	Provide medical insurance program for the elderly (Medicare) and welfare program for low-income population (Medicaid)
Education	**97**	Federal Subsidies for K-12 & Higher Education (1965)	Provide federal subsidies for student loans / school libraries / teacher training / research / textbooks and other items.
Housing	**36**	Federal Housing Administration (1937) / Fannie Mae (1938)	Reduce cost of mortgages and spur home building / purchasing by offering federal mortgage insurance and create secondary market for mortgage loans.
Welfare	**28**	Aid to Dependent Children (1935)	Provide cash assistance to low-income families with children. Replaced by Temporary Assistance for Needy Families program in 1996
Retirement	**584****	Social Security (1935)	Provide retirement income to the elderly
TOTAL	**$1.5 Trillion**	**Or 10% of F2010 GDP / 69% of USA Inc.'s Revenue / 43 of Expense**	

*Note: *Community Development Block Grant was an effort to consolidate various pre-existing categorical community development programs that started with "urban renewal" in the 1950's. **Social Security's F2010 expense excludes ~$123B payments to disabled workers via Disability Insurance program (created in 1956). Source: CATO Institute, White House OMB.*

Entitlement Programs Are the Largest & Growing Expense Items on USA Inc.'s Income Statement in Peace Time

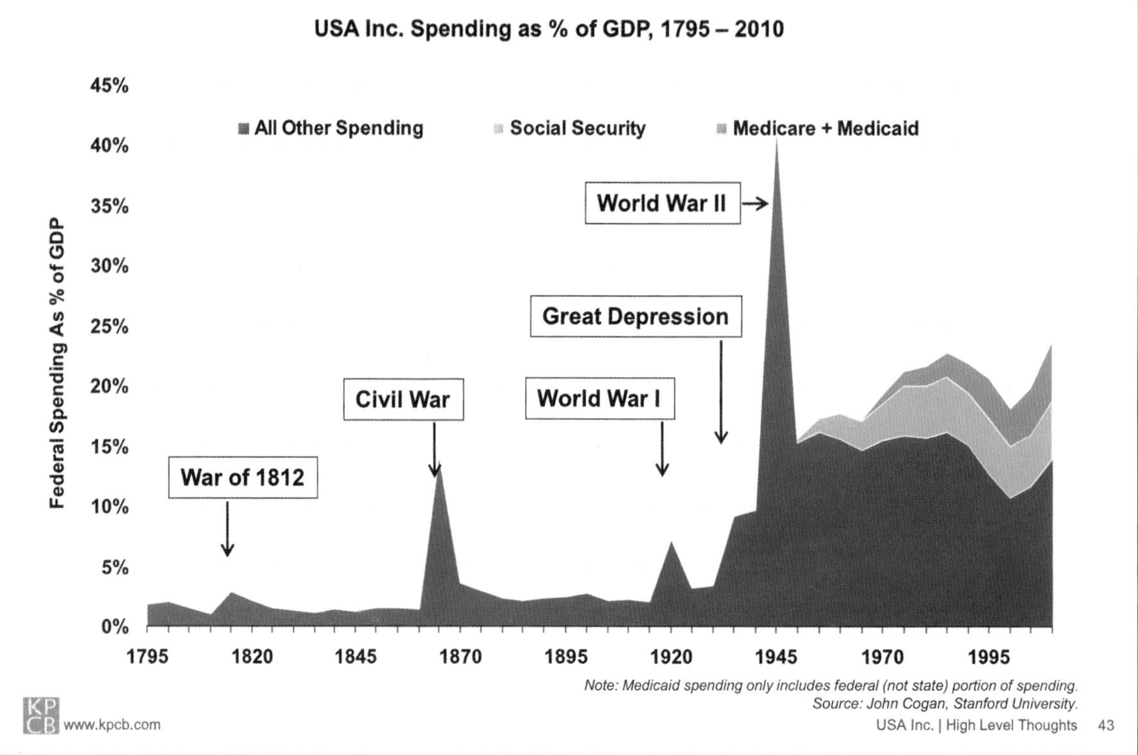

Note: Medicaid spending only includes federal (not state) portion of spending.
Source: John Cogan, Stanford University.

Perspective – USA Entitlement Spending = India's GDP

- With a population of 1.2 billion (vs. USA's 310 million) and 2010 GDP growth of 10% (vs. USA's 3%), India is a well-recognized emerging country on the global stage.

- **It's notable that India's 2010 nominal GDP* of $1.43 trillion was equal to USA's $1.43 trillion in federal government spending on Social Security, Medicare, and Medicaid.**

*Note: *Nominal GDP is not adjusted for purchasing power parity (PPP). Population and GDP data per IMF.*

The Original Estimates of Medicare's Costs Were Vastly Underestimated

- In 1965, the official estimate of Medicare's costs was $500 million per year, roughly $3 billion in 2005 dollars.*
- <u>The actual cost of Medicare has turned out to be 10x that estimate.</u>
  - Medicare's actual net loss (tax receipts + trust fund interest – expenditures) has exceeded $3 billion (adjusted for inflation) every year since 1976 and was $146 billion in 2008 alone. In other words, had the original estimate been accurate, the cumulative 43-year cost since Medicare was created would have been $129 billion, adjusted for inflation.
  - In fact, the actual cumulative spending has been $1.4 trillion** (adjusted for inflation)...in effect, 10x over budget.
- While calculations have been flawed from the beginning for some of USA Inc.'s entitlement programs, little has been done to correct the problems.

An accurate economic forecast might have sunk Medicare.

David Blumenthal and James Morone

"The Lessons of Success – Revisiting the Medicare Story", November 2008

*Sources: * Lyndon B. Johnson Library & Museum. Medicare spending data per White House OMB.*
***Dept. of Health & Human Services, CMS, data adjusted for inflation based on BEA's GDP price index.*

Many Leaders Have <u>**Voiced**</u> Concerns About Entitlement Program Math / Spending

*The **entitlement programs** are not self-funded…they are unfunded liabilities. They are the single biggest component of spending going forward.*

-- Ben Bernanke, Chairman of the Federal Reserve
Testimony before House Budget Committee, June 9, 2010

*The time we have is growing short…there are serious questions, most immediately about the sustainability of our commitment to growing **entitlement programs**.*

-- Paul Volcker, Former Chairman of the Federal Reserve
Chairman of President Obama's Economic Recovery Advisory Board
Speech at Stanford University, May 18, 2010

40-Year USA Inc. Data Points and Trends

	1965		2005	'65-'05 Change
National[1] Healthcare Spending as % of GDP	**6%**	➔	**16%**	**167%**
Federal[2] Healthcare Spending as % of GDP	***1***	➔	***5***	--
Out-of-Pocket Healthcare Spending as % of GDP	***3***	➔	***2***	--
% of Adult Population Considered Obese	**13**	➔	**32**	**146**
% of Americans Receiving Govt. Subsidy[3]	**20**	➔	**35**	**75**
% of Americans that Pay No Federal Income Tax	**20**	➔	**33**	**65**
National[1] Education Spending as % of GDP	**5**	➔	**7**	**48**
Federal Education Spending as % of GDP	***0***	➔	***1***	--
Gross Debt as % of GDP	**47**	➔	**64**	**36**
Interest Payments as % of GDP	**1.2**	➔	**1.5**	**25**
Gini Index of Income Inequality[4]	**0.34[4]**	➔	**0.41**	**20**
Net Debt[5] as % of GDP	**38**	➔	**37**	**-3**
People Below Poverty Level as % of Population	**17**	➔	**13**	**-26**
Defense Spending as % of GDP	**7**	➔	**4**	**-33**
% of Americans that Pay 50% of All Income Tax	**10[6]**	➔	**4**	**-60**
Federal Budget Surplus / Deficit as % of GDP	**-0.2**	➔	**-3**	--

Note: 1) Includes all government and private spending. 2) Includes federal spending on Medicare, Medicaid and other healthcare programs, excludes state spending on Medicaid. 3) % of Americans receiving government subsidy include all recipients of Social Security, Medicare and Medicaid, as well as government employees (incl. federal / state / local / military). Data excludes our estimated duplicates. 4) A Gini index of 0 implies perfect income equality and an index of 1 implies complete inequality, the higher the index, the more inequality there is. Earliest data for USA was measured in 1967. 5) Net debt is federal debt held by the public. 6) Earliest data available in 1980. Source: White House Office of Management and Budget, Department of Health & Human Services, Centers for Disease Control, Internal Revenue Service, Census Bureau.

Summary: 40-Year USA, Inc. Trends*

- **America is spending beyond its means, and the problem – with mounting losses & increasing debt – is getting worse, not better**
- **Healthcare spending and obesity are rising dramatically.**
- **Education spending is growing slower than healthcare spending.**
- **Defense spending is declining on relative basis.**
- **More and more Americans are on the government payroll or receive government subsidies for retirement income, medical care, housing, and food.**
- **Inequality of income and wealth is rising, and fewer Americans pay income taxes to support USA Inc.**
- **Government increasingly resorts to borrowing to fund rising spending levels (primarily for entitlement programs)…**

*Note: *We chose a 40-year period from 1965 to 2005 to examine 'normal' levels of data points and trends. We did not choose the most recent 40-year period (1969 to 2009) as USA was in deep recession in 2008 / 2009 and underwent significant tax policy fluctuations in 1968 /1969 and subsequently many metrics (like individual income and corporate profit as well as federal budget surplus / deficit and debt levels) were significantly off their 'normal' levels.*

What's the Proper Level of This and That? What's Normal?

We begin with the premise that for an enterprise (even a country that can 'print money' and tax) to be sustainable, it cannot lose money on an ongoing basis.

Successful businesses (and households) typically base their expenses on their ability to generate present and future revenue – in other words, they don't spend unless they can pay.

We analyze the data and present scenarios and options for solving the math and financial challenges facing USA Inc.

This page is intentionally left blank.

This page is intentionally left blank.
51
This page is intentionally left blank.
52

Income Statement Drilldown

www.kpcb.com

Income Statement – USA Inc. Shows **-8% Median Net Margin** Over 15 Years

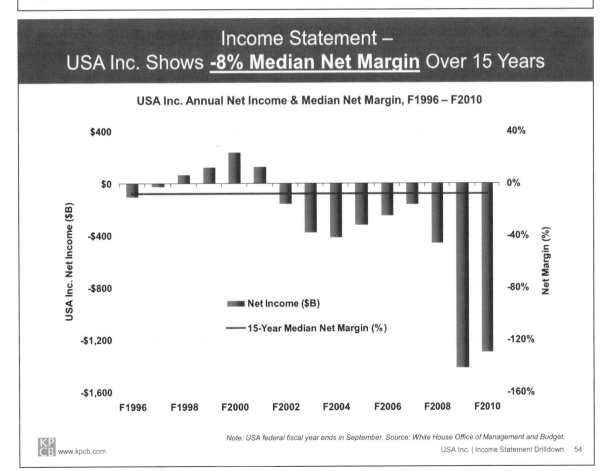

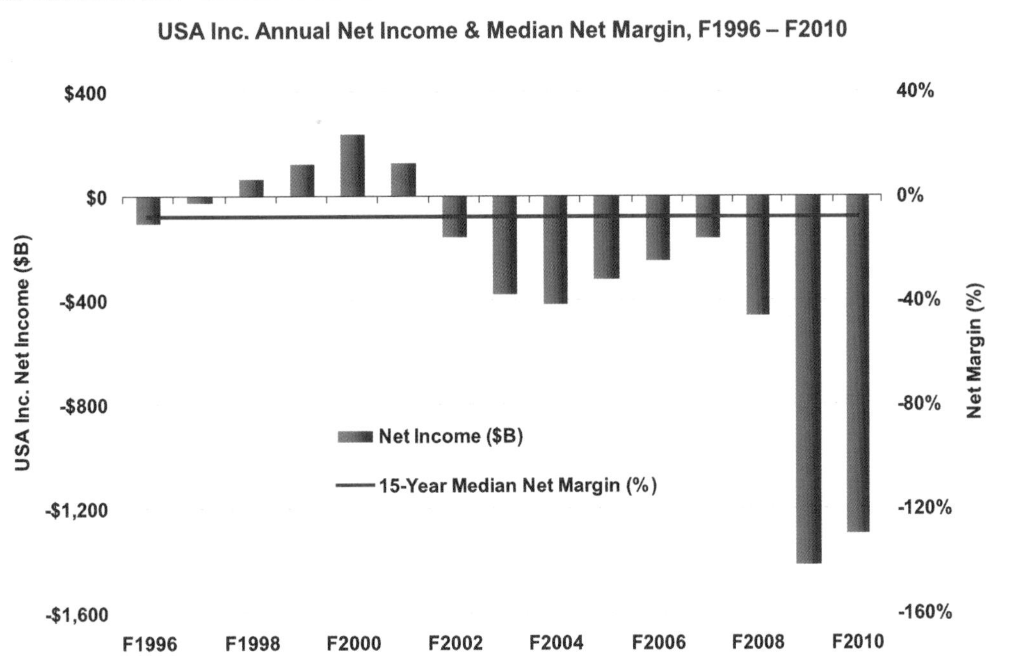

Note: USA federal fiscal year ends in September. Source: White House Office of Management and Budget.

www.kpcb.com

Income Statement – F2010 USA Inc. Revenues + Expenses at a Glance

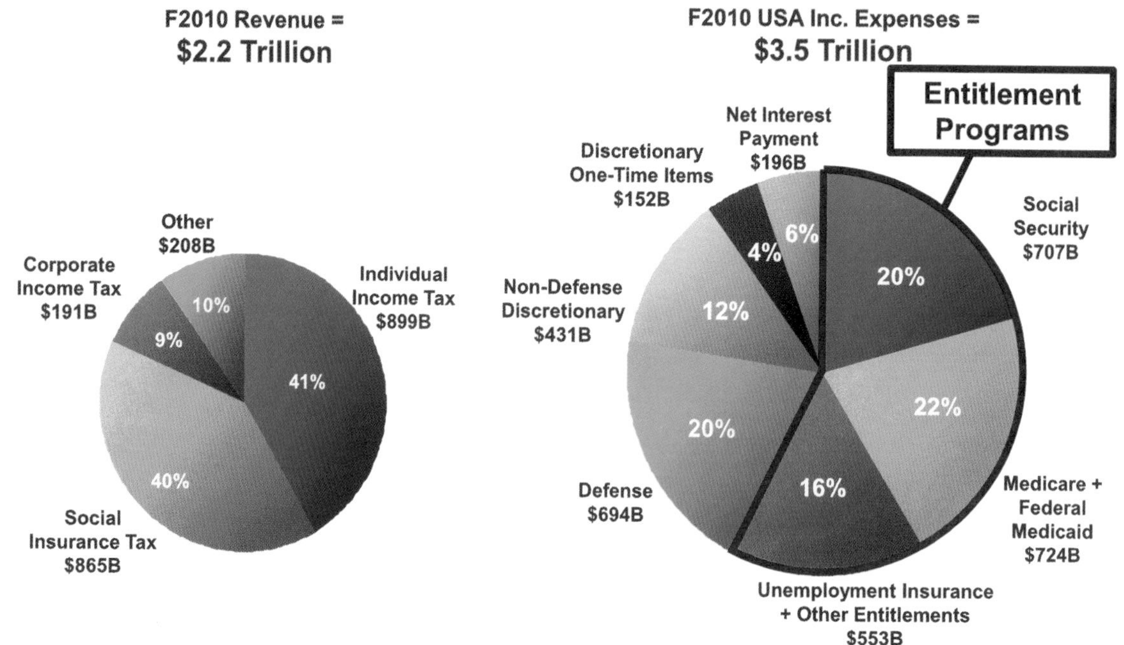

Note: USA federal fiscal year ends in September; *individual & corporate income taxes include capital gains taxes. Non-defense discretionary includes federal spending on education, infrastructure, law enforcement, judiciary functions…
Source: White House Office of Management and Budget.

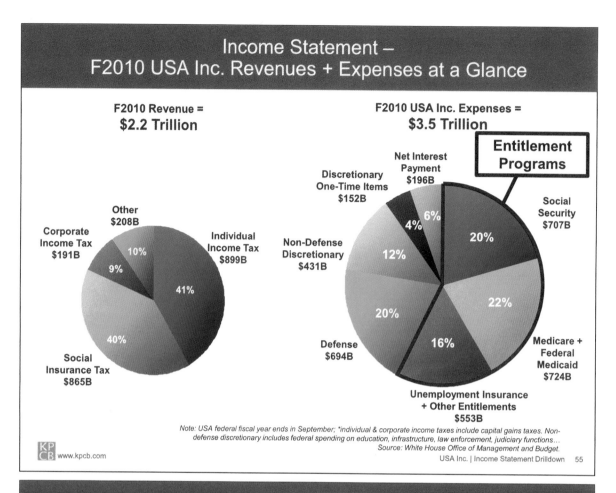

Income Statement – USA Inc. Supported **-60% Net Margin** in F2010

USA Inc. Profit & Loss Statement, F1995 / F2000 / F2005 / F2010

	F1995	… F2000	… F2005	… F2010	Comments
Revenue ($B)	$1,352	$2,026	$2,154	$2,163	**On average, revenue grew 3% Y/Y over past 15 years**
Y/Y Growth	--	***11%***	***15%***	***3%***	
Individual Income Taxes*	$590	$1,005	$927	$899	Largest driver of revenue
% of Revenue	*44%*	*50%*	*43%*	*42%*	
Social Insurance Taxes	$484	$653	$794	$865	Payroll tax on Social Security + Medicare
% of Revenue	*36%*	*32%*	*37%*	*40%*	
Corporate Income Taxes*	$157	$207	$278	$191	Fluctuates significantly with economic conditions
% of Revenue	*12%*	*10%*	*13%*	*9%*	
Other	$120	$161	$154	$208	Includes estate & gift taxes / duties & fees; relatively stable
% of Revenue	*9%*	*8%*	*7%*	*10%*	
Expense ($B)	**$1,516**	**$1,789**	**$2,472**	**$3,456**	**On average, expense grew 6% Y/Y over past 15 years**
Y/Y Growth	--	***5%***	***8%***	***-2%***	
Entitlement / Mandatory	$788	$937	$1,295	$1,984	Significant increase owing to aging population + rising healthcare cost
% of Expense	*52%*	*52%*	*52%*	*57%*	
Non-Defense Discretionary	$223	$335	$497	$431	Includes education / law enforcement / transportation…
% of Expense	*15%*	*19%*	*20%*	*12%*	
"One-Time" Items	--	--	--	$152	Includes discretionary spending on TARP, GSEs, and economic stimulus
% of Expense	--	--	--	*4%*	
Defense	$272	$294	$495	$694	Significant increase owing to on-going War on Terror
% of Expense	*18%*	*16%*	*20%*	*20%*	
Net Interest on Public Debt	$232	$223	$184	$196	Decreased owing to historic low interest rates
% of Expense	*15%*	*12%*	*7%*	*6%*	
Surplus / Deficit ($B)	**-$164**	**$237**	**-$318**	**-$1,293**	**USA Inc. median net margin between 1995 & 2010 = -8%**
Net Margin (%)	***-12%***	***12%***	***-15%***	***-60%***	

Note: USA federal fiscal year ends in September; *individual & corporate income taxes include capital gains taxes. Non-defense discretionary includes federal spending on education, infrastructure, law enforcement, judiciary functions…
Source: White House Office of Management and Budget.

Income Statement – Excluding 'Underfunded' Medicare / Medicaid[1] + One-Time Charges, USA Inc. Shows **4% Median Net Margin** Over 15 Years

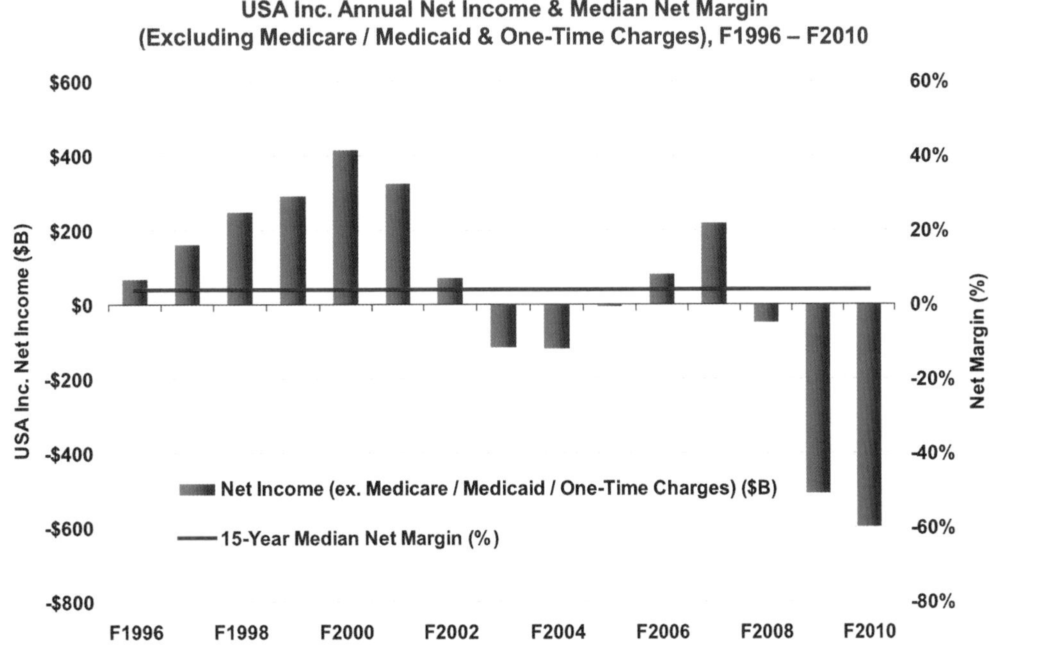

Note: 1) Excludes both 'dedicated' revenue and spending for Medicare and Medicaid. USA federal fiscal year ends in September. Source: White House Office of Management and Budget.

Income Statement: USA Inc. Profit & Loss Statement Is Solid, Excluding 'Underfunded' Medicare / Medicaid Revenue and Spending + One-Time Charges

USA Inc. Profit & Loss Statement (ex. Medicare / Medicaid / One-Time Expense), F1995 / F2000 / F2005 / F2010

	F1995	… F2000	… F2005	… F2010	Comments
Revenue ($B)	$1,256	$1,890	$1,988	$1,983	**On average, revenue (ex. Medicare) grew 3% Y/Y over past 15 years**
Y/Y Growth	--	*11%*	*15%*	*4%*	
Individual Income Taxes*	$590	$1,005	$927	$899	Largest driver of core revenue
% of Revenue	*47%*	*53%*	*47%*	*45%*	
Social Insurance Taxes (ex. Medicare)	$388	$517	$628	$685	Payroll tax on Social Security
% of Revenue	*31%*	*27%*	*32%*	*35%*	
Corporate Income Taxes*	$157	$207	$278	$191	Fluctuates significantly with economic conditions
% of Revenue	*13%*	*11%*	*14%*	*10%*	
Other	$120	$161	$154	$208	Includes estate & gift taxes / duties & fees; relatively stable
% of Revenue	*10%*	*9%*	*8%*	*10%*	
Expense ($B)	**$1,248**	**$1,474**	**$1,992**	**$2,580**	**Expenses(ex. Medicare Medicaid) grew 5% Y/Y over past 15 years**
Y/Y Growth		***5%***	***8%***	***7%***	
Entitlement (ex. Medicare / Medicaid)	$520	$622	$815	$1,259	Significant increase owing to aging population
% of Expense	*42%*	*42%*	*41%*	*49%*	
Non-Defense Discretionary	$223	$335	$497	$431	Includes education / law enforcement / transportation…
% of Expense	*18%*	*23%*	*25%*	*17%*	
Defense	$272	$294	$495	$694	Significant increase owing to on-going War on Terror
% of Expense	*22%*	*20%*	*25%*	*27%*	
Net Interest on Public Debt	$232	$223	$184	$196	Decreased owing to historic low interest rates
% of Expense	*19%*	*15%*	*9%*	*8%*	
Surplus / Deficit ($B)	**$8**	**$416**	**-$4**	**-$597**	**USA Inc. core operations were in surplus 9 out of the past 15 years**
Net Margin (%)	***1%***	***22%***	***0%***	***-30%***	

Note: USA federal fiscal year ends in September; *individual & corporate income taxes include capital gains taxes. Non-defense discretionary includes federal spending on education, infrastructure, law enforcement, judiciary functions… Source: White House Office of Management and Budget.

100-Year Review of USA Inc.'s Basic Income Statement Including Revenue & Expense Drivers as Percent of GDP

	1910	1920	1930	1940	1950	1960	1970	1980	1990	2000	2008	2009	2010
Revenue ($B)	$0.7	$7	$4	$7	$41	$92	$193	$517	$1,032	$2,025	$2,524	$2,105	$2,163
% of GDP	*2%*	*8%*	*4%*	*7%*	*15%*	*18%*	*19%*	*19%*	*18%*	*21%*	*18%*	*15%*	*15%*
Individual Income Taxes	--	$1	$1	$1	$16	$41	$90	$244	$467	$1,004	$1,146	$915	$899
% of GDP	--	*1%*	*1%*	*1%*	*6%*	*8%*	*9%*	*9%*	*8%*	*10%*	*8%*	*6%*	*6%*
Social Insurance Taxes	--	--	--	$2	$4	$15	$45	$158	$380	$653	$900	$891	$865
% of GDP	--	--	--	*2%*	*2%*	*3%*	*4%*	*6%*	*7%*	*7%*	*6%*	*6%*	*6%*
Corporate Income Taxes	--	--	$1	$1	$10	$21	$33	$65	$94	$207	$304	$138	$191
% of GDP	--	--	*1%*	*1%*	*4%*	*4%*	*3%*	*2%*	*2%*	*2%*	*2%*	*1%*	*1%*
Other*	$0.7	$6	$3	$3	$10	$16	$24	$51	$92	$161	$174	$161	$208
% of GDP	*2%*	*6%*	*3%*	*3%*	*4%*	*3%*	*2%*	*2%*	*2%*	*2%*	*1%*	*1%*	*1%*
Expense ($B)	$0.7	$6	$3	$9	$43	$92	$196	$591	$1,253	$1,789	$2,983	$3,518	$3,456
% of GDP	*2%*	*7%*	*4%*	*9%*	*16%*	*18%*	*19%*	*22%*	*22%*	*18%*	*21%*	*25%*	*24%*
Defense	$0.3	$2	$1	$2	$14	$48	$82	$134	$299	$294	$616	$661	$694
% of GDP	*1%*	*3%*	*1%*	*2%*	*5%*	*9%*	*8%*	*5%*	*5%*	*3%*	*4%*	*5%*	*5%*
Interest on the Debt	$0	$1	$1	$1	$5	$7	$14	$53	$184	$223	$253	$187	$196
% of GDP	*0%*	*1%*	*1%*	*1%*	*2%*	*1%*	*1%*	*2%*	*3%*	*2%*	*2%*	*1%*	*1%*
Social Security	--	--	--	$0	$1	$12	$30	$119	$249	$409	$617	$683	$707
% of GDP	--	--	--	*0%*	*0%*	*2%*	*3%*	*4%*	*4%*	*4%*	*4%*	*5%*	*5%*
Healthcare	--	--	--	$0	$0	$1	$12	$55	$156	$352	$671	$764	$821
% of GDP	--	--	--	*0%*	*0%*	*0%*	*1%*	*2%*	*3%*	*4%*	*5%*	*5%*	*6%*
Other**	$0	$3	$2	$6	$23	$25	$57	$231	$365	$511	$825	$1,222	$1,039
% of GDP	--	--	--	*6%*	*8%*	*5%*	*6%*	*8%*	*6%*	*5%*	*6%*	*9%*	*7%*
Surplus / Deficit ($B)	-$0	$0	$1	-$2	-$2	$0	-$3	-$74	-$221	$236	-$459	-$1,413	-$1,293
% of GDP	*0%*	*0%*	*1%*	*-2%*	*-1%*	*0%*	*0%*	*-3%*	*-4%*	*2%*	*-3%*	*-10%*	*-9%*

*Note: Data are not adjusted for inflation. *Other revenue includes customs and excise / estate taxes. **Other expenses include spending on law enforcement / education / public infrastructure / energy, etc. Source: 1910 – 1930 per Census Bureau, 1940-2010 per White House OMB.*

100-Year Review of USA Inc.'s Basic Income Statement Including Revenue & Expense Drivers as Percent of Revenue & Expenses

	1910	1920	1930	1940	1950	1960	1970	1980	1990	2000	2008	2009	2010
Revenue ($B)	$0.7	$7	$4	$7	$41	$92	$193	$517	$1,032	$2,025	$2,524	$2,105	$2,163
% of GDP	*2%*	*8%*	*4%*	*7%*	*15%*	*18%*	*19%*	*19%*	*18%*	*21%*	*18%*	*15%*	*15%*
Individual Income Taxes	--	$1	$1	$1	$16	$41	$90	$244	$467	$1,004	$1,146	$915	$899
% of Revenue	--	*16%*	*28%*	*16%*	*38%*	*44%*	*47%*	*47%*	*45%*	*50%*	*45%*	*43%*	*42%*
Social Insurance Taxes	--	--	--	$2	$4	$15	$45	$158	$380	$653	$900	$891	$865
% of Revenue	--	--	--	*25%*	*11%*	*16%*	*23%*	*31%*	*37%*	*32%*	*36%*	*42%*	*40%*
Corporate Income Taxes	--	--	$1	$1	$10	$21	$33	$65	$94	$207	$304	$138	$191
% of Revenue	--	--	*31%*	*14%*	*26%*	*23%*	*17%*	*12%*	*9%*	*10%*	*12%*	*7%*	*9%*
Other*	$0.7	$6	$3	$3	$10	$16	$24	$51	$92	$161	$174	$161	$208
% of Revenue	*100%*	*84%*	*72%*	*45%*	*25%*	*17%*	*13%*	*10%*	*9%*	*8%*	*7%*	*8%*	*10%*
Expense ($B)	$0.7	$6	$3	$9	$43	$92	$196	$591	$1,253	$1,789	$2,983	$3,518	$3,456
% of GDP	*2%*	*7%*	*4%*	*9%*	*16%*	*18%*	*19%*	*22%*	*22%*	*18%*	*21%*	*25%*	*24%*
Defense	$0.3	$2	$1	$2	$14	$48	$82	$134	$299	$294	$616	$661	$694
% of Expense	*45%*	*37%*	*25%*	*20%*	*32%*	*52%*	*42%*	*23%*	*24%*	*16%*	*21%*	*19%*	*20%*
Interest on the Debt	$0	$1	$1	$1	$5	$7	$14	$53	$184	$223	$253	$187	$196
% of Expense	*3%*	*16%*	*20%*	*11%*	*11%*	*8%*	*7%*	*9%*	*15%*	*12%*	*8%*	*5%*	*6%*
Social Security	--	--	--	$0	$1	$12	$30	$119	$249	$409	$617	$683	$707
% of Expense	--	--	--	*0%*	*2%*	*13%*	*15%*	*20%*	*20%*	*23%*	*21%*	*19%*	*20%*
Healthcare	--	--	--	$0	$0	$1	$12	$55	$156	$352	$671	$764	$821
% of Expense	--	--	--	*1%*	*1%*	*1%*	*6%*	*9%*	*12%*	*20%*	*23%*	*22%*	*24%*
Other**	$0	$3	$2	$6	$23	$25	$57	$231	$365	$511	$825	$1,222	$1,039
% of Expense	*52%*	*47%*	*55%*	*68%*	*54%*	*27%*	*29%*	*39%*	*29%*	*29%*	*28%*	*35%*	*30%*
Surplus / Deficit ($B)	-$0	$0	$1	-$2	-$2	$0	-$3	-$74	-$221	$236	-$459	-$1,413	-$1,293
% of GDP	*0%*	*0%*	*1%*	*-2%*	*-1%*	*0%*	*0%*	*-3%*	*-4%*	*2%*	*-3%*	*-10%*	*-9%*

*Note: Data are not adjusted for inflation. *Other revenue includes customs and excise / estate taxes. **Other expenses include spending on law enforcement / education / public infrastructure / energy, etc. Source: 1910 – 1930 per Census Bureau, 1940-2010 per White House OMB.*

Conclusions: 100-Year Review of USA Inc. Income Statement

- America's government has grown dramatically - USA Inc.'s revenue as percent of GDP has risen from 2% to 15%. Individual / social insurance (Social Security + Medicare) taxes have risen dramatically while customs / excise / estate taxes have declined in relative importance. In addition, USA Inc.'s spending as percent of GDP has risen to 24% in 2010, up from 3% average between 1790 and 1930.
- USA Inc.'s average operating income was at or near breakeven for most of the periods from 1910 to 1970.
- In the 1970s, as healthcare expenses (related to Medicare and Medicaid) began to surge, USA Inc. reported more frequent – and bigger – losses. Since 1970, USA Inc. showed a profit just 4 times (F1998-F2001, when economic growth was especially robust and defense spending was relatively low).
- General expense trends since 1970: non-defense discretionary spending has been flattish (except in recessions with material one-time charges), healthcare spending (largely Medicare + Medicaid) has risen materially, Social Security spending has been flattish, defense spending has been down to flattish, and interest payments varied with interest rates.

Operations of USA Inc. Are Solid, Excluding Medicare / Medicaid and One-Time Charges

Revenues of USA Inc. (largely from individual and corporate income and payroll taxes) can fund most expenses (largely spending on defense, Social Security, unemployment insurance, education, law enforcement, transportation, energy, infrastructure, federal employee & veteran benefits, and interest payments).

In fact, for USA Inc.'s operations besides Medicare / Medicaid and one-time expenses, there's ample scope to increase spending for defense, education, law enforcement, transportation, infrastructure and energy by ~4%* in aggregate and still remain break-even.

*Note: *Excluding Medicare / Medicaid revenue & expenses, USA Inc.'s expenses are, on average, 4% below revenue levels from F1996 to F2010 based on our calculation of White House OMB data.*

Defense Spending Is The Second-Largest Expense Item After Entitlements, But Below Long-Term Trend as Share of GDP

- With budget deficits rising, some advocate cutting back on defense spending, the second-largest expense item after entitlements.
- Defense spending has risen substantially in recent years, due to the wars in Afghanistan and Iraq, and other costs related to the Global War on Terror. As a percentage of GDP, however, defense spending in the U.S. remains below its 60-year trend.
- On an inflation-adjusted basis, U.S. defense spending is at its highest level since World War II. With overhead ~40% of all spending, the Defense Business Board found DoD consistently pays "more for less" and fails to attack overhead as the private sector would.[1]
- The Esquire Commission to Balance the Federal Budget, a group of four former Republican and Democratic senators, found over $300 billion[2] in defense restructuring opportunities, and other analysts proposed gradual cuts to reduce the defense budget by 14% by 2018.[3]

Notes: 1) The Defense Business Board, "Reducing Overhead and Improving Business Operations, "July 2010, http://dbb.defense.gov; 2) see Esquire Commission to Balance the Federal Budget, http://www.esquire.com/blogs/politics/federal-budget-statistics-1110.; 3) Gordon Adams and Matthew Leatherman, "A Leaner and Meaner National Defense," Foreign Affairs, *Jan/Feb 2011)*

Defense Spending Has Risen, Driven by Wars in Afghanistan + Iraq…

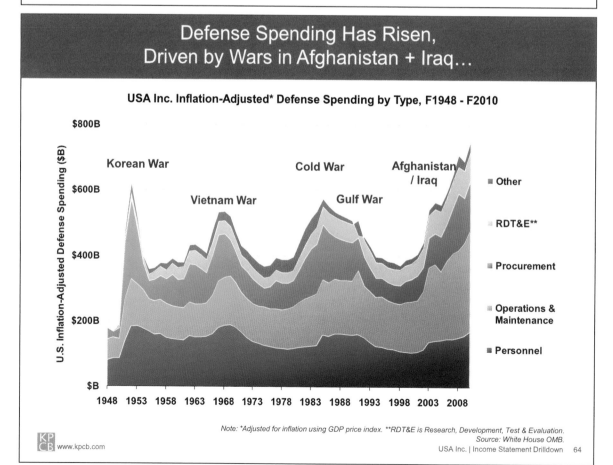

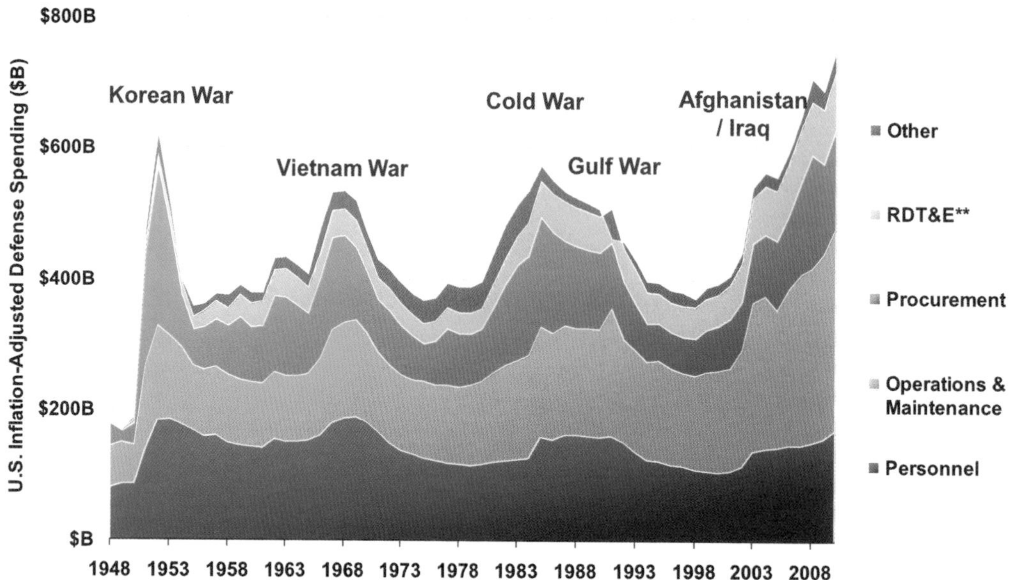

*Note: *Adjusted for inflation using GDP price index. **RDT&E is Research, Development, Test & Evaluation. Source: White House OMB.*

…While Defense Spending Rose to 5% of GDP in F2010 & Is Up from All-Time Historical Low of 3% in F1999 But It Is Still Well Below Post-World War II (1948-2000) Average of 7%

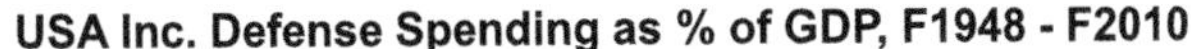

USA Inc. Defense Spending as % of GDP, F1948 - F2010

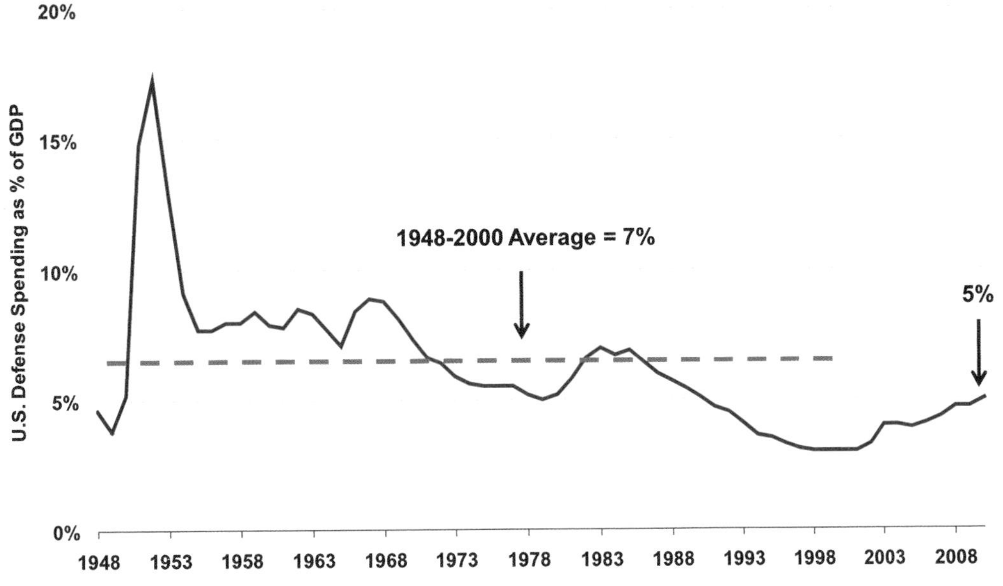

Source: White House OMB.

$950 Billion = Cumulative Cost of Iraq, Afghanistan & Global War on Terror Operations Since 9/11/01 Attacks

Cumulative Cost of Iraq, Afghanistan & Global War on Terror Operations of $950 Billion, as Percent of F2001-F2009 Spending:

4% of Total F2001-F2009 Federal Spending

22% of Total F2001-F2009 Defense Spending

28% of Total F2001-F2009 Federal Budget Deficit

Cumulative Cost of:

$685 Billion = War in Iraq

$231 Billion = War in Afghanistan

$34 Billion = Other Related Operations

Source: White House OMB, Congressional Research Service, "The Cost of Iraq, Afghanistan, and Other Global War on Terror Operations Since 9/11," 9/2/2010.

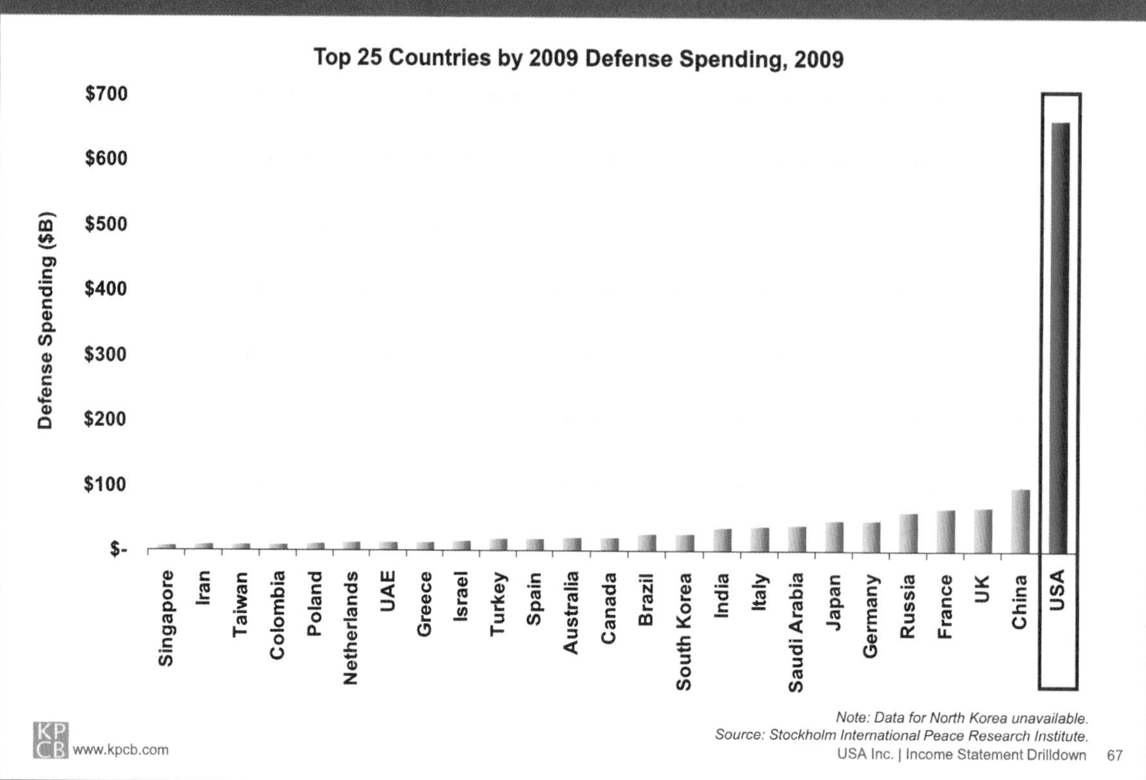
While USA Inc. Ranks # 1 in Defense Spending…
Top 25 Countries by 2009 Defense Spending, 2009
Defense Spending ($B)
$700
$600
$500
$400
$300
$200
$100
$-
Singapore
Iran
Taiwan
Colombia
Poland
Netherlands
UAE
Greece
Israel
Turkey
Spain
Australia
Canada
Brazil
South Korea
India
Italy
Saudi Arabia
Japan
Germany
Russia
France
UK
China
USA
Note: Data for North Korea unavailable.
Source: Stockholm International Peace Research Institute.
KP CB www.kpcb.com
USA Inc. | Income Statement Drilldown 67

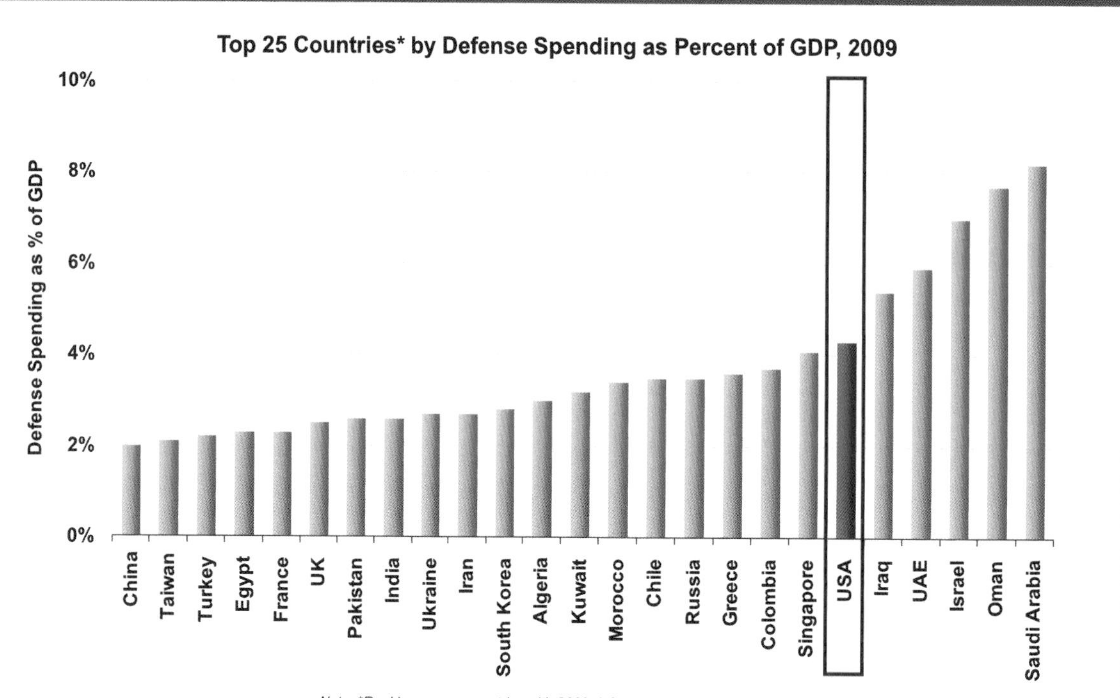
…USA Inc. Ranks # 6 in Defense Spending as Percent of GDP
Top 25 Countries* by Defense Spending as Percent of GDP, 2009
Defense Spending as % of GDP
10%
8%
6%
4%
2%
0%
China
Taiwan
Turkey
Egypt
France
UK
Pakistan
India
Ukraine
Iran
South Korea
Algeria
Kuwait
Morocco
Chile
Russia
Greece
Colombia
Singapore
USA
Iraq
UAE
Israel
Oman
Saudi Arabia
Note: *Ranking among countries with 2009 defense spending of $3 billion or higher; data for North Korea unavailable.
Source: Stockholm International Peace Research Institute.
KP CB www.kpcb.com
USA Inc. | Income Statement Drilldown 68

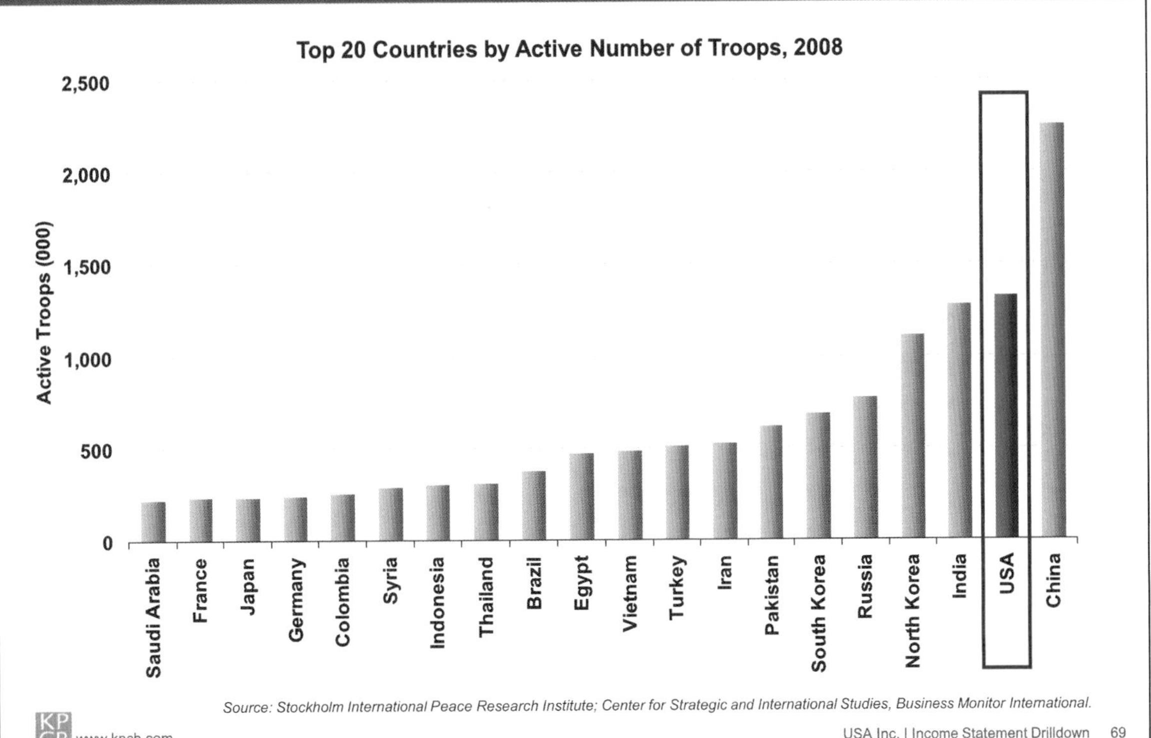
While USA Inc. Ranks # 2 in Number of Troops…
Top 20 Countries by Active Number of Troops, 2008
Active Troops (000)
2,500
2,000
1,500
1,000
500
0
Saudi Arabia
France
Japan
Germany
Colombia
Syria
Indonesia
Thailand
Brazil
Egypt
Vietnam
Turkey
Iran
Pakistan
South Korea
Russia
North Korea
India
USA
China
Source: Stockholm International Peace Research Institute; Center for Strategic and International Studies, Business Monitor International.
KP CB www.kpcb.com
USA Inc. | Income Statement Drilldown 69

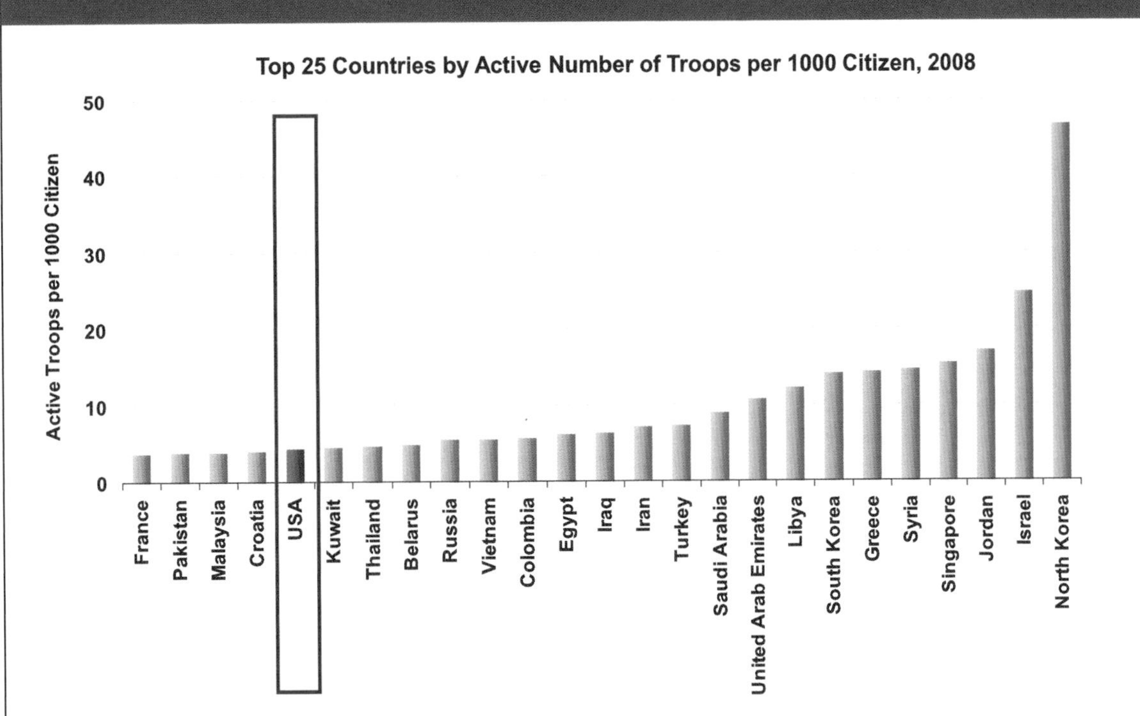
…USA Inc. Ranks # 21 in Number of Troops Per Capita
Top 25 Countries by Active Number of Troops per 1000 Citizen, 2008
Active Troops per 1000 Citizen
50
40
30
20
10
0
France
Pakistan
Malaysia
Croatia
USA
Kuwait
Thailand
Belarus
Russia
Vietnam
Colombia
Egypt
Iraq
Iran
Turkey
Saudi Arabia
United Arab Emirates
Libya
South Korea
Greece
Syria
Singapore
Jordan
Israel
North Korea
Source: Stockholm International Peace Research Institute; Center for Strategic and International Studies, Business Monitor International.
KP CB www.kpcb.com
USA Inc. | Income Statement Drilldown 70

Drill Down on USA Inc.
Entitlement + Interest + One-Time Expenses for F2010

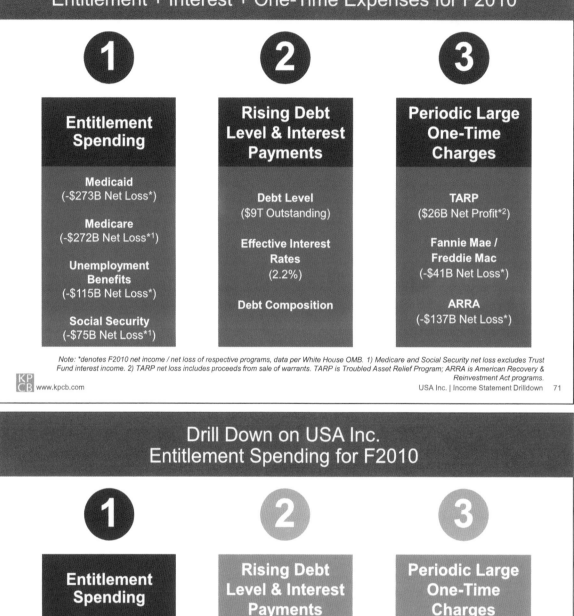

Entitlement Spending

Medicaid
(-$273B Net Loss*)

Medicare
(-$272B Net Loss*[1])

Unemployment Benefits
(-$115B Net Loss*)

Social Security
(-$75B Net Loss*[1])

2

Rising Debt Level & Interest Payments

Debt Level
($9T Outstanding)

Effective Interest Rates
(2.2%)

Debt Composition

3

Periodic Large One-Time Charges

TARP
($26B Net Profit*[2])

Fannie Mae / Freddie Mac
(-$41B Net Loss*)

ARRA
(-$137B Net Loss*)

*Note: *denotes F2010 net income / net loss of respective programs, data per White House OMB. 1) Medicare and Social Security net loss excludes Trust Fund interest income. 2) TARP net loss includes proceeds from sale of warrants. TARP is Troubled Asset Relief Program; ARRA is American Recovery & Reinvestment Act programs.*

Drill Down on USA Inc.
Entitlement Spending for F2010

Entitlement Spending

Medicaid
(-$273B Net Loss*)

Medicare
(-$272B Net Loss*[1])

Unemployment Benefits
(-$115B Net Loss*)

Social Security
(-$75B Net Loss*[1])

2

Rising Debt Level & Interest Payments

Debt Level
($9T Outstanding)

Effective Interest Rates
(2.2%)

Debt Composition

3

Periodic Large One-Time Charges

TARP
($26B Net Profit*[2])

Fannie Mae / Freddie Mac
(-$41B Net Loss*)

ARRA
(-$137B Net Loss*)

*Note: *denotes F2010 net income / net loss of respective programs, data per White House OMB. 1) Medicare and Social Security net loss excludes Trust Fund interest income. 2) TARP net loss includes proceeds from sale of warrants. TARP is Troubled Asset Relief Program; ARRA is American Recovery & Reinvestment Act programs.*

Entitlement Spending: Lacks Sufficient Dedicated Funding

Entitlement programs were created with the best of intentions by the Government. They serve many of the nation's poorest, whose struggles have been made worse by the financial crisis.

However, with the exception of Social Security (which was developed with a pay-as-you-go funding plan and constructed to be legally flexible if conditions change) and unemployment insurance (which was designed to be flexible at State level), other entitlement plans (including Medicaid and Medicare) were developed **without** sufficient dedicated funding.

Here we drill down on the funding trends for entitlement plans …

Entitlement Spending: **Expenses Up 2x** Over 15 Years
Annual Entitlement Spending Per Household = $16,600 per Year

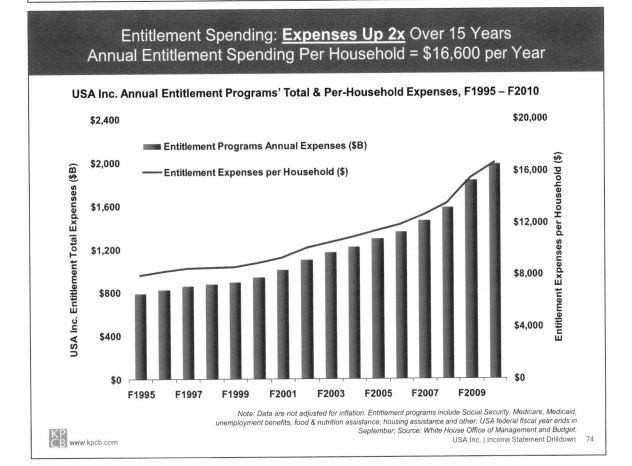

USA Inc. Annual Entitlement Programs' Total & Per-Household Expenses, F1995 – F2010

Entitlement Programs Annual Expenses ($B)
Entitlement Expenses per Household ($)
USA Inc. Entitlement Total Expenses ($B)
$2,400
$2,000
$1,600
$1,200
$800
$400
$0
Entitlement Expenses per Household ($)
$20,000
$16,000
$12,000
$8,000
$4,000
$0
F1995 F1997 F1999 F2001 F2003 F2005 F2007 F2009

Note: Data are not adjusted for inflation. Entitlement programs include Social Security, Medicare, Medicaid, unemployment benefits, food & nutrition assistance, housing assistance and other. USA federal fiscal year ends in September; Source: White House Office of Management and Budget.

Entitlement Spending: Expenses Up **169%** Over Past 15 Years, While Dedicated Funding Up Only **70%****

	F1995 ···	F2000 ···	F2005	F2006	F2007	F2008	F2009	F2010
Entitlement Revenue ($B)	**$484**	**$653**	**$794**	**$838**	**$870**	**$900**	**$891**	**$865**
Y/Y Growth	--	*7%*	*8%*	*6%*	*4%*	*4%*	*-1%*	*-3%*
Social Security	$351	$481	$577	$608	$635	$658	$654	$632
% of Revenue	*72%*	*74%*	*73%*	*73%*	*73%*	*73%*	*73%*	*73%*
Medicare	$96	$136	$166	$177	$185	$194	$191	$180
% of Revenue	*20%*	*21%*	*21%*	*21%*	*21%*	*22%*	*21%*	*21%*
Medicaid	$0	$0	$0	$0	$0	$0	$0	$0
Unemployment Insurance	$29	$28	$42	$43	$41	$40	$38	$45
% of Revenue	*6%*	*4%*	*5%*	*5%*	*5%*	*4%*	*4%*	*5%*
Other*	$8	$9	$9	$9	$9	$9	$8	$8
% of Revenue	*2%*	*1%*	*1%*	*1%*	*1%*	*1%*	*1%*	*1%*
Entitlement Expense ($B)	**$788**	**$937**	**$1,295**	**$1,357**	**$1,462**	**$1,582**	**$1,834**	**$1,984**
Y/Y Growth	--	*5%*	*6%*	*5%*	*8%*	*8%*	*16%*	*8%*
Social Security	$336	$409	$523	$549	$586	$617	$683	$707
% of Expense	*43%*	*44%*	*40%*	*40%*	*40%*	*39%*	*37%*	*36%*
Medicare	$160	$197	$299	$330	$375	$391	$430	$452
% of Expense	*20%*	*21%*	*23%*	*24%*	*26%*	*25%*	*23%*	*23%*
Medicaid	$108	$118	$182	$181	$191	$201	$251	$273
% of Expense	*14%*	*13%*	*14%*	*13%*	*13%*	*13%*	*14%*	*14%*
Unemployment Benefits	$24	$23	$35	$34	$35	$45	$123	$160
% of Expense	*3%*	*2%*	*3%*	*2%*	*2%*	*3%*	*7%*	*8%*
Other*	$161	$189	$256	$264	$275	$328	$347	$392
% of Expense	*20%*	*20%*	*20%*	*19%*	*19%*	*21%*	*19%*	*20%*
Entitlement Surplus / Deficit ($B)	**-$304**	**-$284**	**-$501**	**-$519**	**-$592**	**-$682**	**-$943**	**-$1,119**
Net Margin (%)	***-63%***	***-43%***	***-63%***	***-62%***	***-68%***	***-76%***	***-106%***	***-129%***

*Note: USA federal fiscal year ends in September; Medicaid is jointly funded by federal and state governments, and as a social welfare program (unlike a social insurance program like Medicare), there is no dedicated trust fund. *Other expenses include family & other support assistance, earned income tax credit, child tax credit and payments to states for foster care / adoption assistance. **We exclude Social Security & Medicare Part A trust funds interest income as they are accounting gains rather than real revenue. Source: White House Office of Management and Budget.*

Entitlement Spending: Observation About Social Security & Medicare Part A Trust Fund – More Like Accounting Values Than Real Dollars

- Social Security Trust Fund balance (accumulated annual surpluses + interest income) = $2.5 trillion as of 2009; Medicare Part A Trust Fund balance = $304 billion as of 2009. These surpluses were invested in a special (non-marketable) series of U.S. Treasury securities, which were then used to finance budget deficits in other parts of USA Inc. like Medicaid & Nutrition Assistance.
- As a result, many observers have argued that Social Security and Medicare Part A Trust Funds' balances are no more than accounting gains on paper owing to: 1) no 'real' assets (such as tradable stocks / real estates…) in these Trust Funds as the special U.S. Treasury securities are non-marketable and 2) the Treasury Department needs to raise taxes / cut other programs' spending / borrow more money in the future to meet any withdrawal requests.
- We think that for Social Security and Medicare Part A programs, their Trust Funds' balances have **legal value** as USA Inc. is legally obliged to repay the principal and interest on the Treasury securities held in respective Trust Funds.
- However, we think that these Trust Fund balances have **NO economic value** as these cumulative surpluses have been spent by USA Inc. to reduce the borrowing need in the past. When Social Security & Medicare begin net withdrawal from their Trust Funds (likely in 2017E), USA Inc.'s debt levels + interest payments growth could accelerate, owing to the double whammy of: 1) loss of revenue source (previous surpluses) and 2) additional Treasury redemption costs related to Trust Funds' withdrawal requests.
- Consequently, **we exclude Social Security and Medicare Trust Funds' balances and interest income** from our financial models and **calculate their liabilities on a net basis**.

Data source: Social Security Administration, Dept. of Health & Human Services, CBO. Note: the economic value of Social Security Trust Fund is subject to debate, for a different perspective, refer to Peter Dimond and Peter Orszag, "Saving Social Security: A Balanced Approach," p51 Box 3-5.

Entitlement Spending: Non-Partisan CBO Advises Excluding Social Security / Medicare Trust Funds' Balances + Interest Income in Fiscal Analysis

Trust funds can be useful mechanisms for monitoring the balance between earmarked receipts and a program's spending, but they are basically an accounting device, and their balances, even if "invested" in Treasury securities, provide no resources to the government for meeting future funding commitments. When those payments come due, the government must finance them in the same way that it finances other commitments -- through taxes or borrowing from the public. Thus, assessing the state of the federal government's future finances requires measuring such commitments independently of their trust fund status or the balance recorded in the funds.

-- Congressional Budget Office (CBO)

"Measures of the U.S. Government's Fiscal Position Under Current Law," 8/04

Entitlement Spending: Funding Patterns of Some Entitlement Programs Work Better than Others

Have Worked Relatively Well Financially:

- **Social Security** – Has operated at close to break-even - so far - thanks to sufficient payroll tax income from a relatively large working-age population. In fact, Social Security has worked so well, that its surplus net income has been used to finance other government activities such as Medicaid.
- **Unemployment Insurance** – Has operated at close to break-even thanks to accumulated net incomes during 'good years' (though expenses spiked to $123 billion / $160 billion in 2009 / 2010 from $45 billion in 2008 owing to recession).

Have Worked Relatively Poorly Financially:

- **Medicaid** – Has operated at an average annual loss of $160 billion with, in effect, an average net margin of -100% over past 15 years; the annual dollar loss has risen from $108 billion to $273 billion because of rising healthcare costs and expanded enrollment.
- **Medicare** – Has operated at an average annual loss of $123 billion with, in effect, an average net margin of -83% over past 15 years; the margin has fallen from -66% to -154% (or -$64 billion in annual loss to -$272 billion) because of rising healthcare costs + expanding coverage (added Part D prescription drug benefits through legislation in 2003, rolled out in 2006).

Source: White House Office of Management and Budget.

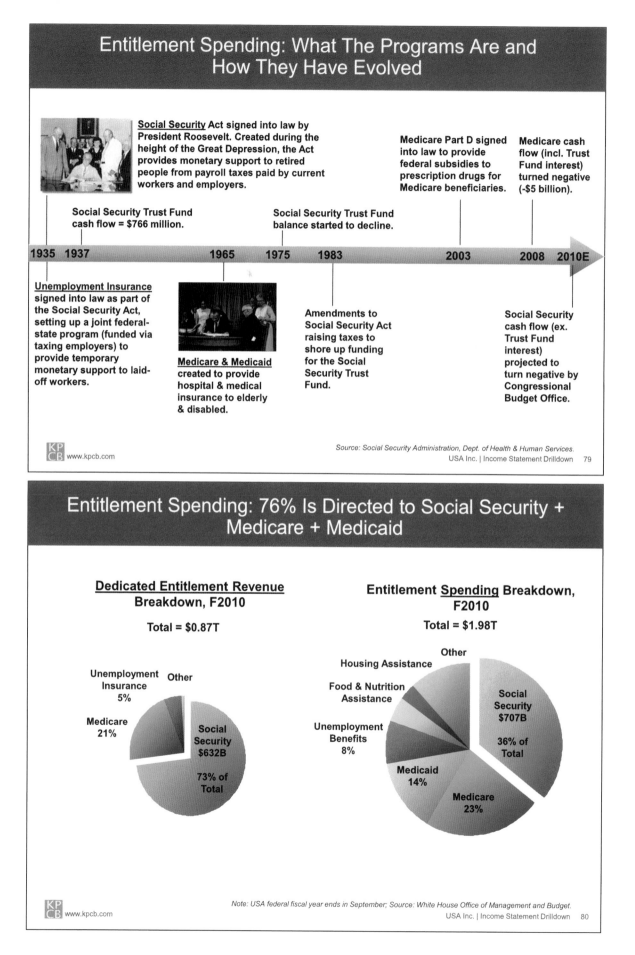

Entitlement Spending: What The Programs Are and How They Have Evolved

1935 — **Social Security** Act signed into law by President Roosevelt. Created during the height of the Great Depression, the Act provides monetary support to retired people from payroll taxes paid by current workers and employers.

1935 — **Unemployment Insurance** signed into law as part of the Social Security Act, setting up a joint federal-state program (funded via taxing employers) to provide temporary monetary support to laid-off workers.

1937 — Social Security Trust Fund cash flow = $766 million.

1965 — **Medicare & Medicaid** created to provide hospital & medical insurance to elderly & disabled.

1975 — Social Security Trust Fund balance started to decline.

1983 — Amendments to Social Security Act raising taxes to shore up funding for the Social Security Trust Fund.

2003 — Medicare Part D signed into law to provide federal subsidies to prescription drugs for Medicare beneficiaries.

2008 — Medicare cash flow (incl. Trust Fund interest) turned negative (-$5 billion).

2010E — Social Security cash flow (ex. Trust Fund interest) projected to turn negative by Congressional Budget Office.

Source: Social Security Administration, Dept. of Health & Human Services.

Entitlement Spending: 76% Is Directed to Social Security + Medicare + Medicaid

Dedicated Entitlement Revenue Breakdown, F2010

Total = $0.87T

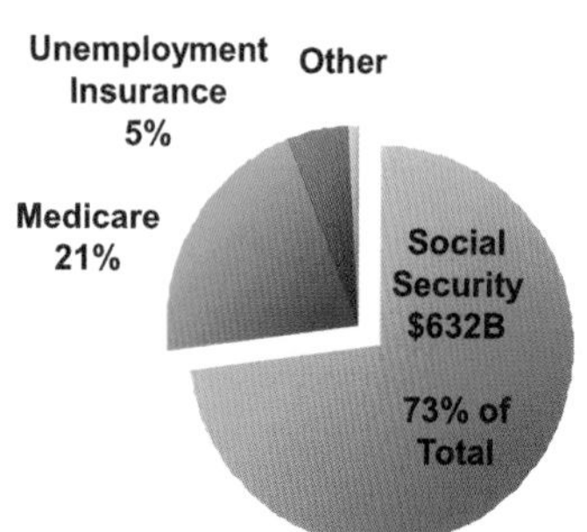

Entitlement Spending Breakdown, F2010

Total = $1.98T

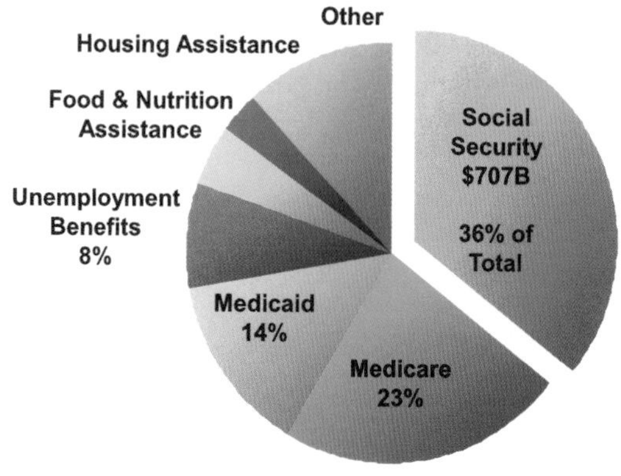

Note: USA federal fiscal year ends in September; Source: White House Office of Management and Budget.

Entitlement Spending: Observations from Previous Slide

- **Entitlement revenue was $0.87 trillion, yet entitlement spending was $1.98 trillion in F2010.**
- **Entitlement spending exceeded entitlement revenue by 129% in F2010.**
- Social Security (ex. Trust Fund interest income) accounted for 73% of dedicated entitlement revenue yet only 36% of entitlement spending in F2010 while Medicare accounted for 21% of revenue and 23% of spending and Medicaid accounted for 0% of revenue and 14% of spending.

Entitlement Spending: Clarification On 'Unfunded' / 'Net Responsibilities'…

- There is debate about the semantics of using words like unfunded / net responsibilities to describe the financial status of entitlement programs like Social Security, Medicare and Medicaid.
- **'Unfunded'** – We define 'unfunded' liabilities for Social Security and Medicare as the present value of future expenditures in excess of dedicated future revenue. We call Social Security and Medicare 'partially unfunded' entitlement programs as their future expenditures are projected to exceed dedicated future revenue.
- **'Net Responsibilities'** – USA Inc. does not record these 'unfunded' financial commitments as explicit liabilities on balance sheet, owing to Federal accounting standards.[1]
  - USA Inc.'s Dept. of Treasury calls these commitments 'net responsibilities' or 'net expenditures' in its annual *Financial Report of the U.S. Government*.
- **Medicaid** – We view Medicaid as an 'unfunded' liability as there is no dedicated revenue source to match expected expenses in our financial analysis. Medicaid is jointly funded on a pay-as-you go basis by Federal and State general tax revenue.

Note: 1) per Dept. of Treasury, "2004 Financial Report of the United States Government."

...Entitlement Spending: Clarification On 'Unfunded' / 'Net Responsibilities'

- Unless they are reduced, USA Inc.'s financial liabilities -- whether they are actual debt or the present value of future promises, whether called 'unfunded' liabilities or 'net responsibilities' and whether funded by dedicated taxes or general revenue – represent significant claims on USA Inc.'s future economic resources.

- To be sure, the projected unfunded liabilities are not the same as debt, because Congress can change the laws that are behind those future promises. With a few exceptions, however, over the past 60 years, lawmakers have acted to boost rather than reduce them.

Entitlement Spending: Social Security Funding Has Worked, So Far While Medicare/Medicaid Are Underfunded by $5.6 Trillion Since Inception in 1965

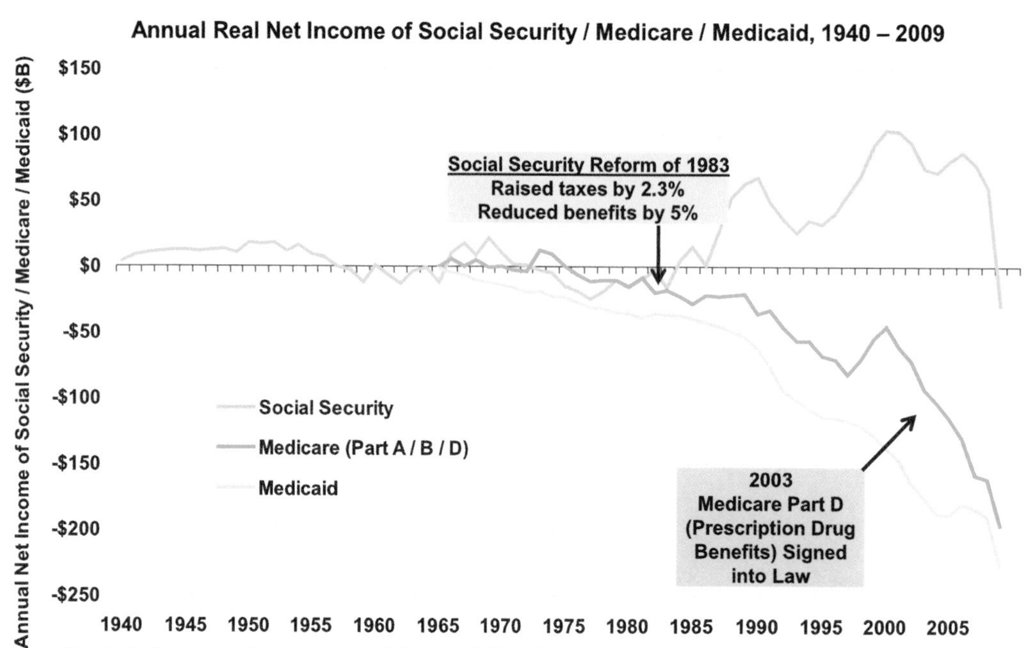

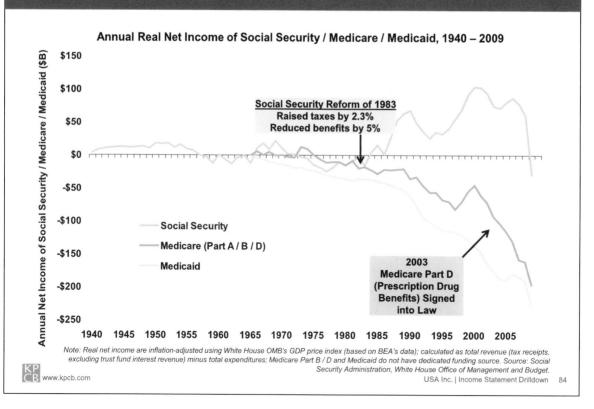

Note: Real net income are inflation-adjusted using White House OMB's GDP price index (based on BEA's data); calculated as total revenue (tax receipts, excluding trust fund interest revenue) minus total expenditures; Medicare Part B / D and Medicaid do not have dedicated funding source. Source: Social Security Administration, White House Office of Management and Budget.

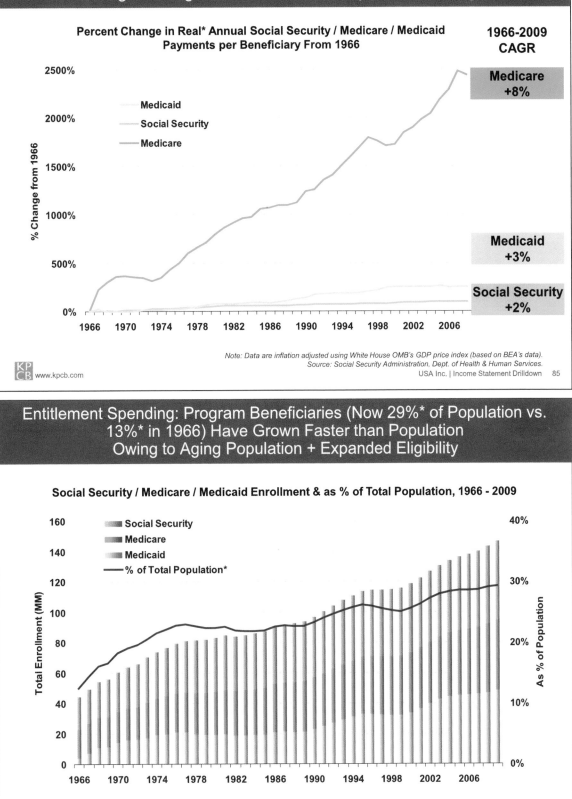

Entitlement Spending: Medicare & Medicaid Payments per Beneficiary Have Risen Faster than Social Security Payments Owing to Rising Healthcare Costs + Expanded Coverage

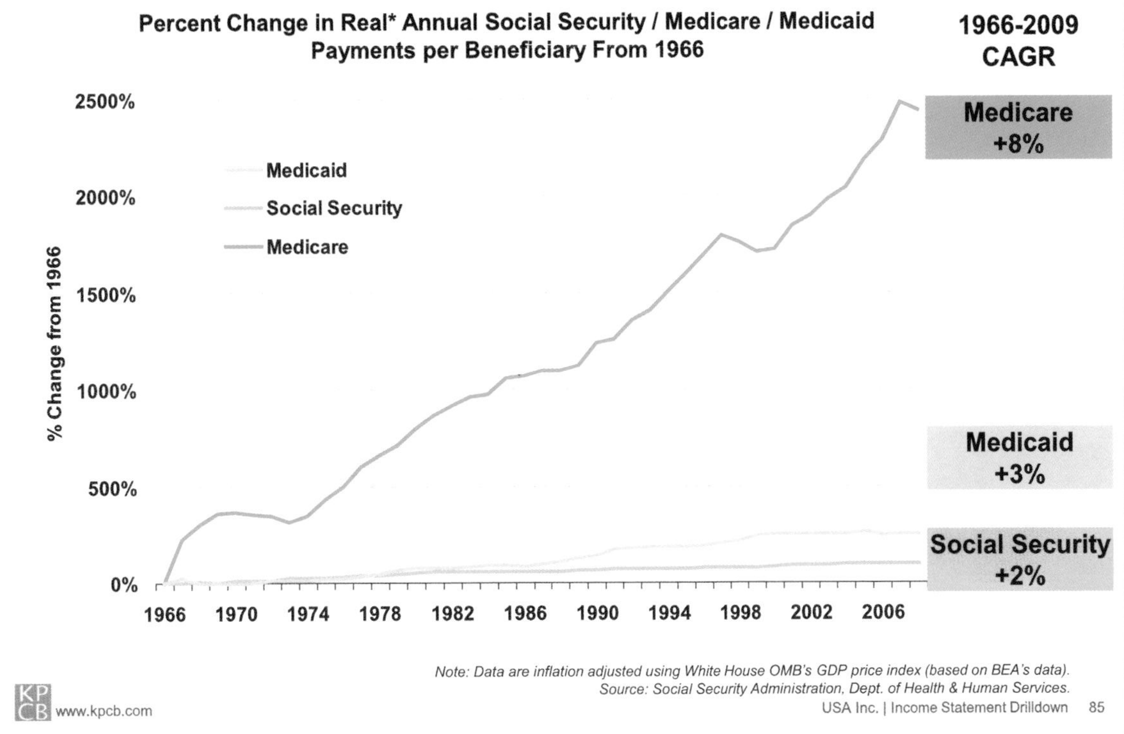

Note: Data are inflation adjusted using White House OMB's GDP price index (based on BEA's data). Source: Social Security Administration, Dept. of Health & Human Services.

Entitlement Spending: Program Beneficiaries (Now 29%* of Population vs. 13%* in 1966) Have Grown Faster than Population Owing to Aging Population + Expanded Eligibility

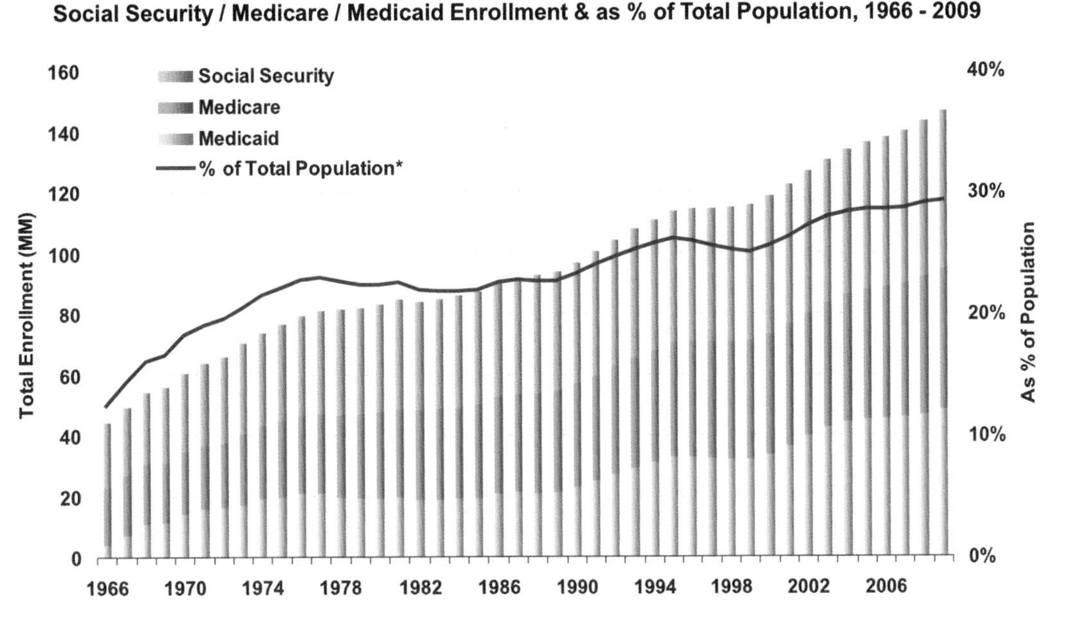

*Note: *Excludes our estimated dual / triple enrollees in Social Security / Medicare / Medicaid. Source: Social Security Administration, Dept. of Health & Human Services.*

Entitlement Spending: While Beneficiaries From Aging Population Rose 2x From 1966 to 2009, Beneficiaries From Expanded Eligibility (Low-Income / Disabled) Rose 10x

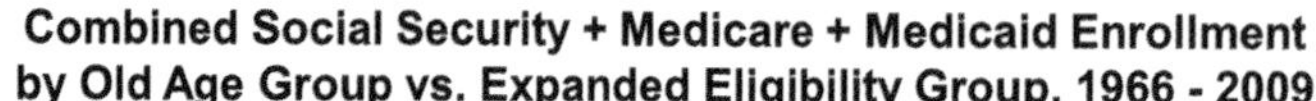

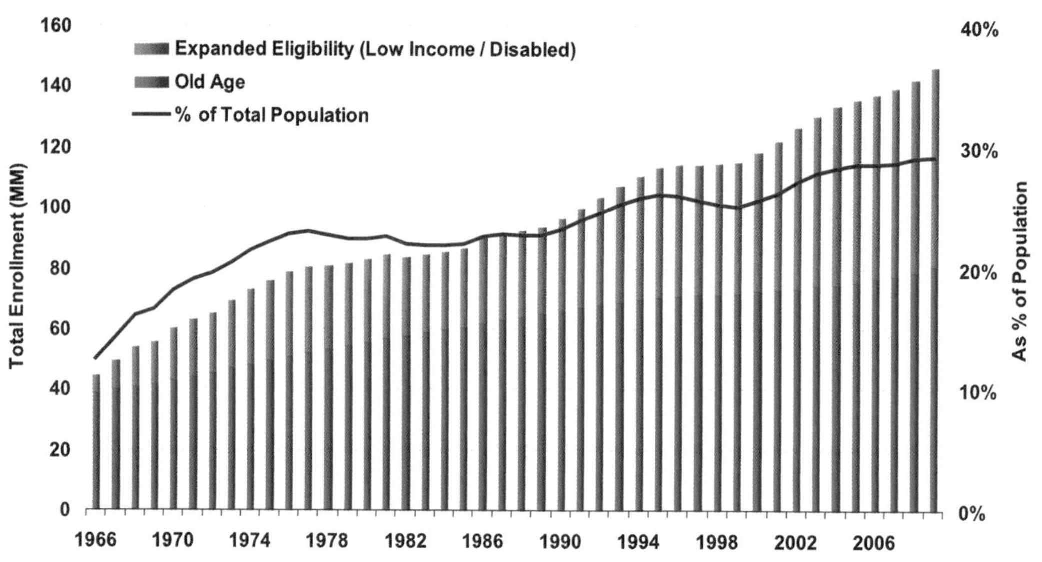

*Note: *Excludes our estimated dual / triple enrollees in Social Security / Medicare / Medicaid. Source: Social Security Administration, Dept. of Health & Human Services.*

Entitlement Spending: Entitlement Program + Government Employee Beneficiaries Are Now 36%* of Population vs. 20%* in 1966

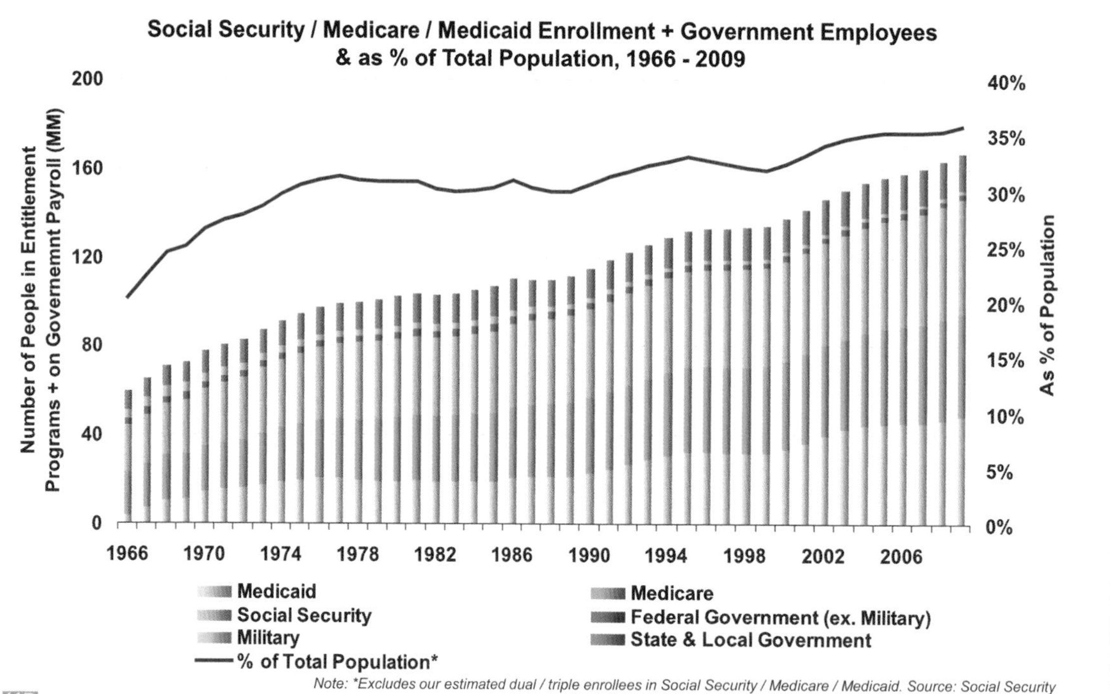

*Note: *Excludes our estimated dual / triple enrollees in Social Security / Medicare / Medicaid. Source: Social Security Administration, Dept. of Health & Human Services, Bureau of Economic Analysis.*

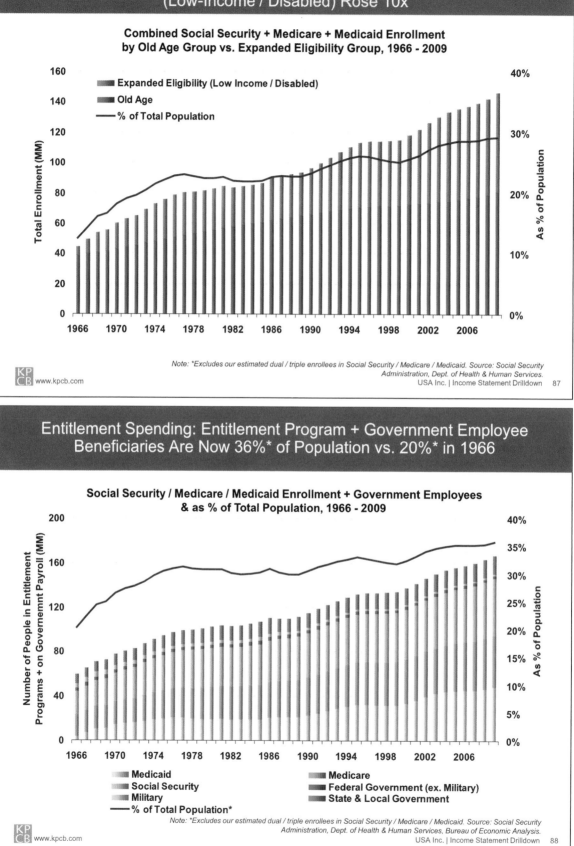

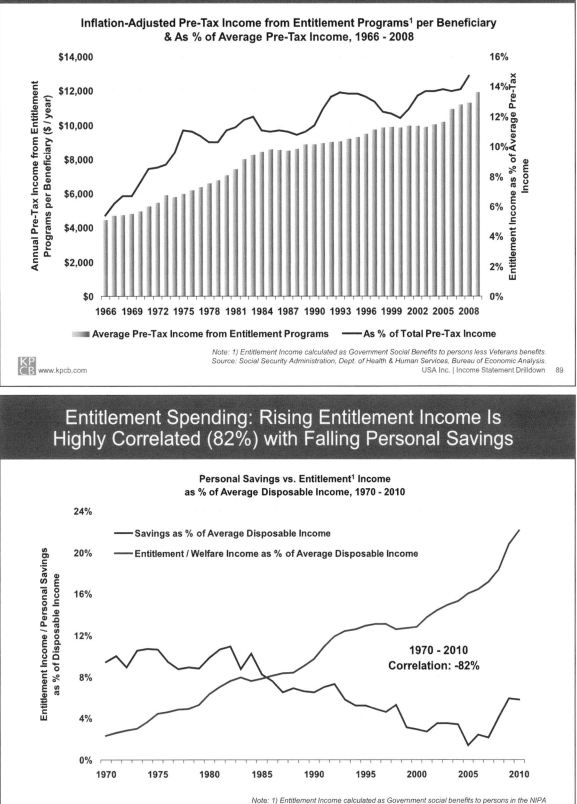

Entitlement Spending per Beneficiary: Inflation-Adjusted Average Pre-Tax Income from Entitlement Programs Has Gone Up 3x Since 1966 to $12K in 2008, or 15% of Average Pre-Tax Income

Inflation-Adjusted Pre-Tax Income from Entitlement Programs[1] per Beneficiary & As % of Average Pre-Tax Income, 1966 - 2008

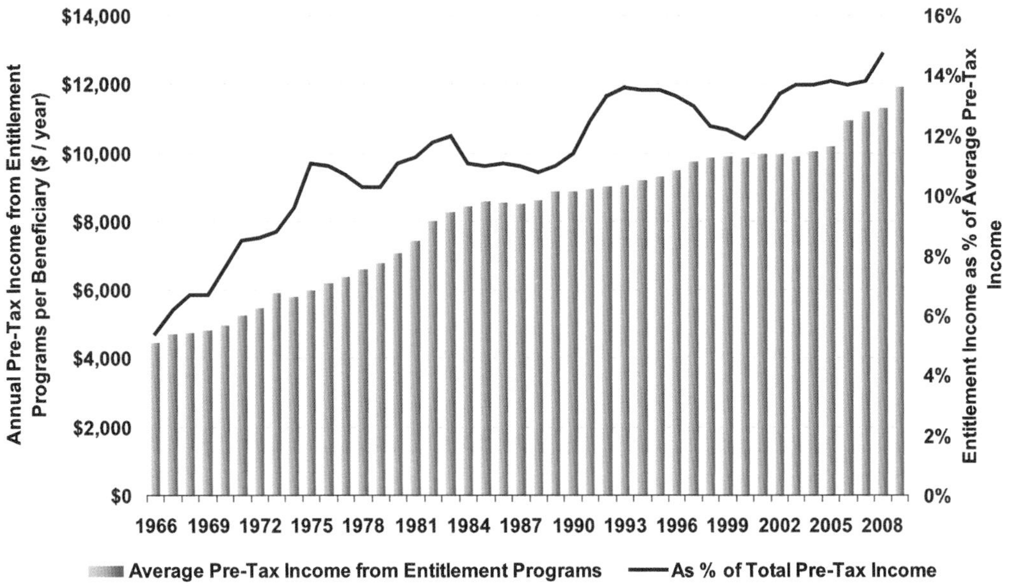

Note: 1) Entitlement Income calculated as Government Social Benefits to persons less Veterans benefits.
Source: Social Security Administration, Dept. of Health & Human Services, Bureau of Economic Analysis.

Entitlement Spending: Rising Entitlement Income Is Highly Correlated (82%) with Falling Personal Savings

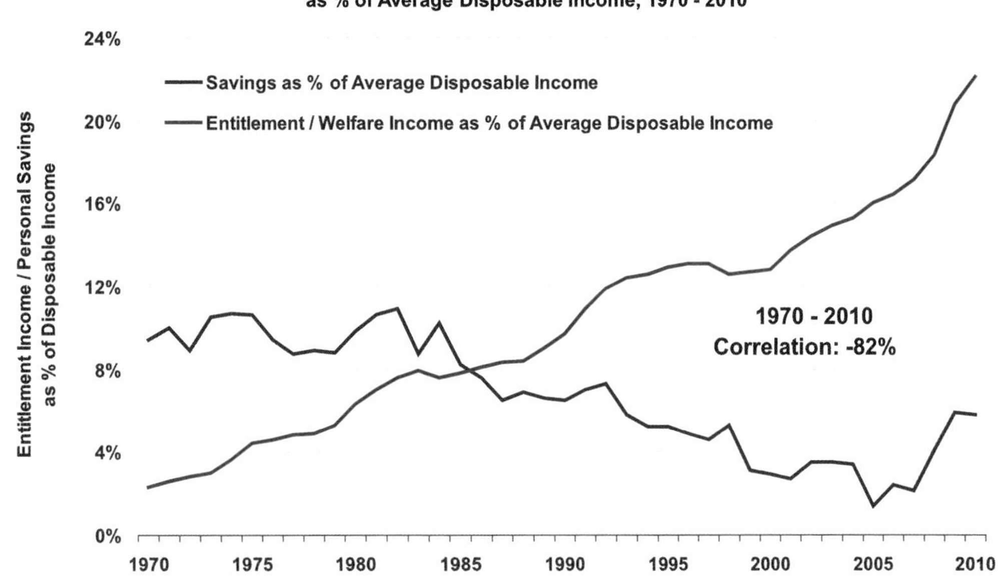

Note: 1) Entitlement Income calculated as Government social benefits to persons in the NIPA series Table 2.1. Savings rate is the amount of money saved divided by income after taxes.
Sources: BEA

Entitlement Spending: Observation from Previous Slide

- Clearly, lower interest rates have allowed Americans to borrow more and save less. But given the high correlation between rising entitlement income for beneficiaries and declining savings rates, one might also wonder if Americans feel less compelled to save money as they feel that they can depend on the government to give them money.

Note: Savings rate is the amount of money saved divided by income after taxes.

Entitlement Spending: Social Security Now Provides 37% of an Average Retiree's Income, Up From 31% in 1962

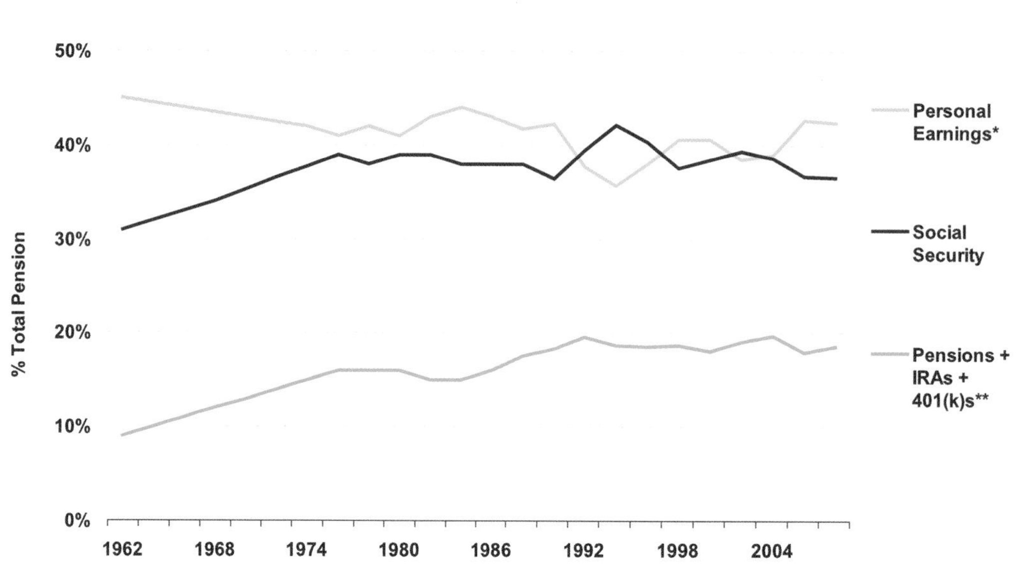

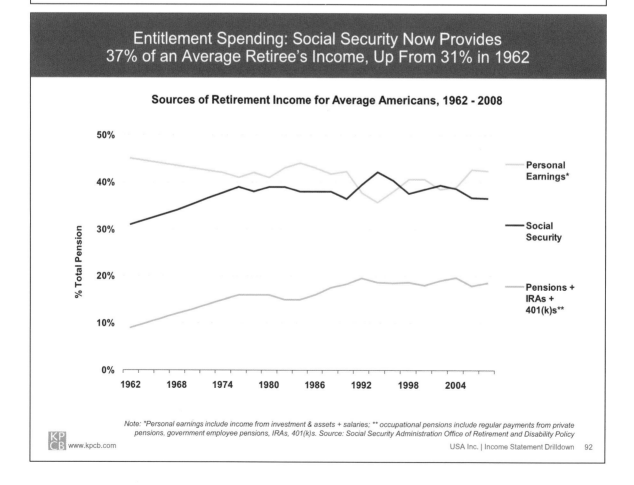

*Note: *Personal earnings include income from investment & assets + salaries; ** occupational pensions include regular payments from private pensions, government employee pensions, IRAs, 401(k)s. Source: Social Security Administration Office of Retirement and Disability Policy*

Next, We Drill Down on Entitlement Programs…

- **We begin with the programs with the least sound financials (Medicaid and Medicare) and end with the programs with the most sound financials (Unemployment Insurance and Social Security), as of today.**

- **We then move to a drilldown of rising healthcare costs after the Medicaid and Medicare drilldowns.**

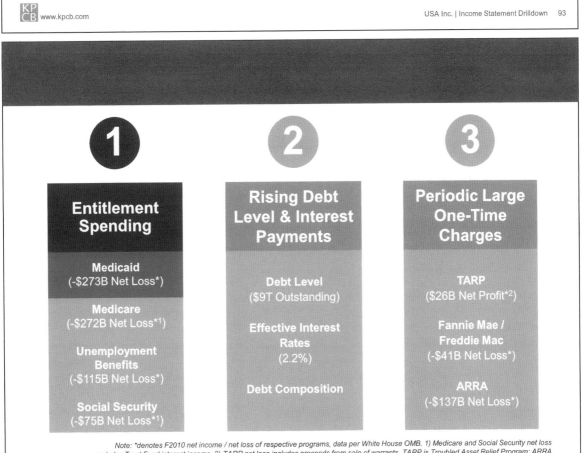

1	2	3
Entitlement Spending	**Rising Debt Level & Interest Payments**	**Periodic Large One-Time Charges**
Medicaid (-$273B Net Loss*)	**Debt Level** ($9T Outstanding)	**TARP** ($26B Net Profit*[2])
Medicare (-$272B Net Loss*[1])	**Effective Interest Rates** (2.2%)	**Fannie Mae / Freddie Mac** (-$41B Net Loss*)
Unemployment Benefits (-$115B Net Loss*)	**Debt Composition**	**ARRA** (-$137B Net Loss*)
Social Security (-$75B Net Loss*[1])		

*Note: *denotes F2010 net income / net loss of respective programs, data per White House OMB. 1) Medicare and Social Security net loss excludes Trust Fund interest income. 2) TARP net loss includes proceeds from sale of warrants. TARP is Troubled Asset Relief Program; ARRA is American Recovery & Reinvestment Act programs.*

Medicaid: Facing Accelerating Cash Flow Deficits

- **Social Welfare Program** – Created in 1965 to provide health insurance to low-income population (2% of Americans under coverage then and 16% now*).
- **No Dedicated Funding** – Federal funding comes from general revenue (all forms of tax receipts).
- **Ever-Growing Expenses** – $273 billion in F2010, up 2x from 10 years ago.
  - **Rising Healthcare Costs** – Owing to aging population + unhealthy life styles + technology advances.
  - **Growing Beneficiary + Benefits** – Covered beneficiaries expanded beyond low-income group in 1980s to include additional groups (like individuals who have high medical expenses and have spent down their assets, and some of those who lost their employer-sponsored healthcare insurance coverage in recession), while covered benefits expanded to include prescription drugs / dental services. **Total expenditures on these new groups and benefits represented ~60% of Medicaid program's spending in 2001, per Kaiser Family Foundation estimates. See slide 319-322 for more details.**
  - **Moral Hazard** – As a "free good," Medicaid reduced demand for private long-term insurance[1] while regulation loopholes + need-based benefit policies created incentives to abuse the Medicaid reimbursement system.

*Note: 1) for more information, please see Jeffrey Brown and Amy Finkelstein, "The Interaction of Public and Private Insurance: Medicaid and the Long-Term Care Insurance Market," 2006. *Medicaid enrollment was 4MM (population 196MM) in 1966 and 50MM (population 305MM) in 2009. Source: National Center for Health Statistics, Kaiser Family Foundation, World Bank, Social Security Administration.*

Medicaid: Underfunded by $3.7 Trillion Over 45 Years, With No Dedicated Funding

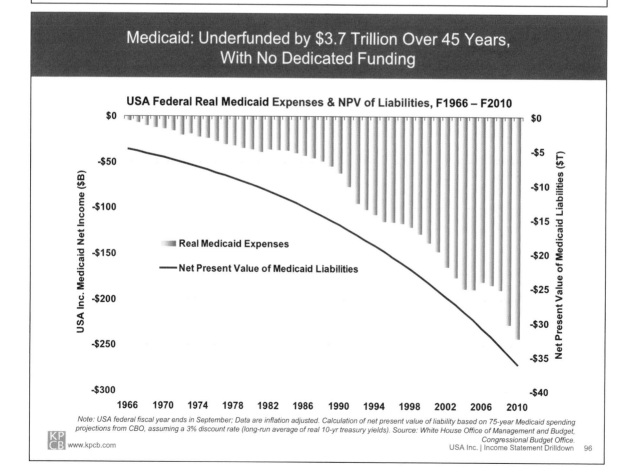

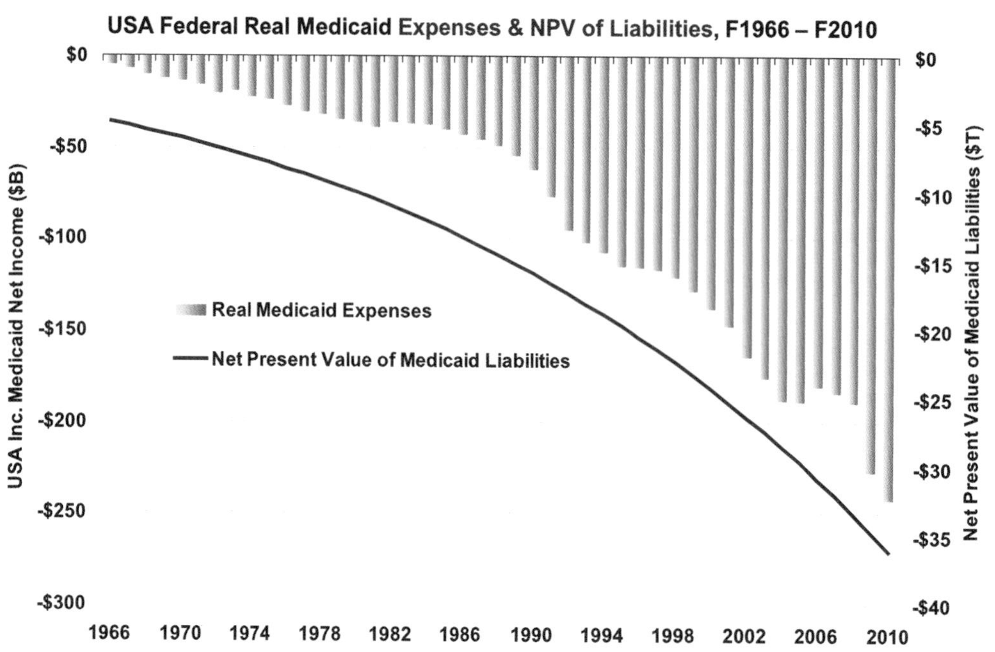

Note: USA federal fiscal year ends in September; Data are inflation adjusted. Calculation of net present value of liability based on 75-year Medicaid spending projections from CBO, assuming a 3% discount rate (long-run average of real 10-yr treasury yields). Source: White House Office of Management and Budget, Congressional Budget Office.

Medicaid: Enrollment Is Up 12x to 49 Million While Annual Payments per Beneficiary Are Up 4x to $5K From 1966 to 2009

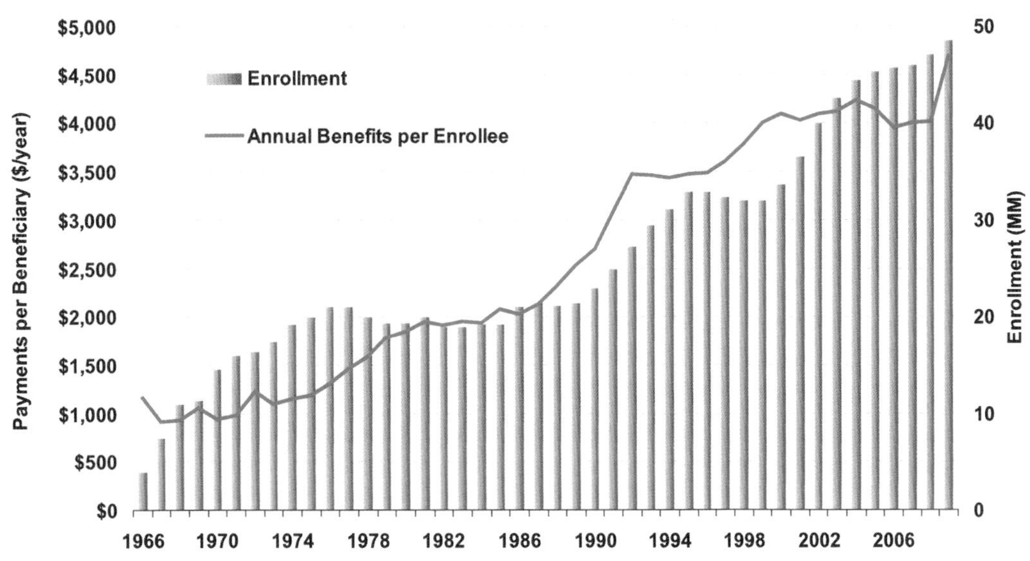

Note: Data are inflation adjusted. Source: Dept. of Health & Human Services.

Medicaid: Observations

- **49 million (26MM low-income children / 12MM low-income adults / 7MM disabled / 4MM elderly) Americans (16% of population) received an average of $4,684 in tax-payer funded payments from the federal government for healthcare in 2009. For context, $6,872 in healthcare benefits is 13% of average annual per-capita income for Americans.**
- When Medicaid was created in 1965 to provide health insurance to low-income Americans, 1 in 50 Americans received Medicaid, now 1 in 6 Americans receives Medicaid.
- That said, Medicaid is an important benefit for recipients as it provides access to healthcare for low-income adults and their children. In recent years, Medicaid beneficiaries and benefit payments have risen faster than population and per-capita income growth owing to expanded coverage, economic difficulties and associated sluggish wage growth for low- and lower-middle-income families, and continued healthcare cost inflation.

Note: Data are inflation adjusted. Source: Dept. of Health & Human Services.

Medicaid: While We Focus on Federal Government Dynamics, It's Notable that State Government Medicaid Funding Also Faces Significant Challenges

- **Medicaid = Major and Growing Expense Line Item for State Governments**
  - Medicaid funding responsibility is shared between federal & state governments. States with higher per-capita income (like New York) pay ~50% of total Medicaid cost while states with lower per-capita income (like Mississippi) pay ~22%.
  - On average, Medicaid accounted for 21% of total state spending in F2009 (ranging from Missouri at 35% to Alaska at 8%). Enrollment growth has been accelerating, in part, owing to more people losing employer-sponsored health insurance in the recession, and thus overall Medicaid costs jumped ~11% Y/Y from October, 2009 to June, 2010.
  - State governments (which unlike the federal government must balance their annual budgets) cannot pay for such elevated levels of Medicaid and maintain normal spending levels for other services (like education and public safety).
- **Enter the Federal Government**
  - ARRA (2009 economic stimulus) provided ~$100 billion in support for the states to pay for elevated levels of Medicaid costs and to avoid large budget cuts in education and public safety. This went a long way toward holding down the states' contribution, but it is a one-time unsustainable fix.
- **Federal Support May Be Expiring by June, 2011**
  - If no action is taken, the Medicaid-related cost burden on the states will rise dramatically in coming years. As a result, many states are on the verge of implementing Medicaid cost containment plans that include cuts in doctor payments, benefit limitations, higher patient co-payments, etc. Moreover, many states are fearful that the recently enacted healthcare reform will lead to additional Medicaid-related costs when it goes into full effect in 2014.

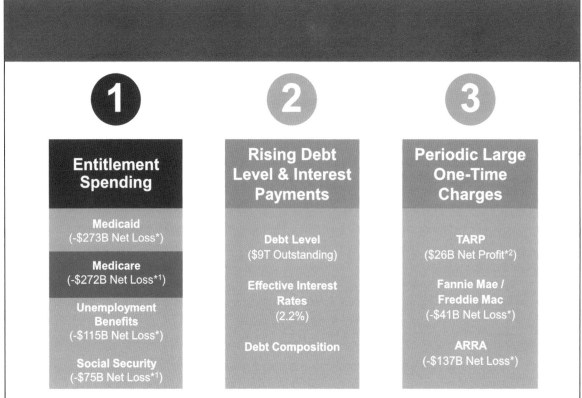

Data Source: National Conference of State Legislatures, "State Budget Update: July 2009."

1 **Entitlement Spending**

- **Medicaid** (-$273B Net Loss*)
- **Medicare** (-$272B Net Loss*1)
- **Unemployment Benefits** (-$115B Net Loss*)
- **Social Security** (-$75B Net Loss*1)

2 **Rising Debt Level & Interest Payments**

- **Debt Level** ($9T Outstanding)
- **Effective Interest Rates** (2.2%)
- **Debt Composition**

3 **Periodic Large One-Time Charges**

- **TARP** ($26B Net Profit*2)
- **Fannie Mae / Freddie Mac** (-$41B Net Loss*)
- **ARRA** (-$137B Net Loss*)

*Note: *denotes F2010 net income / net loss of respective programs, data per White House OMB. 1) Medicare and Social Security net loss excludes Trust Fund interest income. 2) TARP net loss includes proceeds from sale of warrants. TARP is Troubled Asset Relief Program; ARRA is American Recovery & Reinvestment Act programs.*

Medicare: Complex Social Insurance Program With Insufficient Funding

- **Social Insurance Program** – Created in 1965 to provide health insurance to the elderly (65+).
- **Four Parts** – A) Hospital Insurance (to cover inpatient expenses, introduced in 1965); B) Medical Insurance (optional outpatient expenses, 1965); C) Medicare Advantage Plans (private alternative to A&B, 1997) and D) Prescription Drug Coverage (enacted 2003).
- **Funding Mechanism Varies**
  - Part A has dedicated funding via payroll taxes (2.9% of total payroll), though has been running at an annual deficit since 2008 as related payments exceed taxes; Trust Fund is expected to be depleted by 2017E, per Social Security Administration.
  - Part B & D has no dedicated funding (75% of funding came from government allocation / 25% came from enrollees' premium payments).
  - Part C funding came Part A & Part B.
- **Ever-Growing Expenses – $452 billion expenses in F2010, up 2x from 10 years ago**
  - Rising Healthcare Costs – Owing to aging population + unhealthy life styles + technology advances.
  - Moral Hazard – As a "free good," Medicare reduced demand for private long-term insurance[1] while loopholes in the regulations + need-based benefit policies created incentives to abuse the system.

Note: 1) for more information, please see Jeffrey Brown and Amy Finkelstein, "The Interaction of Public and Private Insurance: Medicaid and the Long-Term Care Insurance Market," 2006. Source: National Center for Health Statistics, Kaiser Family Foundation, World Bank, Social Security Administration.

Medicare: Underfunded by $1.9 Trillion Over 45 Years

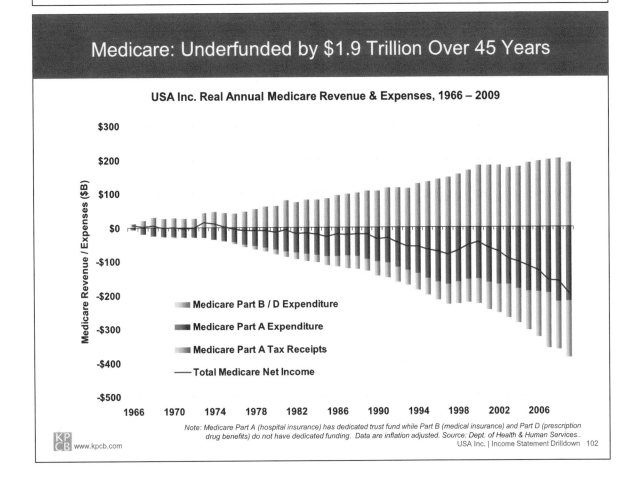

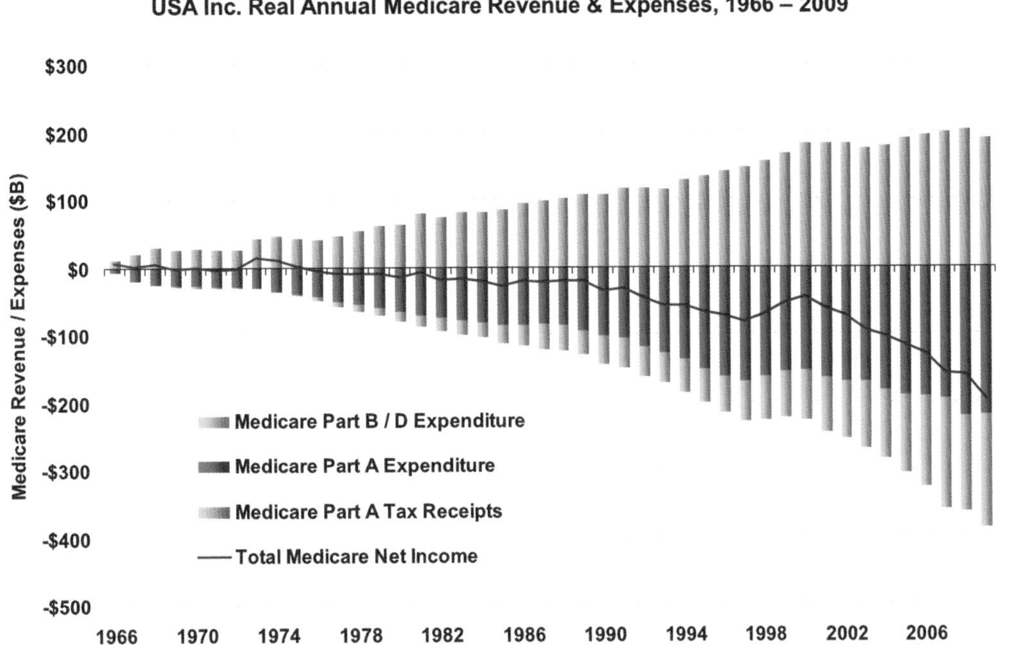

Note: Medicare Part A (hospital insurance) has dedicated trust fund while Part B (medical insurance) and Part D (prescription drug benefits) do not have dedicated funding. Data are inflation adjusted. Source: Dept. of Health & Human Services..

Medicare: Enrollment Up 2x to 46 Million While Annual Payments per Beneficiary Up 26x to $8,325 From 1966 to 2009

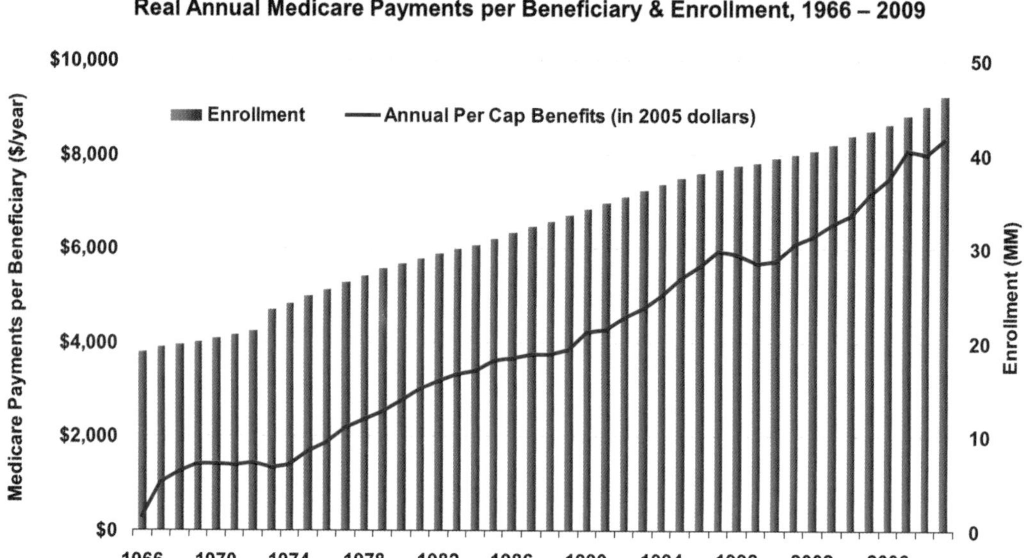

Note: Data are inflation adjusted using BEA's GDP price index. Source: Dept. of Health & Human Services.

Medicare: Observations

- **46 million elderly Americans (15% of population) received an average of $8,325 in tax-payer funded payments for healthcare in 2009 ($5,079 for hospital care; $3,246 for medical insurance & prescription drugs).**
- **On the surface, $8,325 in free healthcare benefits every year certainly seems like a high number – 23% of annual per-capita income – (although working Medicare recipients do pay Medicare taxes).**
- As with employer-sponsored health insurance plans, if people, in effect, get a free benefit (with little personal financial commitment), they may not be especially diligent and frugal about how they 'spend' it. The same concept extends beyond healthcare recipients to the healthcare providers.*
- When Medicare was created in 1965 to provide health insurance to elderly Americans, 1 in 10 Americans received Medicare, now 1 in 7 Americans receives Medicare…above the initial 'plan.'

*Note: *The issue that people overuse services for which they do not have personal financial commitment applies to most private insurance as well. For a more detailed discussion, see slide 293. Data are inflation adjusted using BEA's GDP price index. Source: Dept. of Health & Human Services.*

Total Government* Healthcare Spending Increases are Staggering – Up 7x as % of GDP Over Five Decades vs. Education Spending, Only Up 0.6x

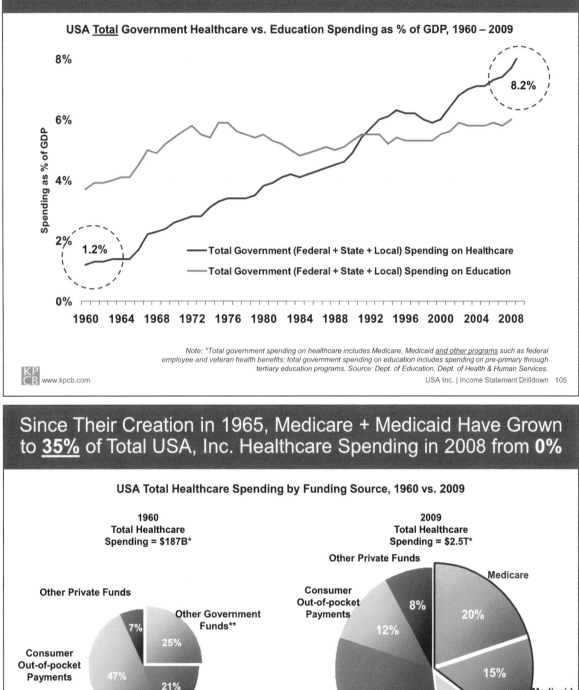

USA Total Government Healthcare vs. Education Spending as % of GDP, 1960 – 2009

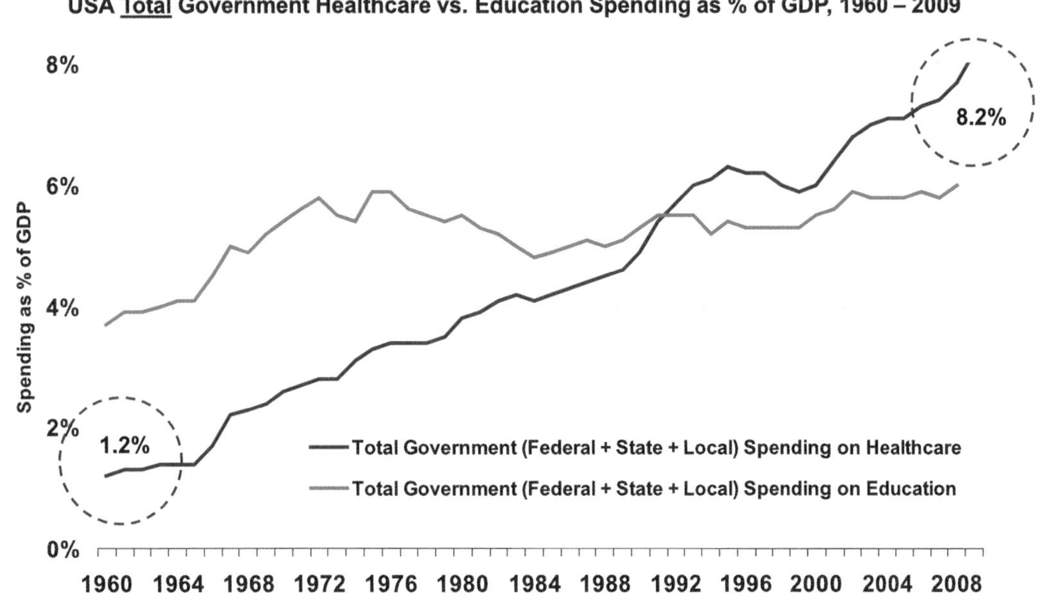

*Note: *Total government spending on healthcare includes Medicare, Medicaid and other programs such as federal employee and veteran health benefits; total government spending on education includes spending on pre-primary through tertiary education programs. Source: Dept. of Education, Dept. of Health & Human Services.*

Since Their Creation in 1965, Medicare + Medicaid Have Grown to 35% of Total USA, Inc. Healthcare Spending in 2008 from 0%

USA Total Healthcare Spending by Funding Source, 1960 vs. 2009

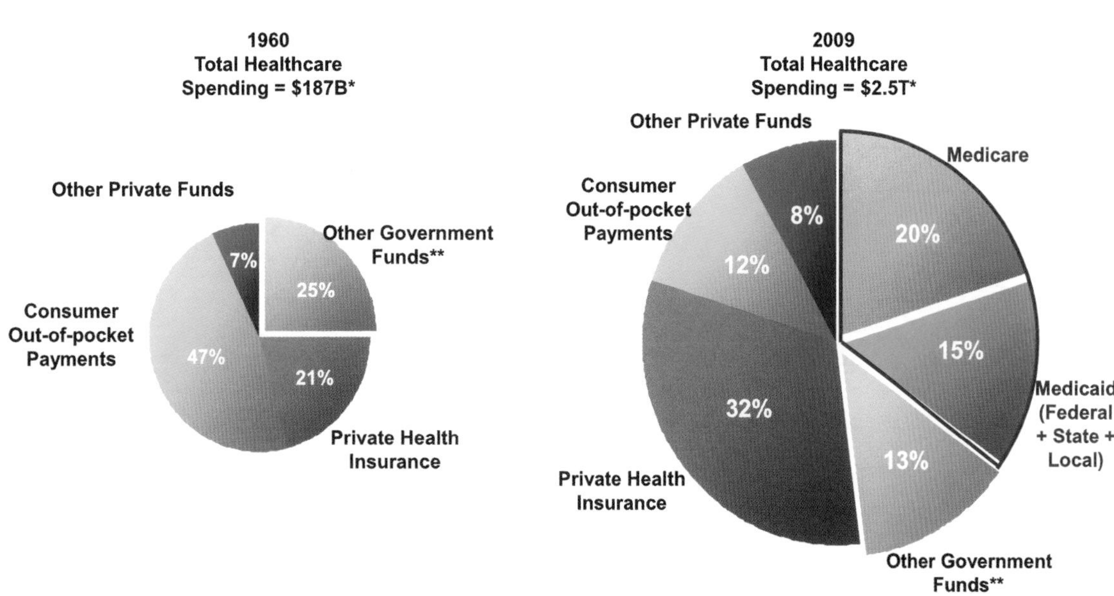

*Note: *Adjusted for inflation, in 2005 dollars. ** Other government funds include those from Dept. of Defense, Veterans' Administration and federal funding for healthcare research and public health activities. Source: U.S. Department of Health & Human Services.*

Think About That…

- **Total government spending on healthcare (including Medicare, Medicaid and <u>other programs</u>) has risen 7x from 1.2% of GDP in 1960 to 8.2% in 2009 while total government spending on education has risen only 0.6x from 4% of GDP in 1960 to 6% in 2009.**
- Medicare and Medicaid, which did not exist in 1960, rose to 35% of total healthcare spending in 2009, while out-of-pocket spending declined to 12% of total healthcare spending in 2009 (or $894 per person per year*), down from 47% in 1960 (or $478 per person*).
- Lifetime healthcare costs for the average American are $631,000, of which the government pays for an estimated 48% while private insurers (like UnitedHealth and Blue Cross Blue Shield) pay 32% and consumers pay just 12%.
- When citizens don't need to pay directly for something (like healthcare) and are given an expensive good / service for free (or well below cost), they tend to consume more of it – it's basic supply and demand economics.
- This approach faces increasing challenges as USA, Inc. has gone deeper and deeper in debt to pay for it…

*Note: *Adjusted for inflation, in 2005 dollars. Nominal amount would be $972 out-of-pocket healthcare spending per person in 2008 and $70 per person in 1960. Source: U.S. Department of Health & Human Services.*

USA Healthcare Spending Is Higher Than All Other OECD Countries Combined (with 35% of Other OECD Countries' Combined Population)

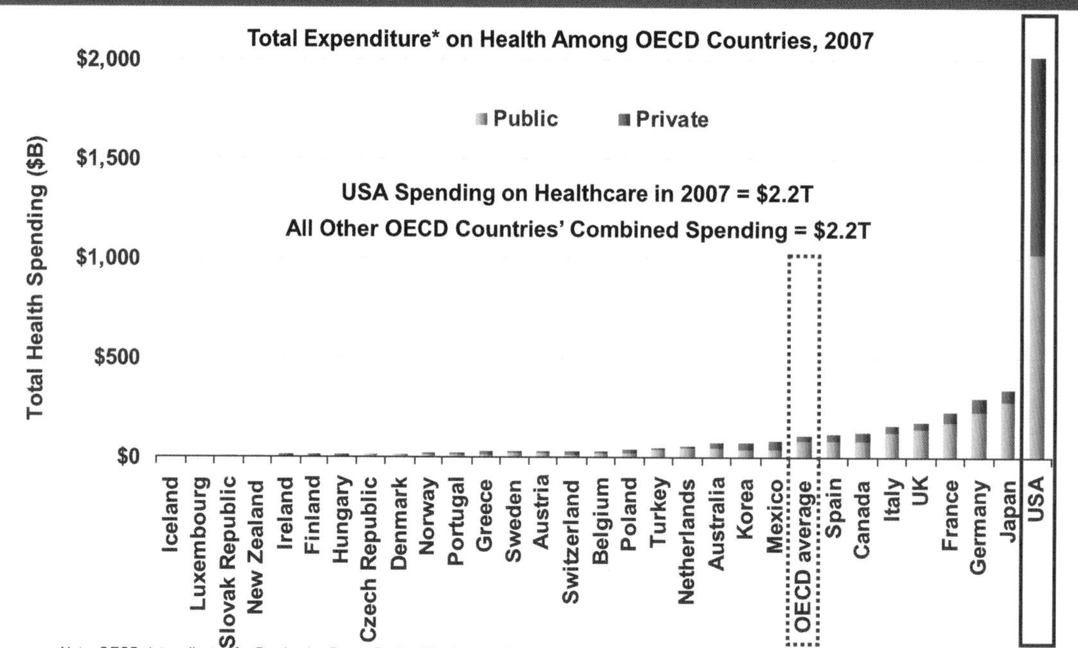

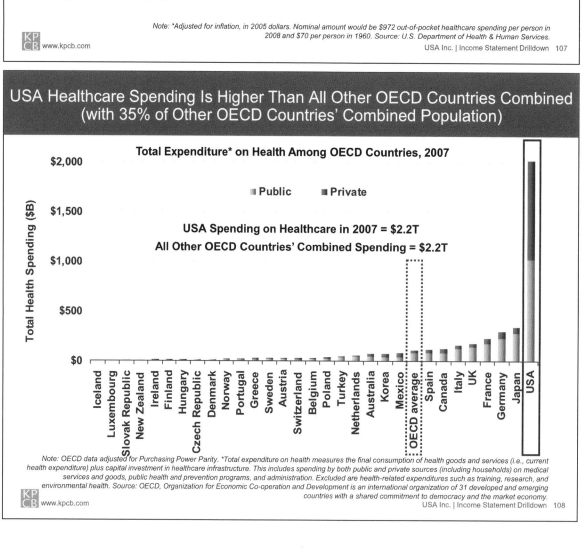

*Note: OECD data adjusted for Purchasing Power Parity. *Total expenditure on health measures the final consumption of health goods and services (i.e., current health expenditure) plus capital investment in healthcare infrastructure. This includes spending by both public and private sources (including households) on medical services and goods, public health and prevention programs, and administration. Excluded are health-related expenditures such as training, research, and environmental health. Source: OECD, Organization for Economic Co-operation and Development is an international organization of 31 developed and emerging countries with a shared commitment to democracy and the market economy.*

USA Per Capita Spending on Healthcare = 3x OECD Average

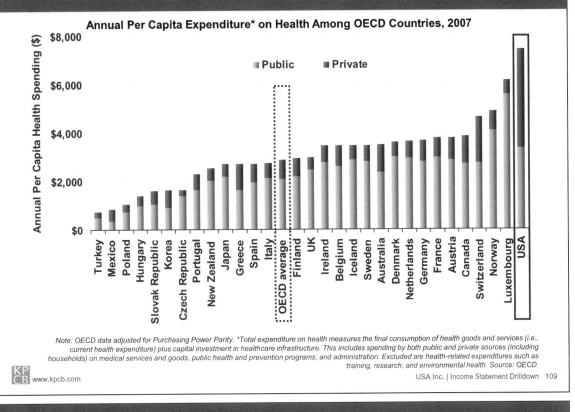

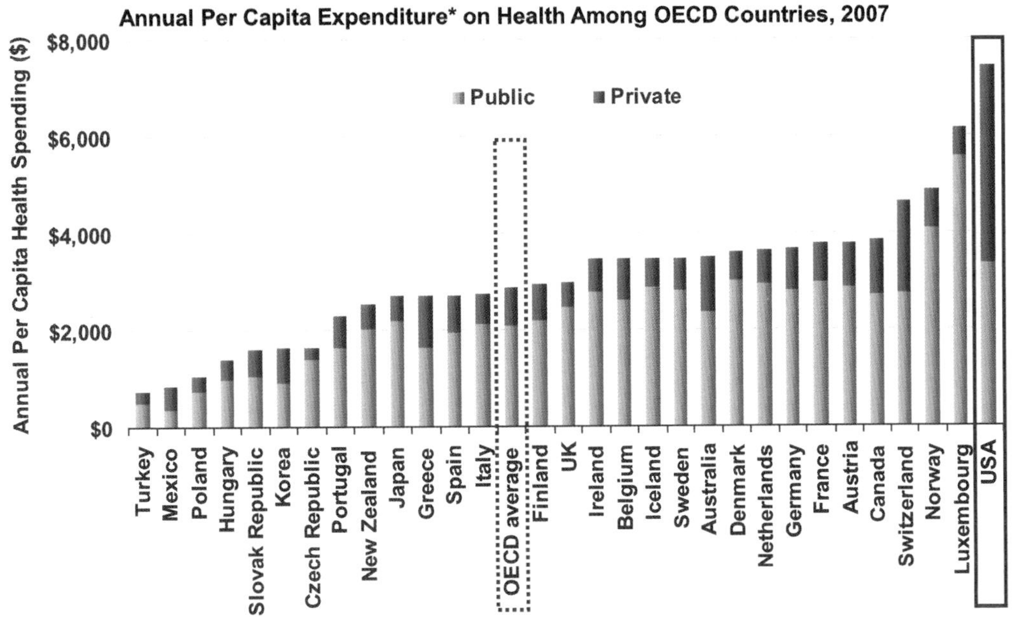

*Note: OECD data adjusted for Purchasing Power Parity. *Total expenditure on health measures the final consumption of health goods and services (i.e., current health expenditure) plus capital investment in healthcare infrastructure. This includes spending by both public and private sources (including households) on medical services and goods, public health and prevention programs, and administration. Excluded are health-related expenditures such as training, research, and environmental health. Source: OECD.*

USA Spending on Healthcare as % of GDP = 2x OECD Average

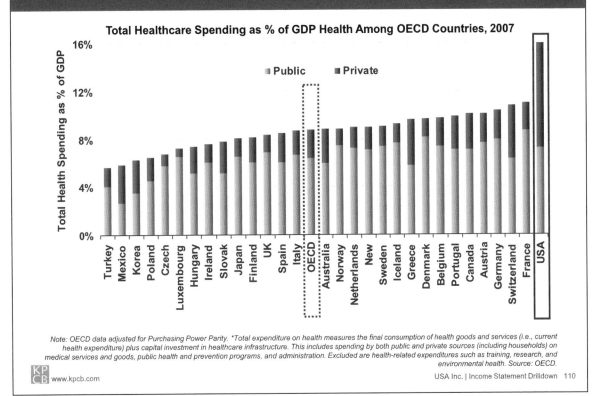

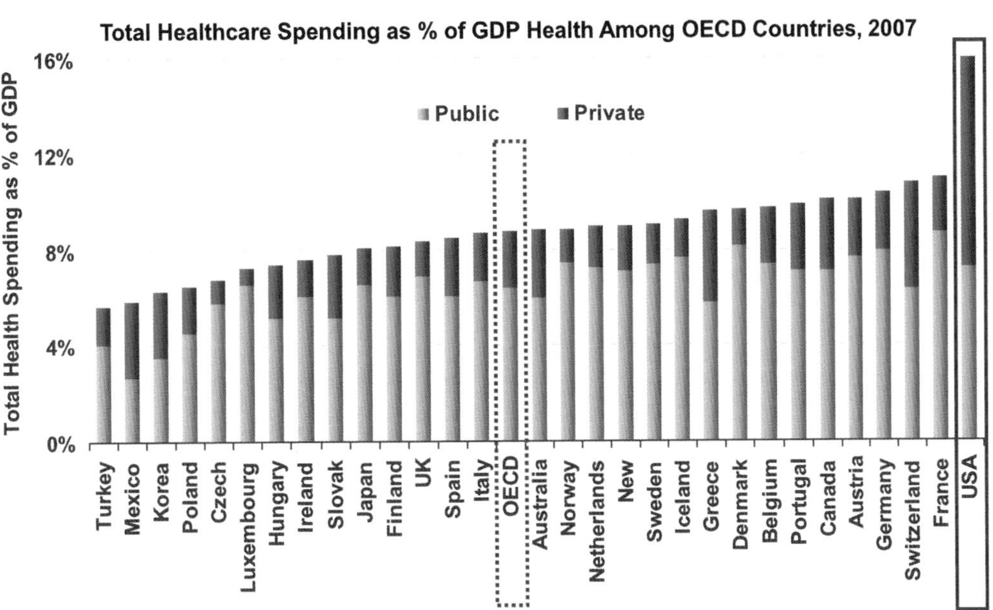

*Note: OECD data adjusted for Purchasing Power Parity. *Total expenditure on health measures the final consumption of health goods and services (i.e., current health expenditure) plus capital investment in healthcare infrastructure. This includes spending by both public and private sources (including households) on medical services and goods, public health and prevention programs, and administration. Excluded are health-related expenditures such as training, research, and environmental health. Source: OECD.*

USA Spending on Healthcare **IS NOT** Performance-Based and **IS NOT** Correlated to Longer Life Expectancy

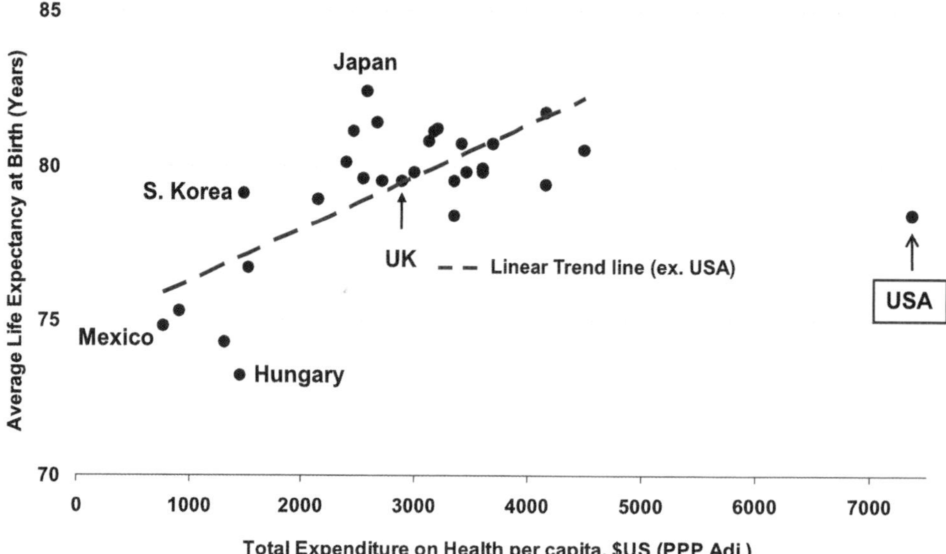

In Addition to Life Expectancy, USA Falls Behind OECD Averages in Many Other Health Indicators

2007 Health Indicators	USA	OECD Median	USA Ranking (1 = Best, 30 = Worst) RED = Below Average
Obesity (% of total population)	34	15	30
Infant Mortality (per 1,000 live births)	7	4	27
Medical Resources Available (per 1,000 population)			
Total Hospital Beds	3	6	25
Practicing Physicians	2	3	22
Doctors' Consultations per Year	4	6	19
MRI Machines* (per million population)	26	9	1
Cause of Death (per 100,000 population)			
Heart Attack	216	178	22
Respiratory Diseases	60	45	21
Diabetes	20	12	20
Cancer	158	159	14
Stroke	33	45	8

*Note: *MRI is Magnetic Resonance Imaging. Source: OECD.*

Think About That…

- USA per capita healthcare spending is 3x OECD average, yet the average life expectancy and a variety of health indicators in the US fall below average.
- But if you spend way more than everyone else, shouldn't your results (a.k.a. 'performance') be better than everyone else's, or at least near the top?
- Should you examine sources of waste/inefficiency given lower output despite greater input?
- Definition of 'Performance' = Amount of useful work accomplished given certain amount of time and resources.
- Definition of 'Efficient' = Obtains maximum benefit from a given level of input of cost, time, or effort.

*Note: OECD data adjusted for Purchasing Power Parity. * Lifetime healthcare costs = life expectancy (years) x per capita healthcare spending ($ per year, 2006). Source: OECD, US Dept. of Health & Human Services.*

Patient Protection and Affordable Care Act (PPACA)

PPACA – America's new healthcare reform legislation, signed into law on 3/23/10 – creates some reason for concern that it could become an unfunded entitlement.

PPACA: A Detailed Drilldown into Costs of Recent Healthcare Reform Is Key as it **May Increase** Budget Deficit…

- **Congressional Budget Office expects Reform to *lower* the deficit by $143 billion during 2010-19**
  - Gross cost of $938 billion for expanded coverage, per CBO.
  - Less: $511 billion in spending cuts from lower Medicare reimbursement rate + $420 billion in tax revenues (excl. excise tax) from higher payroll tax rates on high-income families and indoor tanning services + $149 billion in penalty payments by employers/individuals and excise tax on "Cadillac" insurance plans with annual cost exceeding $10,000 for individual / $28,000 for families.

Source: CBO.

PPACA – Verdict Is Still Out on Eventual Costs / Deficit Impact

- Issues With Official Cost Estimates to Consider
  - Deficit neutral status somewhat reliant on future lawmakers' willingness to implement Medicare savings/reimbursement reductions:
    - Reductions in payment rates for many types of Healthcare providers relative to the rates that would have been paid under prior law (always a politically difficult decision).
    - However the good news is that recommendations from the Independent Payment Advisory Board focused on reducing growth in per capita Medicare spending if it exceeds target automatically become the law without congressional intervention if Congress allows IPAB to operate as planned.
  - CBO estimates the effects of proposals as written: CBO acknowledges that it is unclear whether reform can actually reduce the annual growth rate in Medicare spending from 4% (historical average) to 2% for the next two decades, as PPACA estimates assume.
  - Relies on excise taxes on sectors of the healthcare industry that could be passed through to consumers via price increases.
  - Starting in 2018, assumes taxation of high premium employment-based health insurance plans.
- Opportunities For Cost Savings to Consider
  - Increased access to preventative care could potentially slow down overall healthcare cost growth. Such potential effect is not captured in CBO scoring.
  - Investments in information technology and new provider & consumer incentives can drive better and more efficient care.

Source: Morgan Stanley Healthcare Research.

PPACA – There Is Potential for 'Unintended' Consequences

- The new law changes some system incentives, which may lead to new behavior patterns, many of which are complex and hard to predict.
  - The market may adapt to new MLR (Medical Loss Ratio) rules that incentivize and reward a very specific (but ultimately arbitrary) cost structure.
  - The cost/benefit analysis for employers and consumers may change, and some may opt to re-evaluate their current employer-sponsored coverage offerings.

- Health plans that are no longer economically viable may exit markets, potentially adding to the uninsured problem prior to 2014.

- Likely acceleration in consolidation of payers as well as providers.

Source: Doug Simpson, Morgan Stanley Healthcare Research.

Historical Anecdote – "An Accurate Economic Forecast Might Have Sunk Medicare & Medicaid [in 1965]"

- In 1965, the official estimate of Medicare's costs was $500 million per year, roughly $3 billion in 2005 dollars.*
- The actual cost of Medicare has turned out to be 10x that estimate.
  - Medicare's actual net loss (tax receipts + trust fund interest – expenditures) has exceeded $3 billion (adjusted for inflation) every year since 1976 and was $146 billion in 2008 alone. In other words, had the original estimate been accurate, the cumulative 43-year cost since Medicare was created would have been $129 billion, adjusted for inflation.
  - In fact, the actual cumulative spending has been $1.4 trillion** (adjusted for inflation)...in effect, 10x over budget.
- While calculations have been flawed from the beginning for some of USA Inc.'s entitlement programs, little has been done to correct the problems.

> ***An accurate economic forecast might have sunk Medicare.***
>
> *David Blumenthal and James Morone*
>
> *"The Lessons of Success – Revisiting the Medicare Story", November 2008*

*Sources: * Lyndon B. Johnson Library & Museum. Medicare spending data per White House OMB.*
***Dept. of Health & Human Services, CMS, data adjusted for inflation based on BEA's GDP price index.*

If History is a Guide, There is Potential for Estimates to Understate Eventual Costs – Medicare Is 10x Higher Than Spending Forecast

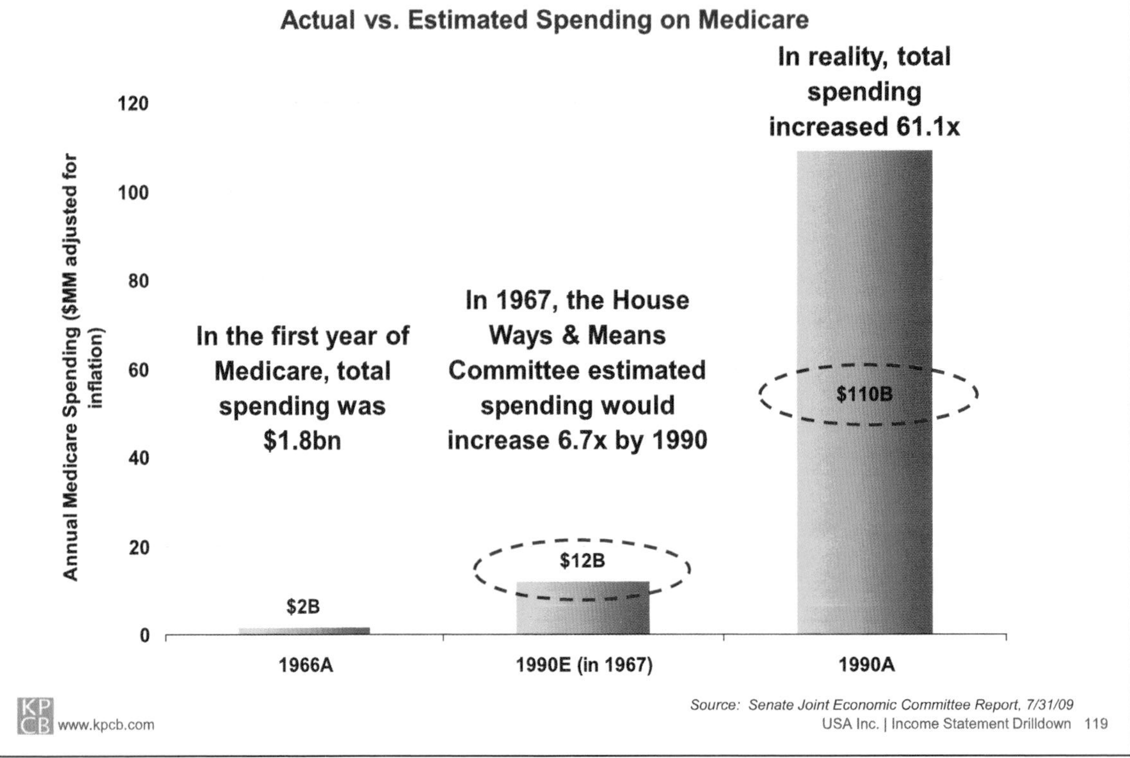

Actual vs. Estimated Spending on Medicare
Annual Medicare Spending ($MM adjusted for inflation)
120
100
80
60
40
20
0
In the first year of Medicare, total spending was $1.8bn
In 1967, the House Ways & Means Committee estimated spending would increase 6.7x by 1990
In reality, total spending increased 61.1x
$2B
$12B
$110B
1966A
1990E (in 1967)
1990A

Source: Senate Joint Economic Committee Report, 7/31/09

However, More Recent Healthcare Entitlement Such as Medicare part D Has Cost Less Than Expected

- Medicare Part D (the 2006 outpatient drug benefit for seniors) was projected to cost $111 billion annually.
- In 2009, Medicare Part D's actual cost = $61 billion, 45% below projection.
- The government originally projected 43 million beneficiaries in 2009, but only 33 million seniors (23% below projection) elected to participate in 2009.
- Medicare Part D was outsourced to the private sector, and seniors elected to enroll in plans operated primarily by managed care organizations, which utilize a variety of techniques to reduce costs and improve the quality of care.
- *The Washington Times* stated on August 16th 2010 – "The lower cost - a result of slowing demand for prescription drugs, higher use of generic drugs and fewer people signing up - has surprised even some of the law's most pessimistic critics."
- The Part D experience has given some observers hope that PPACA will not cost more than anticipated.

Source: Morgan Stanley Healthcare Research.

2

3

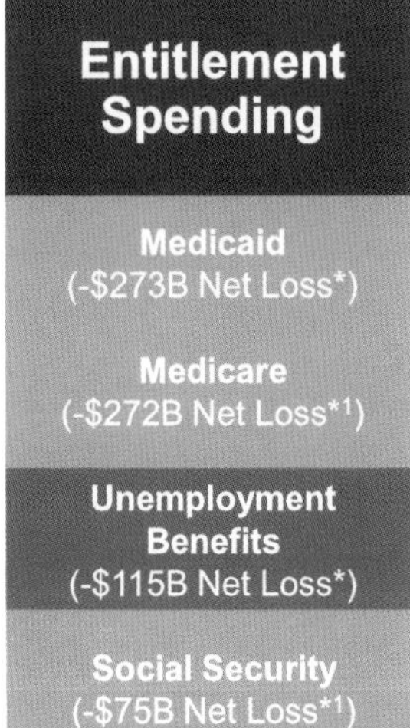

Rising Debt Level & Interest Payments

Debt Level
($9T Outstanding)

Effective Interest Rates
(2.2%)

Debt Composition

Periodic Large One-Time Charges

TARP
($26B Net Profit*2)

Fannie Mae / Freddie Mac
(-$41B Net Loss*)

ARRA
(-$137B Net Loss*)

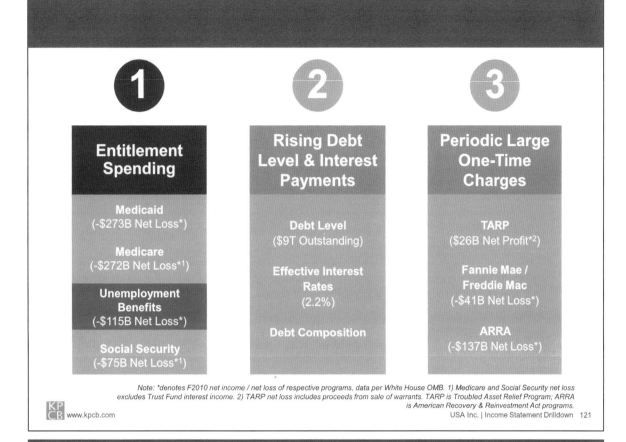

*Note: *denotes F2010 net income / net loss of respective programs, data per White House OMB. 1) Medicare and Social Security net loss excludes Trust Fund interest income. 2) TARP net loss includes proceeds from sale of warrants. TARP is Troubled Asset Relief Program; ARRA is American Recovery & Reinvestment Act programs.*

Unemployment Benefits: Long-Term Break-Even, Though Prone to Cyclicality

- **Social Insurance Program** – Created in 1935 as part of the Social Security Act to provide temporary financial assistance to eligible workers who are unemployed through no fault of their own (via layoffs or natural disasters).
- **Funded via Taxing Employers** – Employers pay federal government 0.8% of payroll (in addition to various levels of state unemployment insurance taxes) to fund the Federal Unemployment Insurance Trust Fund.
- **Funding = Pro-Cyclical** – Rising employment increases revenue and reduces benefit payments, generally leading to surpluses, while falling employment reduces revenue and increases benefits payments, leading to periodically large deficits during recessions.
- **Flexible at the State Level by Design** – State governments set policies on unemployment benefit eligibility / duration / tax levels, while federal government provide financial and legal oversight.
- **Generally Break-Even** – In 29 of the past 49 years, Federal unemployment insurance programs have had surpluses. Excluding the 2009 / 2010 loss, unemployment insurance had a cumulative surplus of $53 billion from 1962 to 2008.

Source: White House OMB.

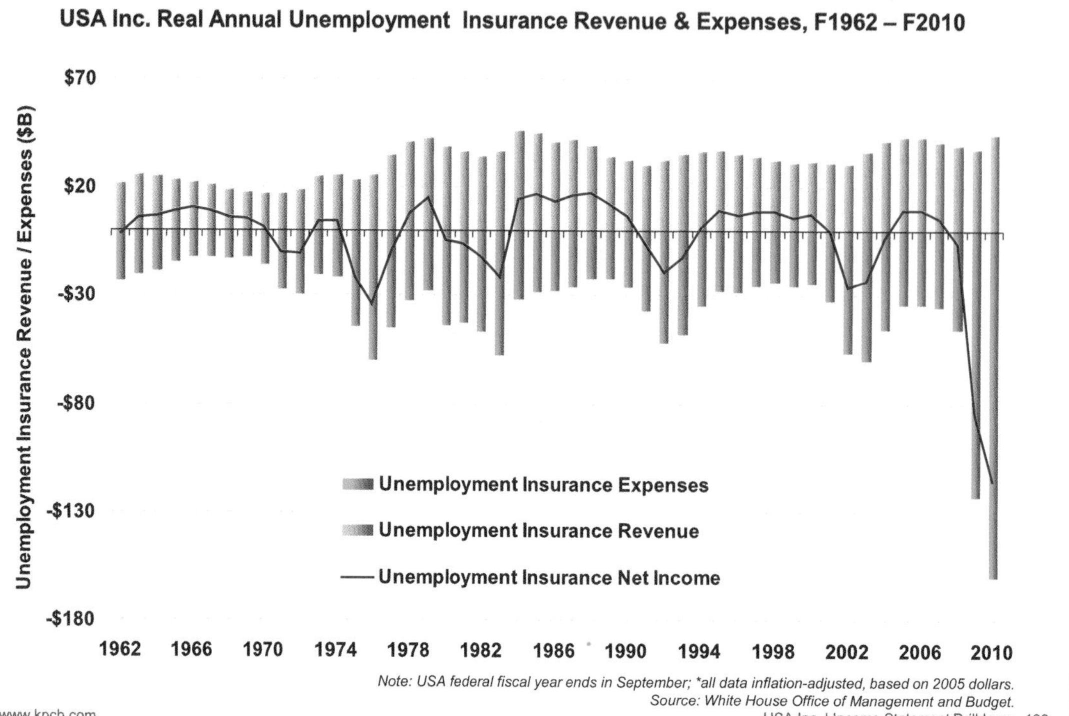
Unemployment Benefits: Solid, Though Cyclical, Funding
But Underfunded by $150B Over 49 Years Owing to -$115B* Deficits in 2010
USA Inc. Real Annual Unemployment Insurance Revenue & Expenses, F1962 – F2010
$70
$20
-$30
-$80
-$130
-$180
Unemployment Insurance Revenue / Expenses ($B)
Unemployment Insurance Expenses
Unemployment Insurance Revenue
Unemployment Insurance Net Income
1962
1966
1970
1974
1978
1982
1986
1990
1994
1998
2002
2006
2010
Note: USA federal fiscal year ends in September; *all data inflation-adjusted, based on 2005 dollars.
Source: White House Office of Management and Budget.
KP CB www.kpcb.com
USA Inc. | Income Statement Drilldown 123

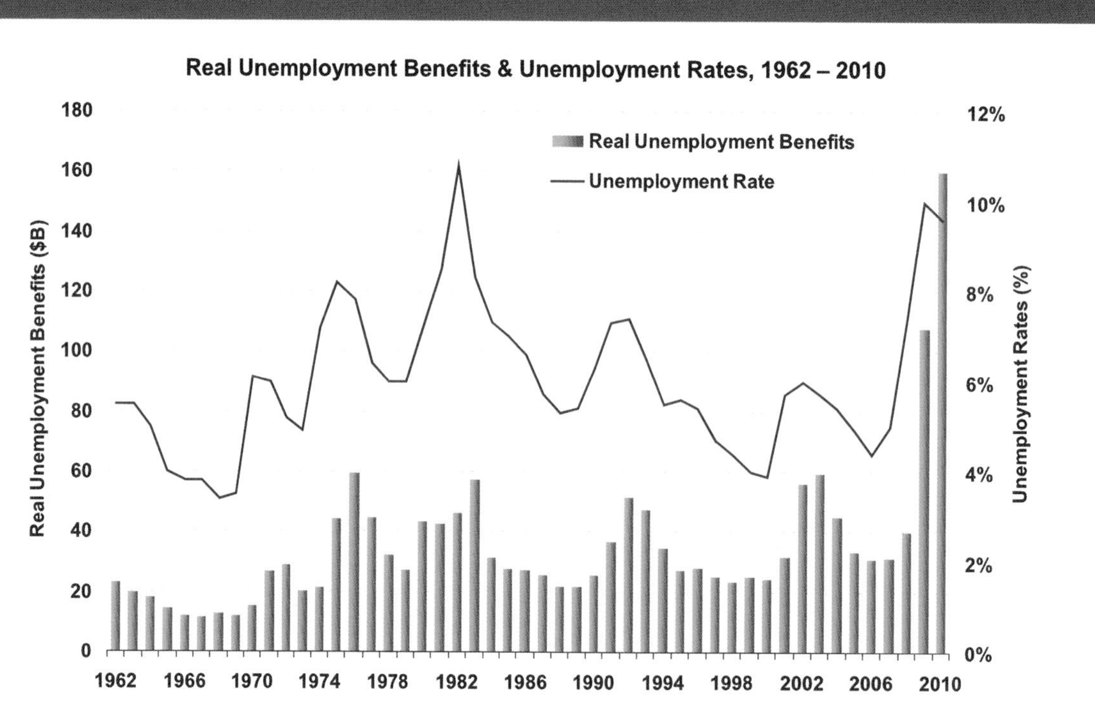
Unemployment Benefits: In the Past, Benefits Paid
Have High (70%) Correlation to Unemployment Rate
Real Unemployment Benefits & Unemployment Rates, 1962 – 2010
180
160
140
120
100
80
60
40
20
0
Real Unemployment Benefits ($B)
12%
10%
8%
6%
4%
2%
0%
Unemployment Rates (%)
Real Unemployment Benefits
Unemployment Rate
1962
1966
1970
1974
1978
1982
1986
1990
1994
1998
2002
2006
2010
Note: Fiscal year ends in September. Source: White House Office of Management & Budget, Bureau of Labor Statistics.
KP CB www.kpcb.com
USA Inc. | Income Statement Drilldown 124

Unemployment Benefits: Good News—Unemployment Change In the Past Has Strong (71%) Inverse Correlation with Real GDP Change, so Economic Growth Should Reduce Unemployment

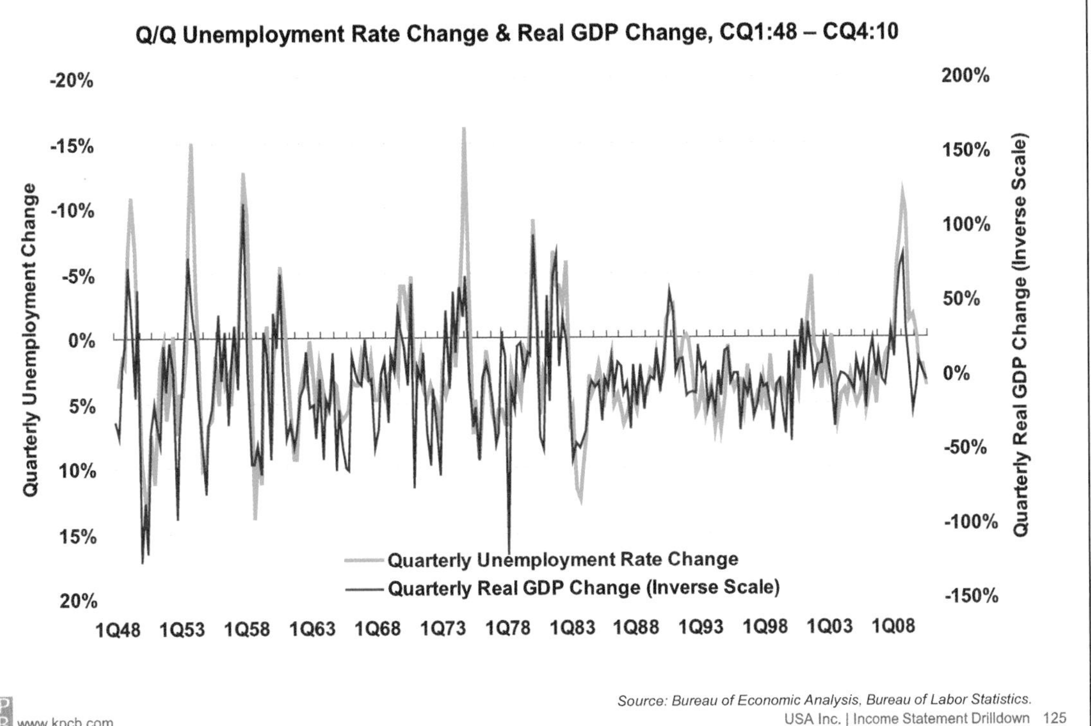

Source: Bureau of Economic Analysis, Bureau of Labor Statistics.

Unemployment Benefits: Bad News—Newly Extended Unemployment Benefits Could Cost USA Inc. $34 Billion in Next Two Years

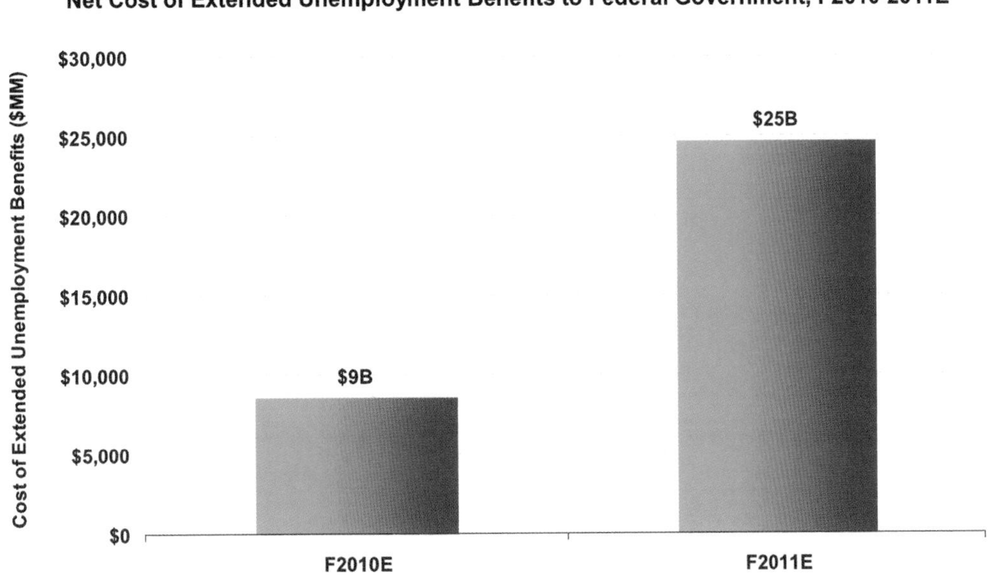

Note: Net cost of the Unemployment Compensation Extension Act of 2010 is expected to decline substantially in F2012E because the deadline to file for extended unemployment benefits expires in November 2010 and federal extended unemployment insurance provides benefits for up to 99 weeks (less than two years). Source: Congressional Budget Office, 7/10.

Unemployment Benefits: Bad News—Structural Problems in Labor Force Could Lead to Prolonged Duration/Increased Rate of Unemployment

- **Structural Problems in USA Labor Force**
  - **Healthcare costs may be a barrier to hiring for employers**
    - Healthcare benefits = 8% of average total employee compensation; grew at 6.9% CAGR from 1998 to 2008 compared with 4.5% CAGR in salaries.
    - Healthcare benefits are fixed costs as they are paid on an annual per-worker basis and do not vary with hours worked.
    - As employers try to lower fixed costs to right-size to their reduced revenue levels, layoffs are the only way to reduce fixed healthcare costs.
  - **Skills mismatch may be a barrier to hiring for employers**
    - A large portion of the long-term unemployed may lack requisite skills.
    - 14% of firms reported difficulty filling positions due to the lack of suitable talent, per 5/10 Manpower Research survey.
  - **Labor immobility resulting from the housing bust may be a barrier to hiring**
    - One in four homeowners are "trapped" because they owe more than their houses are worth, so they cannot move to take another job – until they sell or walk away.

Source: Richard Berner, "Why is US Employment So Weak" (7/23/10), Morgan Stanley Research.

Unemployment Benefits: Bad News

Although economists have shown that extended availability of UI [unemployment insurance] benefits will increase unemployment duration, the effect in the latest downturn appears quite small compared with other determinants of the unemployment rate. Our analyses suggest that extended UI benefits account for about 0.4 percentage point of the nearly 6 percentage point increase in the national unemployment rate over the past few years. It is not surprising that the disincentive effects of UI would loom small in the midst of the most severe labor market downturn since the Great Depression.

Despite the relatively minor influence of extended UI, it is important to note that the 0.4 percentage point increase in the unemployment rate represents about 600,000 potential workers who could become virtually unemployable if their reliance on UI benefits were to continue indefinitely.

Rob Valletta and Katherine Kuang, Federal Reserve Board of San Francisco
"Extended Unemployment and UI Benefits," April 19, 2010.

1 **Entitlement Spending**

Medicaid
(-$273B Net Loss*)

Medicare
(-$272B Net Loss*1)

Unemployment Benefits
(-$115B Net Loss*)

Social Security
(-$75B Net Loss*1)

2 **Rising Debt Level & Interest Payments**

Debt Level
($9T Outstanding)

Effective Interest Rates
(2.2%)

Debt Composition

3 **Periodic Large One-Time Charges**

TARP
($26B Net Profit*2)

Fannie Mae / Freddie Mac
(-$41B Net Loss*)

ARRA
(-$137B Net Loss*)

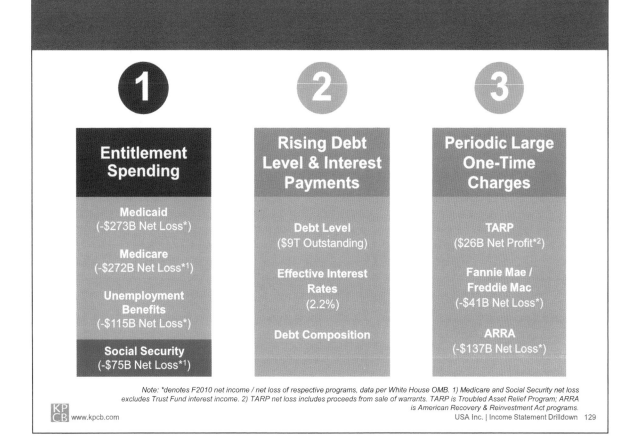

*Note: *denotes F2010 net income / net loss of respective programs, data per White House OMB. 1) Medicare and Social Security net loss excludes Trust Fund interest income. 2) TARP net loss includes proceeds from sale of warrants. TARP is Troubled Asset Relief Program; ARRA is American Recovery & Reinvestment Act programs.*

Social Security: In Good Shape Now, Yet Challenged in Future by Aging Population

- **Social Insurance Program Created in 1935** – During height of the Great Depression to help elderly (65+*) and disabled people avoid poverty.
- **Pay-as-You-Go Funding** – Social Security taxes deducted from current payrolls to pay out to current eligible recipients of Social Security.
- **For Most of its 8 Decades (1935-1970; 1985 - 2009), Annual Social Security Payments Have Been Funded by Annual Social Security Taxes** – However, based on estimates from Congressional Budget Office (CBO), beginning in 2016 (or earlier), Social Security will begin running an annual deficit as payments exceed taxes (at unchanged flat tax rate of 12.4%[1] of annual gross wages) – this is a problem!
- **Social Security Has Been Struck by Annual Deficit Crisis Before** – From 1975 to 1981, Social Security expenses exceeded revenue every year, which caused a 45% reduction in the Social Security Trust Fund balance. Legislation recommended by the Greenspan Commission in 1983 reduced average benefits by ~5%[2] and raised social insurance tax rates for individuals by ~2.3%.[3] But the Greenspan Commission fix will run out soon as Social Security turns to operating loss in 2016.

*Note: *Early retirees (62+) could receive partial benefits between 62 and 65. 1) 6.2% taxes paid by employees and matched by employers on gross wages up to but not exceeding the Social Security wage base of ~$100K; 2) total benefit cuts included $27B savings from benefit taxation for the wealthy and $66B savings from delay in cost of living adjustments over 1984-1989; 3) average increase in entitlement payroll tax rates between 1982 and 1988, includes Medicare payroll taxes, per estimates from CBO. Source: Social Security Administration.*

Social Security: Financially Sound – So Far – Owing to Increased Revenue / Reduced Spending Post 1983 Reform, But 'Operating Loss' Resumed in 2009

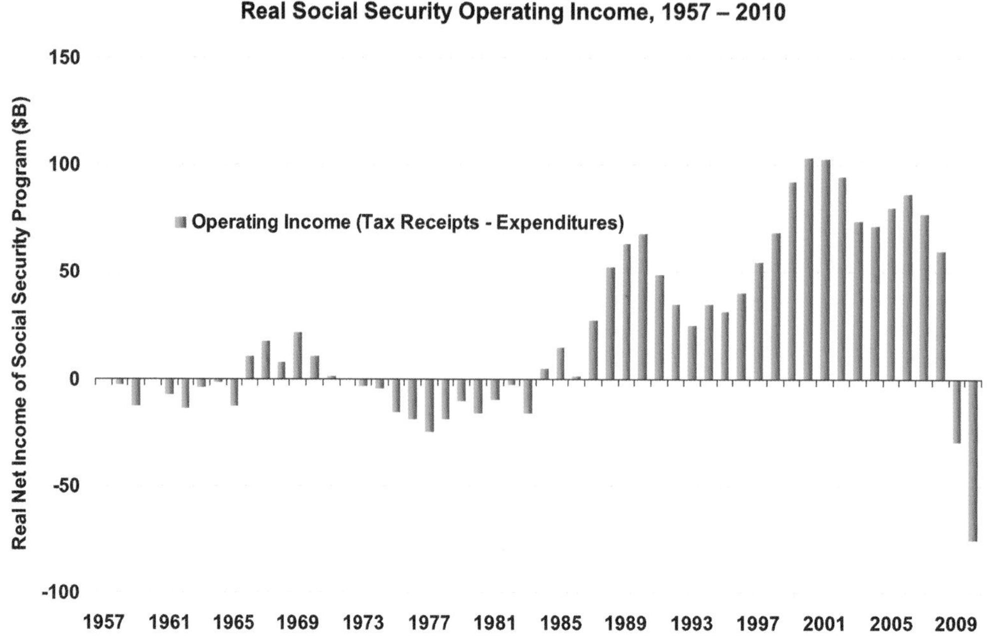

*Note: *Data is adjusted for inflation using White House OMB's GDP price index (based on BEA's data). USA federal fiscal year ends in September; Source: Social Security Administration.*

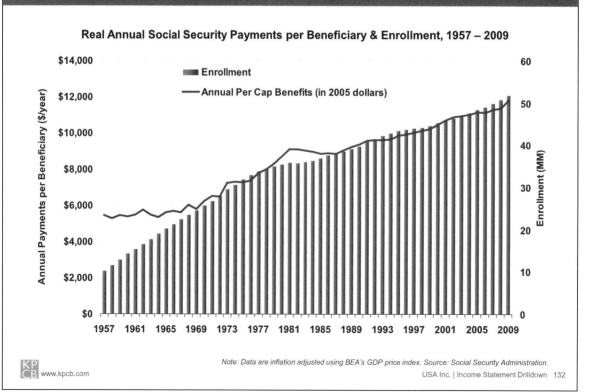

Social Security: Enrollment Up 5x to 52 Million While Inflation-Adjusted Annual Payments per Beneficiary Up 2x to $12K From 1957 to 2009

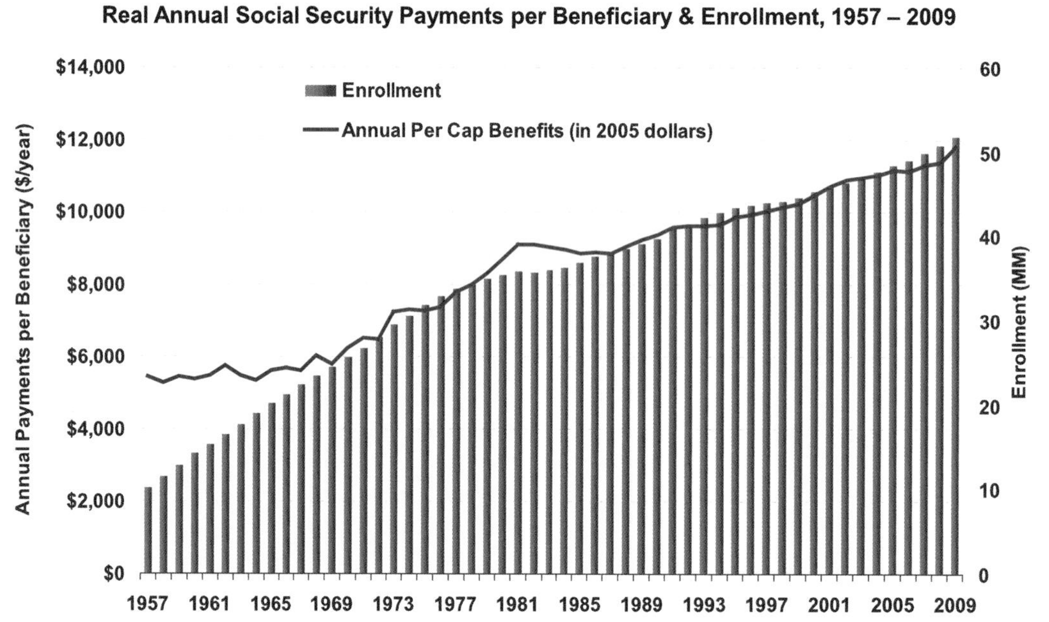

Note: Data are inflation adjusted using BEA's GDP price index. Source: Social Security Administration.

Social Security: Observations

- **52 million retired Americans (17% of population) received an average of $11,826 (in 2005 dollars) in Social Security payments (32% of USA per-capita income) in 2009.**
- By comparison, 10 million retired Americans (6% of population) received an average of $5,447 (in 2005 dollars) in Social Security payments (51% of per-capita income) in 1957.
- When Social Security was created in early 20th century to provide retirement income to elderly Americans, 1 in 127 Americans[1] (<1% of population) received Social Security payments. Now 1 in 6 Americans (17%) receive Social Security payments…well above the initial 'plan.'

Note: 1) Social Security was created in 1935, full data on enrollees not available until 1945.
Source: Social Security Administration.

Social Security: America is Aging, and USA, Inc. Workers Are Required to Support 5x More Beneficiaries (and Rising) than They Did in 1950!

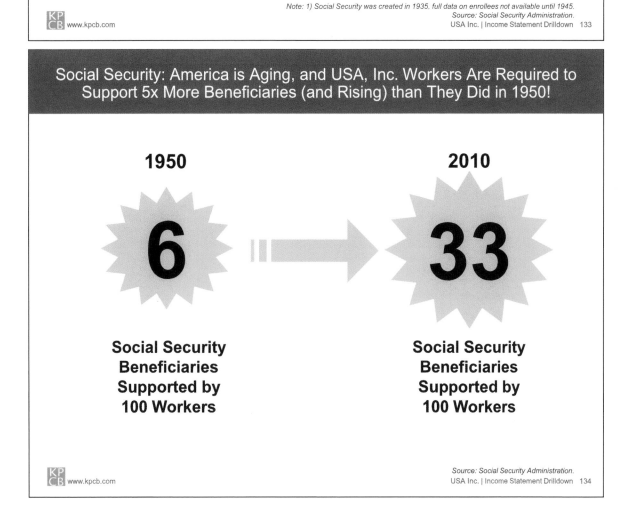

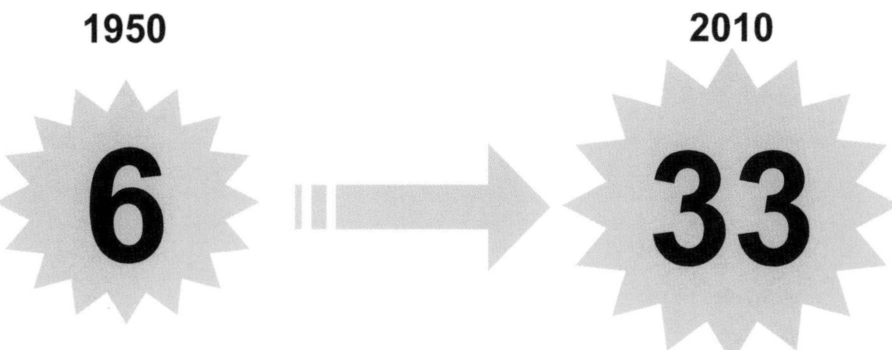

Social Security Beneficiaries Supported by 100 Workers

Social Security Beneficiaries Supported by 100 Workers

Source: Social Security Administration.

Social Security: Each Retiree Was Supported by __42__ Workers in 1945 & Just __3__ Workers in 2009

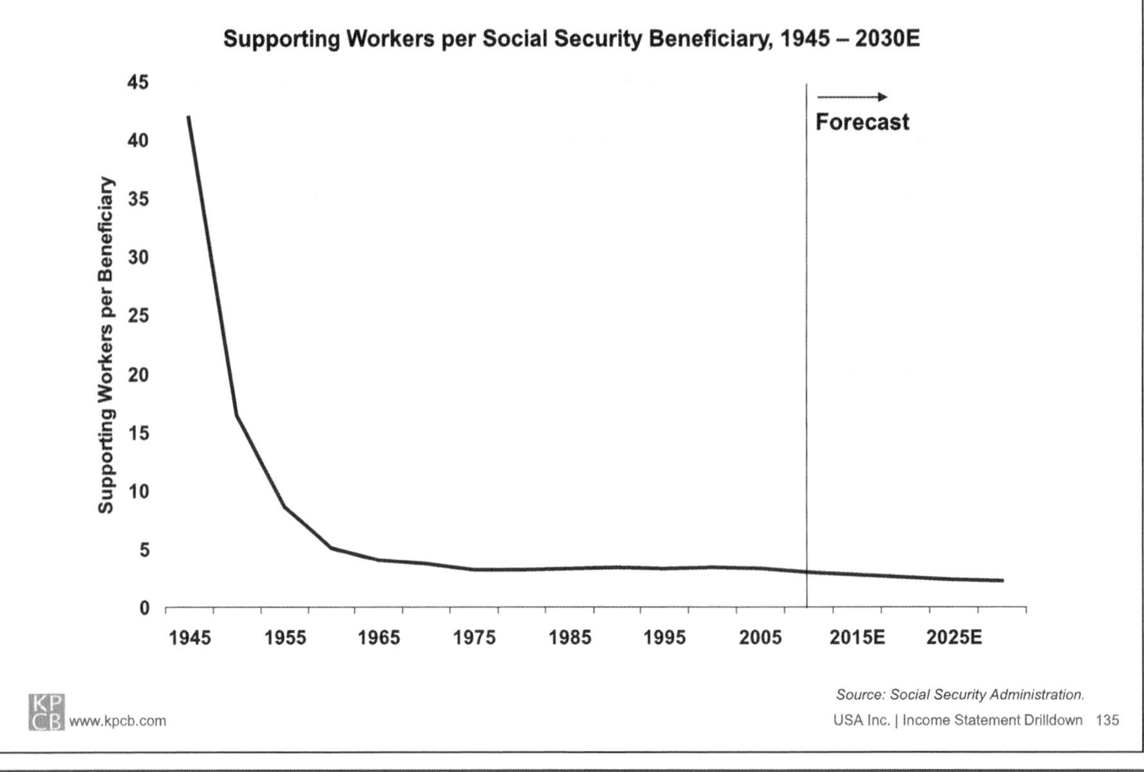

Source: Social Security Administration.

Think About That…

If you are a worker in USA, Inc. (as 81 million tax-paying Americans are), in effect, you have 5 times more 'dependents*' than your parents had and 15 times more than your grandparents.

*Note: * 'Dependents' = retirees who receive Social Security benefits primarily funded via payroll taxes on current working population.*

Analysts Often Think of Things as Math Problems…

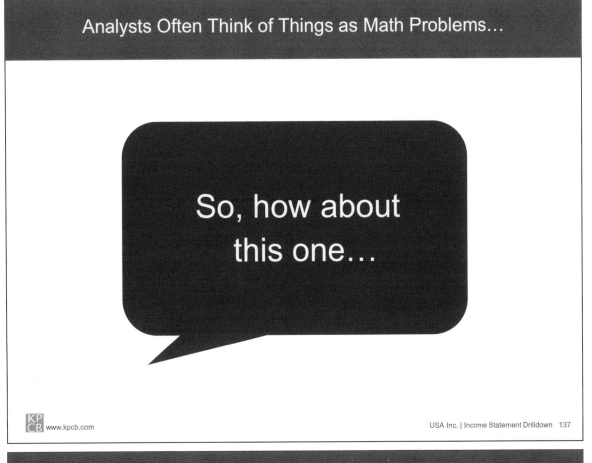

Americans Are Living 26% Longer, But Social Security 'Retirement Age' Has Increased Only 3% Since Social Security Was Created in 1935…

USA Life Expectancy at Birth, 1935 & 2009

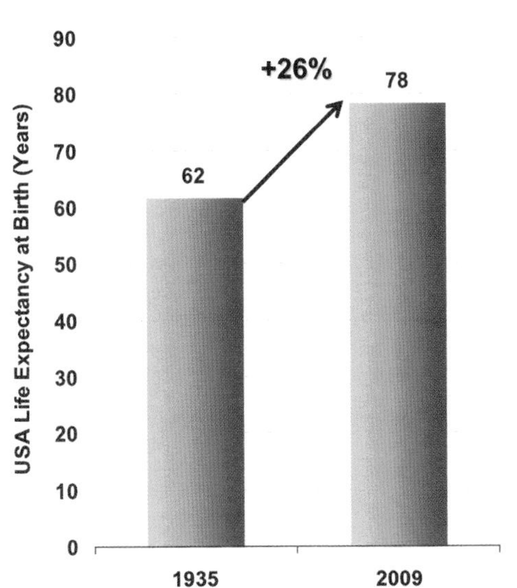

USA Full Retirement Age, 1935 & 2009

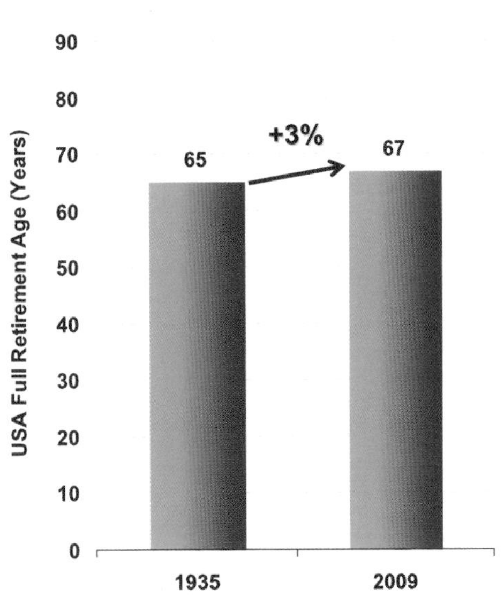

Note: Full retirement age is 65 for people born in 1930; 67 for people born in 2009; Social Security Amendments of 1961 allowed early retirement to start at 62+ with reduced benefits. Source: National Center for Health Statistics, World Bank, Social Security Administration.

That's a Math Problem…

- **If an expense rises by 26% and the ability to pay rises by only 3%, the math doesn't work.** A computer in a science fiction movie might blurt out, 'does not compute…does not compute…'
- ''Something's Gotta Give…' as the 2003 film put it.
- A mathematician or economist would say, 'the expense must go down or the ability to pay must rise to match the expense.'
- Simple math implies that the age for collecting full benefits should rise from 67 to 72, so that expenses more closely match workers' ability to pay. Under this scenario, while Americans are living 30% longer, the 'retirement' age would rise just 7%, still well below the increase in life expectancy since Social Security was created.

Social Security: Unless The Program Is Restructured, Cash Flow Will Turn Negative by 2015E Owing to Aging Population

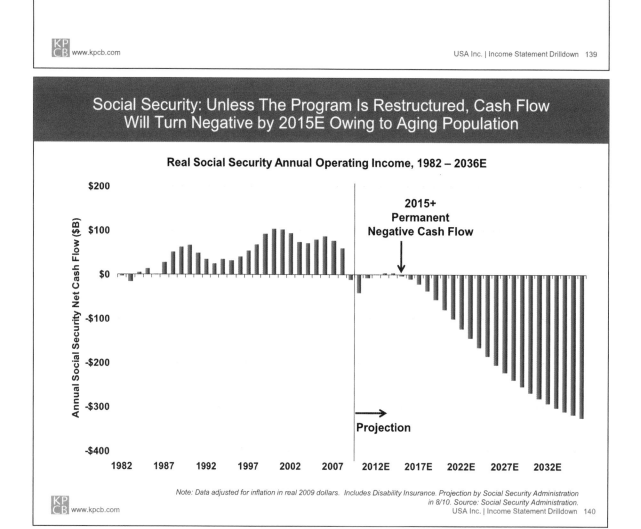

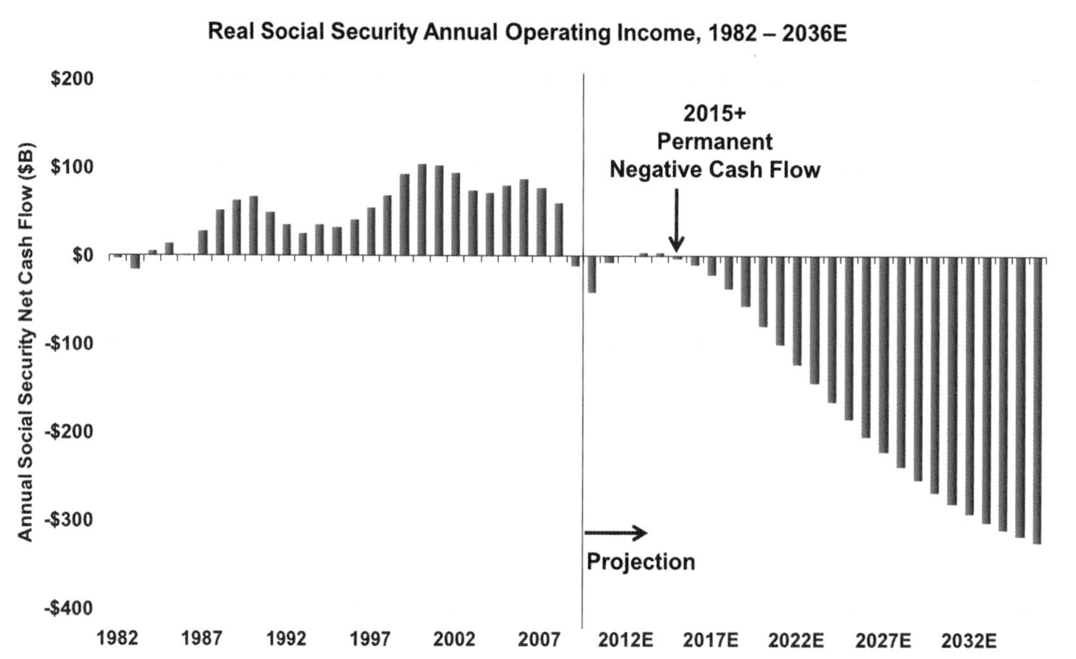

Note: Data adjusted for inflation in real 2009 dollars. Includes Disability Insurance. Projection by Social Security Administration in 8/10. Source: Social Security Administration.

In Sum…

Heretofore, Social Security and Unemployment Insurance have been effectively funded, but two significant entitlement programs (Medicaid and Medicare) were created without effective funding plans / programs. Only one of these (Medicaid) is means-tested (indicating that one is eligible for Medicaid only if he / she does not sufficient financial means).

Left unchanged, Unemployment Insurance funding should improve as economic growth resumes, but Social Security will no longer be self-funded within 5-10 years, and the underfunding of Medicaid and Medicare will simply go from bad to worse.

Drill Down on USA Inc.
Rising Debt Level and Interest Payments

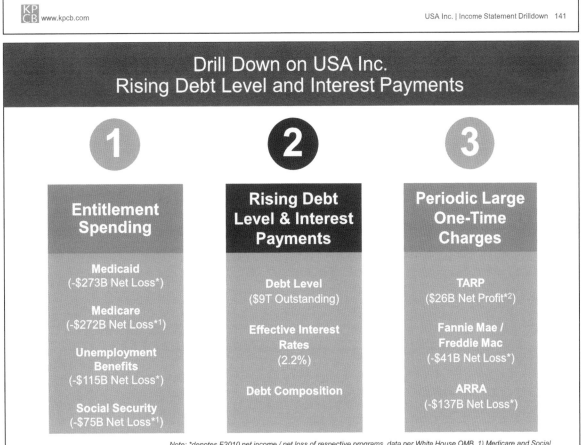

1

Entitlement Spending

Medicaid
(-$273B Net Loss*)

Medicare
(-$272B Net Loss*1)

Unemployment Benefits
(-$115B Net Loss*)

Social Security
(-$75B Net Loss*1)

2

Rising Debt Level & Interest Payments

Debt Level
($9T Outstanding)

Effective Interest Rates
(2.2%)

Debt Composition

3

Periodic Large One-Time Charges

TARP
($26B Net Profit*2)

Fannie Mae / Freddie Mac
(-$41B Net Loss*)

ARRA
(-$137B Net Loss*)

*Note: *denotes F2010 net income / net loss of respective programs, data per White House OMB. 1) Medicare and Social Security net loss excludes Trust Fund interest income. 2) TARP net loss includes proceeds from sale of warrants. TARP is Troubled Asset Relief Program; ARRA is American Recovery & Reinvestment Act programs.*

Interest Payments:
3 Determinants = Debt Level + Interest Rates + Maturity

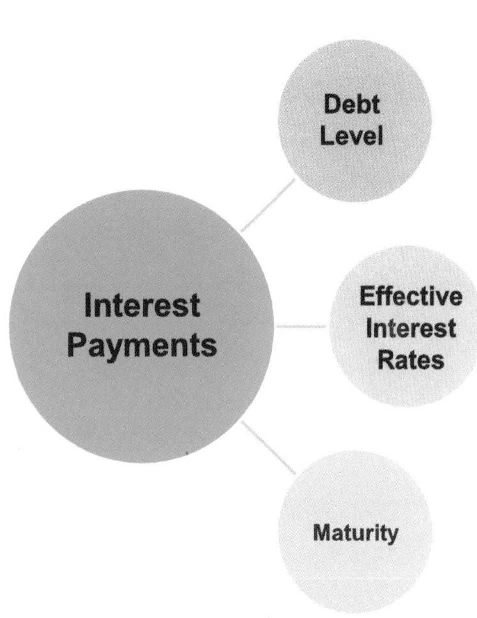

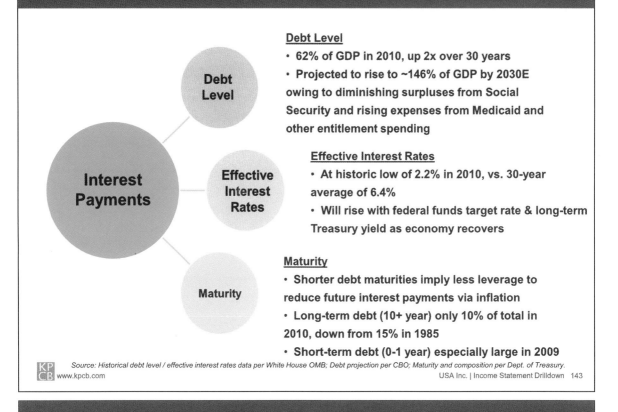

Debt Level
- 62% of GDP in 2010, up 2x over 30 years
- Projected to rise to ~146% of GDP by 2030E owing to diminishing surpluses from Social Security and rising expenses from Medicaid and other entitlement spending

Effective Interest Rates
- At historic low of 2.2% in 2010, vs. 30-year average of 6.4%
- Will rise with federal funds target rate & long-term Treasury yield as economy recovers

Maturity
- Shorter debt maturities imply less leverage to reduce future interest payments via inflation
- Long-term debt (10+ year) only 10% of total in 2010, down from 15% in 1985
- Short-term debt (0-1 year) especially large in 2009

Source: Historical debt level / effective interest rates data per White House OMB; Debt projection per CBO; Maturity and composition per Dept. of Treasury.

Drill Down on Debt Levels & Related Expenses

We begin with a simple study of current and historical debt levels and key drivers of why debt has risen so much, then we look at interest rates (which are low by historical standards) and the impact they have on interest expense, then we look at the short-term vs. long-term composition of USA Inc.'s debt.

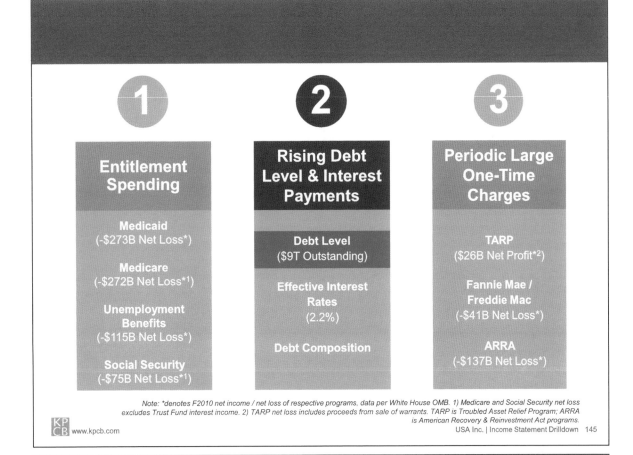

1
Entitlement Spending

Medicaid
(-$273B Net Loss*)

Medicare
(-$272B Net Loss*1)

Unemployment Benefits
(-$115B Net Loss*)

Social Security
(-$75B Net Loss*1)

2
Rising Debt Level & Interest Payments

Debt Level
($9T Outstanding)

Effective Interest Rates
(2.2%)

Debt Composition

3
Periodic Large One-Time Charges

TARP
($26B Net Profit*2)

Fannie Mae / Freddie Mac
(-$41B Net Loss*)

ARRA
(-$137B Net Loss*)

*Note: *denotes F2010 net income / net loss of respective programs, data per White House OMB. 1) Medicare and Social Security net loss excludes Trust Fund interest income. 2) TARP net loss includes proceeds from sale of warrants. TARP is Troubled Asset Relief Program; ARRA is American Recovery & Reinvestment Act programs.*

Debt Level: Highest (as % of GDP) Since World War II and Rising Rapidly

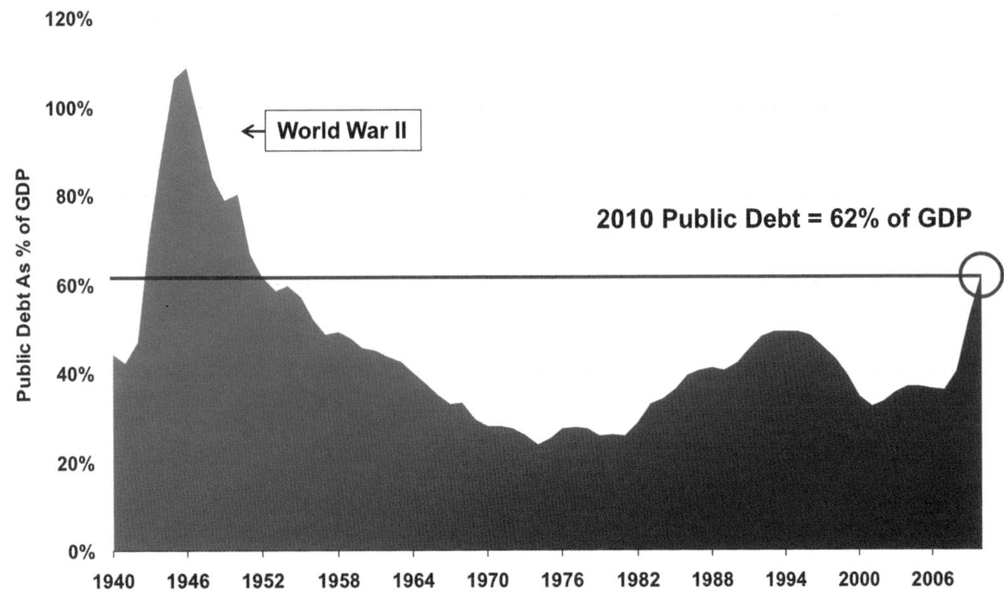

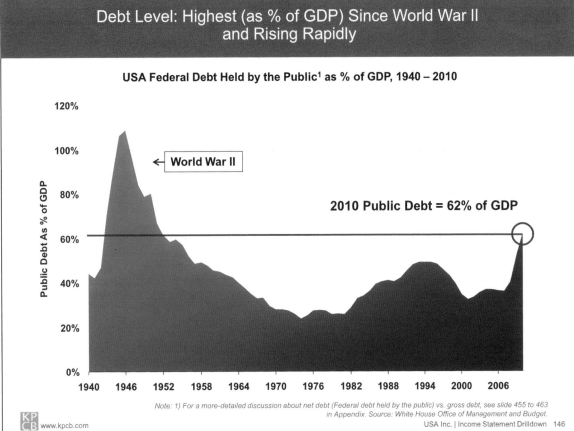

Note: 1) For a more-detailed discussion about net debt (Federal debt held by the public) vs. gross debt, see slide 455 to 463 in Appendix. Source: White House Office of Management and Budget.

Why Has Debt Risen So Much? Public Debt Up **2x** Over Past 3 Decades

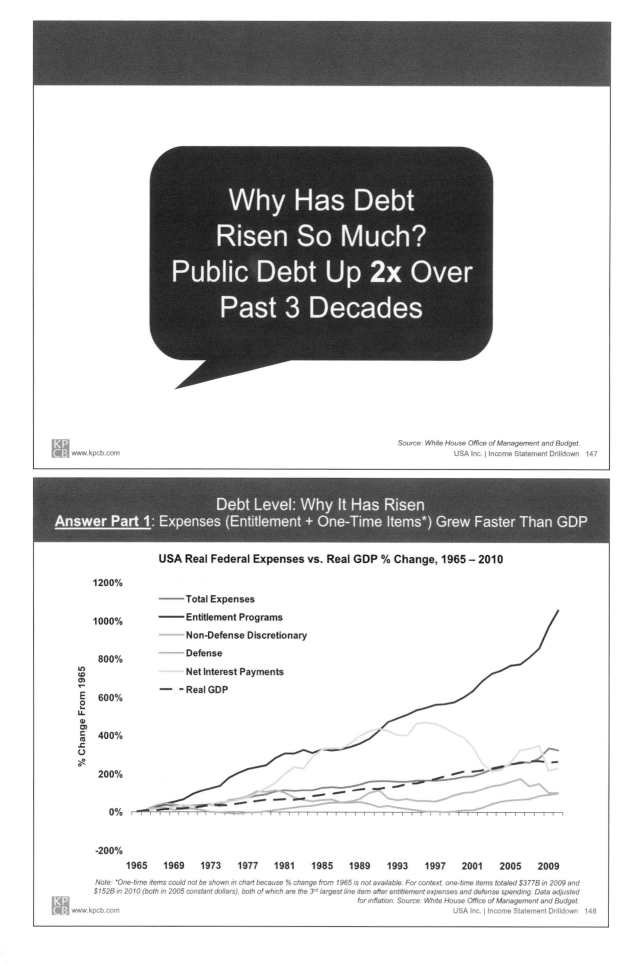

Debt Level: Why It Has Risen

Answer Part 1: Expenses (Entitlement + One-Time Items*) Grew Faster Than GDP

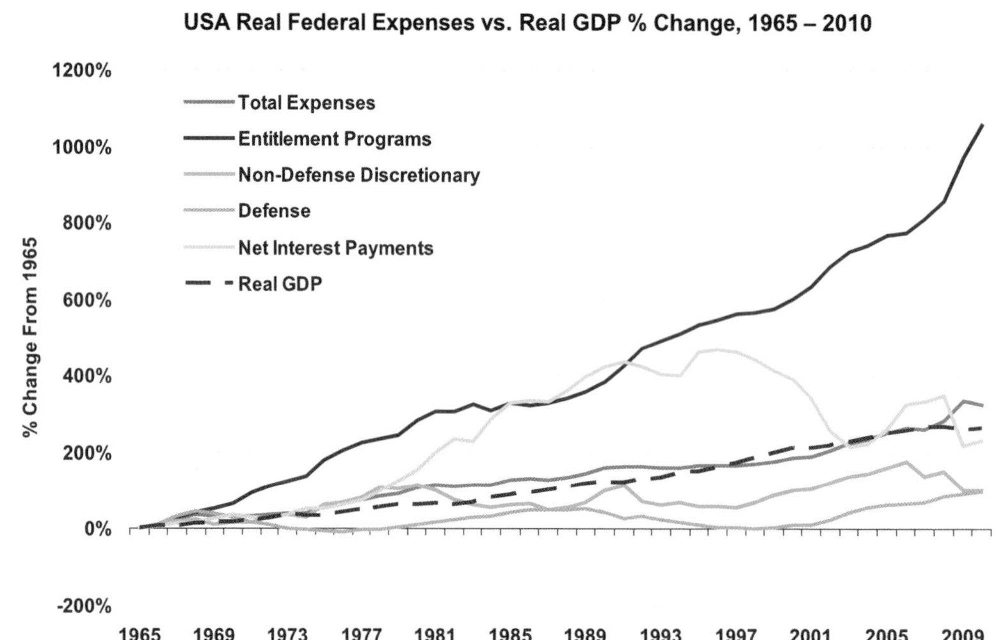

*Note: *One-time items could not be shown in chart because % change from 1965 is not available. For context, one-time items totaled $377B in 2009 and $152B in 2010 (both in 2005 constant dollars), both of which are the 3rd largest line item after entitlement expenses and defense spending. Data adjusted for inflation. Source: White House Office of Management and Budget.*

Debt Level: Entitlement Spending Increased **11x** (1965 to 2010), While Real GDP Grew **3x**

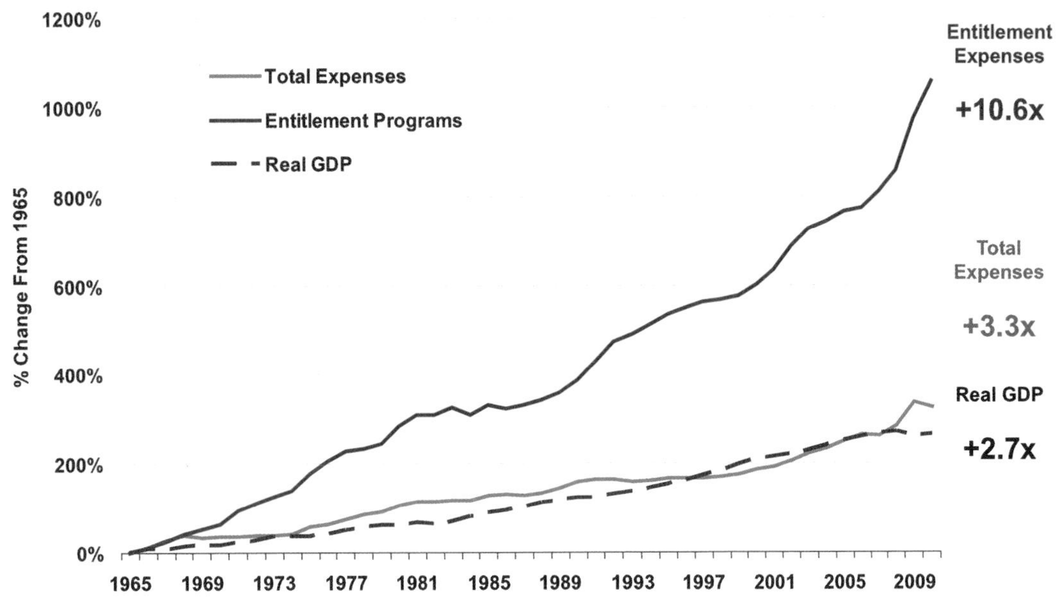

Note: Data adjusted for inflation. Source: White House Office of Management and Budget.

Debt Level: Why It Has Risen
Answer Part 2: Revenue (Esp. Corporate Taxes) Fell Below GDP Growth

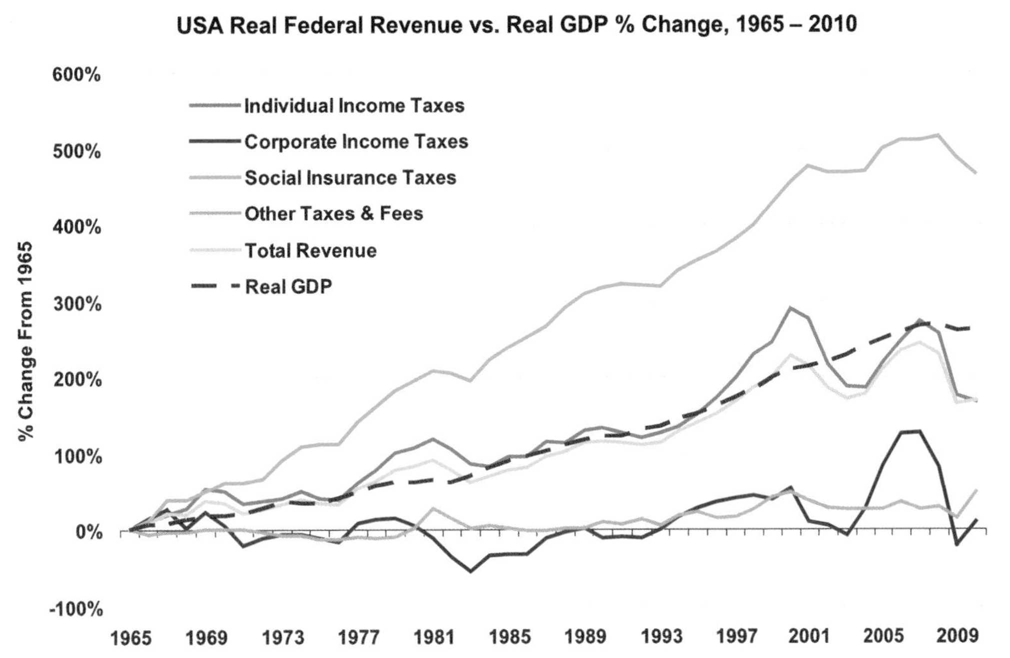

Note: All data adjusted for inflation. Source: White House Office of Management and Budget, Bureau of Economic Analysis.

Debt Level: Recessions + Corporate Tax Accounting Changes Led to Revenue Underperformance (Relative to GDP Growth)

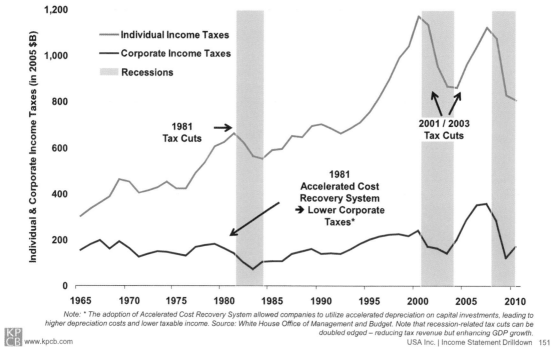

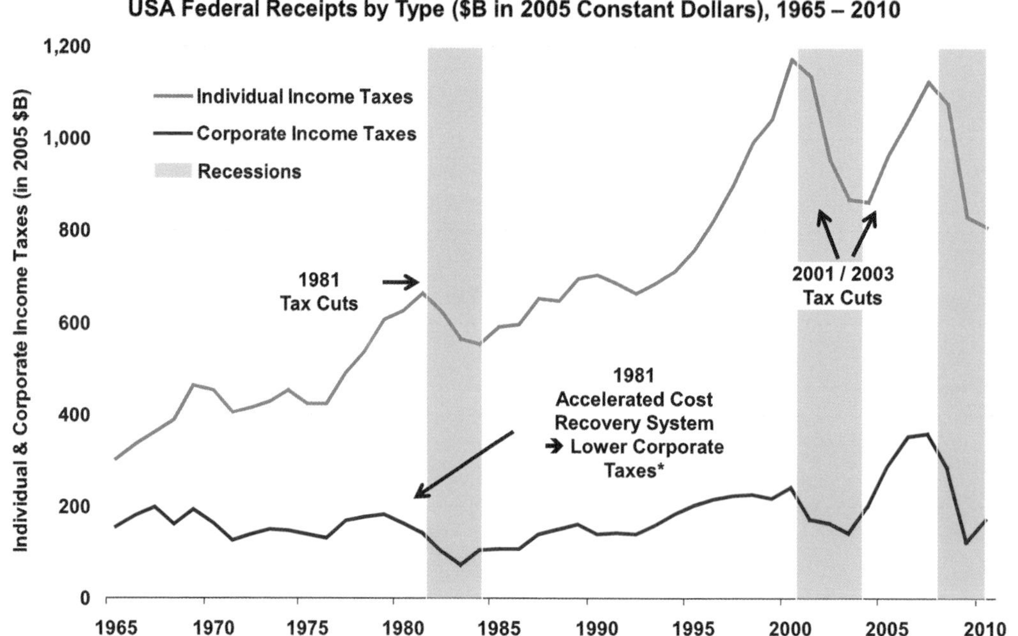

*Note: * The adoption of Accelerated Cost Recovery System allowed companies to utilize accelerated depreciation on capital investments, leading to higher depreciation costs and lower taxable income. Source: White House Office of Management and Budget. Note that recession-related tax cuts can be doubled edged – reducing tax revenue but enhancing GDP growth.*

Debt Level: In the Past, Social Security's Surpluses Have Masked USA Inc.'s True Borrowing Needs by $1.4T

- Social Security tax receipts exceeded outlays in every year between 1984 and 2008, leading to a cumulative surplus of $1.4 trillion.
- These surpluses have been used to fund other parts of federal government operations (including Medicaid, infrastructure and defense...) under the unified budget accounting rules.
- Without these past Social Security surpluses, USA Inc. would have to have issued $1.4 trillion more debt (or 16% higher than current level of debt) to fund its operations.

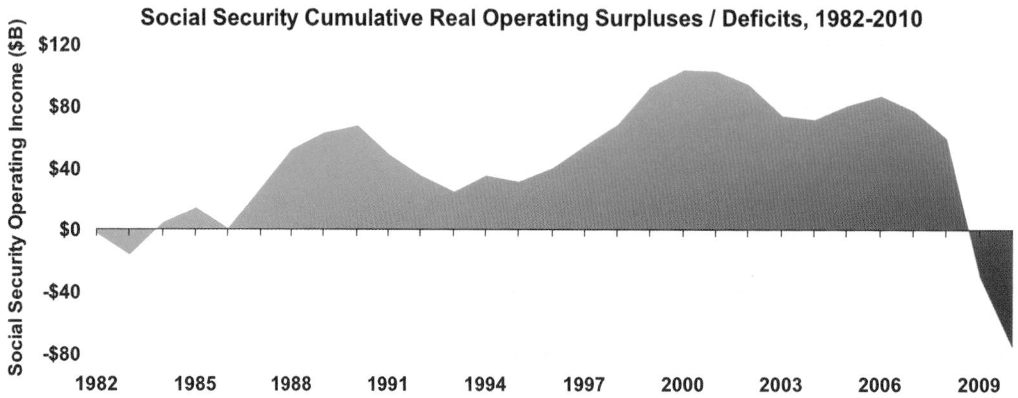

Note: Surpluses & deficits exclude Trust Fund interest income, adjusted for inflation. Data source: Congressional Budget Office.

Why Will Debt Level Continue to Rise? Public Debt Projected to Rise **2x** Over Next 3 Decades

Source: Congressional Budget Office Long-Term Budget Outlook (6/10), Alternative Fiscal Scenario (assuming a continuation of today's underlying fiscal policy. This scenario deviates from CBO's baseline because it incorporates some policy changes that are widely expected to occur and that policymakers have regularly made in the past).

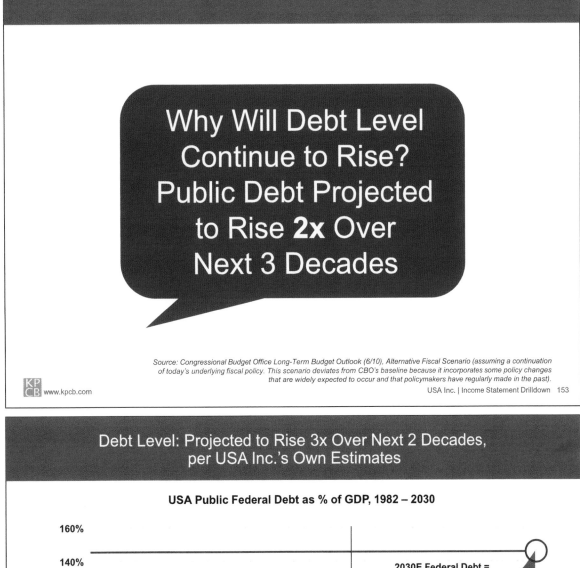

Debt Level: Projected to Rise 3x Over Next 2 Decades, per USA Inc.'s Own Estimates

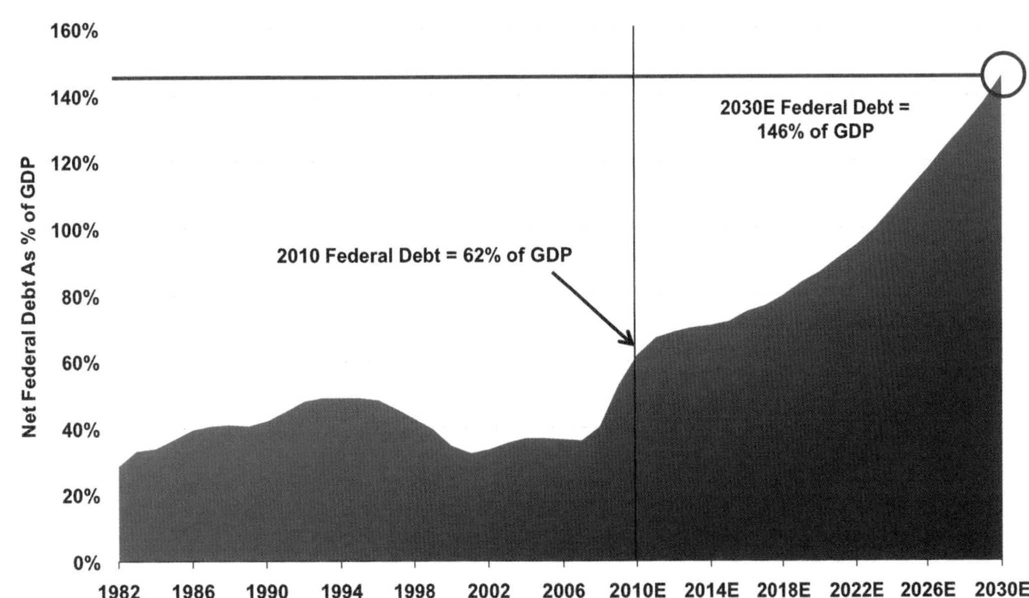

Source: Congressional Budget Office Long-Term Budget Outlook (6/10), Alternative Fiscal Scenario (assuming a continuation of today's underlying fiscal policy. This scenario deviates from CBO's baseline because it incorporates some policy changes that are widely expected to occur and that policymakers have regularly made in the past).

Debt Level: Why Will It Continue to Rise?
Answer Part 1: Notional Social Security "Trust Fund" Surpluses Likely Turning Into Deficits Owing to Aging Population

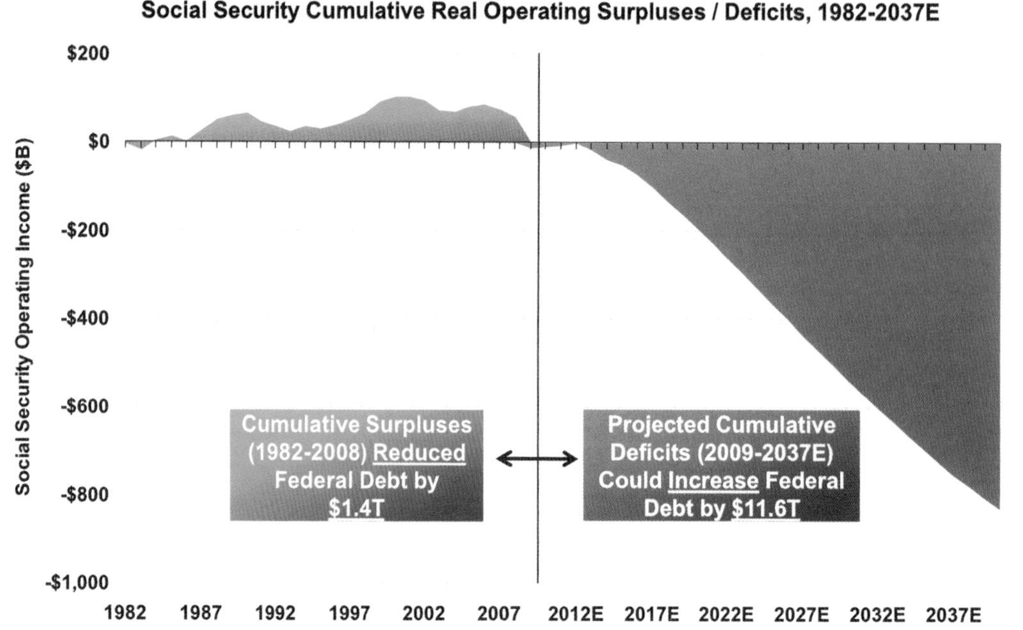

Note: Surpluses & deficits exclude Trust Fund interest income, adjusted for inflation in 2009 dollars.
Source: Congressional Budget Office.

Debt Level: Why Will It Continue to Rise?
Answer Part 2: Notional Medicare* "Trust Fund" Surpluses Likely Turning Into Deficits Owing to Aging Population

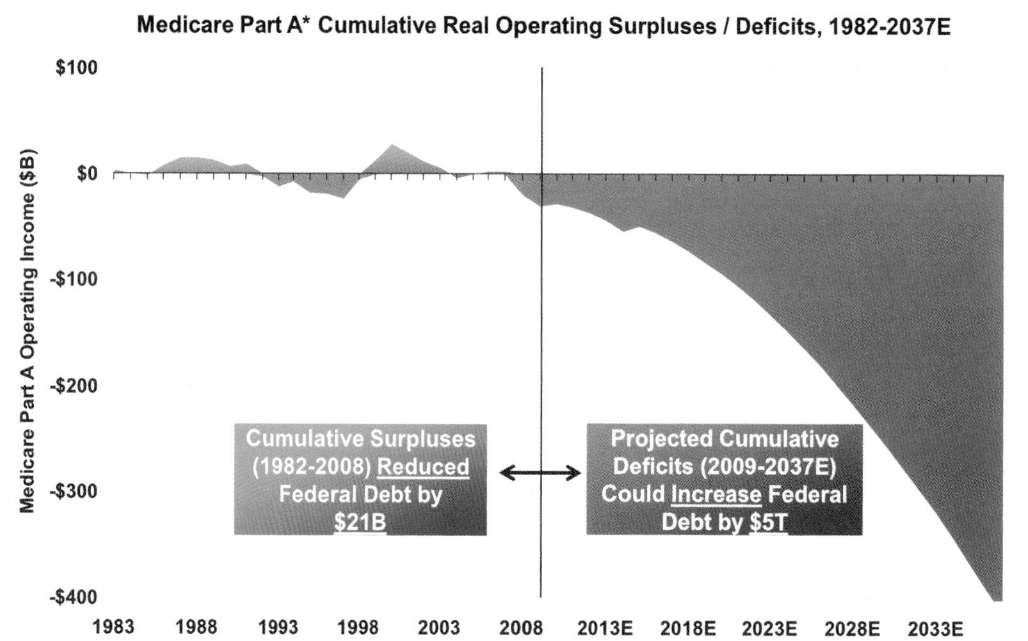

*Note: Data are adjusted for inflation in 2009 dollars. *Only Medicare Part A (hospital insurance) has a trust fund (funded by payroll taxes), Part B (medical insurance) and Part D (prescription drug benefits) are primarily funded by general tax revenue and premium / co-payments. Source: Medicare Trustees.*

Debt Level: Why Will It Continue to Rise?
Answer Part 3: Potential Loss on Guarantees on Fannie Mae / Freddie Mac Originations Could Rise

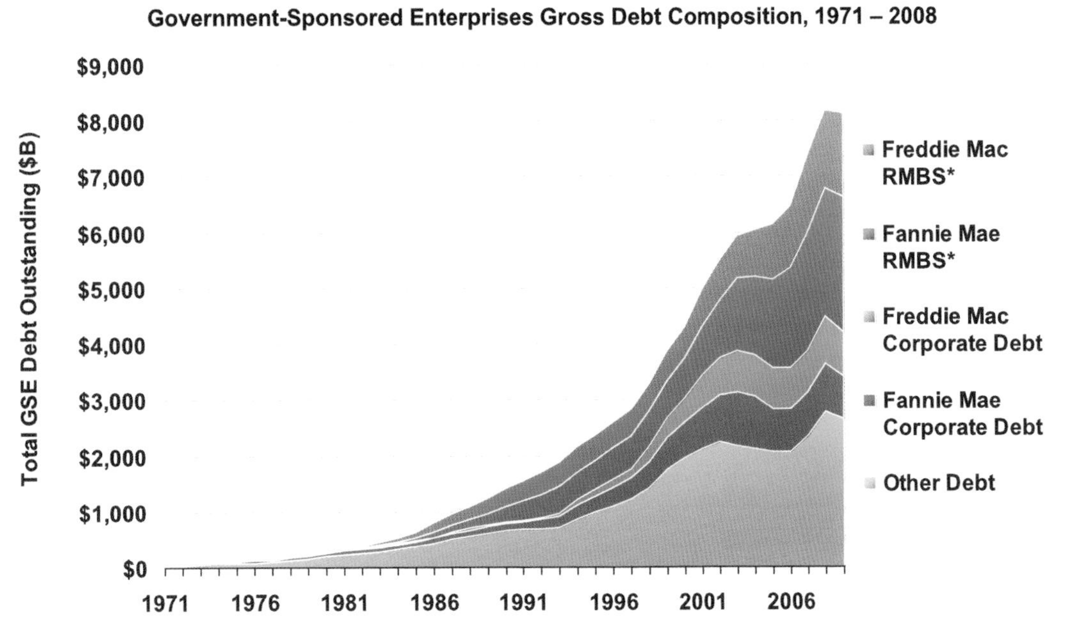

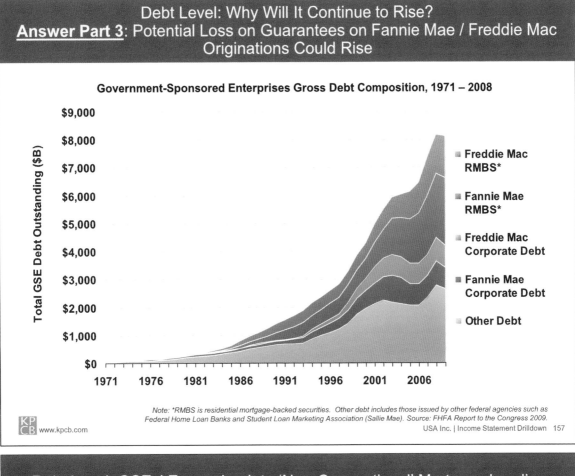

*Note: *RMBS is residential mortgage-backed securities. Other debt includes those issued by other federal agencies such as Federal Home Loan Banks and Student Loan Marketing Association (Sallie Mae). Source: FHFA Report to the Congress 2009.*

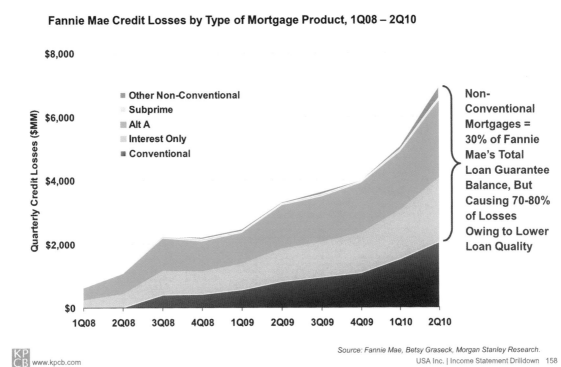

Debt Level: GSEs' Expansion Into 'Non-Conventional' Mortgage Lending Business Has Proved to Be Costly So Far

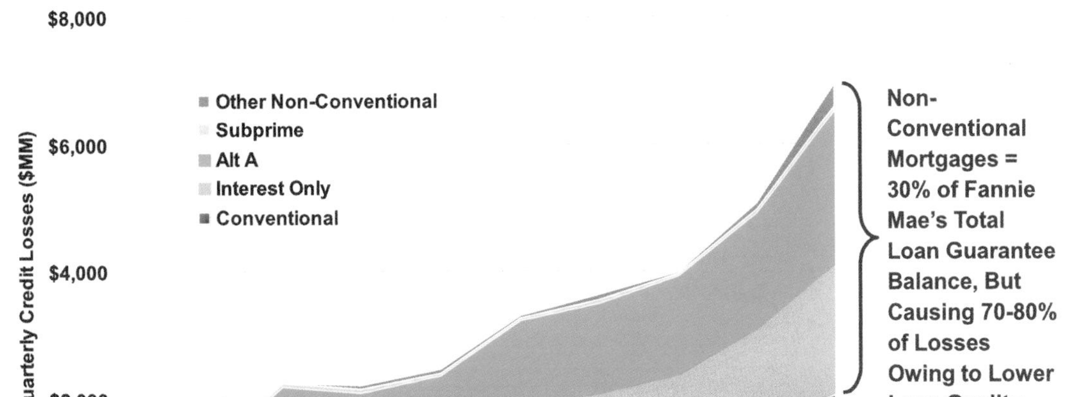

Source: Fannie Mae, Betsy Graseck, Morgan Stanley Research.

Debt Level: Fannie Mae + Freddie Mac = Latest Estimated Ultimate Cost to Taxpayers Varies*

Base-Case Estimated Ultimate Net Loss**	Source	Comments / Assumptions
$389 Billion	**Congressional Budget Office (CBO)**	**Net accrued loss to be borne by taxpayers, including net cash infusions (with implied default rate of ~5-10%) and risk premiums associated with federal government's implicit guarantee on GSEs' credit.** **Bulk of the net loss ($291B) occurred prior to and during F2009.** **On a cash basis, CBO's estimate would have been in line with White House OMB's estimate.**
$160 Billion	**White House Office of Management and Budget (OMB)**	**Net cash outlay to be borne by Treasury Dept. (and ultimately taxpayers), including Treasury Dept.'s cash outlays to purchase Fannie Mae & Freddie Mac preferred stock (with implied default rate of ~5-10%), minus cash received from dividends.** **Bulk of the net cash outlay ($112B) occurred prior to and during F2009.**

*Note: *Latest estimated cost to taxpayers varies and continues to rise. **By F2019E. Source: CBO, OMB.*

Debt Level: Scenario Math – What Various Default Rates Could Mean for Taxpayer Ultimate Cash Cost of Fannie Mae & Freddie Mac

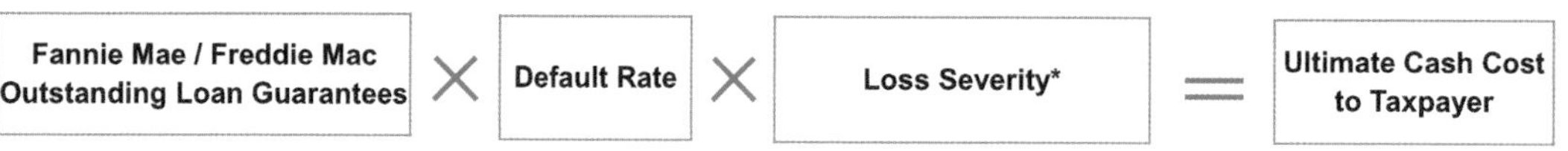

Outstanding Loan Guarantees	Default Rate	Loss Severity*	Ultimate Cash Cost to Taxpayer
$5 Trillion[1] (before government conservatorship in 9/08)	2%	50%	$50 Billion
	5%		$125 Billion
	10%		$250 Billion
	15%		$375 Billion
	20%		$500 Billion
	25%		$625 Billion

$160 Billion

Current CBO / OMB Forecasts of Ultimate Cash Cost of Fannie Mae / Freddie Mac ← (between $125 Billion and $250 Billion)

*Note: * Loss severity is liquidation value (foreclosure auction or other means) as a % of the loan amount adjusted for any advances and fees. Source: 1) Fannie Mae, Freddie Mac.*

1

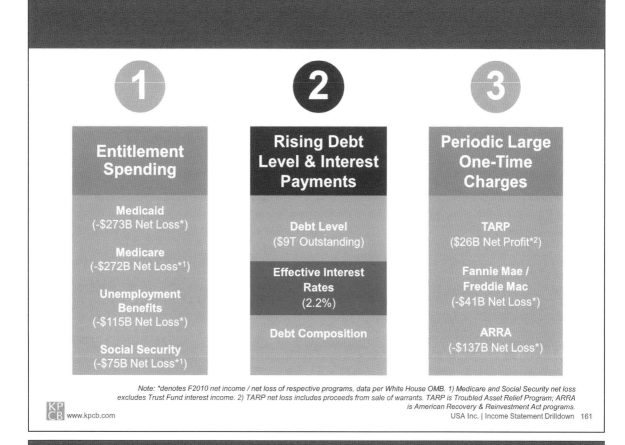

Entitlement Spending

Medicaid
(-$273B Net Loss*)

Medicare
(-$272B Net Loss*[1])

Unemployment Benefits
(-$115B Net Loss*)

Social Security
(-$75B Net Loss*[1])

2

Rising Debt Level & Interest Payments

Debt Level
($9T Outstanding)

Effective Interest Rates
(2.2%)

Debt Composition

3

Periodic Large One-Time Charges

TARP
($26B Net Profit*[2])

Fannie Mae / Freddie Mac
(-$41B Net Loss*)

ARRA
(-$137B Net Loss*)

*Note: *denotes F2010 net income / net loss of respective programs, data per White House OMB. 1) Medicare and Social Security net loss excludes Trust Fund interest income. 2) TARP net loss includes proceeds from sale of warrants. TARP is Troubled Asset Relief Program; ARRA is American Recovery & Reinvestment Act programs.*

Effective Interest Rates: While USA Debt Has Risen Steadily Since 1981, Rates Have Fallen Steadily, so the Cost of Debt Has Potentially Been Held Artificially Low

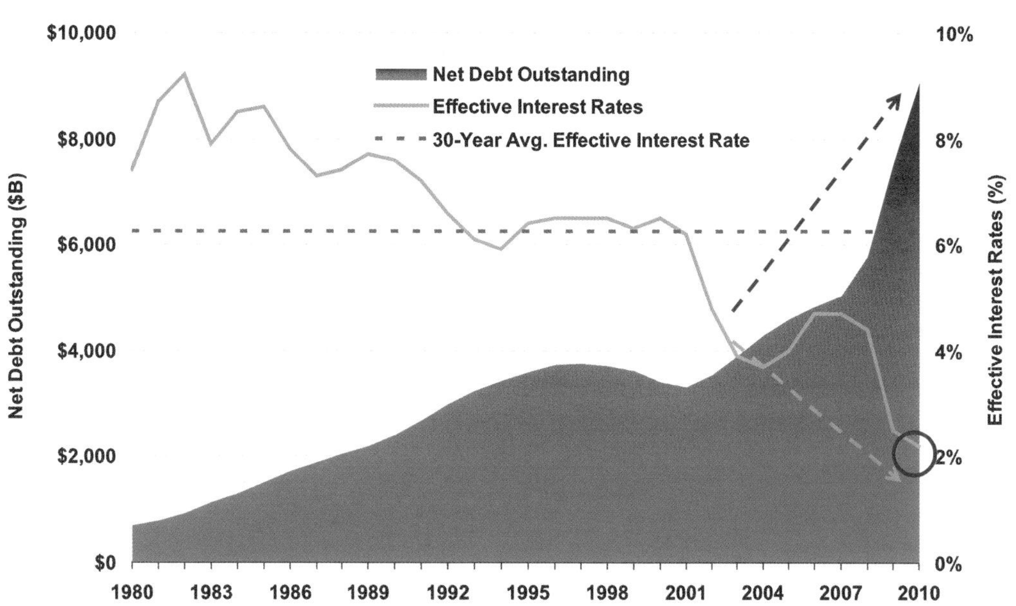

Source: White House Office of Management and Budget.

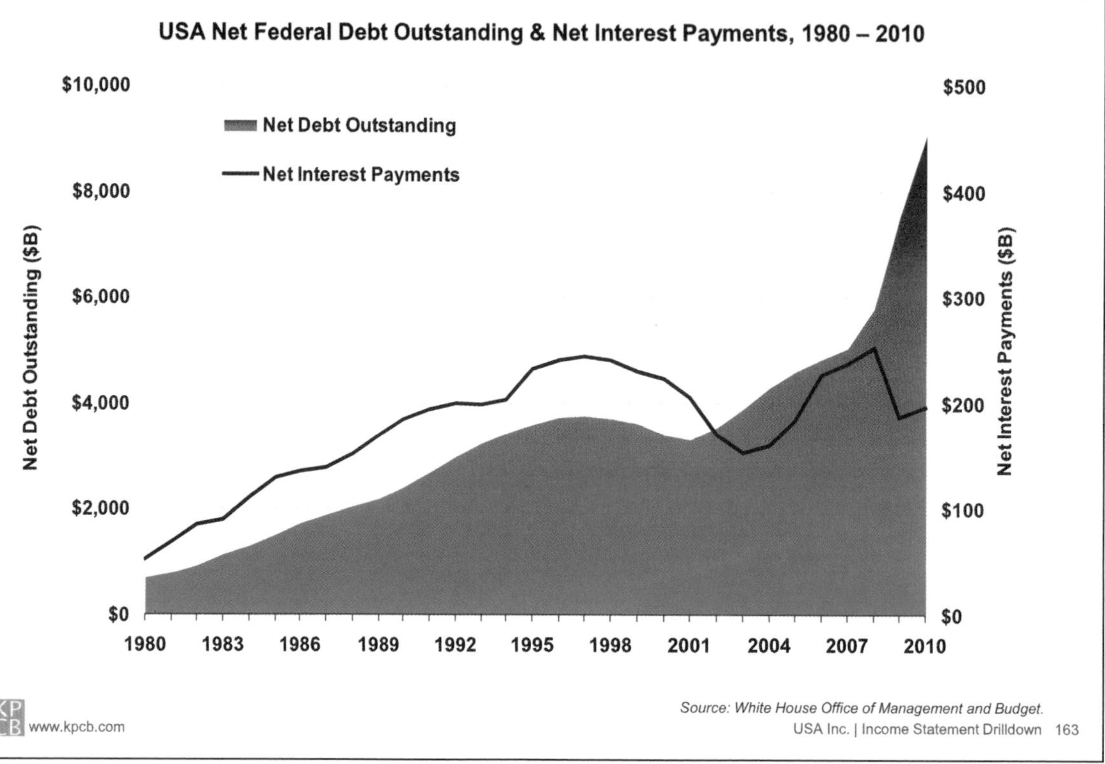

Effective Interest Rates: While USA Debt Has Risen, Net Interest Payments Have Fallen
USA Net Federal Debt Outstanding & Net Interest Payments, 1980 – 2010
Net Debt Outstanding
Net Interest Payments
Net Debt Outstanding ($B)
Net Interest Payments ($B)
$10,000
$8,000
$6,000
$4,000
$2,000
$0
$500
$400
$300
$200
$100
$0
1980
1983
1986
1989
1992
1995
1998
2001
2004
2007
2010
Source: White House Office of Management and Budget.
www.kpcb.com
USA Inc. | Income Statement Drilldown 163

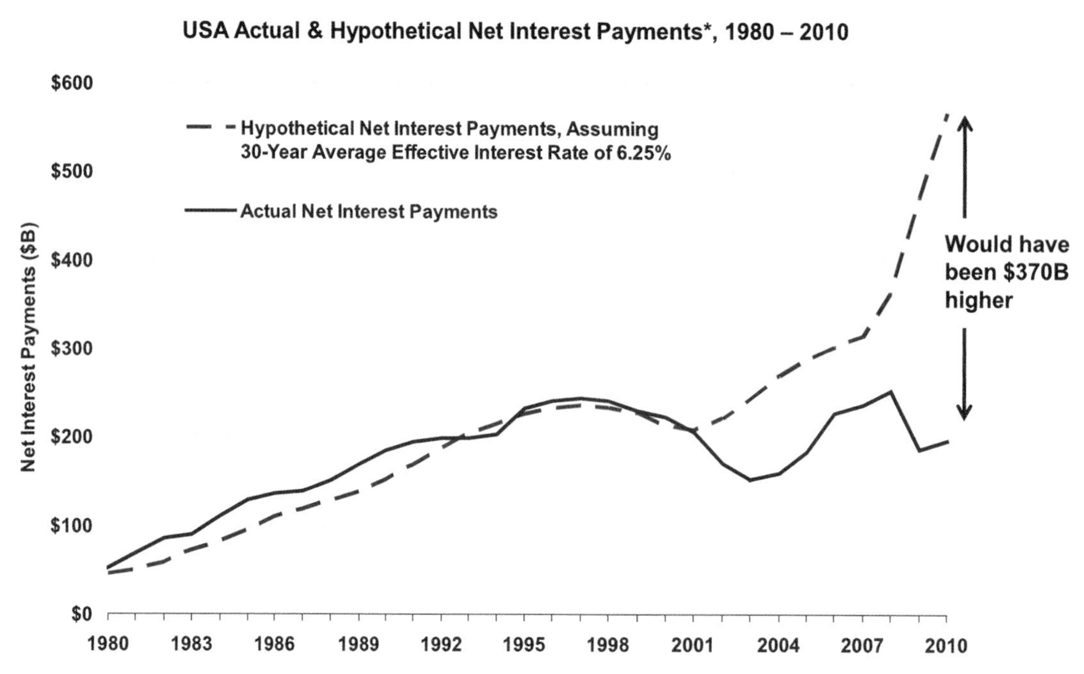

Effective Interest Rates: Hypothetical Exercise – If USA 2009 Cost of Debt Was Paid at 30-Year Average Interest Rate Level of 6% vs. Current 2%, Annual Interest Cost Would Rise 3x to $566 Billion from $196 Billion
USA Actual & Hypothetical Net Interest Payments*, 1980 – 2010
Hypothetical Net Interest Payments, Assuming 30-Year Average Effective Interest Rate of 6.25%
Actual Net Interest Payments
Net Interest Payments ($B)
$600
$500
$400
$300
$200
$100
$0
Would have been $370B higher
1980
1983
1986
1989
1992
1995
1998
2001
2004
2007
2010
Note: * Hypothetical net interest payments calculation assumes all other variables (such as GDP, revenue, spending, debt levels, etc.) are held constant. Source: White House Office of Management and Budget.
www.kpcb.com
USA Inc. | Income Statement Drilldown 164

Effective Interest Rates: But Cost of Debt Unlikely to Continue to Decline For Extended Period If Economy Improves

USA Federal Debt Weighted Average Yields, 1980 – 2010

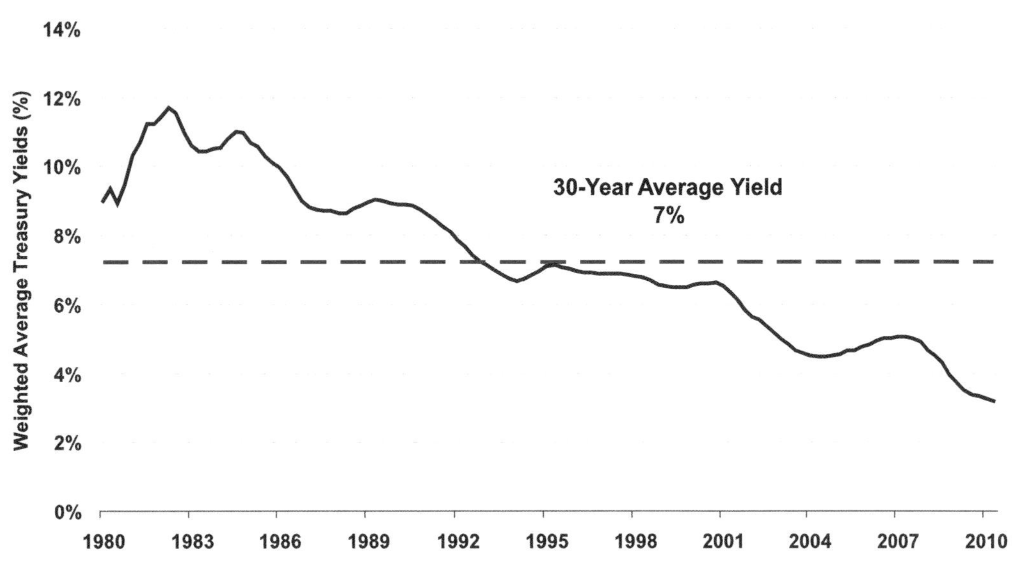

Source: US Treasury.

Effective Interest Rates: If Debt Levels & Interest Rates Rise Dramatically Beyond 2010, Net Interest Payments Could Soar…

USA Federal Net Debt Outstanding / Effective Interest Rates / Net Interest Payments, 2009 – 2016E

	2009	2010	2011E	2012E	2013E	2014E	2015E	2016E	11-16E CAGR
Net Debt Outstanding ($B)	$7,545	$9,019	$10,856	$11,881	$12,784	$13,562	$14,301	$15,064	7%
Y/Y Growth	30%	20%	20%	9%	8%	6%	5%	5%	
Effective Interest Rate (%)	2.5%	2.2%	1.9%	2.0%	2.5%	3.1%	3.5%	3.7%	--
Net Interest Payments ($B)	$187	$196	$207	$242	$321	$418	$494	$562	22%
Y/Y Growth	-26%	5%	5%	17%	33%	30%	18%	14%	
% of Federal Tax Receipts	9	9	10	9	11	13	14	15	

Note: CAGR is compound annual growth rate. Source: White House Office of Management and Budget.

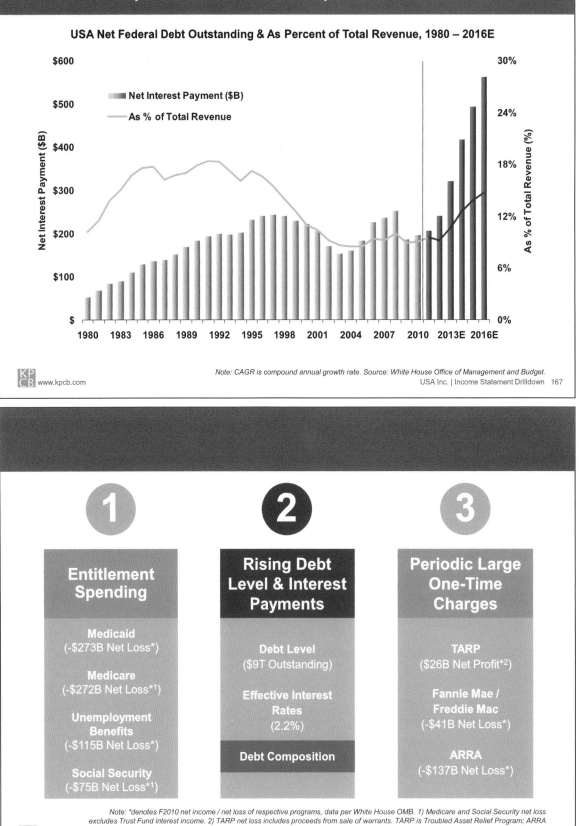

Effective Interest Rates: If Debt Levels & Interest Rates Rise Dramatically Beyond 2010, Net Interest Payments Could Soar

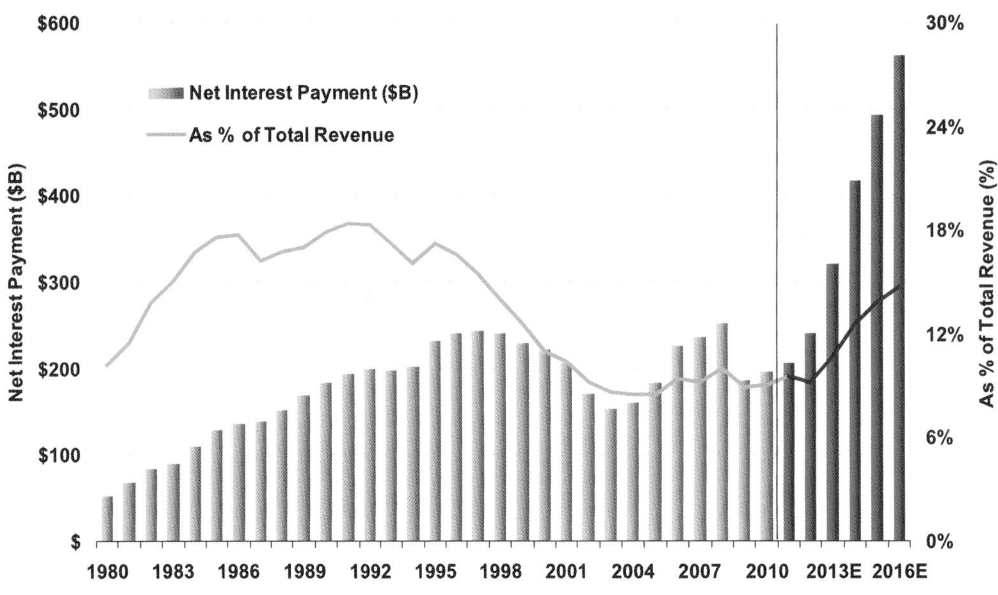

Note: CAGR is compound annual growth rate. Source: White House Office of Management and Budget.

1

Entitlement Spending

Medicaid (-$273B Net Loss*)

Medicare (-$272B Net Loss*1)

Unemployment Benefits (-$115B Net Loss*)

Social Security (-$75B Net Loss*1)

2

Rising Debt Level & Interest Payments

Debt Level ($9T Outstanding)

Effective Interest Rates (2.2%)

Debt Composition

3

Periodic Large One-Time Charges

TARP ($26B Net Profit*2)

Fannie Mae / Freddie Mac (-$41B Net Loss*)

ARRA (-$137B Net Loss*)

*Note: *denotes F2010 net income / net loss of respective programs, data per White House OMB. 1) Medicare and Social Security net loss excludes Trust Fund interest income. 2) TARP net loss includes proceeds from sale of warrants. TARP is Troubled Asset Relief Program; ARRA is American Recovery & Reinvestment Act programs.*

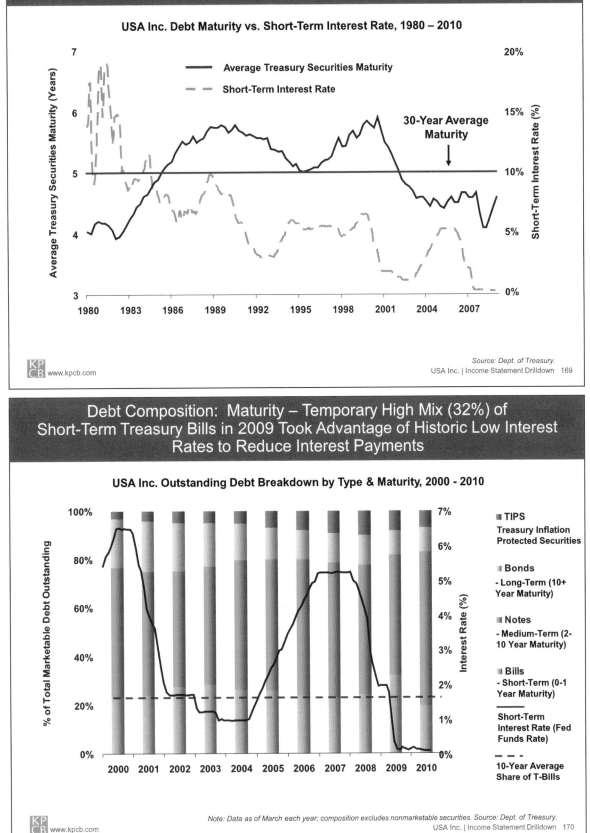

Debt Composition: Average Debt Maturity Declining Since 2000, Combined With Declining Interest Rate, Leading to "Artificially Low" Interest Payments

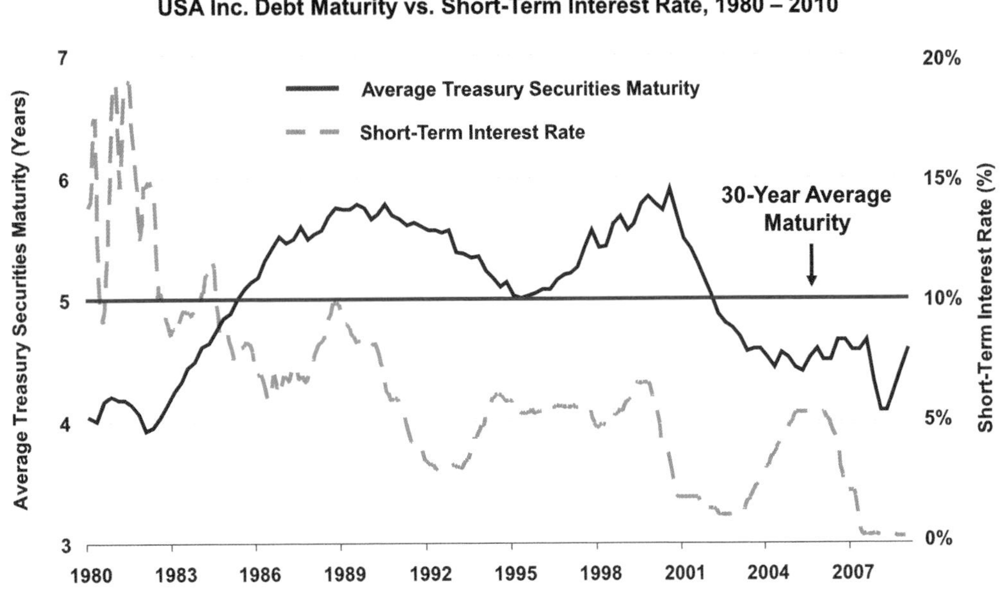

Source: Dept. of Treasury.

Debt Composition: Maturity – Temporary High Mix (32%) of Short-Term Treasury Bills in 2009 Took Advantage of Historic Low Interest Rates to Reduce Interest Payments

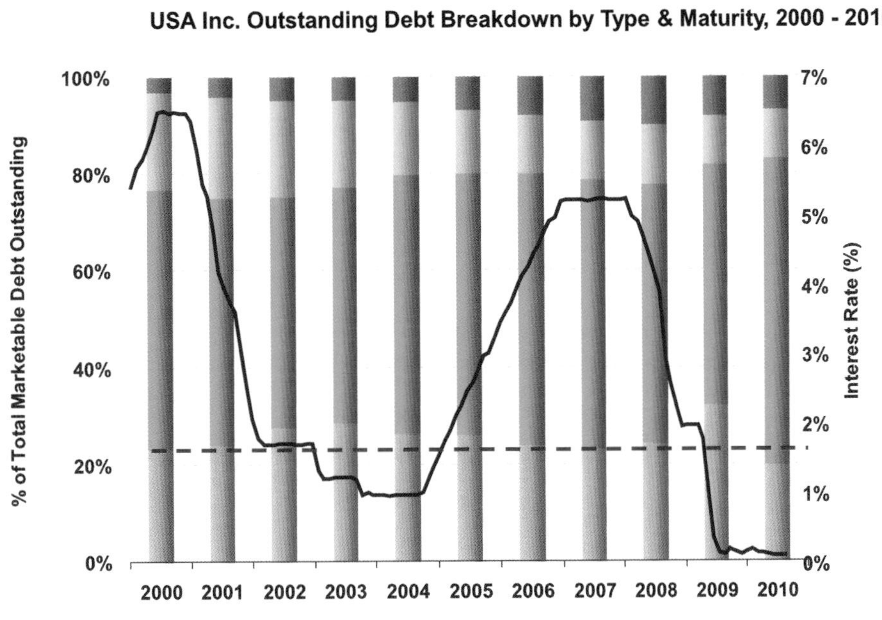

TIPS
Treasury Inflation Protected Securities

Bonds
- Long-Term (10+ Year Maturity)

Notes
- Medium-Term (2-10 Year Maturity)

Bills
- Short-Term (0-1 Year Maturity)

Short-Term Interest Rate (Fed Funds Rate)

10-Year Average Share of T-Bills

Note: Data as of March each year; composition excludes nonmarketable securities. Source: Dept. of Treasury.

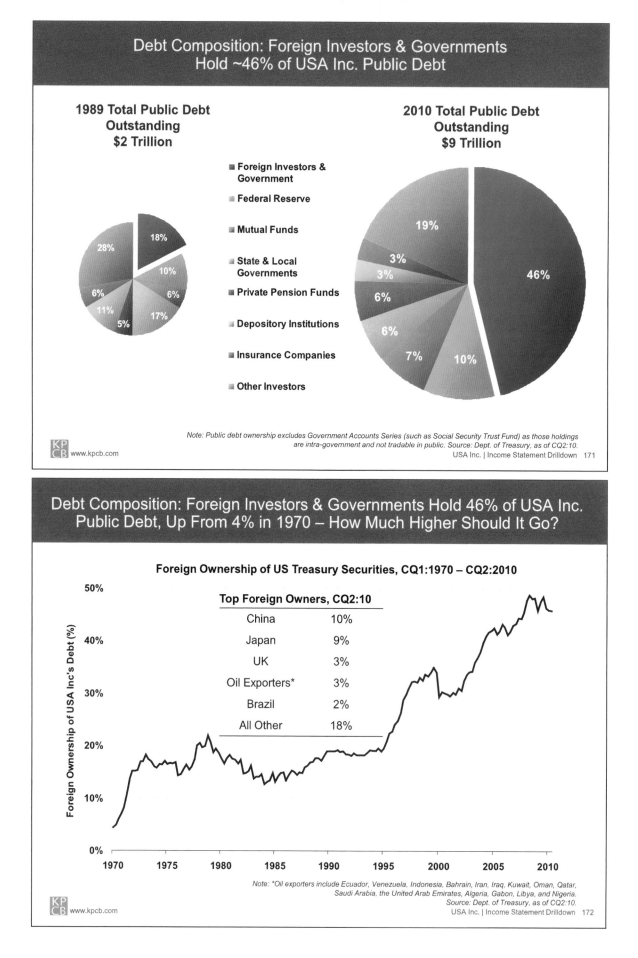

Debt Composition: Foreign Investors & Governments Hold ~46% of USA Inc. Public Debt

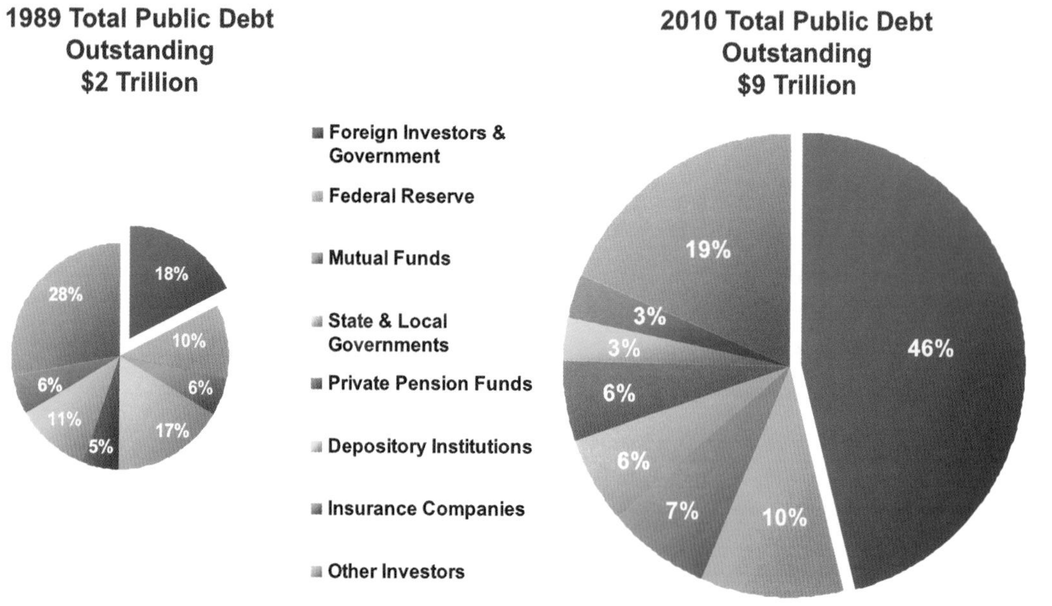

Note: Public debt ownership excludes Government Accounts Series (such as Social Security Trust Fund) as those holdings are intra-government and not tradable in public. Source: Dept. of Treasury, as of CQ2:10.

Debt Composition: Foreign Investors & Governments Hold 46% of USA Inc. Public Debt, Up From 4% in 1970 – How Much Higher Should It Go?

Foreign Ownership of US Treasury Securities, CQ1:1970 – CQ2:2010

Top Foreign Owners, CQ2:10	
China	10%
Japan	9%
UK	3%
Oil Exporters*	3%
Brazil	2%
All Other	18%

*Note: *Oil exporters include Ecuador, Venezuela, Indonesia, Bahrain, Iran, Iraq, Kuwait, Oman, Qatar, Saudi Arabia, the United Arab Emirates, Algeria, Gabon, Libya, and Nigeria. Source: Dept. of Treasury, as of CQ2:10.*

And – You Guessed It – Here's the Punch Line…

Entitlement Spending + Interest Payments Alone Should Exceed USA Inc. Total Revenue by 2025E!

Entitlement Spending + Interest Payments vs. Revenue as % of GDP, 1980 – 2050E

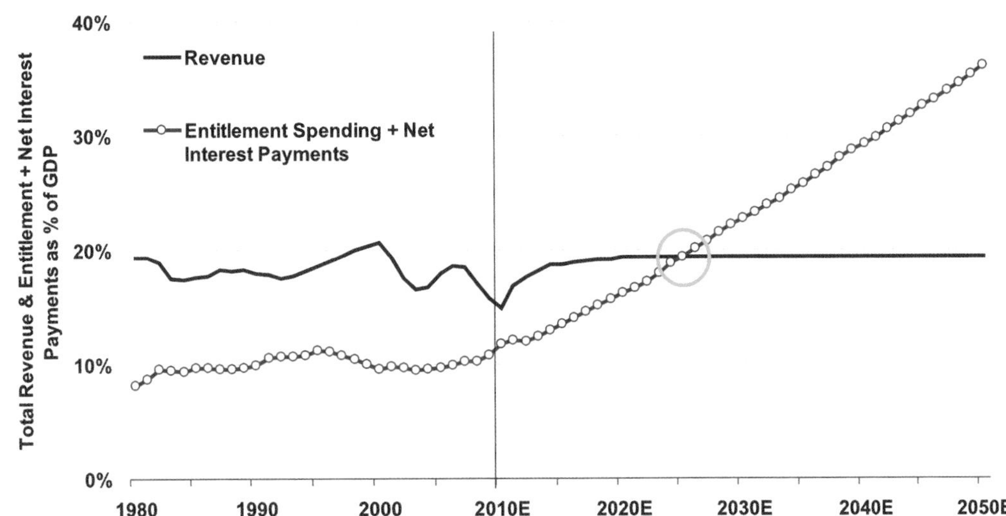

Source: Congressional Budget Office (CBO) Long-Term Budget Outlook (6/10). Note that entitlement spending includes federal government expenditures on Social Security, Medicare and Medicaid. Data in our chart is based on CBO's 'alternative fiscal scenario' forecast, which assumes a continuation of today's underlying fiscal policy. Note that CBO also maintains an 'extended-baseline' scenario, which adheres closely to current law. The alternative fiscal scenario deviates from CBO's baseline because it incorporates some policy changes that are widely expected to occur (such as extending the 2001-2003 tax cuts rather than letting them expire as scheduled by current law and adjusting physician payment rates to be in line with the Medicare economic index rather than at lower scheduled rates) and that policymakers have regularly made in the past.

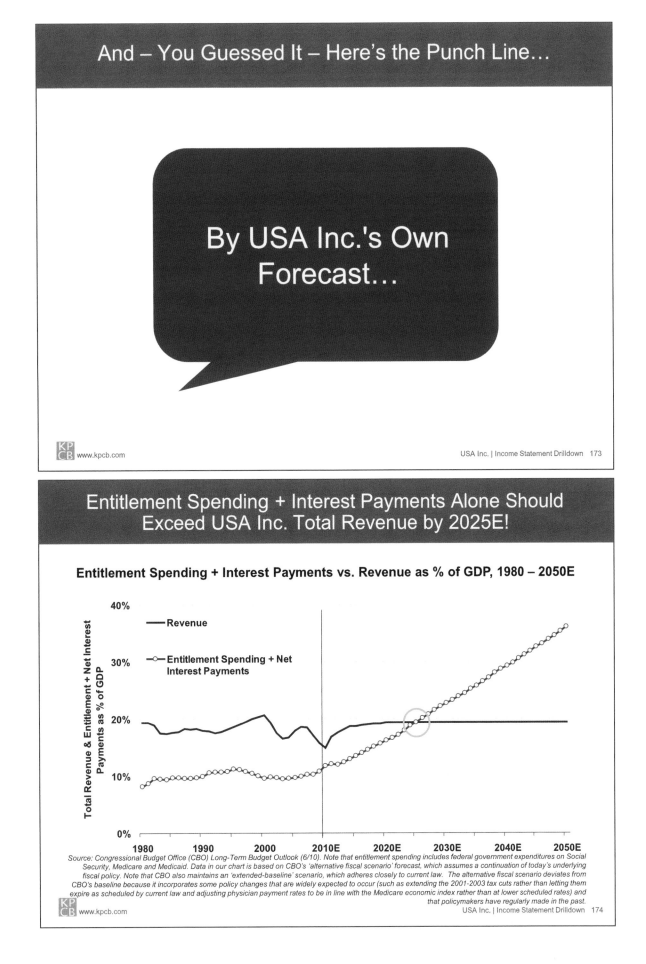

CBO's Projection from 10 Years Ago (in 1999) Showed Federal Revenue Sufficient to Support Entitlement Spending + Interest Payments Until 2060E – 35 Years Later than Current Projection

CBO's Projection in the '1999 Long-Term Budget Outlook' on Entitlement Spending + Interest Payments vs. Revenue as % of GDP, 1980 – 2070E

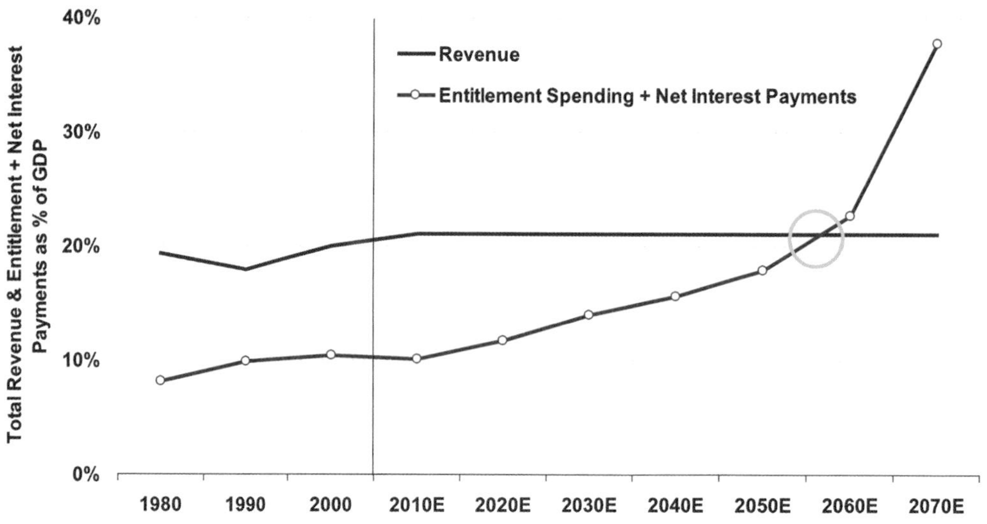

Source: Congressional Budget Office Long-Term Budget Outlook (1999). Note that there was no alternative fiscal scenario in CBO's forecast back then.

If the Previous Two Slides…

aren't a
wake-up call,
we don't know
what is…

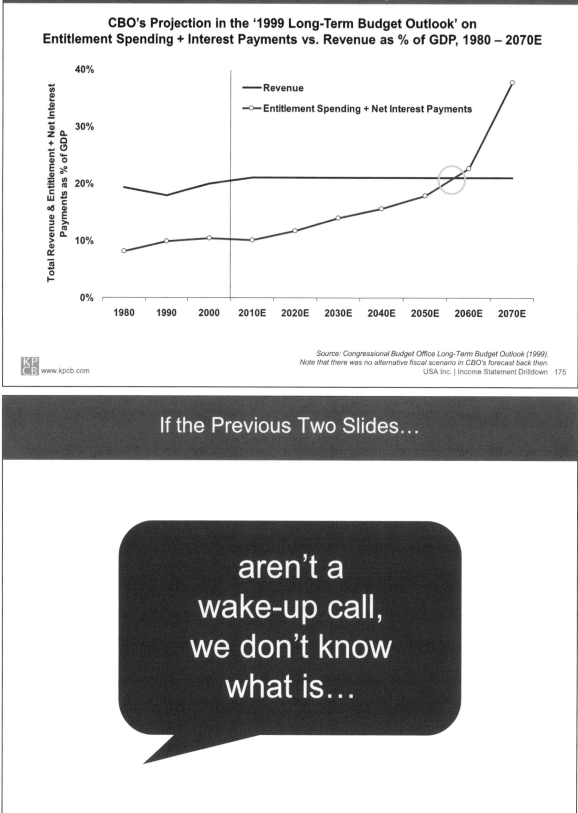

Drill Down on USA Inc. Periodic Large One-Time Charges

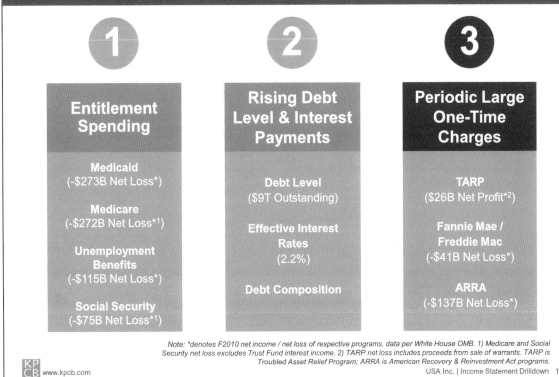

1 — Entitlement Spending

Medicaid
(-$273B Net Loss*)

Medicare
(-$272B Net Loss*1)

Unemployment Benefits
(-$115B Net Loss*)

Social Security
(-$75B Net Loss*1)

2 — Rising Debt Level & Interest Payments

Debt Level
($9T Outstanding)

Effective Interest Rates
(2.2%)

Debt Composition

3 — Periodic Large One-Time Charges

TARP
($26B Net Profit*2)

Fannie Mae / Freddie Mac
(-$41B Net Loss*)

ARRA
(-$137B Net Loss*)

*Note: *denotes F2010 net income / net loss of respective programs, data per White House OMB. 1) Medicare and Social Security net loss excludes Trust Fund interest income. 2) TARP net loss includes proceeds from sale of warrants. TARP is Troubled Asset Relief Program; ARRA is American Recovery & Reinvestment Act programs.*

One-Time Charges: Unusually High in F2009 & F2010 with Financial + Economic Crisis

Net One-Time Charges to USA Inc. ($B)	F2008	F2009	F2010	F2011 YTD*	Net Sum of 4 Years
Government-Sponsored Enterprises (GSEs)	**$14**	**$97**	**$41**	–	**$152**
Fannie Mae	–	60	23	–	83
Freddie Mac	$14	37	18	–	69
Troubled Asset Relief Program (TARP)*	–	**$261**	**-$26**	**-$23**	**$213**
Banks	–	134	-85	-28	21
Automakers	–	78	-6	-14	58
AIG	–	49	–	20	69
Individual Homeowners	–	0	39	-1	38
Other Financial Institutions	–	–	22	–	22
Consumers & Small Businesses	–	–	4	–	4
American Recovery and Reinvestment Act (ARRA)**	–	**$40**	**$137**	–	**$177**
Education	–	21	50	–	71
Nutrition Assistance	–	5	11	–	16
Transportation	–	4	15	–	19
Tax Credits	–	2	33	–	35
Energy	–	1	5	–	6
Other	–	7	23	–	30
Net Total One-Time Charges ($B)	**$14**	**$398**	**$152**	**-$23**	**$542**

*Note: Federal fiscal year ends in September. *TARP one-time charges include repayments & dividends; F2011 TARP data as of 2/11, per US Treasury; F2011 YTD GSE & ARRA data not available. **ARRA one-time charges exclude funds used by entitlement programs such as Social Security / Medicare / Medicaid / Unemployment. Source: Congressional Budget Office, Dept of Treasury.*

One-Time Charges: What Charges from F2008-F2010 May Look Like on Net Basis Over Next 10 Years

One-Time Charges from the 'Financial Crisis' are Not Created Equal – While TARP Was the Headliner, When All's Said & Done, TARP may be Smallest Component, by a Long Shot

	Current Cost ($B, as of 2/11)	Ultimate Cash Cost ($B, by F2020E)	Comments
TARP	$213B – –	– ➔ <$51B[1]	May fall from net $213 billion to $51 billion or less[1] as banks continue to pay back their loans and automakers / AIG seek IPOs / sales to realize value of USA Inc.'s equity stake.
GSE	$152 – –	– ➔ ~$160[2]	May grow from net $152 billion to ~$160 billion (or higher)[2] as Fannie Mae and Freddie Mac losses on loan guarantees stabilize and they continue to pay dividends on USA Inc.'s shares.
ARRA	$177 – –	– ➔ $417	Should rise from $177 billion to $417 billion[3] based on commitments…and a payback plan was never factored into these payments.

Note: 1) Latest Treasury estimate as of 12/10, includes net profits from banks of $16B, net costs from AIG ($5B) / Automakers ($17B) / Consumers & Housing programs ($-46B) and other. AIG net costs excludes potential gains from selling AIG's common shares held by the Treasury, which could turn out to be a $22B profit for the Treasury based on 10/1/10 closing price. Including this potential gain, TARP ultimate cost to the Treasury would be $29B. 2) White House OMB estimates ultimate cash cost of Fannie Mae / Freddie Mac at $165B while the CBO estimates the ultimate cash costs at $160B. Both estimates imply an average default rate of 5-10% on Fannie Mae + Freddie Mac's $5T loan guarantee portfolio and a loss severity of 50%. The Federal Housing Finance Agency (FHFA) estimates ultimate costs to range from $142B to $259B. 3) Net cash costs are limited to discretionary spending items in ARRA. Source: CBO, U.S. Dept of Treasury, White House OMB, FHFA.

Recipients of $ from USA One-Time Charges (F2008-2011YTD)

Total Net 2008-2011 One-Time Charges = $542 Billion (as of 2/11)

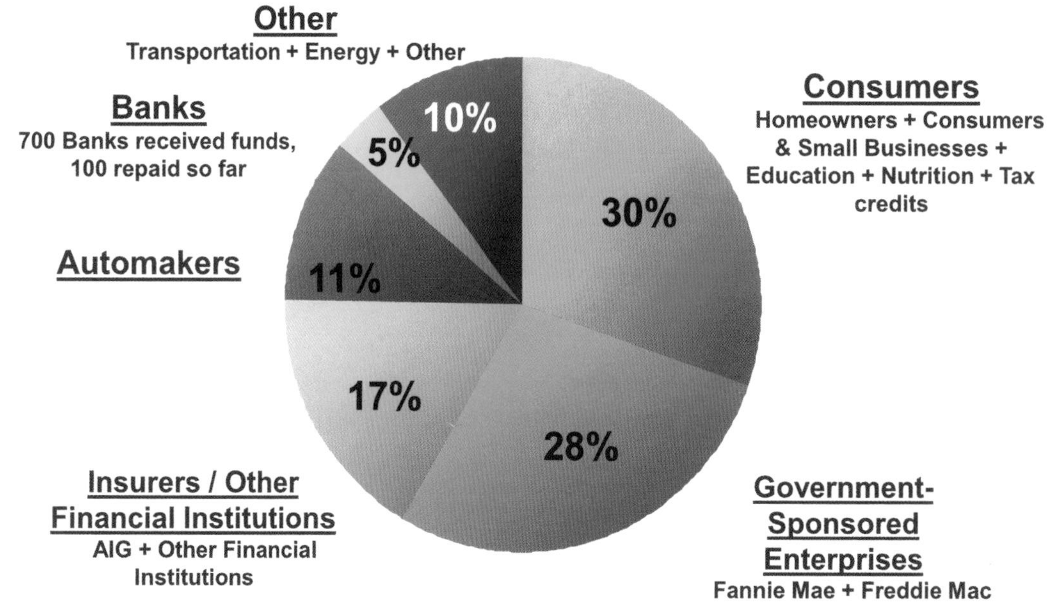

Source: Dept. of Treasury, as of 2/11.

Drill Down on One-Time Charges

Most of USA Inc.'s recent one-time charges are directly or indirectly related to America's real estate bubble and aggressive borrowing.

First we look at the drivers of the real estate bubble (we call it 'anatomy of a real estate bubble'), then we drill down on the past / present / future financial impact of the three types of one-time charges and the recipients:

1) TARP (Troubled Asset Relief Program)
2) GSEs (Government-Sponsored Enterprises)
2) ARRA (American Recovery and Reinvestment Act)

What created the real estate bubble?

Real Estate Bubble: Root Causes—Government Home Ownership Push + Declining Interest & Savings Rates + Aggressive Borrowing and Lending Led to 10+ Years of Rising Home Ownership

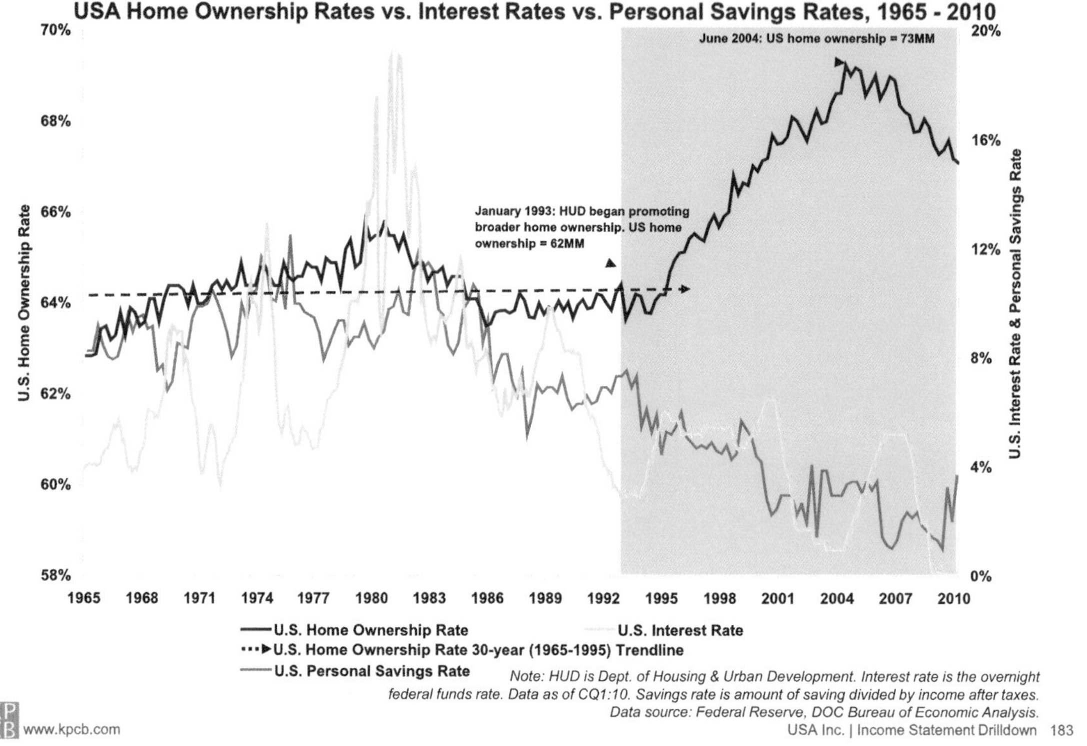

Note: HUD is Dept. of Housing & Urban Development. Interest rate is the overnight federal funds rate. Data as of CQ1:10. Savings rate is amount of saving divided by income after taxes. Data source: Federal Reserve, DOC Bureau of Economic Analysis.

Real Estate Bubble: Home Prices Rose Dramatically (7% Annually) for 10 Years – Up ~2x Over 10-Year Period Ending 2007

USA Real Home Price & Building Cost Indexes, % Change 1965 – 2008

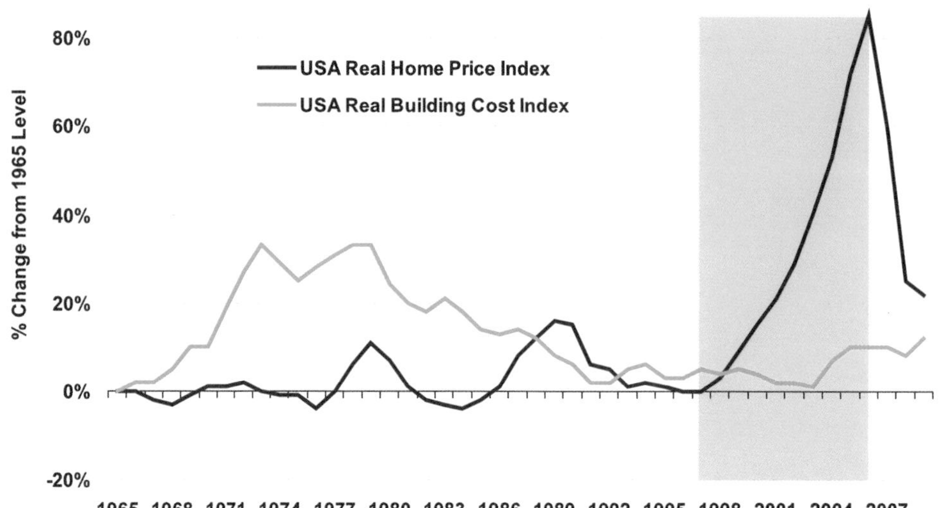

Note: Real home prices & building costs are inflation-adjusted. Source: Robert Shiller, Yale University.

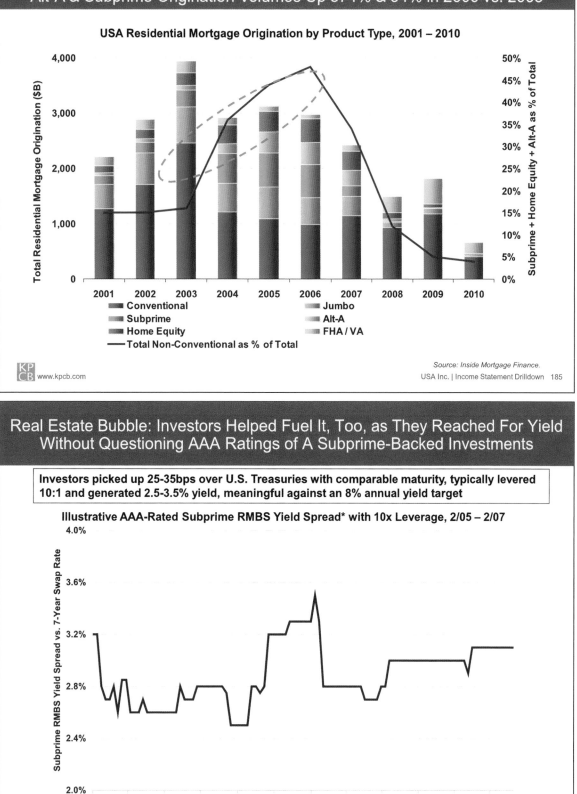

Banks & Other Mortgage Originators Helped Fuel Housing Bubble as They Originated Lower Quality Mortgages – Alt-A & Subprime Origination Volumes Up 374% & 94% in 2006 vs. 2003

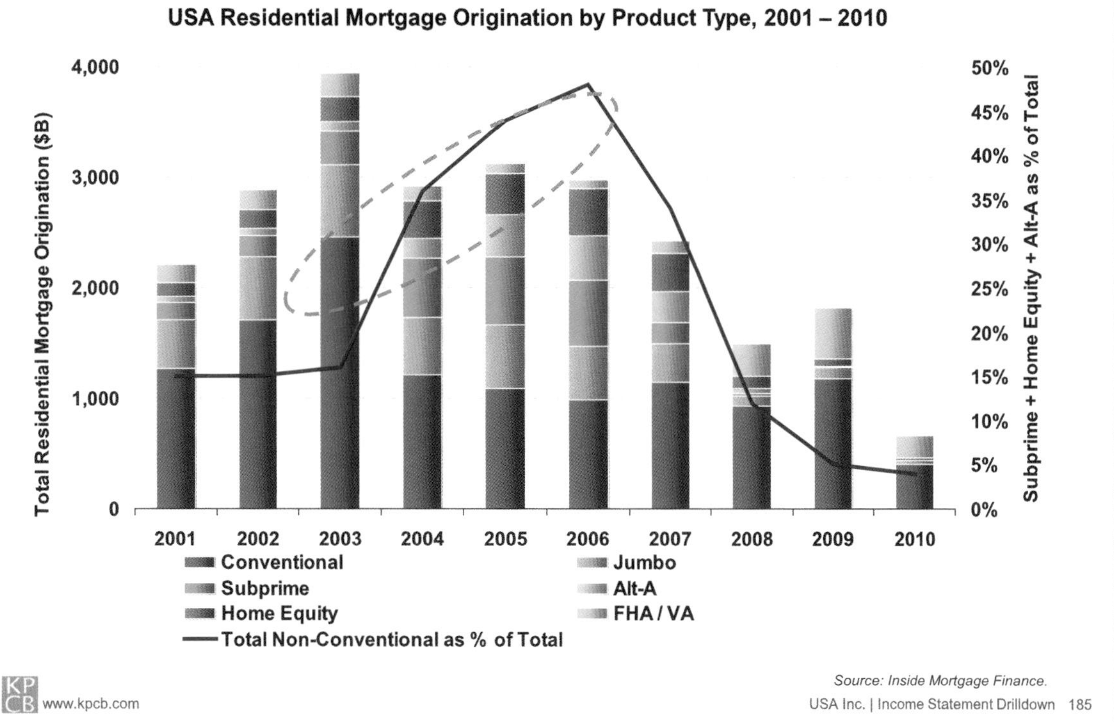

Source: Inside Mortgage Finance.

Real Estate Bubble: Investors Helped Fuel It, Too, as They Reached For Yield Without Questioning AAA Ratings of A Subprime-Backed Investments

Investors picked up 25-35bps over U.S. Treasuries with comparable maturity, typically levered 10:1 and generated 2.5-3.5% yield, meaningful against an 8% annual yield target

Illustrative AAA-Rated Subprime RMBS Yield Spread* with 10x Leverage, 2/05 – 2/07

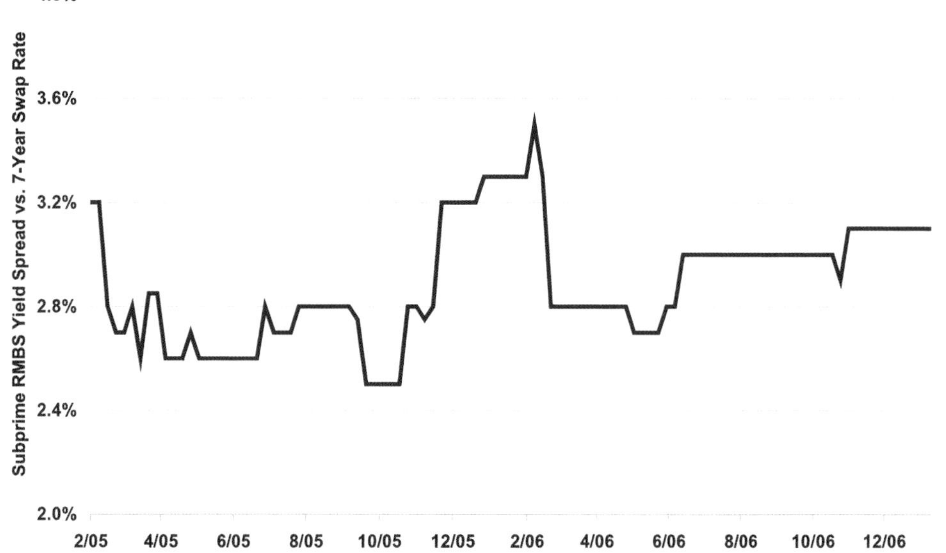

Note: Illustrative AAA-rated subprime RMBS spread represented as Mezzanine CDO spread vs. 7-year swap rate.
Source: Betsy Graseck, Morgan Stanley Research.

Investors Struggle with Today's Low ~4% Risk Free Rate

- Pension funds & other investors look for ~8% annual returns in order to meet promised payouts.
- The challenge is far greater than before given:
  - Rising obligations relative to income
  - Lower interest rates
- Promises (e.g., pension, healthcare) made during an 8% interest rate environment are much harder to meet when the risk free rate has fallen from 8% to 3.6%.[1]
- The choice is either to reduce obligations…

  or

  …Invest in riskier assets.

Note: 10-year Treasury coupon rate as of 2/18/2010. Source: Betsy Graseck, Morgan Stanley Research.

1	2	3
Entitlement Spending	**Rising Debt Level & Interest Payments**	**Periodic Large One-Time Charges**
Medicaid (-$273B Net Loss*)	**Debt Level** ($9T Outstanding)	**TARP** ($26B Net Profit*[2])
Medicare (-$272B Net Loss*[1])	**Effective Interest Rates** (2.2%)	**Fannie Mae / Freddie Mac** (-$41B Net Loss*)
Unemployment Benefits (-$115B Net Loss*)	**Debt Composition**	**ARRA** (-$137B Net Loss*)
Social Security (-$75B Net Loss*[1])		

*Note: *denotes F2010 net income / net loss of respective programs, data per White House OMB. 1) Medicare and Social Security net loss excludes Trust Fund interest income. 2) TARP net loss includes proceeds from sale of warrants. TARP is Troubled Asset Relief Program; ARRA is American Recovery & Reinvestment Act programs.*

Troubled Asset Relief Program (TARP): Recipient of 38% of Net Government (Taxpayer) Funding*

In TARP, the financial rescue program (created in October, 2008), USA Inc. purchased assets and equity from financial institutions to provide the capital and liquidity needed during the 2008 financial crisis (which followed the real estate bubble).

In 2009, TARP recipients were broadened to include automakers, an insurance company (AIG), individual homeowners, small & medium-sized businesses and other non-bank financial institutions.

To date, USA Inc. loaned these institutions $464 billion and received $250 billion in repayment and warrant proceeds for a net outstanding loan balance of $214 billion.

*Note: *As of 2/11, numbers are rounded. Source: Dept. of Treasury.*

TARP Distribution – Equally Distributed Among Financial Institutions / Automakers / Insurer / Individuals as of 2/11

Outstanding Troubled Asset Relief Program (TARP) Balance of $214B[1] as of 2/11

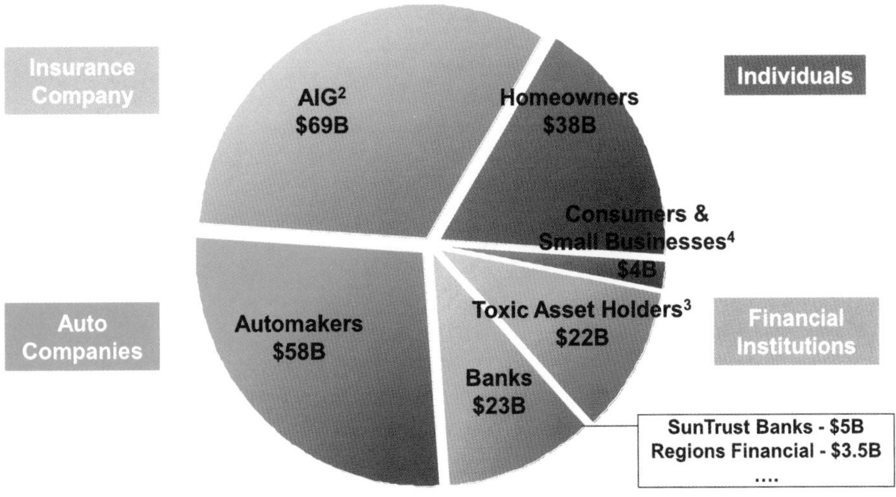

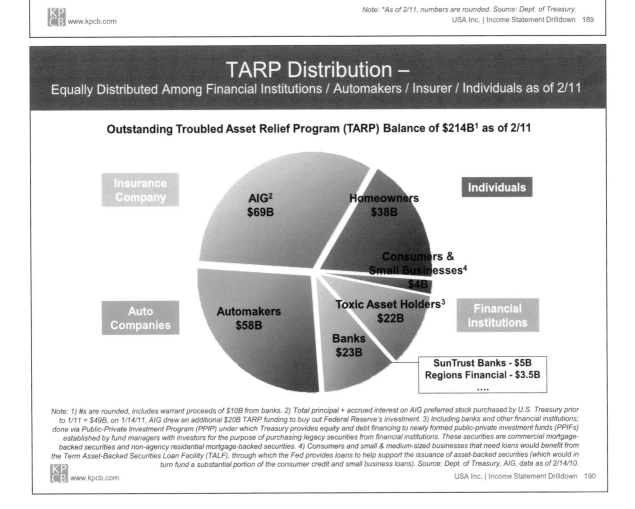

Note: 1) #s are rounded, includes warrant proceeds of $10B from banks. 2) Total principal + accrued interest on AIG preferred stock purchased by U.S. Treasury prior to 1/11 = $49B, on 1/14/11, AIG drew an additional $20B TARP funding to buy out Federal Reserve's investment. 3) Including banks and other financial institutions; done via Public-Private Investment Program (PPIP) under which Treasury provides equity and debt financing to newly formed public-private investment funds (PPIFs) established by fund managers with investors for the purpose of purchasing legacy securities from financial institutions. These securities are commercial mortgage-backed securities and non-agency residential mortgage-backed securities. 4) Consumers and small & medium-sized businesses that need loans would benefit from the Term Asset-Backed Securities Loan Facility (TALF), through which the Fed provides loans to help support the issuance of asset-backed securities (which would in turn fund a substantial portion of the consumer credit and small business loans). Source: Dept. of Treasury, AIG, data as of 2/14/10.

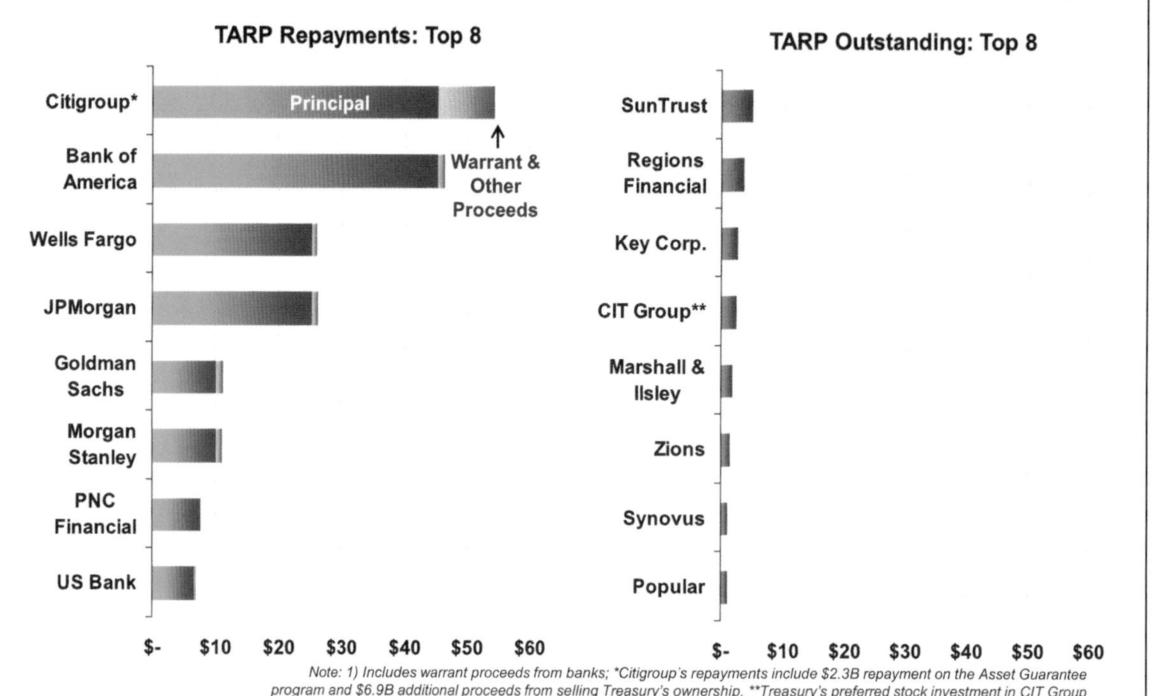
TARP Repayments and Outstanding Loans: Most Large Banks Have Repaid
$222 Billion Paid Back1, $23 Billion Outstanding
TARP Repayments: Top 8
Citigroup*
Bank of America
Wells Fargo
JPMorgan
Goldman Sachs
Morgan Stanley
PNC Financial
US Bank
Principal
Warrant & Other Proceeds
$-
$10
$20
$30
$40
$50
$60
TARP Outstanding: Top 8
SunTrust
Regions Financial
Key Corp.
CIT Group**
Marshall & Ilsley
Zions
Synovus
Popular
$-
$10
$20
$30
$40
$50
$60
Note: 1) Includes warrant proceeds from banks; *Citigroup's repayments include $2.3B repayment on the Asset Guarantee program and $6.9B additional proceeds from selling Treasury's ownership. **Treasury's preferred stock investment in CIT Group was lost as a result of CIT's bankruptcy filing. Source: Dept of Treasury, data as of 2/11.
KP CB www.kpcb.com
USA Inc. | Income Statement Drilldown 191

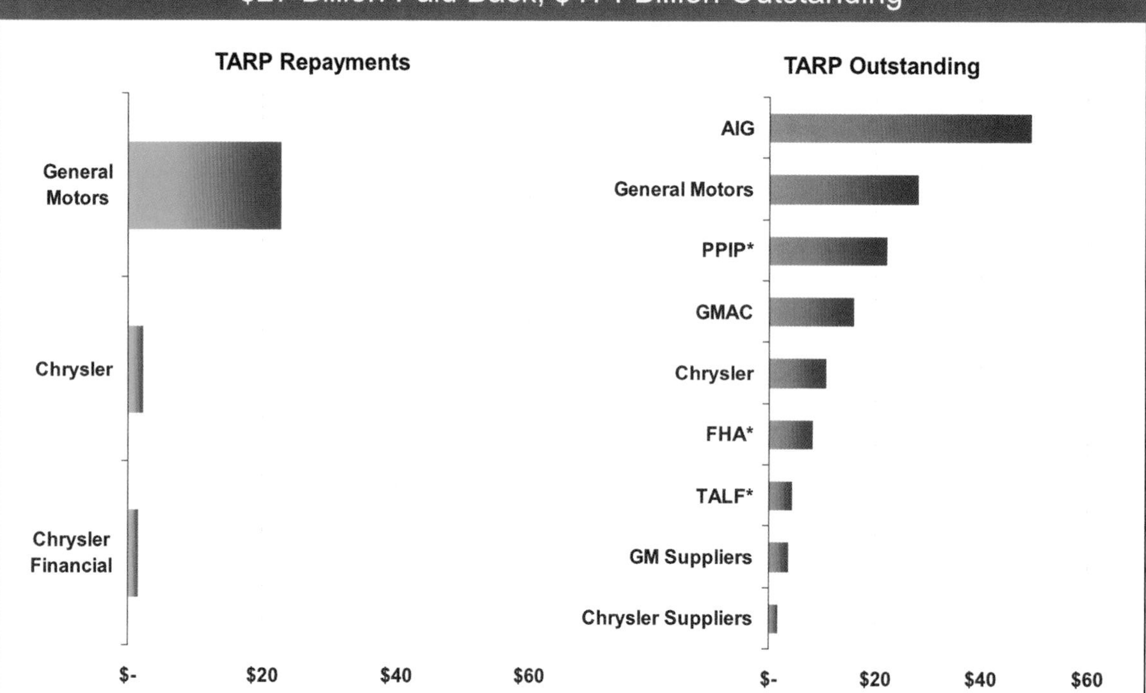
TARP Repayments And Outstanding Loans:
Most Non-Bank TARP Recipients Have Not Repaid
$27 Billion Paid Back, $171 Billion Outstanding
TARP Repayments
General Motors
Chrysler
Chrysler Financial
$-
$20
$40
$60
TARP Outstanding
AIG
General Motors
PPIP*
GMAC
Chrysler
FHA*
TALF*
GM Suppliers
Chrysler Suppliers
$-
$20
$40
$60
Note: * PPIP is Public-Private Investment Program, FHA represents the FHA Short Refinance Program, TALF is Term Asset-Backed Securities Loan Facility.
Source: Dept of Treasury, data as of 1/11.
KP CB www.kpcb.com
USA Inc. | Income Statement Drilldown 192

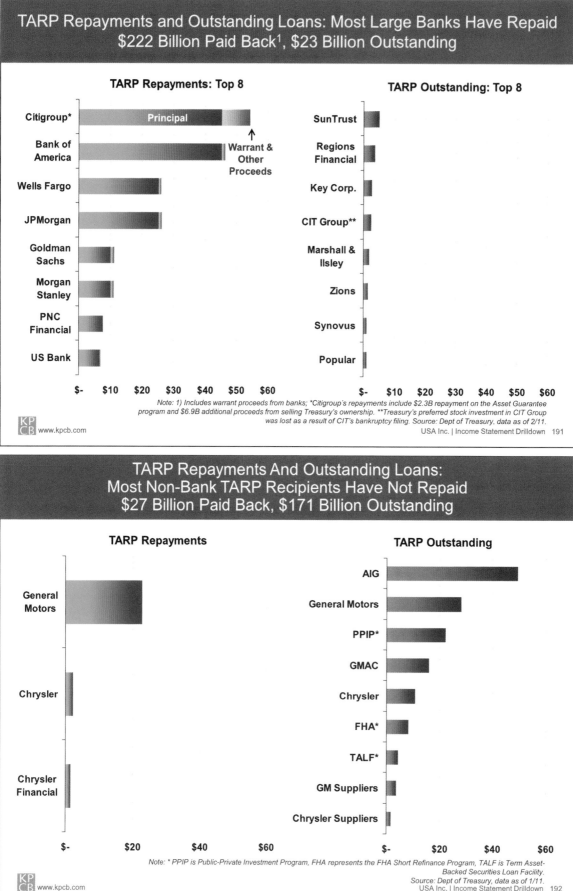

2

3

Entitlement Spending	Rising Debt Level & Interest Payments	Periodic Large One-Time Charges
Medicaid (-\$273B Net Loss*)	**Debt Level** (\$9T Outstanding)	**TARP** (\$26B Net Profit*2)
Medicare (-\$272B Net Loss*1)	**Effective Interest Rates** (2.2%)	**Fannie Mae / Freddie Mac** (-\$41B Net Loss*)
Unemployment Benefits (-\$115B Net Loss*)	**Debt Composition**	**ARRA** (-\$137B Net Loss*)
Social Security (-\$75B Net Loss*1)		

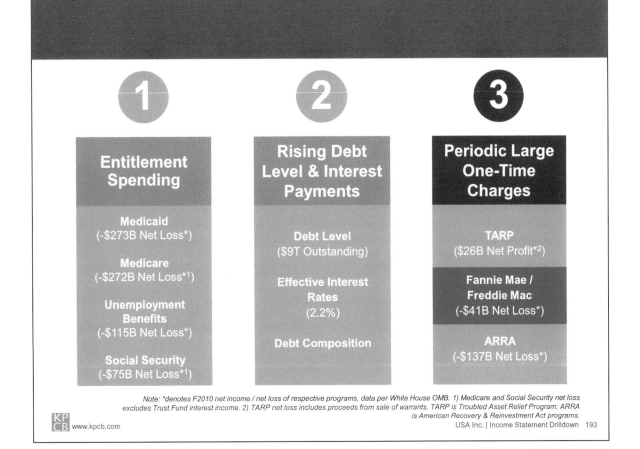

*Note: *denotes F2010 net income / net loss of respective programs, data per White House OMB. 1) Medicare and Social Security net loss excludes Trust Fund interest income. 2) TARP net loss includes proceeds from sale of warrants. TARP is Troubled Asset Relief Program; ARRA is American Recovery & Reinvestment Act programs.*

Government-Sponsored Enterprises (GSEs): Recipients of 28% of Net Government (Taxpayer) Funding

- **GSEs Fannie Mae & Freddie Mac extended their guarantees on residential mortgages from conventional loans into Alt-A, interest-only and subprime loans.**
- While technically not part of the federal government, Fannie Mae & Freddie Mac have enjoyed an implicit government guarantee on their debt and RMBS securities as investors believed (correctly, as it turned out) that the federal government would support these entities if they failed. As a result, GSEs' long-term debt securities receive AAA/Aaa ratings from all rating agencies and are classified by financial markets as "agency securities" with interest rates above USA Treasuries but below AAA corporate debts.
- Post placing Fannie Mae & Freddie Mac into a government conservatorship, USA Inc. has so far invested \$152B[1] into these two GSEs with an estimated \$8-13B[2] more likely over the next 10 years, given the ongoing weakness in housing market and the poor underwriting by Fannie Mae & Freddie Mac.

Source: 1) U.S. Dept of Treasury, as of 12/10, 2) White House OMB / U.S. Congressional Budget Office.

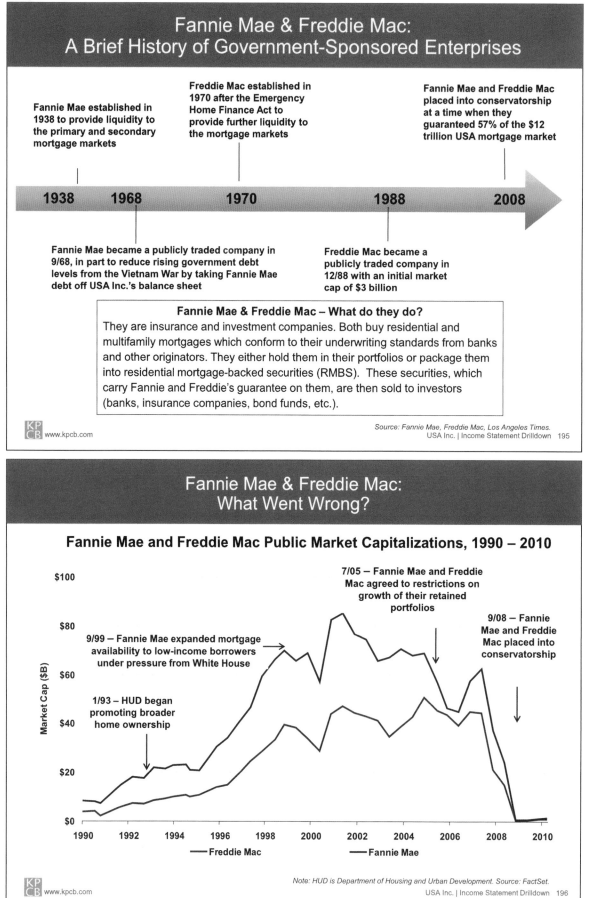

Fannie Mae & Freddie Mac: A Brief History of Government-Sponsored Enterprises

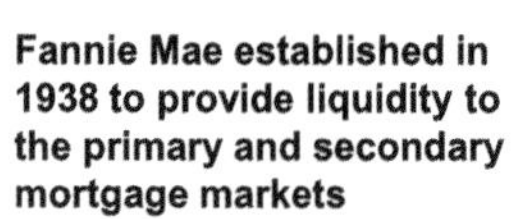

Fannie Mae established in 1938 to provide liquidity to the primary and secondary mortgage markets

Freddie Mac established in 1970 after the Emergency Home Finance Act to provide further liquidity to the mortgage markets

Fannie Mae and Freddie Mac placed into conservatorship at a time when they guaranteed 57% of the $12 trillion USA mortgage market

1938 1968 1970 1988 2008

Fannie Mae became a publicly traded company in 9/68, in part to reduce rising government debt levels from the Vietnam War by taking Fannie Mae debt off USA Inc.'s balance sheet

Freddie Mac became a publicly traded company in 12/88 with an initial market cap of $3 billion

Fannie Mae & Freddie Mac – What do they do?

They are insurance and investment companies. Both buy residential and multifamily mortgages which conform to their underwriting standards from banks and other originators. They either hold them in their portfolios or package them into residential mortgage-backed securities (RMBS). These securities, which carry Fannie and Freddie's guarantee on them, are then sold to investors (banks, insurance companies, bond funds, etc.).

Source: Fannie Mae, Freddie Mac, Los Angeles Times.

Fannie Mae & Freddie Mac: What Went Wrong?

Fannie Mae and Freddie Mac Public Market Capitalizations, 1990 – 2010

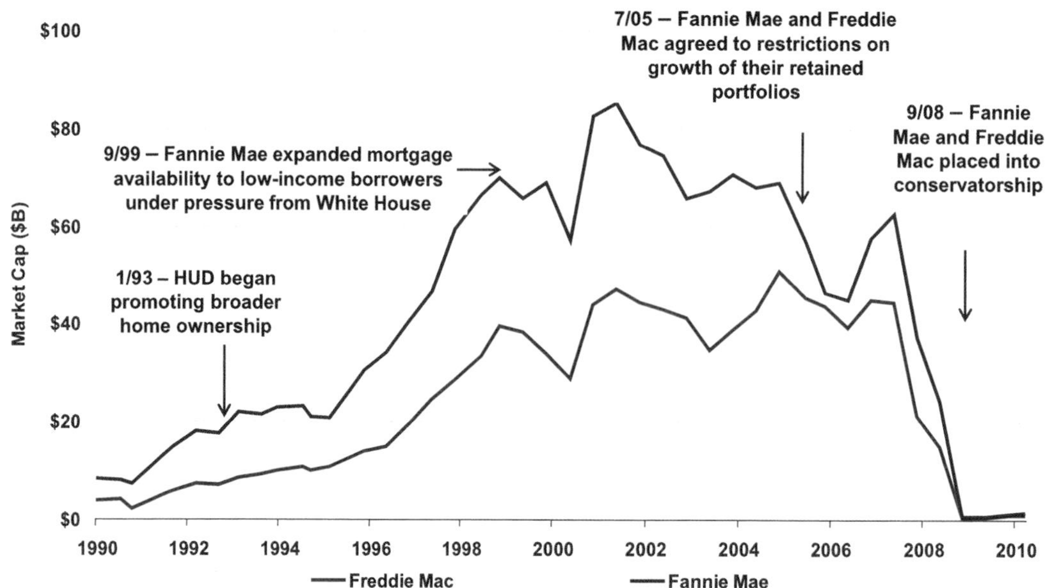

9/99 – Fannie Mae expanded mortgage availability to low-income borrowers under pressure from White House
1/93 – HUD began promoting broader home ownership

Note: HUD is Department of Housing and Urban Development. Source: FactSet.

Fannie Mae & Freddie Mac: Accounted for Majority of Total Residential Mortgage-Backed Securities (RMBS) Issuance Since 1990s

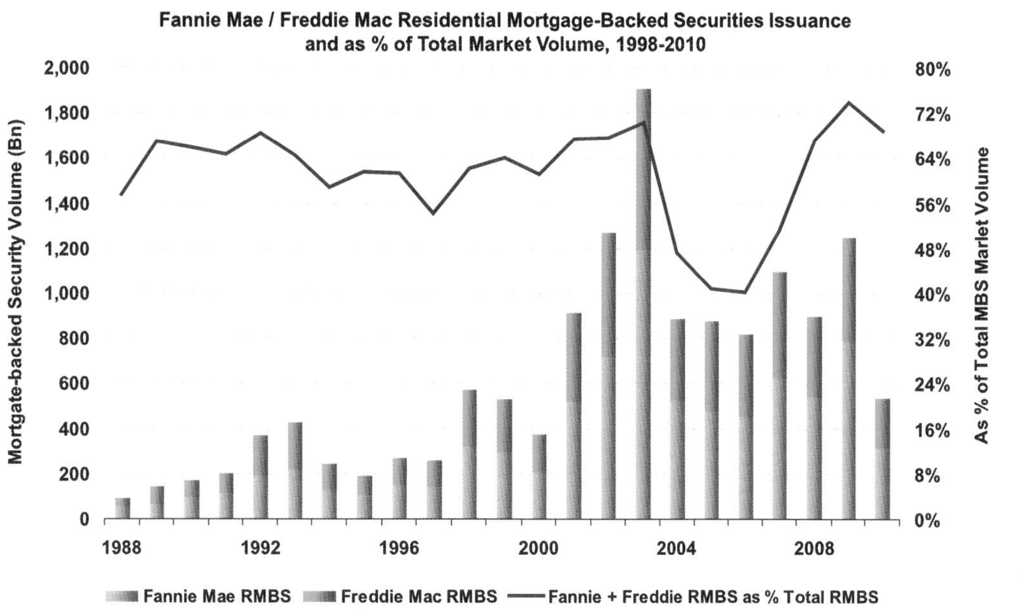

Sources: 1988-2006 data from Calculated Risk; Fannie Mae / Freddie Mac data from FHFA Annual Report to the Congress 2009, 2009 / 2010 data per EMBS and Hybrid Weekly.

Fannie Mae & Freddie Mac: Latest Estimated Ultimate Cost to Taxpayers Varies*

Base-Case Estimated Ultimate Net Loss**	Source	Comments / Assumptions
$389 Billion	Congressional Budget Office (CBO)	Net accrued loss to be borne by taxpayers, including net cash infusions (with implied default rate of ~5-10%) and risk premiums associated with federal government's implicit guarantee on GSEs' credit. Bulk of the net loss ($291B) occurred prior to and during F2009. On a cash basis, CBO's estimate would have been in line with White House OMB's estimate.
$160 Billion	White House Office of Management and Budget (OMB)	Net cash outlay to be borne by Treasury Dept. (and ultimately taxpayers), including Treasury Dept.'s cash outlays to purchase Fannie Mae & Freddie Mac preferred stock (with implied default rate of ~5-10%), minus cash received from dividends. Bulk of the net cash outlay ($112B) occurred prior to and during F2009.

*Note: *Latest estimated cost to taxpayers varies and continues to rise. **By F2019E. Source: CBO, OMB.*

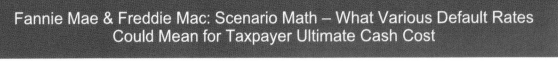

Fannie Mae & Freddie Mac: Scenario Math – What Various Default Rates Could Mean for Taxpayer Ultimate Cash Cost

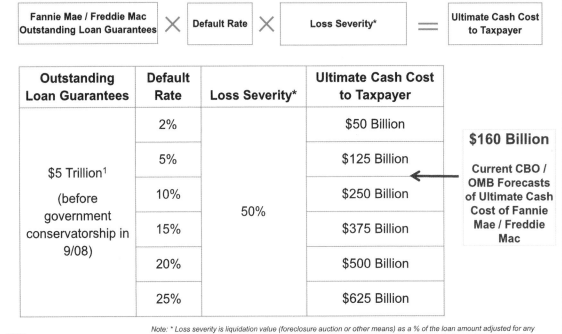

Fannie Mae / Freddie Mac Outstanding Loan Guarantees × **Default Rate** × **Loss Severity*** = **Ultimate Cash Cost to Taxpayer**

Outstanding Loan Guarantees	Default Rate	Loss Severity*	Ultimate Cash Cost to Taxpayer
$5 Trillion[1] (before government conservatorship in 9/08)	2%	50%	$50 Billion
	5%		$125 Billion
	10%		$250 Billion
	15%		$375 Billion
	20%		$500 Billion
	25%		$625 Billion

$160 Billion

Current CBO / OMB Forecasts of Ultimate Cash Cost of Fannie Mae / Freddie Mac

*Note: * Loss severity is liquidation value (foreclosure auction or other means) as a % of the loan amount adjusted for any advances and fees. Source: 1) Fannie Mae, Freddie Mac.*

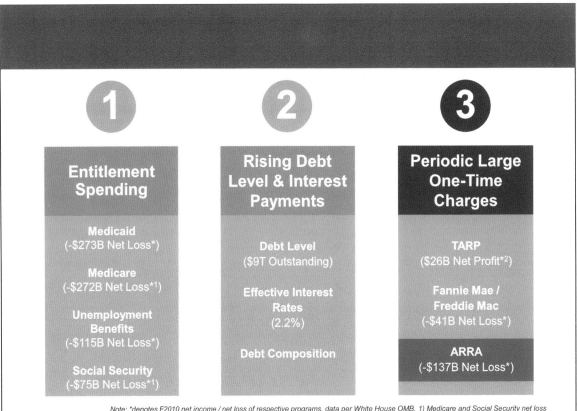

KP CB www.kpcb.com

1

Entitlement Spending

Medicaid
(-$273B Net Loss*)

Medicare
(-$272B Net Loss*[1])

Unemployment Benefits
(-$115B Net Loss*)

Social Security
(-$75B Net Loss*[1])

2

Rising Debt Level & Interest Payments

Debt Level
($9T Outstanding)

Effective Interest Rates
(2.2%)

Debt Composition

3

Periodic Large One-Time Charges

TARP
($26B Net Profit*[2])

Fannie Mae / Freddie Mac
(-$41B Net Loss*)

ARRA
(-$137B Net Loss*)

*Note: *denotes F2010 net income / net loss of respective programs, data per White House OMB. 1) Medicare and Social Security net loss excludes Trust Fund interest income. 2) TARP net loss includes proceeds from sale of warrants. TARP is Troubled Asset Relief Program; ARRA is American Recovery & Reinvestment Act programs.*

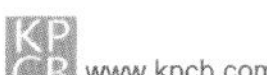

America Recovery & Reinvestment Act (ARRA): Recipient of 34% of Net Government (Taxpayer) Funding

In ARRA (the economic stimulus program created in February, 2009), USA Inc. aims to create jobs and promote investment and consumer spending by cutting taxes, expanding unemployment benefits, and increasing spending in education, healthcare, infrastructure, and energy.

These measures are projected to increase federal spending by $500+ billion while reducing federal tax receipts by $275 billion over 10 years ($177 billion of which occurred in F2009 and F2010).

Source: White House Office of Management & Budget.

ARRA*: Negative Effect on Discretionary Budgets Should Peak in F2010, But Spending Commitments through F2019E Total $417 Billion

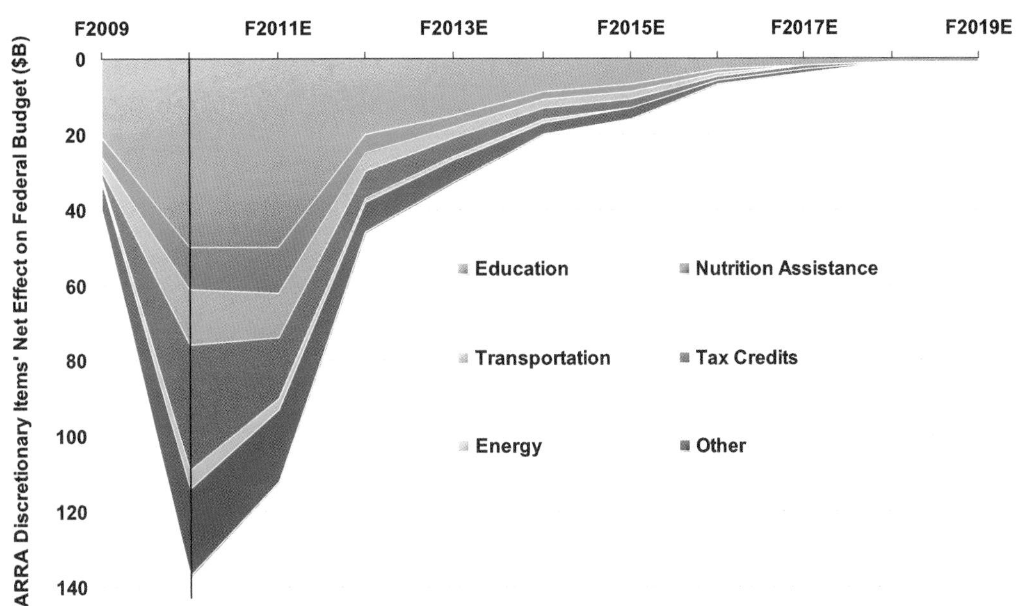

*Note: *ARRA is American Recovery and Reinvestment Act of 2009. US federal fiscal year ends in September. Net effects on budgets are limited to discretionary spending items in ARRA. Source: Congressional Budget Office.*

ARRA: Spending Examples

Education – Used ARRA funding and saved education jobs, such as teachers, principals, librarians, and counselors

Tax Credits – Provided higher Earned Income Tax Credits

Transportation – Repaired roads and bridges

Energy – Provided additional funding for renewable energy and energy efficiency projects

Nutrition Assistance – Provided additional assistance for low-income families to purchase food

Other – Funding for various programs related to homeland security and law enforcement…

Longer-term taxpayer impact of GSE Loans + ARRA + TARP varies…regardless, it is material

What 'One-Time Charges' from F2008-F2010 May Look Like on Net Basis Over Next 10 Years

One-Time Charges from the 'Financial Crisis' are Not Created Equal – While TARP Was the Headliner, When All's Said & Done, TARP may be Smallest Component, by a Long Shot

	Current Cost ($B, as of 2/11)	Ultimate Cash Cost ($B, by F2020E)	Comments
TARP	$214B – –	– → <$51B[1]	May fall from net $214 billion to $51 billion or less[1] as banks continue to pay back their loans and automakers / AIG seek IPOs / sales to realize value of USA Inc.'s equity stake.
GSE	$152 – –	– → ~$160[2]	May grow from net $152 billion to ~$160 billion (or higher)[2] as Fannie Mae and Freddie Mac losses on loan guarantees stabilize and they continue to pay dividends on USA Inc.'s shares.
ARRA	$177 – –	– → $417	Should rise from $177 billion to $417 billion[3] based on commitments…and a payback plan was never factored into these payments.

Note: 1) Latest Treasury estimate as of 12/10, includes net profits from banks of $16B, net costs from AIG ($5B) / Automakers ($17B) / Consumers & Housing programs ($-46B) and other. AIG net costs excludes potential gains from selling AIG's common shares held by the Treasury, which could turn out to be a $22B profit for the Treasury based on 10/1/10 closing price. Including this potential gain, TARP ultimate cost to the Treasury would be $29B. 2) White House OMB estimates ultimate cash cost of Fannie Mae / Freddie Mac at $165B while the CBO estimates the ultimate cash costs at $160B. Both estimates imply an average default rate of 5-10% on Fannie Mae + Freddie Mac's $5T loan guarantee portfolio and a loss severity of 50%. The Federal Housing Finance Agency (FHFA) estimates ultimate costs to range from $142B to $259B. 3) Net cash costs are limited to discretionary spending items in ARRA. Source: CBO, U.S. Dept of Treasury, White House OMB, FHFA.

This page is intentionally left blank.

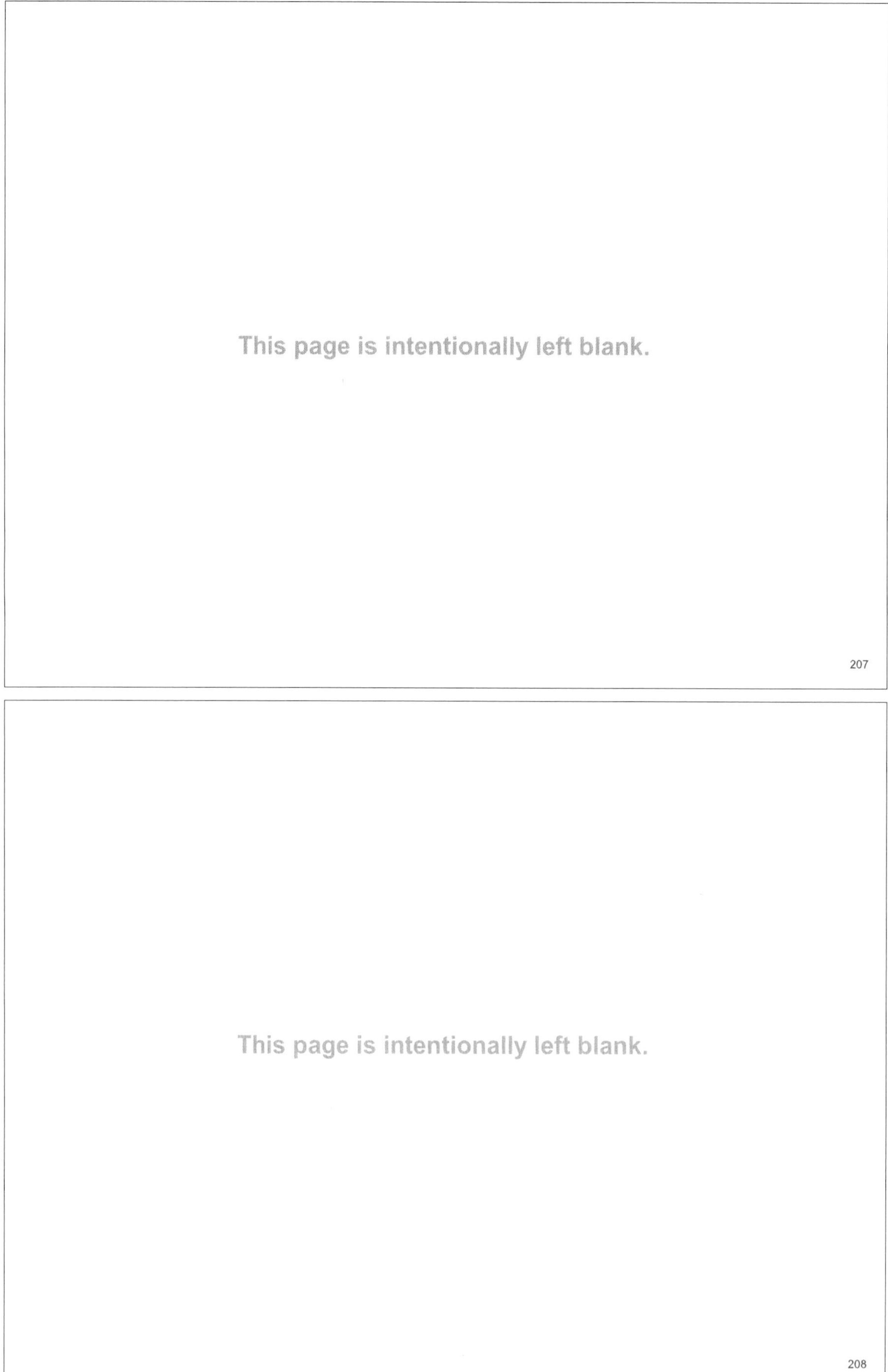
This page is intentionally left blank.
207
This page is intentionally left blank.
208

Balance Sheet Drilldown

Balance Sheet: USA Inc. Federal Debt + Unfunded Entitlement Liabilities (Social Security + Medicare…) Exceed Stated Assets

	F1996	…	F2003	…	F2009	F2010	Comments
ASSETS ($B)							
Cash & Other Monetary Assets	$193		$120		$393	$429	$200B cash balance owing to
Accounts / Loans / Taxes Receivable	206		278		626	783	temporary Fed market stabilization
Inventories	232		241		285	286	initiatives
Property, Plant & Equipment	969		658		784	829	
TARP + GSE Investments	–		–		304	254	Includes $145B TARP direct loans &
Other assets	124		97		275	303	equity investment + $109B in GSEs
Total Assets ($B)	1,724		1,394		2,668	2,884	Growth primarily owing to TARP
Y/Y Growth	*33%*		*40%*		*35%*	*8%*	capitalization + Fed liquidity program
LIABILITIES ($B)							
Accounts Payable	$162		$62		$73	$73	Significant rise in debt owing to on-
Accrued Payroll & Benefits	–		100		161	164	going budget deficits + stimulus
Federal Debt	3,730		3,945		7,583	9,060	spending
Federal Employee & Veteran Benefits Payak	1,652		3,880		5,284	5,720	Federal employee & veteran benefits
Liability to GSEs	–		–		92	360	rose 3x owing to scheduled annual
Other Liabilities	530		512		932	979	pay raises + rising benefit costs
Unfunded Net Entitlement Liabilities	5,415		20,825		45,878	30,857	Unfunded entitlement liabilities up 6x
Y/Y Growth	–		*16%*		*7%*	*-33%*	between F1996 and F2010.
NPV of Unfunded Social Security	$3,600		$4,927		$7,677	$7,947	Medicare NPV down sharply Y/Y
NPV of Unfunded Medicare	1,815		15,819		38,107	22,813	owing to new assumptions from the
NPV of Unfunded Other Benefits			79		94	97	Healthcare reform legislation
Total Liabilities ($B)	11,488		29,324		60,002	47,214	Significant increase from rising levels
Y/Y Growth	--		*14%*		*9%*	*-21%*	of debt + unfunded future benefits
NET WORTH ($B)	-$9,764		-$27,930		-$57,334	-$44,330	-$44T of net worth for USA Inc. more
Y/Y Growth	--		*13%*		*8%*	*-23%*	than tripled, from -$10T in 1996

Note: USA Inc.'s balance sheet presented here does not include the financial value of the Government's sovereign powers to tax, regulate commerce, and set monetary policy. It also excludes its control over nonoperational resources, including national and natural resources, for which the Government is a steward. Total liabilities include the net present value (NPV) of unfunded entitlement liabilities like Social Security / Medicare / other payments, which the Treasury Dept. considers 'off-balance sheet' responsibilities. U.S. government fiscal year ends in September. Source: U.S. Department of the Treasury, Financial Report on the U.S. Government, 1996 – 2010.

USA Inc. Net Worth: **-$44 Trillion** in Perspective

There are doubts about the accuracy of such a big negative number, especially when the value of USA Inc.'s assets is so hard to calculate. The value of natural resources, the power to tax, the ability to print the world's reserve currency, the human capital in our educational system – these and other assets would clearly reduce that number, if they could be accurately calculated.

Given the differences between government and corporate accounting, what matters is not the exact number, but the trend – which is clearly moving in the wrong direction. Liabilities have been growing faster than assets. Just to put that $57 trillion into context…

-$44 Trillion = $142,999 per Person in USA[1]

$370,961 per Household[1]

20x USA Inc. Annual Revenue[2]

3.8x S&P500 Total Market Capitalization[3]

3.0x USA Annual GDP[4]

0.9x Global Stock Market Capitalization[5]

0.8x Total USA Household Wealth[6]

Source: 1) Population & household data as of 1/10, per Census Bureau estimates; 2) annual federal income in F2010, per Dept. of Treasury; 3) as of 1/11, per S&P; 4) GDP is 2010 nominal figure, per BEA; 5) as of 1/10, per World Federation of Exchanges; 6) as of CQ3:10, calculated as total net worth of households & nonprofit organizations, per Federal Reserve (12/10 data).

We Believe Citizens Should Consider These 'Off-Balance Sheet' Liabilities For A 'More Complete' Understanding of USA Inc.'s Finances

"…the Government's responsibilities to make future payments for social insurance and certain other programs are not shown as liabilities according to Federal accounting standards…These programmatic commitments remain Federal responsibilities and as currently structured will have a significant claim on budgetary resources in the future…The reader needs to understand these responsibilities to get a more complete understanding of the Government's finances."

Department of the Treasury,

"2004 Financial Report of the United States Government"

Balance Sheet: USA Inc. Total Liabilities*: $47 Trillion in F2010, or $395,093 per Household Owing Largely to Entitlement Spending

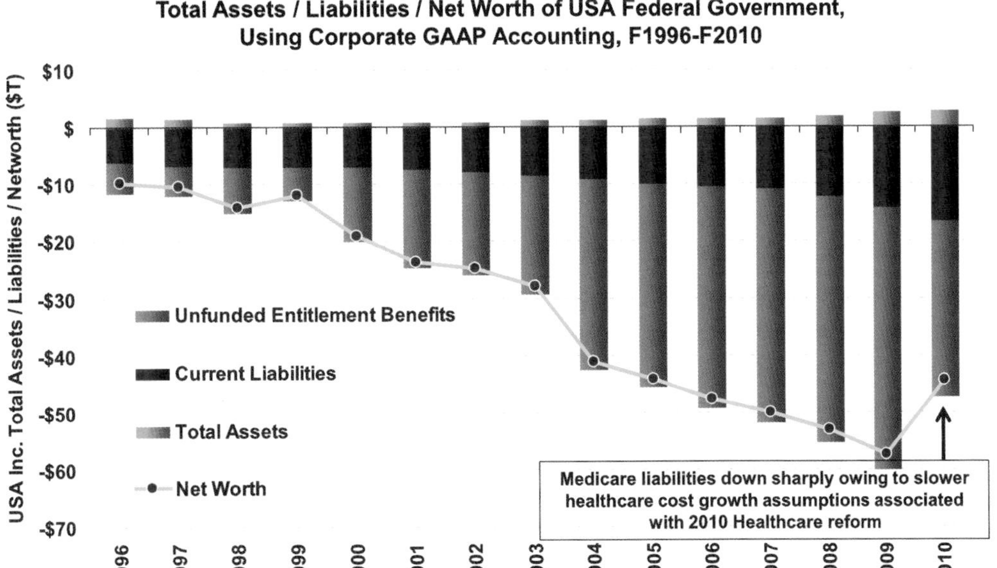

Note: USA Inc.'s balance sheet presented here does not include the financial value of the Government's sovereign powers to tax, regulate commerce, and set monetary policy. It also excludes its control over nonoperational resources, including national and natural resources, for which the Government is a steward. Total liabilities include the net present value (NPV) of unfunded entitlement liabilities like Social Security / Medicare / other payments, which the Treasury Dept. considers 'off-balance sheet' responsibilities. U.S. government fiscal year ends in September. Source: U.S. Department of the Treasury, Financial Report on the U.S. Government, 1996 – 2009.

Balance Sheet: USA Inc. Total Liabilities: $47 Trillion in F2010 Up 5x From 1996, Driven by Medicare Liabilities

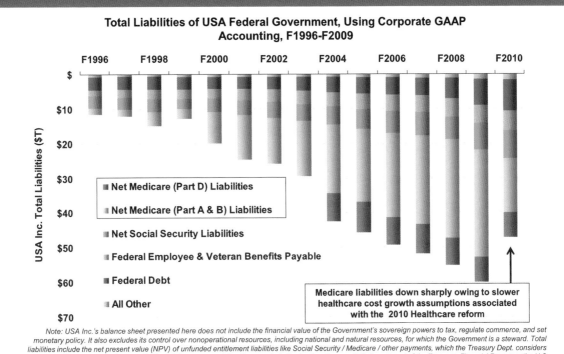

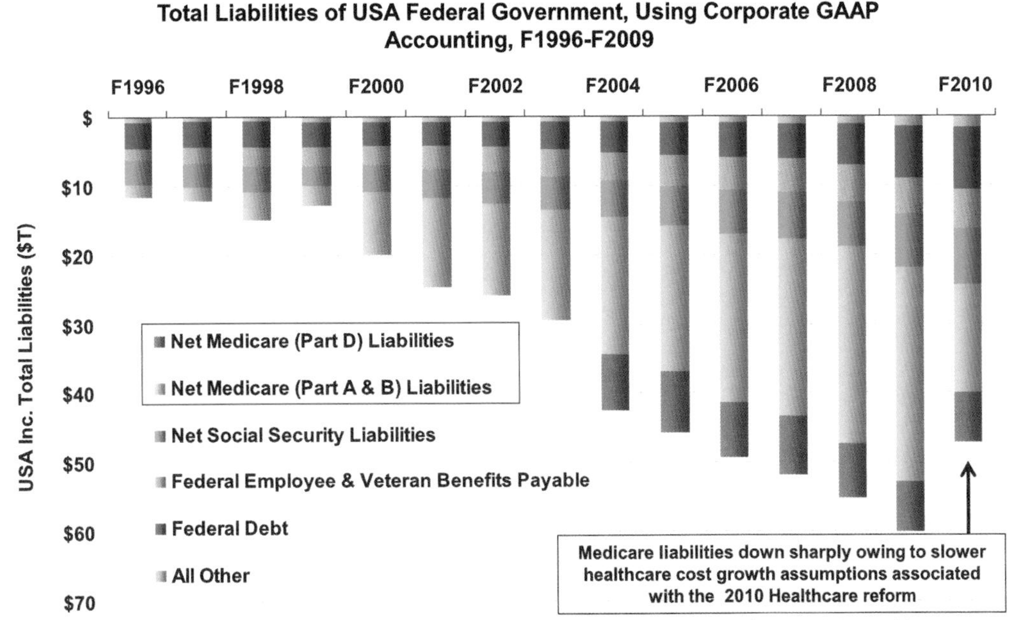

Note: USA Inc.'s balance sheet presented here does not include the financial value of the Government's sovereign powers to tax, regulate commerce, and set monetary policy. It also excludes its control over nonoperational resources, including national and natural resources, for which the Government is a steward. Total liabilities include the net present value (NPV) of unfunded entitlement liabilities like Social Security / Medicare / other payments, which the Treasury Dept. considers 'off-balance sheet' responsibilities. U.S. government fiscal year ends in September. Source: U.S. Department of the Treasury, Financial Report on the U.S .Government, 1996 – 2009.

Important Caveats on F2010 Medicare Liability Improvement

- Medicare Part A and Part B unfunded liability improved to -$16 trillion in F2010, up 47% from -$31 trillion in F2009, per the Board of Medicare Trustees.
- The improvement was driven primarily by downward revisions of future cost growth assumptions following enactment of healthcare reform in 2010.
- However, Medicare's Chief Actuary Richard Foster noted that "*while the Patient Protection and Affordable Care Act, as amended, makes important changes to the Medicare program and substantially improves its financial outlook,* ***there is a strong likelihood that certain of these changes will not be viable in the long range****...Without major changes in health care delivery systems, the prices paid by Medicare for health services [as scheduled by current law] are very likely to fall increasingly short of the costs of providing these services...Congress would have to intervene to prevent the withdrawal of providers from the Medicare market and the severe problems with beneficiary access to care that would result. Overriding the productivity adjustments, as Congress has done repeatedly in the case of physician payment rates,* ***would lead to far higher costs for Medicare in the long range than those projected under current law...For these reasons, the financial projections shown [here] for Medicare do not represent a reasonable expectation for actual program operations in either the short range*** *(as a result of the unsustainable reductions in physician payment rates)* ***or the long range*** *(because of the strong likelihood that the statutory reductions in price updates for most categories of Medicare provider services will not be viable).*"

Note: Emphasis added. Source: Statement of Actuarial Opinion, 2010 Annual Report of the Boards of Trustees of the Federal Hospital Insurance and Federal Supplementary Medical Insurance Trust Funds.

Balance Sheet: Even Excluding Unfunded Entitlement Benefits, USA Inc.'s Net Worth = -$13 Trillion in F2010, Owing to $9 Trillion of Debt

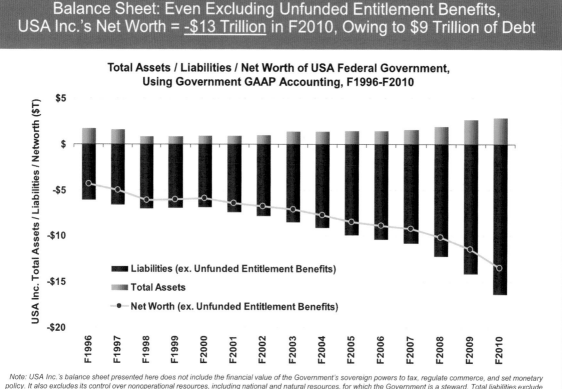

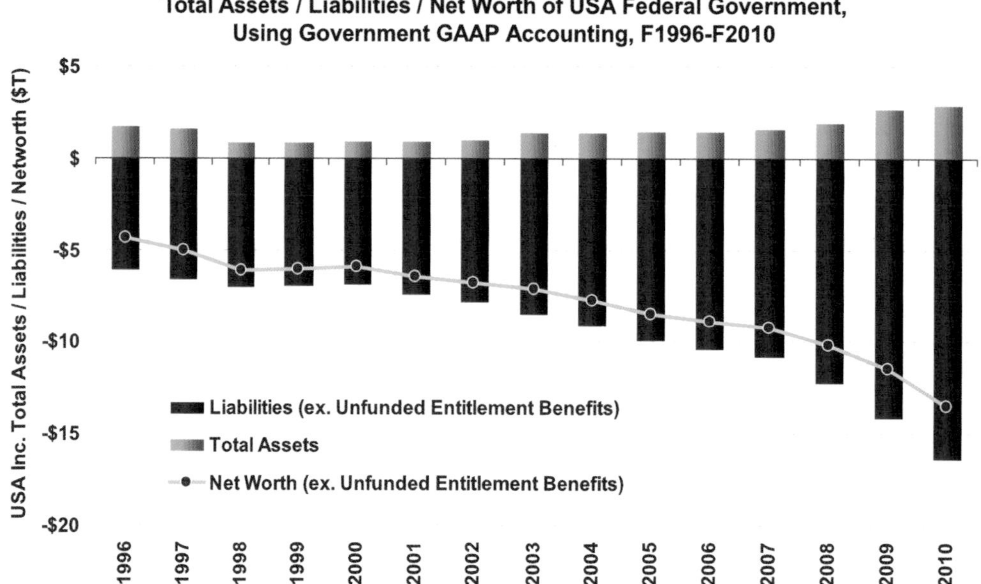

Note: USA Inc.'s balance sheet presented here does not include the financial value of the Government's sovereign powers to tax, regulate commerce, and set monetary policy. It also excludes its control over nonoperational resources, including national and natural resources, for which the Government is a steward. Total liabilities exclude the net present value (NPV) of unfunded entitlement liabilities like Social Security / Medicare / other payments, which the Treasury Dept. considers 'off-balance sheet' responsibilities. U.S. government fiscal year ends in September. Source: U.S. Department of the Treasury, Financial Report on the U.S. Government, 1996 – 2010.

Balance Sheet: Observations of Last Ten Years

- **Unfunded promise of future entitlement spending** grew 6x to -$31 trillion, owing to rapidly rising healthcare cost + new Medicare Part D program + aging population in the medium-future.
- **Federal net debt outstanding more than doubled** to $9 trillion **on the back of** chronic budget deficits, two major recessions in 2001 and 2008, and growing entitlement spending.
- **Federal employee & veteran benefits outstanding also more than doubled,** to $5.7 trillion, thanks to rising healthcare costs and ongoing war on terror.

This page is intentionally left blank.

This page is intentionally left blank.

This page is intentionally left blank.

What Might a Turnaround Expert—Empowered to Improve USA Inc.'s Financials—Consider?

First, Examine USA Inc. Key Drivers of Revenue & Expenses...

- **USA Inc.'s Revenue = Highly Correlated (83%) with GDP Growth***
  - 90% of USA Inc.'s 2010 revenue derived from taxing individual and corporate income, which depends on GDP growth and changes to tax rates / composition.

- **USA Inc.'s Expenses = Less (73%) Correlated with GDP Growth***
  - *Entitlement Programs* = 57% of USA Inc.'s expenses in 2010
    - driven by government policy + demographic changes
  - *Defense Programs* = 20% of expenses
    - driven by external threat levels and policy
  - *Net Interest Payments* = 6% of expenses
    - driven by net debt level + interest rates + composition of debt maturity

Observation: while revenue is highly correlated with GDP growth, expenses are less so.

*Note: *Historical inflation-adjusted correlation between GDP and revenue / expense Y/Y growth rates from 1940 to 2010, GDP / revenue adjusted using GDP deflator; expenses adjusted using White House OMB's composite outlay deflator. Nominal revenue / GDP correlation over the same period is 84%; expense / GDP correlation is 71%. Data source: White House Office of Management & Budget, CBO.*

Then, Aim to Determine What 'Normal' Is…

- We review **40-year income statement patterns** and focus on 'average' / 'normal' levels of USA Inc.'s revenue drivers (primarily related to taxes) and expense drivers (by category) as a percent of revenue, as a starting point to help define 'average' / 'normal.'
- Established businesses typically determine their expense levels based on their revenue trend / outlook.
- In a perfect world, the government (and its citizens) would continually review the multiple variables in the income statement of USA Inc. (in a bipartisan way) and would **work hard to foster compromise, in order to optimize** revenue and expenses for the long term AND the short term.

Considering USA Inc. 'Normal' / Average Financial Metrics / Ratios For…

1) Revenue Growth

2) Revenue Drivers as Percent of Revenue

3) Expense Growth by Category

4) Category Expenses as Percent of Expenses

Revenue Growth: Average Federal Revenue (Driven by Taxes) In-Line With GDP Growth

1965 – 2005 USA Real Federal Income Growth by Category vs. Real GDP Growth

	Revenue Growth				
	1965 Y/Y	2005 Y/Y	40-yr CAGR	*'05 vs 40-yr Variance*	Comments
Individual Income Taxes	11%	11%	3%	*8%*	Individual & corporate income taxes are cyclical; 2005 Y/Y growth were significantly affected by economic recovery post 2001 recession.
Corporate Income Taxes	15	43	2	*41*	
Social Insurance Taxes	12	5	5	*1*	Social insurance taxes & other fees are less cyclical. Social insurance taxes grew significantly faster than GDP.
Other Taxes & Fees	-5	1	1	*0*	
Total Federal Revenue	9%	11%	3%	*8%*	
Real GDP	7%	3%	3%	*0%*	

"Normal"

Note: All data are inflation adjusted using GDP price index from BEA; '05 vs. 40-yr variance is rounded.
Data source: White House Office of Management & Budget.

Revenue Growth: Observations from Previous Slide

We chose a 40-year period from 1965 to 2005 to examine 'normal' levels of revenue and expenses. We did not choose the most recent 40-year period (1969 to 2009) as USA was in deep recession in 2008 / 2009 and underwent significant tax policy fluctuations in 1968 /1969 and subsequently many metrics (like individual income and corporate profit) varied significantly from 'normal' levels.

Total USA Inc. revenue (collected via taxes) has grown at an average 3% annual rate, in-line with 40-year GDP growth rate. Corporate taxes have – on average – grown at 2% annually over 40 years. Social insurance taxes (for Social Security and Medicare) have grown at an average 5% annual rate, above the 3% GDP growth.

Questions:

1) How crucial is the role played by lower relative tax rates – especially for corporations – in stimulating job and GDP growth and helping American maintain / gain / constrain loss of global competitive advantage?

2) Should social insurance tax growth be more closely aligned with GDP growth?

Note: All data are inflation adjusted using GDP price index from BEA; '05 vs. 40-yr variance is rounded.
Data source: White House Office of Management & Budget.

Revenue Drivers as Percent of Total Revenue: Average Federal Revenue Are Skewed to Social Insurance (Entitlement) Taxes and Away from Corporate Income Taxes

1965 – 2005 USA Real Federal Income Mix by Category

	Share of Total Revenue			
	1965	2005	40-yr Average	*'05 vs 40-yr Variance*
Individual Income Taxes	42%	43%	46%	*-3%*
Corporate Income Taxes	22	13	12	*1*
Social Insurance Taxes	19	37	33	*4*
Other Taxes & Fees	17	7	10	*-3*
Total Federal Revenue	**100%**	**100%**	**100%**	***0%***

"Normal"

Note: All data are inflation adjusted using GDP price index from BEA; '05 vs. 40-yr variance is rounded.
Data source: White House Office of Management & Budget.

Revenue Drivers as Percent of Revenue: Observations from Previous Slide

Social Insurance taxes (for entitlement programs) have risen materially to 37% of revenue (vs. 33% 40-year average), and have risen aggressively from 19% in 1965, owing to introduction of Medicare in 1965 and the 1983 reform of social security taxes.

Questions:

1) What level of social insurance / entitlement 'tax' can USA Inc. support on an on-going basis? Rising from 19% of revenue in 1965 to 33% of revenue in 2005 – of which 75% was spent on healthcare – takes its toll on other areas of spending / growth. There are serious tradeoffs - every dollar that goes to entitlement programs is not spent on education, infrastructure, and defense.

2) Why have corporate income taxes fallen to 13% of revenue in 2009 from 22% in 1965 aside from recession? How crucial has this been to maintain global competitive advantage and stimulating American job and GDP growth?

Note: All data are inflation adjusted using GDP price index from BEA; '05 vs. 40-yr variance is rounded.
Data source: White House Office of Management & Budget.

Expense Growth by Category: Entitlement Spending Growing Much Faster than Other Expenses and 2% Higher than GDP Growth

1965 – 2005 USA Real Federal Expenses Growth by Category vs. Real GDP Growth

	Expenses Growth				
	1965 Y/Y	2005 Y/Y	40-yr CAGR	*'05 vs. 40-yr Variance*	Comments
Entitlement Expenses	12%	3%	6%	*-3%*	Entitlement expenses grew 2 percentage points faster than GDP and overall expenses
Defense	12	6	1	*4*	Defense spending grew 2 percentage points below overall expenses
Non-Defense Discretionary*	10	6	2	*4*	
Net Interest Payments	7	12	3	*8*	
Total Federal Expenses	11%	5%	3%	*2%*	
Real GDP	7%	3%	3%	*0%*	

↑ **Normal**

*Note: All data are inflation adjusted using GDP price index from BEA; '05 vs. 40-yr variance is rounded. *Non-defense discretionary spending includes education, infrastructure, agriculture, housing, etc. Data source: White House Office of Management & Budget.*

Expense Growth by Category: Observations from Previous Slide

While GDP and USA Inc. tax revenue have grown at a 3% annual rate for 40 years, entitlement spending has grown 5%, net interest payments have risen 3%, and defense plus non-defense discretionary spending (including education, infrastructure, law enforcement and judiciary) have risen by 1%. These different growth rates have become even more pronounced in recent years.

Questions:

1) Isn't it time for a re-set and acknowledgment of trade-offs? Should taxes, non-defense discretionary spending, and defense spending grow in line with GDP over time? Should entitlement spending be restructured to be more efficient and supportable by the ongoing financial dynamics of USA, Inc. and also grow in line with or below GDP?

Note: All data are inflation adjusted using GDP price index from BEA; '05 vs. 40-yr variance is rounded. Data source: White House Office of Management & Budget.

Expense Drivers as Percent of Total Expenses: Entitlement + One-Time Items Are Crowding Out Other Federal Spending

1965 – 2005 USA Real Federal Expenses Mix by Category

	Share of Total Expenses			
	1965	**2005**	**40-yr Average**	***'05 vs. 40-yr Variance***
Entitlement Expenses	**21%**	**51%**	**42%**	***9%***
Defense	**43**	**20**	**24**	***-4***
Non-Defense Discretionary*	**29**	**22**	**23**	***-1***
Net Interest Payments	**7**	**7**	**11**	***-4***
Total Federal Expenses	**100%**	**100%**	**100%**	***0%***

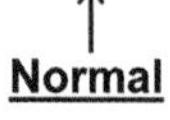

*Note: All data are inflation adjusted using GDP price index from BEA; '05 vs. 40-yr variance is rounded. *Non-defense discretionary spending includes education, infrastructure, agriculture, housing, etc. Data source: White House Office of Management & Budget.*

Category Expenses as Percent of Expenses: Observations from Previous Slide

Entitlement spending has risen to 51% of total spending, higher than 40-year average of 42% (and much higher than the 21% in 1965), defense spending has fallen to 20% from 24% average, non-defense discretionary spending (including education, infrastructure, energy, law enforcement and veteran services) has fallen to 22% from 23%, and net interest payments have fallen to 7% from 11%, despite higher debt (largely because of declining interest rates). These trends have become more pronounced in recent years.

Questions:

1) Should entitlement spending account for 51% (and rising) share of total USA Inc.'s spending, while other key areas (such as education, infrastructure, energy, law enforcement…) account for only 22% (and falling) of spending?

Note: All data are inflation adjusted using GDP price index from BEA; '05 vs. 40-yr variance is rounded. Data source: White House Office of Management & Budget.

Bottom Line, as Data in This Presentation Indicate…

USA Inc.'s expenses far exceed revenue – and government projections imply this trend will get worse, not better.

In addition - while not addressed in depth in this presentation - USA Inc. (while still a global powerhouse), at the margin, is losing competitive advantage to many other countries.

Instead of ignoring the problems, we simply ask the question…
How would a financial / turnaround expert look at USA Inc.'s financials, business model, strategic plans, efficiency and aim to drive the 'business' to break-even (or a modest profit) over the next 5-10 years?

Matching Expenses & Revenue: Imperatives & Constraints

There are many reasons to make changes

- USA Inc. is losing money, and forecasts imply it will continue to lose money.
- Net debt levels (62% in F2010) are expected to surpass 90% threshold* – above which real GDP growth could slow by more than one percentage point – by 2021E.
- Spending (primarily related to entitlement programs) is at unsustainable levels based on USA Inc.'s ability to fund the spending (without increasing debt levels).
- Americans rank 'reducing America's debt' as one of country's top priorities, according to a national survey by Peter G. Peterson Foundation in 11/09.
- We are now in the midst of a major generational baton-passing (from the Baby Boomers to Generation X) which requires preparation for policy change.
- Foreigners own 46% (and rising) of USA Inc.'s debt, per Treasury Department – Are they going to keep funding USA Inc.'s spending?

*Note: *Carmen Reinhart and Kenneth Rogoff observed from 3,700 historical annual data points from 44 countries that the relationship between government debt and real GDP growth is weak for debt/GDP ratios below a threshold of 90 percent of GDP. Above 90 percent, median growth rates fall by one percent, and average growth falls considerably more. We note that while Reinhart and Rogoff's observations are based on 'gross debt' data, in the U.S., debt held by the public is closer to the European countries' definition of government gross debt. For more information, see Reinhart and Rogoff, "Growth in a Time of Debt," 1/10.*

Matching Expenses & Revenue: Imperatives & Constraints

There are many constraints to making changes

- ~90 million citizens (29% of Americans)[1] have grown accustomed to entitlement programs - 47MM on Medicaid, 45MM on Medicare, and 51MM on Social Security, and many of them vote.
- Politicians depend on re-election campaigns, which can create conflicts, especially given that only 12% of the population are willing to cut Social Security and Medicare benefits, per Pew survey in 2/11.
- Low personal savings rates (near 6% of disposable income in CQ2:10), high unemployment (near 10%) and economic uncertainty, which can limit ability to make radical change.
- 14 million healthcare-related workers[2] have grown accustomed to relatively high healthcare spending.

Note: 1) as of 2008, excludes double counting of beneficiaries of multiple entitlement programs; 2) as of 2008, per BEA. Source: Social Security Administration, Dept. of Health & Human Services, BEA.

And Then There's the Constraint of USA Inc.'s Weak Economy

[The] typical error most countries make coming out of a financial crisis is they shift too quickly to premature restraint. You saw that in the United States in the 30s, you saw that in Japan in the 90s. It is very important for us to avoid that mistake. If the government does nothing going forward, then the impact of policy in Washington will shift from supporting economic growth to hurting economic growth.

Timothy Geithner, Secretary of US Treasury

The Wall Street Journal, September 12, 2010

High-Level Thoughts on How to Turn Around USA Inc.'s Financial Outlook

Negative Cash Flow = USA Inc.'s Fundamental Financial Problem

- **Negative cash flow implies that USA Inc. can't afford the services it is providing to 'customers' (citizens).**
- **USA Inc. needs to re-prioritize its services and offer them in a more cost-effective way to stop losing (and borrowing) money.**
- **The financial data imply that USA Inc.'s operations must be restructured.**

The First Step to a 'Turnaround' is Acknowledging There is a Problem

A turnaround situation is first recognized when there is serious concern or dissatisfaction with the firm's [organization's] performance, results, and/or near-term forecasts of [financial] performance and results.

- Richard Sloma, *The Turnaround Manager's Handbook*

If your organization is in trouble, be honest. Make it absolutely clear to everyone in the company that survival [long-term viability] depends on cost management.

- Jon Meliones, “Saving Money, Saving Lives,” *Harvard Business Review on Turnarounds*

How Might a 'Turnaround Expert' Look at an Organization that Needs to be 'Turned Around?'

The recovery of a [challenged] company [or country]…depends on the implementation of an appropriate rescue plan or turnaround prescription. Characteristics of the appropriate remedy are that it must: 1) address the fundamental problems; 2) tackle the underlying causes (rather than the symptoms) and 3) be broad and deep enough in scope to resolve all the key issues.

- Stuart Slatter, David Lovett, Laura Barlow, *Leading Corporate Turnaround*

Aim to Answer Questions Like These About USA Inc.…

Strategy / Financial Model

- Which countries (or states) have 'best practices' (based on productivity and outcomes) in key areas of operations (like healthcare, retirement plans, welfare, defense, education, infrastructure) – which of these best practices can / should be implemented by USA Inc.?
- What is the organization trying to solve for - what is USA Inc.'s mission? / Who are USA Inc.'s customers?
- Is USA Inc. providing its customers an optimized mix of services, based, in part, on ability to fund the services?
- Are there 'business lines' that USA Inc. should exit / scale back / expand?
- Why is USA Inc. spending more money than it brings in (and borrowing more money) – what are the checks and balances?
- What do USA Inc.'s financials tell us about the health of the business?
- Should USA Inc. consider a capital budget separated from the operating budget to ensure sufficient levels of investment in education, technology and infrastructure?
- What are the best attributes / biggest problems of USA Inc.'s business?
- Does USA Inc. have a path to profitability (or break-even)?
- How should the government improve transparency in long-term budgeting and projections? How can USA Inc. engage the public in this process?

Source: KPCB and Alvarez & Marsal Public Sector Services, LLC.

…Aim to Answer Questions Like These About USA Inc.…

People / Organizational Structure

- Has management effectively articulated a sound mission to its employees and constituents - is USA Inc. properly organized to effectively achieve its mission?
- Does the organization have the right people, in the right places, at the right time?
- Does the business have a best-in-class leadership team and are they empowered to make change?
- Are employees motivated / empowered / accountable for maximum performance?
- Are employees properly trained and compensated?
- Has the organization 'run the numbers' and effectively quantified the things that are quantifiable?
- Do leading performance measures exist that support proactive management?
- How do you change the culture to be one that is steeped with focus on costs savings and operating efficiency?

Source: KPCB and Alvarez & Marsal Public Sector Services, LLC.

…Aim to Answer Questions Like These About USA Inc.

Productivity / Operations

- How does USA Inc. measure performance and progress – are tools in place to measure success / failure?
- Should USA Inc. empower an independent / 3rd party auditor with expertise in government operations around the world AND corporate turnarounds to conduct a broad-ranging audit of USA Inc.'s operations to measure efficiency and productivity of each business lines?
- Does USA Inc. have tight management and financial controls?
- What is the best way to measure and improve individual program performance? Can Congress, the administration and the agencies agree on common metrics?
- Are there operations that should be centralized (like procurement, human resources, employee payroll and benefits) and decentralized?
- Are there operations that USA Inc. can outsource to local private companies to improve efficiency and reduce costs?
- Where should USA Inc. increase and or decrease investment?
- Is USA Inc. investing for the future in a responsible way?
- Should USA Inc. drive public / private partnership in infrastructure investment with collective 'skin in the game?'
- Is the organization leveraging technology to improve productivity and connect with customers and suppliers?
- How can USA Inc. improve business process related to time, cost and quality?
- Does USA Inc. own assets it doesn't need that it can sell at attractive prices?

Source: KPCB and Alvarez & Marsal Public Sector Services, LLC.

Three Principles for a USA Inc. 'Turnaround' from Louis Gerstner

- **Do not impose "across-the-board" cost reductions**
  - This is a simple and tempting remedy for an organization in fiscal trouble. But it is almost always unproductive. A truly effective organization needs incremental investments in programs that drive innovation and higher productivity. Moreover, across-the-board cuts are almost guaranteed to reduce morale, promote short-sighted choices, and encourage accounting gimmicks that send people looking for loopholes instead of creative solutions.
- **Focus on programs, not costs**
  - The greatest productivity gains come from asking questions such as: What things are we doing now that we do not need as much in the future? Can we eliminate them? Reduce their size? Provide them in a totally restructured fashion?
- **Allow no exceptions**
  - To drive a truly effective restructuring program, everything must be on the table. There can be no sacred cows—no part of the organization that is exempt from scrutiny. Every unit of the organization may not face a cut, but every unit needs to be rethought.

Source: Louis V. Gerstner Jr. "Don't Just Cut Government, Reinvent It," Opinion in The Wall Street Journal, 2/1/2011.

Financial Experts Tend to 'Assume What Can Go Wrong, Will Go Wrong,' and Usually Manage Expenses in that Way

- In projecting scenarios, financial experts would note that USA Inc.'s revenue and expenses are highly correlated to economic changes – for example, a 0.1 percentage point slowdown in real GDP annual growth rate could worsen USA Inc.'s F2011-F2020E budget deficit by $288B, or 5% owing to lower tax revenue and higher welfare spending.

Key Economic Variables	CBO Base-Case Assumption	What if...	F2011-F2020E Impact on USA Inc.'s		
			Revenue ($B / % of Base-Case)	Spending ($B / % of Base-Case)	Deficit ($B / % of Base-Case)
Real GDP Y/Y Growth Rate	2.1% F2011E 4.4% F2012-14E 2.4% F2015-20E	Real GDP growth rates are <u>0.1 percentage point lower per year</u>	-$247B (-1%)	+$41B (--%)	-$288B (-5%)
Interest Rates	4.6% on 3-month T-bills 5.5% on 10-year T-notes	Interest rates are <u>1 percentage point higher</u>	+$94B (+0.3%)	+$1,214B (+3%)	-$1,120B (-19%)
Inflation	1.7%	Inflation is <u>1 percentage point higher</u>	+$2,475B (+7%)	+$3,191B (+7%)	-$715B (-12%)

Source: CBO, "The Budget and Economic Outlook: Fiscal Years 2010 to 2020," 1/10.

Past Performance Does Not Guarantee Future Results – Japan's Economic Miracle From 1960 to 1990 Rapidly Deteriorated Into the 'Lost Decades' of 1990's & 2000's

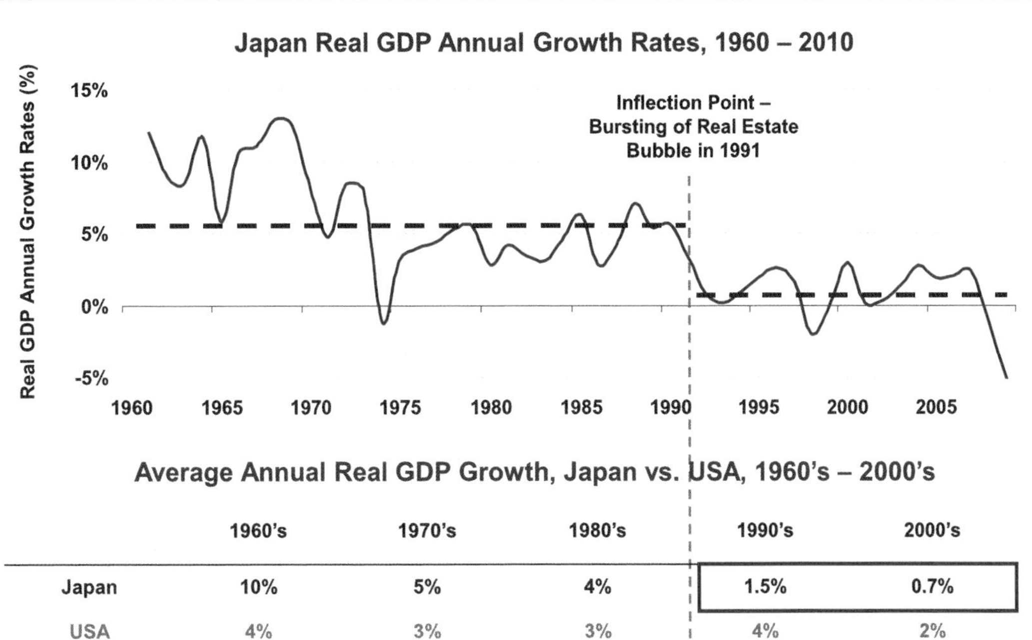

Average Annual Real GDP Growth, Japan vs. USA, 1960's – 2000's

	1960's	1970's	1980's	1990's	2000's
Japan	10%	5%	4%	1.5%	0.7%
USA	4%	3%	3%	4%	2%

Source: World Bank, IMF.

Unfunded Entitlement (Medicare + Social Security) + Underfunded Entitlement Expenditures (Medicaid) = Among Largest Long-Term Liabilities on USA Inc.'s Balance Sheet

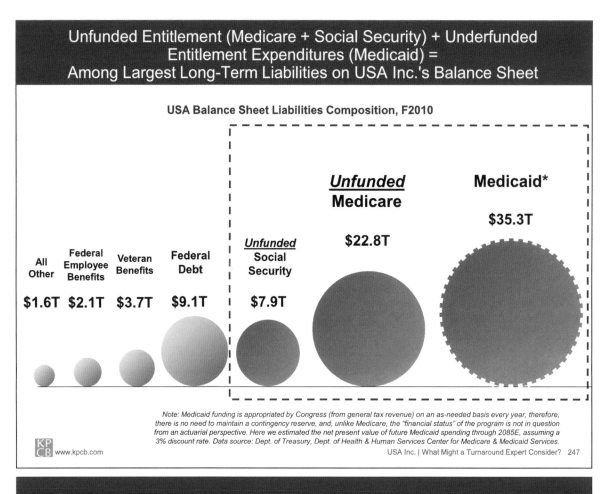

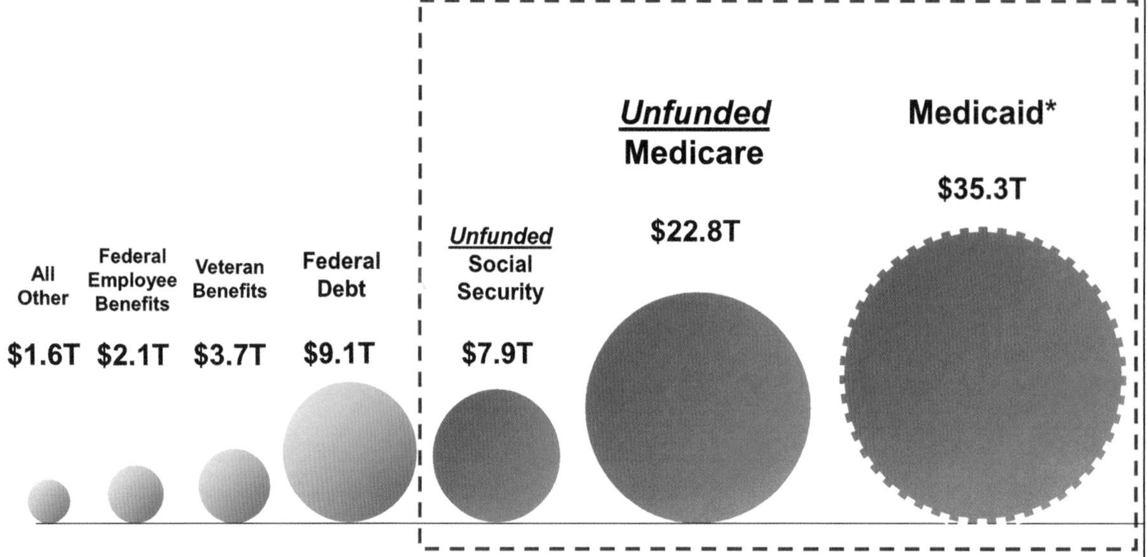

Note: Medicaid funding is appropriated by Congress (from general tax revenue) on an as-needed basis every year, therefore, there is no need to maintain a contingency reserve, and, unlike Medicare, the "financial status" of the program is not in question from an actuarial perspective. Here we estimated the net present value of future Medicaid spending through 2085E, assuming a 3% discount rate. Data source: Dept. of Treasury, Dept. of Health & Human Services Center for Medicare & Medicaid Services.

USA Inc.'s Financial Disconnect

The country faces a fundamental disconnect between the services the people expect the government to provide, particularly in the form of benefits for older Americans, and the tax revenues that people are willing to send to the government to finance those services. That fundamental disconnect will have to be addressed in some way if the budget is to be placed on a sustainable course.

- Douglas Elmendorf, Director of U.S. Congressional Budget Office, 11/10/2009

An Observation from Ben Bernanke, Current Chairman of the Federal Reserve

A famous economist once said anything that can't go on forever will eventually stop, and this [government liabilities from entitlement programs] will stop, but it might stop in a very unpleasant way in terms of sharp cuts, a financial crisis, high interest rates that stop growth, continued borrowing from abroad. So, clearly we need to get control of this over the medium term, and ***specifically we're going to have to look at entitlements because that's a very big part of the obligations of the federal government going forward****.*

-- Ben Bernanke, Chairman of the Federal Reserve

Testimony before House Budget Committee, June 9, 2010

Note: *Emphasis added.*

Bad News: USA Inc.'s Entitlement Programs are Inflation Indexed, Thus Potential Inflation – Which Would Reduce General Consumer Purchasing Power – Would Not Reduce Entitlement Liabilities

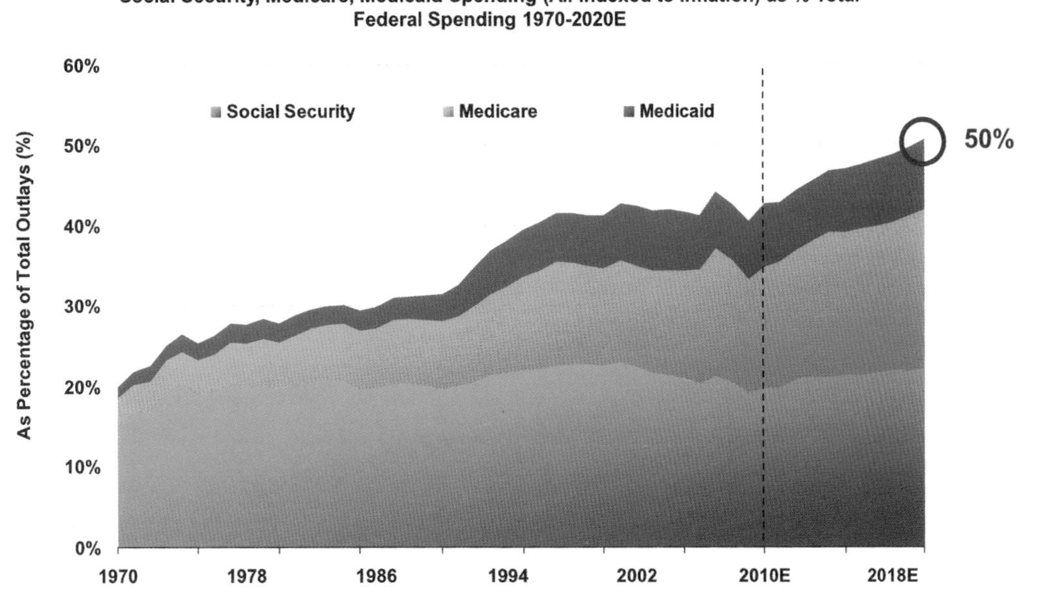

Data sources: The Budget and Economic Outlook, CBO 6/10.

Good News: While 'Unfunded' Liabilities Have Helped Bankrupt Companies, USA Inc.'s Unfunded Liabilities are Not Legal Contracts

- **Medicare / Social Security** – While beneficiaries have a legal entitlement to receive benefits as set forth under the Social Security Act, **Congress has the legal authority to change the levels of benefits and/or the conditions under which they are paid**. Congress's authority to modify provisions of the Social Security program was affirmed in the 1960 Supreme Court decision in *Flemming v. Nestor*, wherein the Court held that an individual does not have an accrued "property right" in Social Security benefits. The Court has made clear in subsequent decisions that the payment of Social Security taxes conveys **no contractual rights to Social Security benefits.**
- **Medicaid** – Benefit levels & eligibility are determined jointly by Federal and State governments. Federal funding is met through an appropriation by Congress (and can be adjusted annually).

Source: Congressional Research Service, Social Security Reform: Legal Analysis of Social Security Benefits Entitlement Issues.

What Might a Turnaround Expert Consider?

2

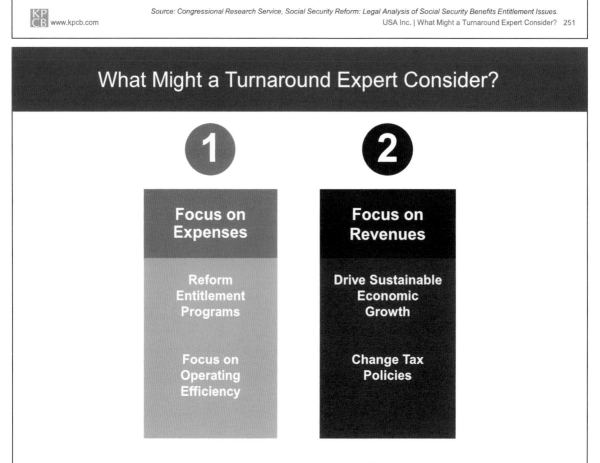

Focus on Expenses	Focus on Revenues
Reform Entitlement Programs	Drive Sustainable Economic Growth
Focus on Operating Efficiency	Change Tax Policies

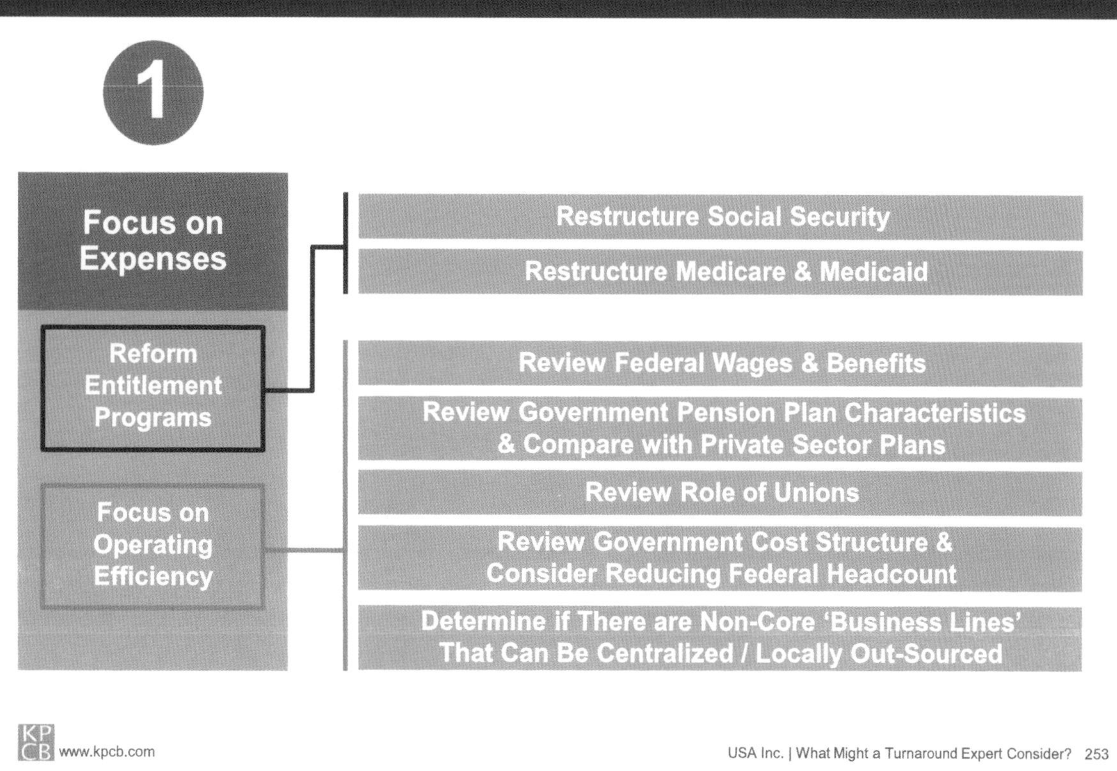

For Each of the Major Problems, We Highlight: 1) Mathematical Illustrations and 2) Policy Options

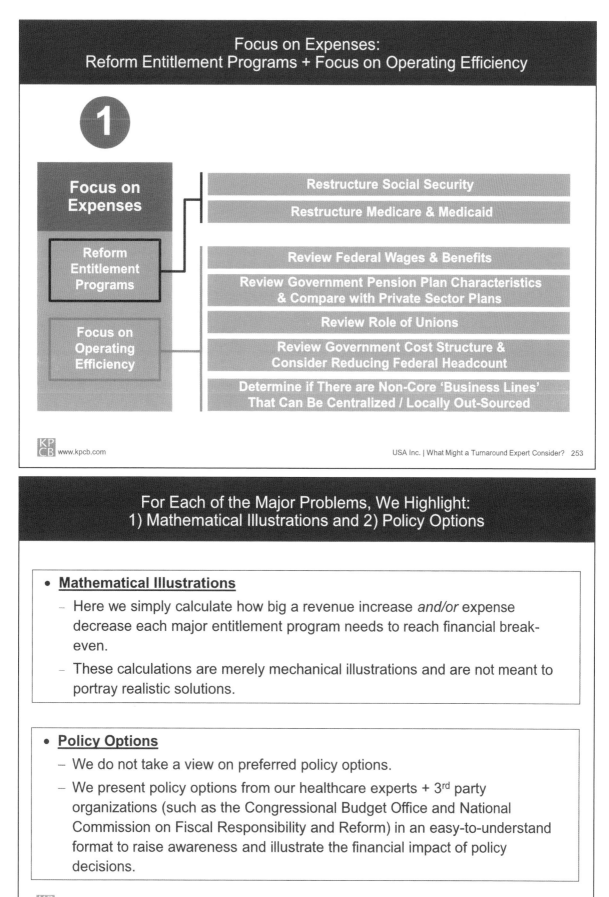

- **Mathematical Illustrations**
  - Here we simply calculate how big a revenue increase *and/or* expense decrease each major entitlement program needs to reach financial break-even.
  - These calculations are merely mechanical illustrations and are not meant to portray realistic solutions.

- **Policy Options**
  - We do not take a view on preferred policy options.
  - We present policy options from our healthcare experts + 3rd party organizations (such as the Congressional Budget Office and National Commission on Fiscal Responsibility and Reform) in an easy-to-understand format to raise awareness and illustrate the financial impact of policy decisions.

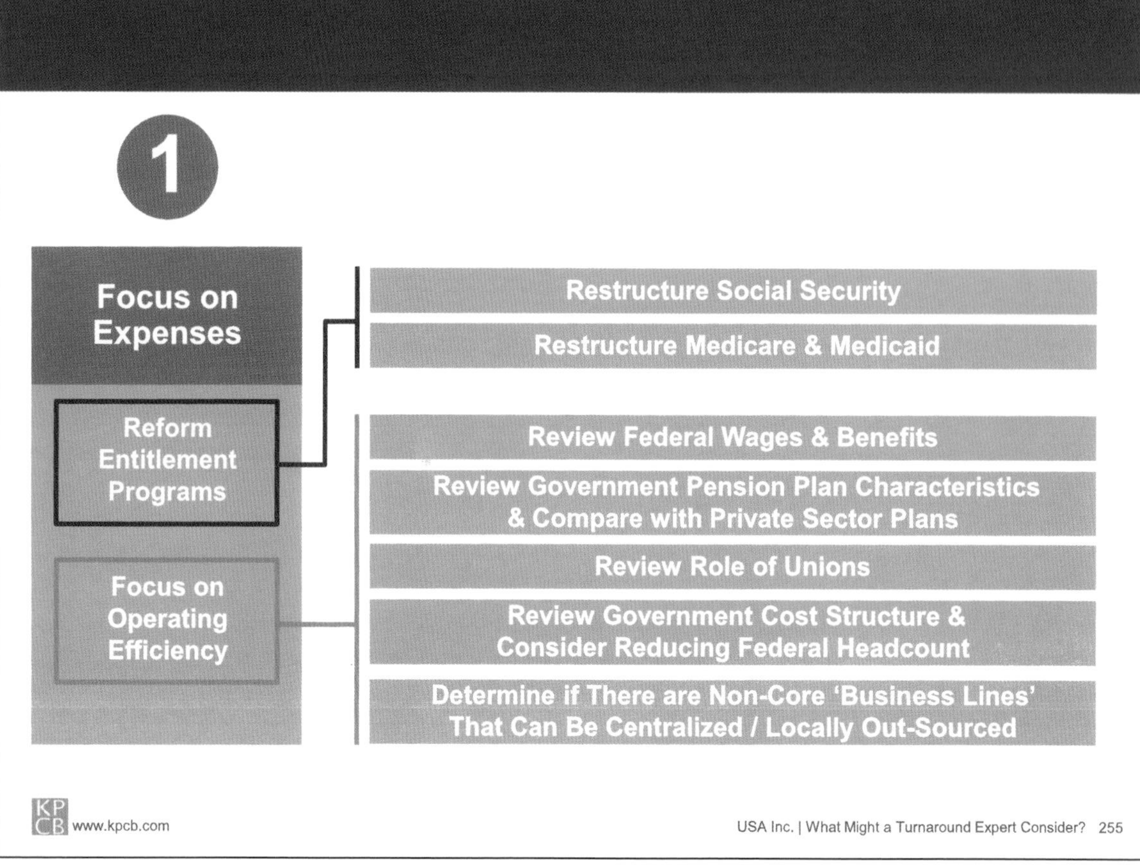
1
Focus on Expenses
Reform Entitlement Programs
Focus on Operating Efficiency
Restructure Social Security
Restructure Medicare & Medicaid
Review Federal Wages & Benefits
Review Government Pension Plan Characteristics & Compare with Private Sector Plans
Review Role of Unions
Review Government Cost Structure & Consider Reducing Federal Headcount
Determine if There are Non-Core 'Business Lines' That Can Be Centralized / Locally Out-Sourced
www.kpcb.com
USA Inc. | What Might a Turnaround Expert Consider? 255

Restructure Social Security: Variables To Make the Program Financially Break-Even for the Long-Term

Mathematical Illustrations* Slide 257–259

1) Retirement age – increase it to 73, from 67? ***or***

2) Social Security benefits – decrease them by 12%? ***or***

3) Social Security tax rate – increase it by 2 percentage points?

Policy Options Slide 261–267

1) Combination of some / all mathematical illustrations above? ***and/or***

2) Consider / implement CBO's various policy options on Social Security's tax rates / taxable payroll / initial benefit formulas / cost-of-living adjustment… (July 2010)**? ***and/or***

3) Consider / implement National Commission on Fiscal Responsibility and Reform's policy proposals (November 2010)***?

*Note: *For mathematical illustrations, we simply calculate how big a revenue increase AND / OR expense decrease each major entitlement program needs to reach financial break-even. These calculations are merely mechanical illustrations and are not meant to portray realistic solutions. **See: CBO, "Social Security Options 2010." ***See: National Commission on Fiscal Responsibility and Reform, CoChairs' Proposal, 11.10.10 Draft Document.*

Restructure Social Security: Mathematical Illustration #1 – Increase Retirement Age From 67 to 73

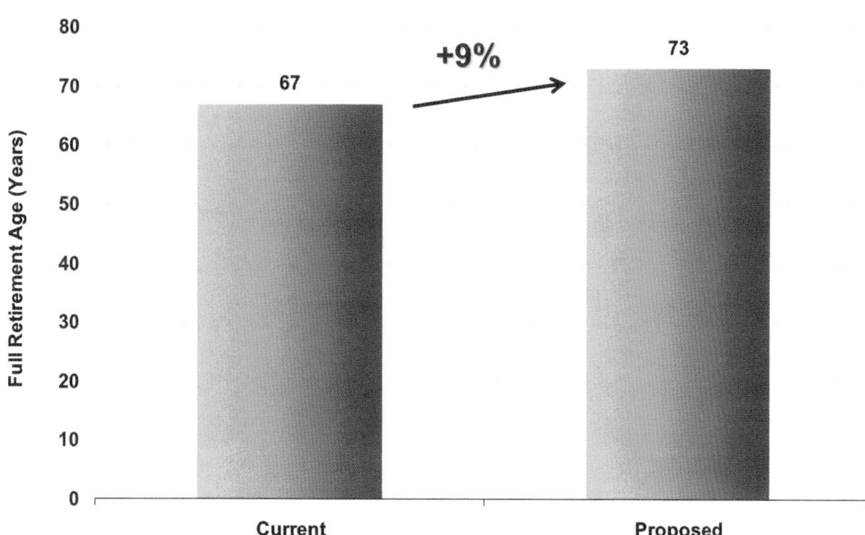

Note: For mathematical illustrations, we simply calculate how big a revenue increase AND / OR expense decrease each major entitlement program needs to reach financial break-even. These calculations are merely mechanical illustrations and are not meant to portray realistic solutions.
Note: Increase full retirement age to 73 will reduce average life expectancy at retirement to the same level as when Social Security was introduced in the late 1930s. Source: Melissa M. Favreault and Richard W. Johnson, The Urban Institute, "Raising Social Security's Retirement Age," 7/10.

Restructure Social Security: Mathematical Illustration #2 – Reduce Social Security Expenses (Benefits) By 12%

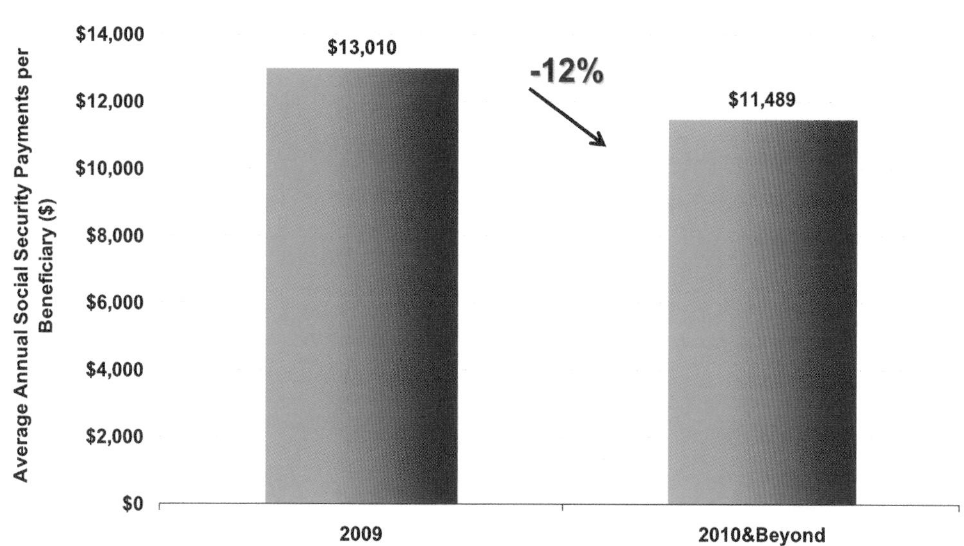

Note: For mathematical illustrations, we simply calculate how big a revenue increase AND / OR expense decrease each major entitlement program needs to reach financial break-even. These calculations are merely mechanical illustrations and are not meant to portray realistic solutions.
Source: Social Security Administration forecast in "The 2010 Annual Report of the Board of Trustees of the Federal Old-Age and Survivors Insurance and Federal Disability Insurance Trust Funds," 8/10.

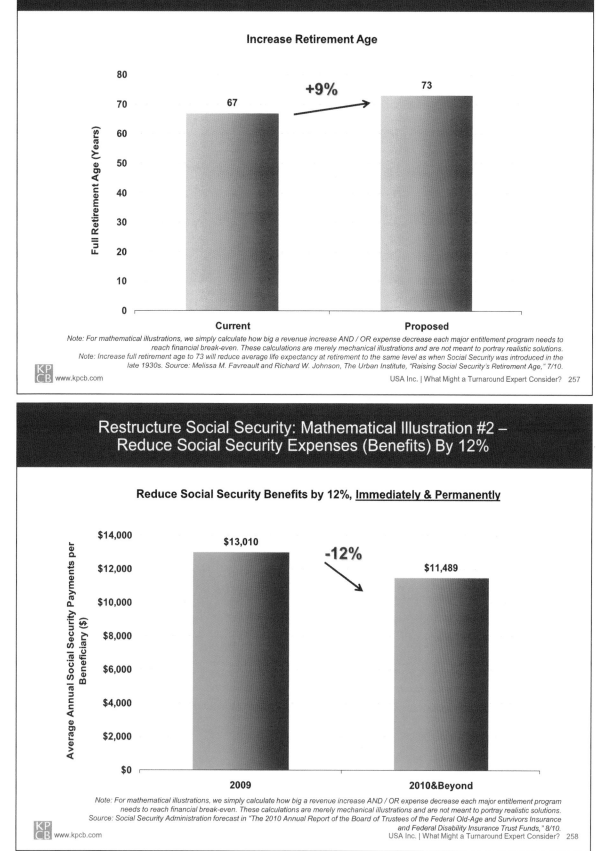

Restructure Social Security: Mathematical Illustration #3 – Increase Social Security Tax Rate From 12.4% to 14.2%

Increase Social Security Tax Rate by 1.92 Percentage Points, <u>Immediately & Permanently</u>

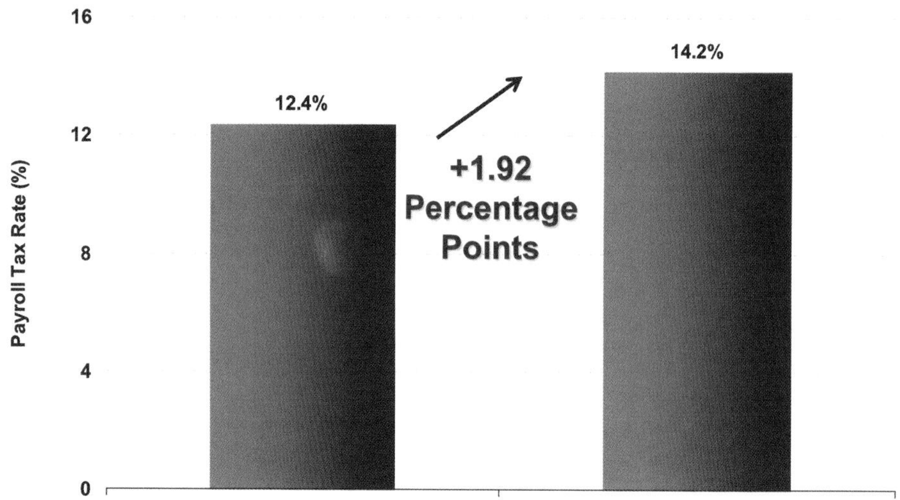

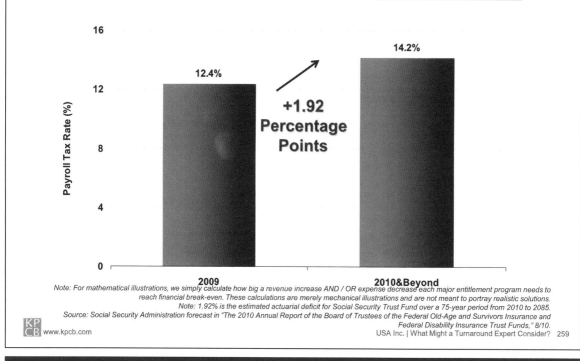

Note: For mathematical illustrations, we simply calculate how big a revenue increase AND / OR expense decrease each major entitlement program needs to reach financial break-even. These calculations are merely mechanical illustrations and are not meant to portray realistic solutions.
Note: 1.92% is the estimated actuarial deficit for Social Security Trust Fund over a 75-year period from 2010 to 2085.
Source: Social Security Administration forecast in "The 2010 Annual Report of the Board of Trustees of the Federal Old-Age and Survivors Insurance and Federal Disability Insurance Trust Funds," 8/10.

Good News: Mathematical Illustrations to Fix Social Security's Financial Problems Do Not Seem Drastic

In fact, when Social Security was nearing bankruptcy in 1983, a combination of moderate reforms led to 25 consecutive years of operating surpluses.

<u>Highlights of 1983 Social Security Reform</u>

1) Raised full retirement age to 67 by 2027 (from 65)*

2) Reduced annual benefits by 5% (via a 6-month delay in cost-of-living adjustment in 1983 & subsequent changes in benefit formulas and tax schemes) .

3) Raised Social Security tax rates by 2.3% (via an advancement in scheduled tax increase).

4) Made Social Security benefits (up to 50%) taxable income.

*Note: *For people born in 1937 or earlier, full retirement age (with 100% Social Security benefit) remained at 65. For people born after 1960, full retirement age was raised to 67. For people born between 1937 and 1960, the full retirement age progressively increases from 65 to 67. Source: Social Security Administration archive.*

Restructure Social Security: Policy Options #1 – Combining Raising Retirement Age + Reducing Benefits + Raising Tax Rates

Consider:

1) Increase retirement age by 0-9% ***and/or***

2) Reduce social security benefits by 0-12%? ***and/or***

3) Increase social security tax rate from 12.4% to 14.2%? ***and/or***

4) Combination of some / all of the above & more?

Restructure Social Security: Policy Options From the Congressional Budget Office (CBO) to Reduce Social Security Future Deficits By 1) Changing Tax Codes[1]

Policy Options		Future Deficit Reduction[2] (%)
Increase Payroll Tax Rate by …	2% gradually over a 20-year period	100%
	3% gradually over a 60-year period	83
	1% in 2012	50
Raise the Taxable Earnings Limit[3] to …	No limit, without Increasing benefits	150%
	No limit	100
	$250,000, without Increasing benefits	83
	90% of earnings	33
Impose 4% Tax on Earnings Above …	$106,800, without Increasing benefits	50%
	$250,000, without Increasing benefits	17

Note: 1) Benefits are adjusted as taxation is changed, unless specified otherwise 2) As % of the estimated present value of Social Security trust fund cumulative deficit in future 75 years. 3) Currently at $106,800

Source: CBO, "Social Security Options 2010."

Restructure Social Security: CBO's Policy Options to Reduce Social Security Future Deficits By 2) Changing Benefit Formula

Policy Options		Future Deficit Reduction (%)
Reduce Primary Insurance Amount[1] Factors ...	To Index Initial Benefits to Prices Rather Than Earnings	167 %
	By ~33% for top 2 tiers of earnings[3]	117
	By 15% for all tiers of earnings	83
	By 0.5% every year for all tiers of earnings	67
	By ~33% for the top tier of earnings	17
Index ...	Earnings in AIME[2] + Bend Points in PIA[1] to price	100%
	Bend Points in PIA[1] formula to price	83
	Earnings in AIME[2] formula to price	33
	Initial benefits to changes in life expectancy	33
Lower Initial Benefits[4] for ..	The top 70% of earners	83%
	The top 50% of earners	67

Note: 1) Primary Insurance Amount (PIA): the benefit a person would receive if he/she elects to begin receiving retirement benefits at his/her normal retirement age 2) Average Indexed Monthly Earnings (AIME): an average of monthly income received by a beneficiary during their work life 3) Currently there are 3 tiers of earnings in calculation of PIA – top tier = 15% of monthly earnings over $4,586; tier 2 = 32% of monthly earnings between $761 and $4,586; tier 3 = 90% of monthly earnings below $761 4) Benefits for newly qualified individuals. Source: CBO, "Social Security Options 2010."

Restructure Social Security: CBO's Policy Solutions to Reduce Social Security Future Deficits By 3) Raising Retirement Age / Lower Cost-of-Living Adjustment

Policy Options		Future Deficit Reduction (%)
Adjust Full Retirement Age	To 70	50%
	Index to life expectancy	33
	To 68	17
Adjust Cost-of-living Adjustment[1]	Reduce It by 0.5 Percentage Points	50%
	Base It on the Chained CPI for All Urban Consumers	33

Notes: 1) Cost-of-Living Adjustment (COLA): increases of Social Security's general benefit based on cost of living, as currently measured by CPI for Urban Wage Earners and Clerical Workers (CPI-W). Source: CBO, "Social Security Options 2010."

Restructure Social Security: Policy Options From Report of the National Commission on Fiscal Responsibility and Reform

Policy Options	Future Social Security Deficit Reduction[1]
Gradually reduce future benefit payments to high earners while increasing them for low earners by 2050	37%
Gradually increase taxable maximum to 90% of covered earnings by 2050	35%
Apply refined inflation measure (chained-CPI) to cost-of-living index	26%
Gradually increase retirement ages to 68 by 2050 / 69 by 2075	21%
Other[2]	--
Total Future Social Security Deficit Reduction	**116%[3]**

Note: 1) As % of the estimated present value of Social Security trust fund cumulative deficit in future 75 years. 2) Other measures include boosting benefit to oldest old retirees and covering newly hired state and local workers after 2020. 3) total deficit reduction does not equal to the sum of individual reductions owing to policy interplay. Source: National Commission on Fiscal Responsibility and Reform, "The Moment of Truth: Report of the National Commission on Fiscal Responsibility and Reform," 12/1/10.

Restructure Social Security: Declining USA Household Savings Rate Creates Challenge to Reducing Benefits as Americans are Under-Saving, Thus Limiting Financial Cushion

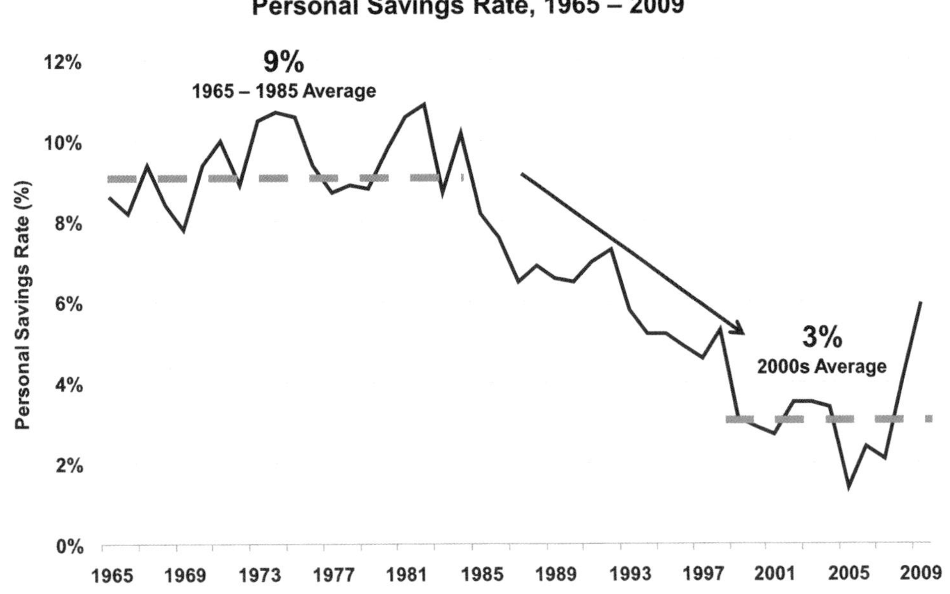

Note: Personal savings rate is calculated as the amount of savings divided by disposable income (income after taxes). Source: BEA.

Restructure Social Security: Especially High Unemployment Levels Also Create Challenge to Reducing Benefits

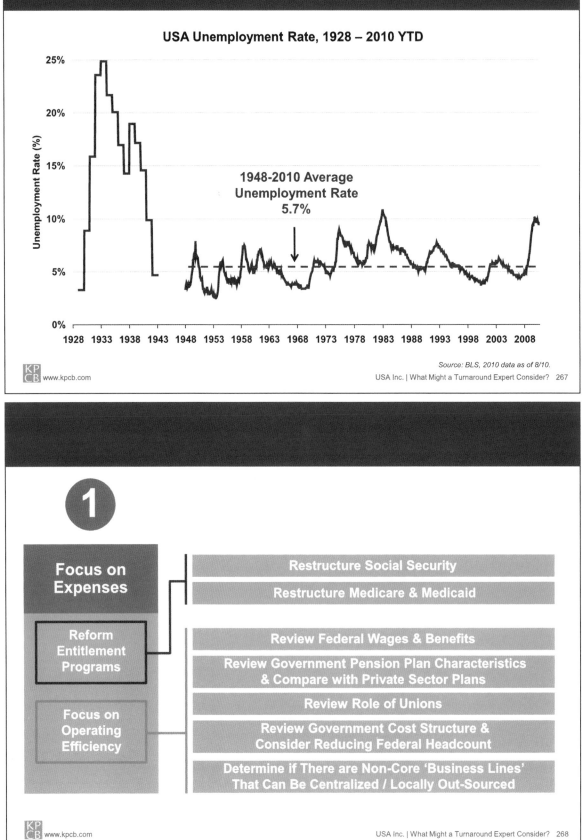

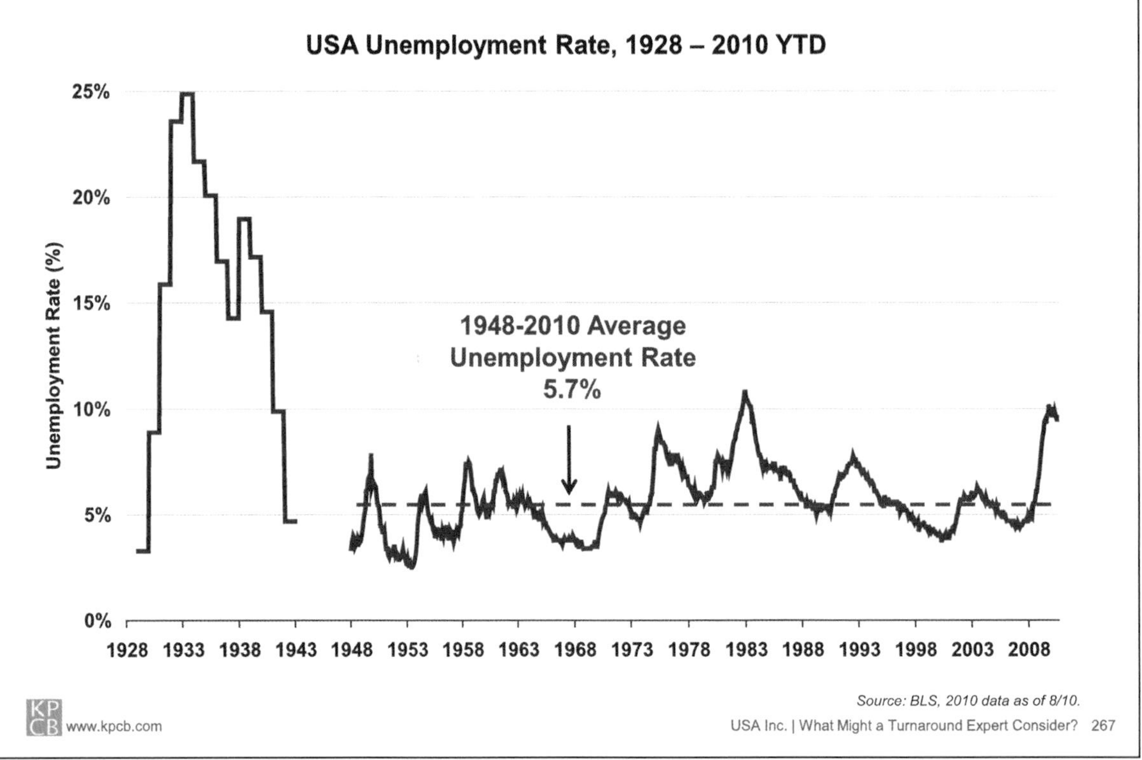

Source: BLS, 2010 data as of 8/10.

1

Focus on Expenses

- **Reform Entitlement Programs**
  - Restructure Social Security
  - Restructure Medicare & Medicaid
- **Focus on Operating Efficiency**
  - Review Federal Wages & Benefits
  - Review Government Pension Plan Characteristics & Compare with Private Sector Plans
  - Review Role of Unions
  - Review Government Cost Structure & Consider Reducing Federal Headcount
  - Determine if There are Non-Core 'Business Lines' That Can Be Centralized / Locally Out-Sourced

Restructure Medicare & Medicaid: Observations About America's Healthcare System

1) **High Expenses** – however measured, the costs are high: a) total dollars; b) share of GDP relative to other countries; c) cost relative to ability to pay (government, business, or individual), and

2) **Inefficiencies** – both the data and the insights of doctors, nurses, patients, and healthcare professionals identify opportunities for more efficient communication, data sharing and cost saving.

Restructure Medicare & Medicaid: Mathematical Challenge Related to Government Healthcare Programs Facing USA Inc. per CBO Forecasts

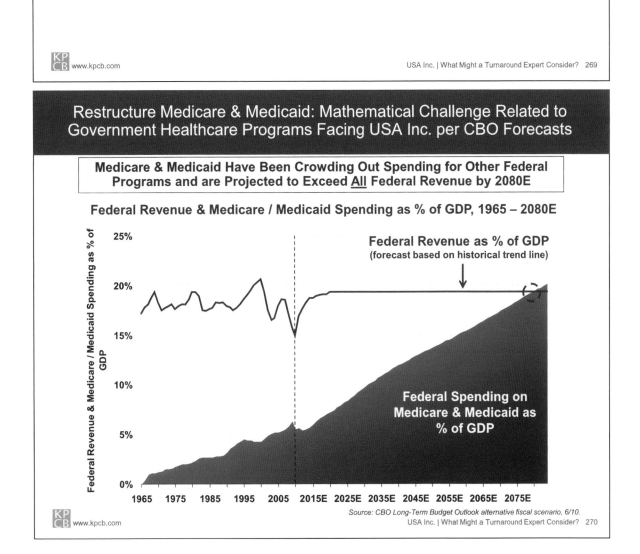

Medicare & Medicaid Have Been Crowding Out Spending for Other Federal Programs and are Projected to Exceed All Federal Revenue by 2080E

Federal Revenue & Medicare / Medicaid Spending as % of GDP, 1965 – 2080E

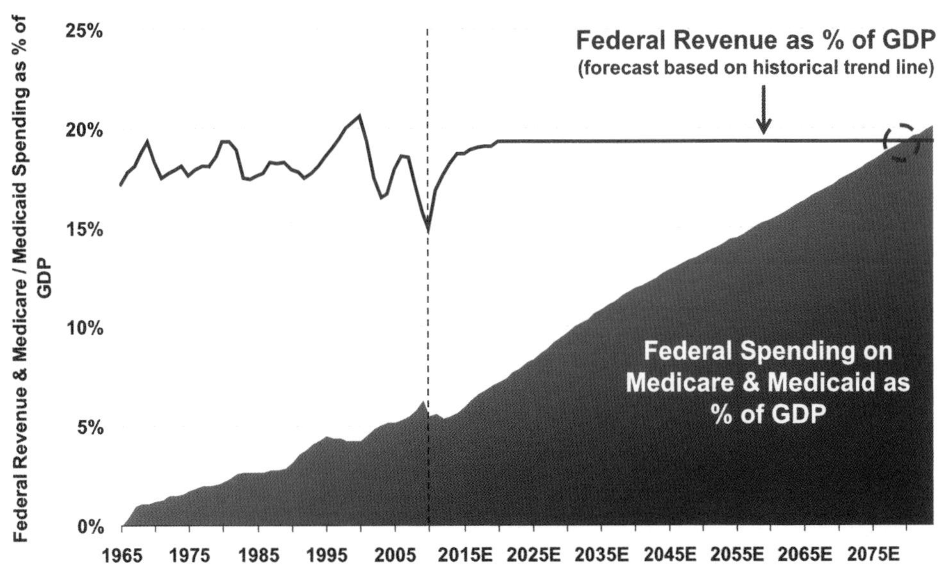

Source: CBO Long-Term Budget Outlook alternative fiscal scenario, 6/10.

Restructure Medicare & Medicaid: Variables in Restructuring Medicare & Medicaid to Reduce Material Impact on USA Inc.'s Expenses

<u>Mathematical Illustrations*</u> Slide 273–274

1) Medicare benefits – reduce them by 53% (or cap them)? ***or***

2) Medicare tax rate – increase it by 4 percentage points?

<u>Policy Options</u> Slide 275–328

1) Combination of mathematical illustrations – reduce benefits ***and/or*** increase taxes? ***and/or***

2) Isolate and address the drivers of medical cost inflation? ***and***

3) Improve efficiency / productivity of healthcare system? ***and***

4) Reduce services for some Medicaid beneficiaries? ***and***

5) Consider / implement CBO's 26 policy options that could reduce annual budget deficit by up to 38%?** ***and/or***

6) Consider / Implement National Commission on Fiscal Responsibility and Reform's medium- and long-term policy options***

*Note: *Each mathematical illustration would bring Medicare Part A into long-term (75-year) actuarial balance. There is no mathematical illustration for Medicaid or Medicare Part B & D as there's no 'dedicated' funding.*
***See: CBO, "Budget Options, Volume 1: Health Care," 12/2008.*
****See: National Commission on Fiscal Responsibility and Reform, "Co-Chairs' Proposal," 11/10/10.*

Restructure Medicare & Medicaid: Mathematical Illustrations*

<u>Mathematical Illustrations*</u>

1) Medicare benefits – reduce / cap them?

or

2) Medicare tax rate – increase it?

*Note: *For mathematical illustrations, we simply calculate how big a revenue increase AND / OR expense decrease each major entitlement program needs to reach financial break-even. These calculations are merely mechanical illustrations and are not meant to portray realistic solutions.*

Restructure Medicare & Medicaid: Mathematical Illustration #1 – Reduce Medicare Benefits* By 53%

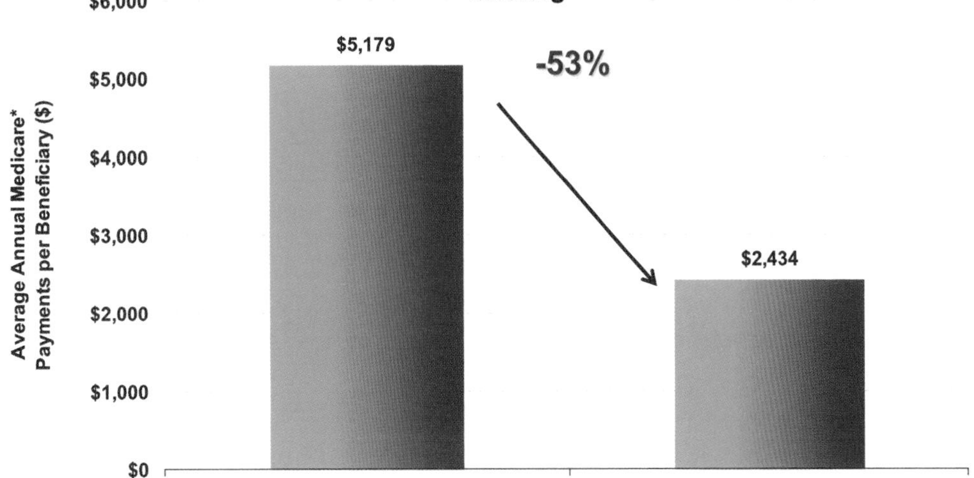

Note: For mathematical illustrations, we simply calculate how big a revenue increase AND / OR expense decrease each major entitlement program needs to reach financial break-even. These calculations are merely mechanical illustrations and are not meant to portray realistic solutions.

*Source: Dept. of Health & Human Services forecast in "2009 Annual Report of the Boards of Trustees of the Federal Hospital Insurance and Federal Supplementary Medical Insurance Trust Funds," 5/09. *Note that data presented here are limited to Medicare Part A (Hospital Insurance) Trust Fund. Medicare Part B (Medical Insurance) and Part D (Prescription Drug Benefits) are primarily funded via insurance premiums and general tax revenue transfers. Note also that data presented here are estimates prior to PPACA (2009 healthcare reform).*

Restructure Medicare & Medicaid: Mathematical Illustration #2 – Increase Medicare Tax Rate From 2.9% to 6.8%

Sizing the problem:
It would take massive (3.9 percentage points) payroll tax hikes on individual and businesses to address the Medicare* funding shortfall

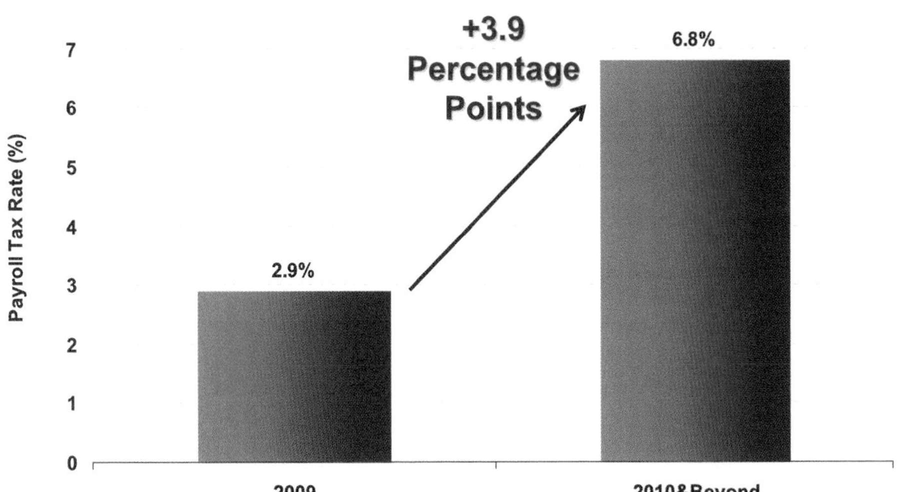

Note: For mathematical illustrations, we simply calculate how big a revenue increase AND / OR expense decrease each major entitlement program needs to reach financial break-even. These calculations are merely mechanical illustrations and are not meant to portray realistic solutions.

*Source: Dept. of Health & Human Services forecast in "2009 Annual Report of the Boards of Trustees of the Federal Hospital Insurance and Federal Supplementary Medical Insurance Trust Funds," 5/09. *Note that data presented here are limited to Medicare Part A (Hospital Insurance) Trust Fund. Medicare Part B (Medical Insurance) and Part D (Prescription Drug Benefits) are primarily funded via insurance premiums and general tax revenue transfers. Note also that data presented here are estimates prior to PPACA (2009 healthcare reform).*

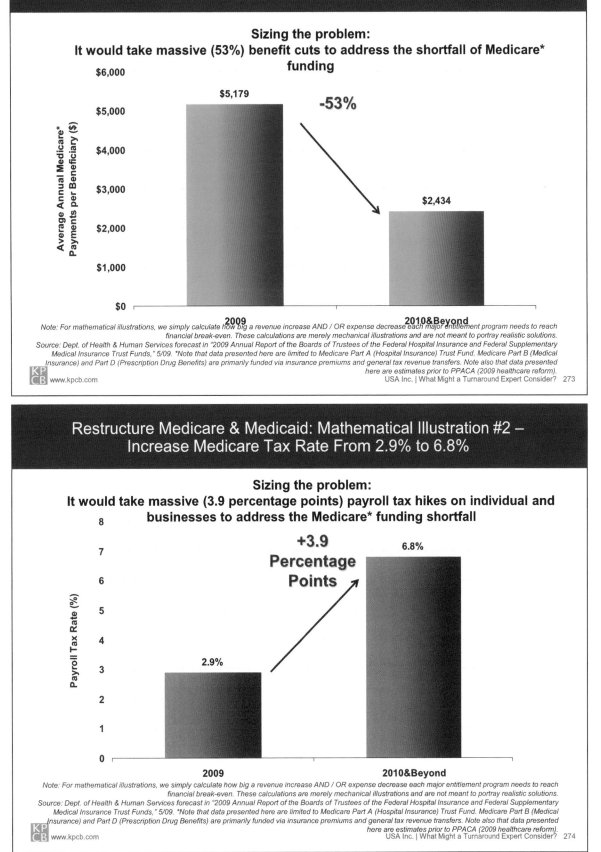

Restructure Medicare & Medicaid: Policy Options

Policy Options

1) Combination of mathematical solutions – reduce benefits and / or increase taxes? ***and/or***

2) Isolate and address the drivers of rising healthcare costs? ***and***

3) Improve efficiency / productivity of healthcare system? ***and***

4) Reduce services for some Medicaid beneficiaries? ***and***

5) Consider / implement CBO's 26 policy options that could reduce annual budget deficit by up to 38%? ***and/or***

6) Consider / Implement National Commission on Fiscal Responsibility and Reform's medium- and long-term policy options?

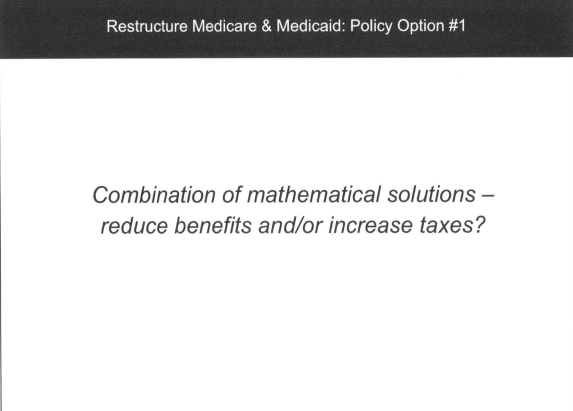

Restructure Medicare & Medicaid: Policy Option #1

Combination of mathematical solutions – reduce benefits and/or increase taxes?

Restructure Medicare & Medicaid: Combination of Reducing Benefits (Including Covered Lives) & / or Raising Taxes

Consider:

1) Reduce Medicare benefits by 53%? ***and/or***

2) Increase Medicare tax rate from 2.9% to 6.8%? ***and/or***

3) Some combination of all / some the above

However you look at it, this math is draconian. A 53% cut in Medicare benefits and / or more than doubling taxes are unrealistic. The situation for Medicaid is even worse, as Medicaid has no dedicated funding source.

Neither Medicare nor Medicaid has yet fully faced up to the crisis and reform that Social Security experienced in the early 1980s.

Restructure Medicare & Medicaid: Policy Option #2

Isolate and address the drivers of rising healthcare costs

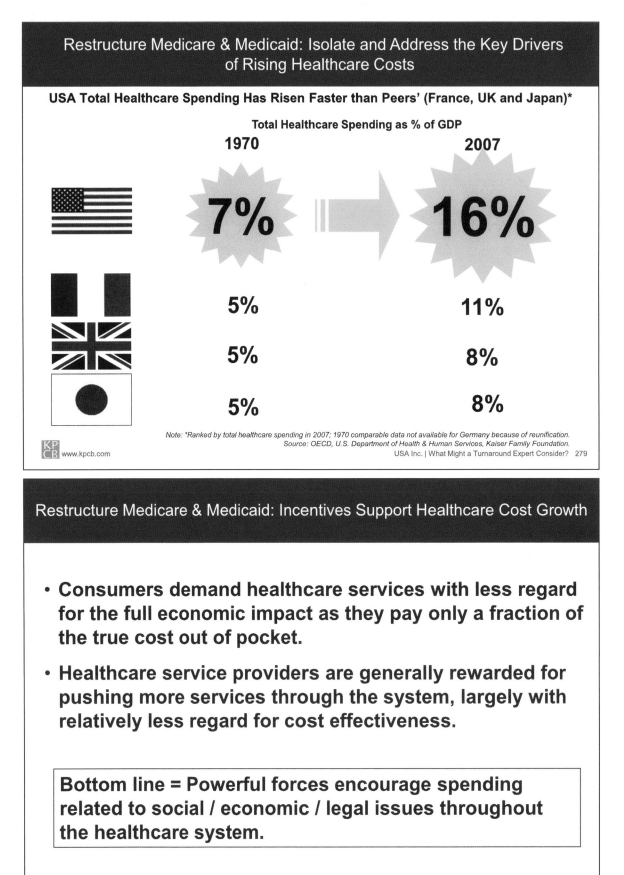

Restructure Medicare & Medicaid: Isolate and Address the Key Drivers of Rising Healthcare Costs

USA Total Healthcare Spending Has Risen Faster than Peers' (France, UK and Japan)*

Total Healthcare Spending as % of GDP

	1970	2007
USA	7%	16%
France	5%	11%
UK	5%	8%
Japan	5%	8%

*Note: *Ranked by total healthcare spending in 2007; 1970 comparable data not available for Germany because of reunification.*
Source: OECD, U.S. Department of Health & Human Services, Kaiser Family Foundation.

Restructure Medicare & Medicaid: Incentives Support Healthcare Cost Growth

- **Consumers demand healthcare services with less regard for the full economic impact as they pay only a fraction of the true cost out of pocket.**
- **Healthcare service providers are generally rewarded for pushing more services through the system, largely with relatively less regard for cost effectiveness.**

Bottom line = Powerful forces encourage spending related to social / economic / legal issues throughout the healthcare system.

Source: Doug Simpson, Morgan Stanley Healthcare Research.

Restructure Medicare & Medicaid: Social + Economic + Legal Factors Drive Incentives to Spend

1) ***Social*** – Growing + aging population (with related disproportionate spending on end-of-life care) and unhealthy lifestyles.
2) ***Economic*** – Healthcare service providers have financial incentives to perform more services and drive revenue while consumers often have little incentive to manage incremental cost.
3) ***Legal*** - Rising overhead from defensive medicine (to avoid lawsuits) and from regulatory compliance costs.

Source: Morgan Stanley Healthcare Research.

Restructure Medicare & Medicaid: Social Forces that Push Up Healthcare Spending

1) Growing and Aging Population
2) Unhealthy Lifestyles
3) Possible Solutions

1) Growing and Aging Population

2) Unhealthy Lifestyles

3) Possible Solutions

Restructure Medicare & Medicaid: Social Factors— USA is Aging…13% of Americans Over 65 Years Old, Up from 5% in 1930

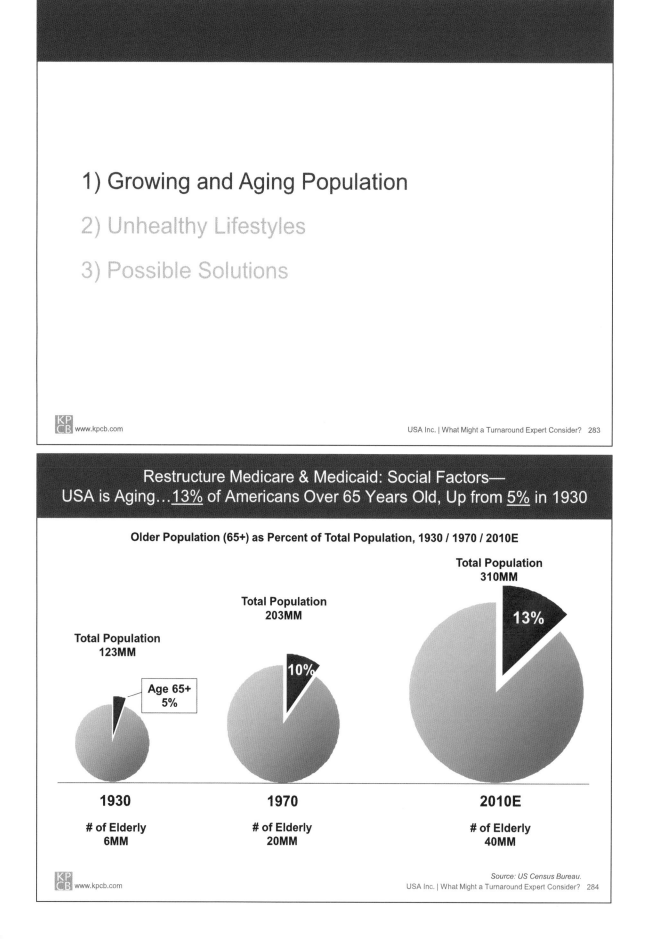

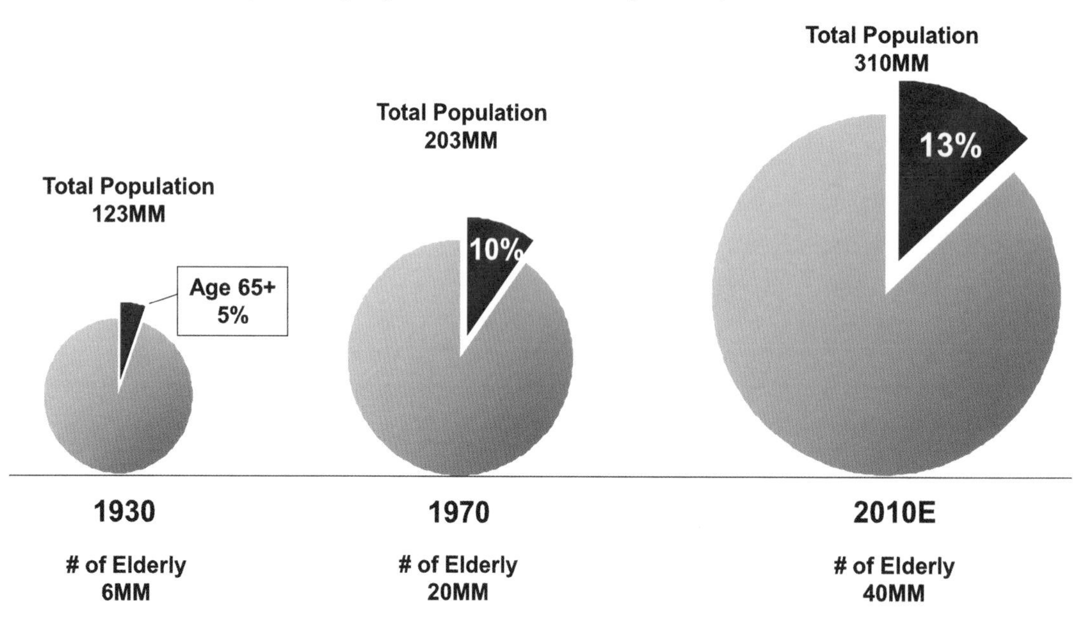

Source: US Census Bureau.

Restructure Medicare & Medicaid: Social Factors— Older People Spend 2x More per Year on Healthcare than Younger Americans

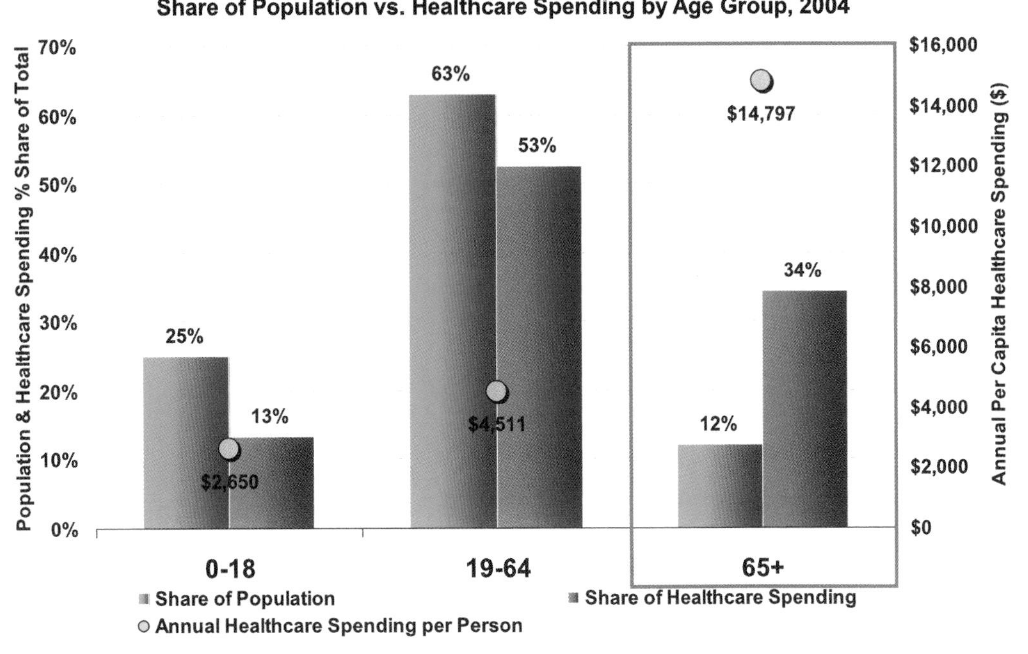

Source: Dept. of Health & Human Services, US Census Bureau.

Restructure Medicare & Medicaid: Social Factors— ~28% of Annual Medicare Spending Geared Toward End-of-Life Care (Last 12 Months)

2008 Medicare Total Benefit Expense $363B

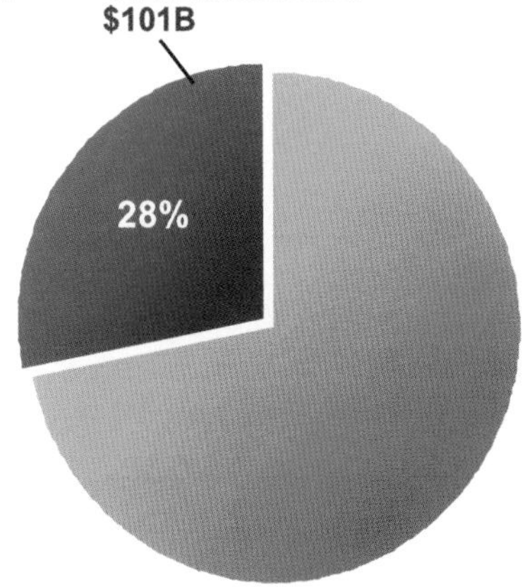

- **People 65+ spent $14,797 per year on healthcare on average in 2004, 3x what working-age people (19-64) spend.**
- It's notable that ~28% of average Medicare recipient spending occurs in the final year of life and 12% occurs in the final two months of life.

Sources: CMS, Medpac, Report to the Congress: Medicare Payment Policy, 3/10

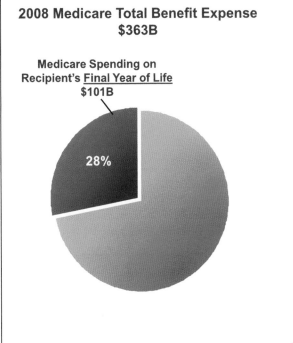

1) Growing and Aging Population

2) Unhealthy Lifestyles

3) Possible Solutions

Restructure Medicare & Medicaid: Social Factors— 32% of Americans Considered Obese in 2008, Up from 15% in 1990…

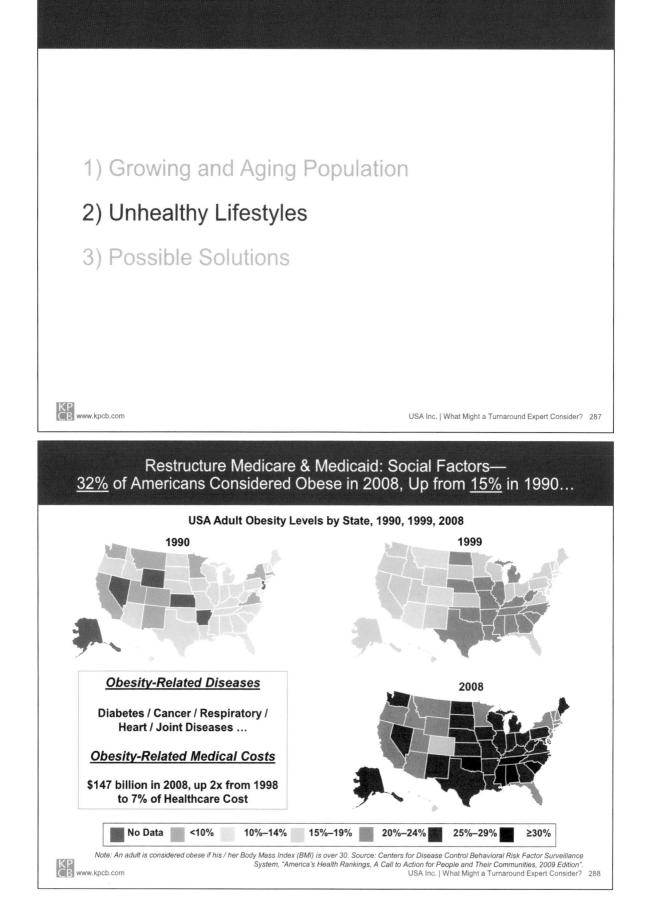

USA Adult Obesity Levels by State, 1990, 1999, 2008

1990

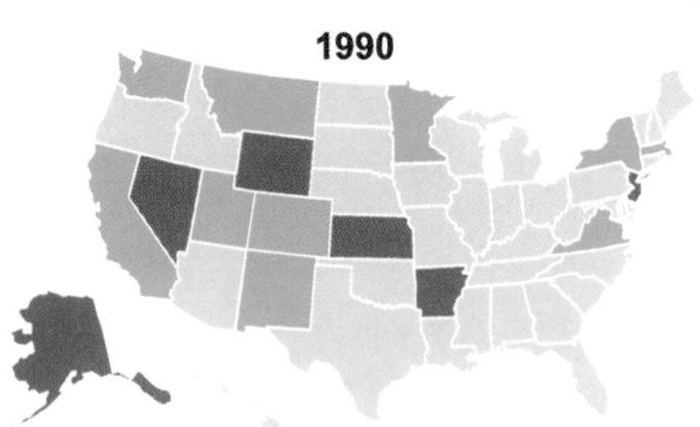

1999

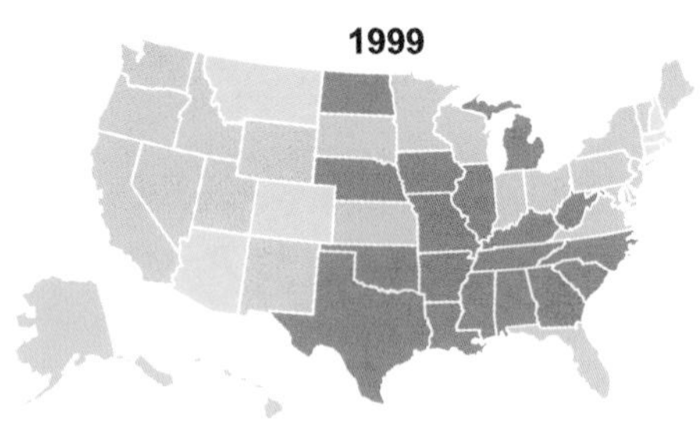

Obesity-Related Diseases

Diabetes / Cancer / Respiratory / Heart / Joint Diseases …

Obesity-Related Medical Costs

$147 billion in 2008, up 2x from 1998 to 7% of Healthcare Cost

2008

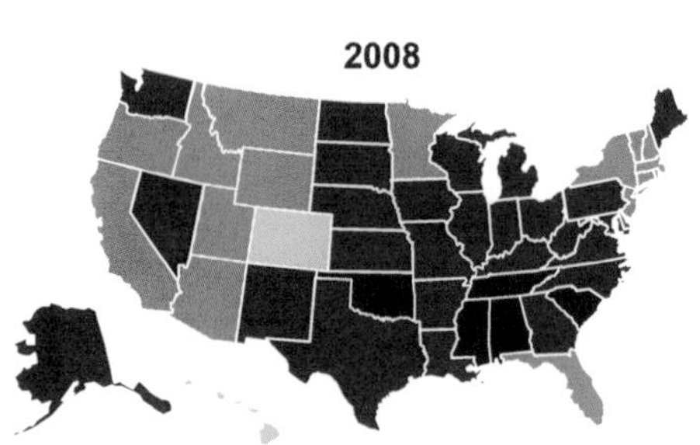

No Data | <10% | 10%–14% | 15%–19% | 20%–24% | 25%–29% | ≥30%

Note: An adult is considered obese if his / her Body Mass Index (BMI) is over 30. Source: Centers for Disease Control Behavioral Risk Factor Surveillance System, "America's Health Rankings, A Call to Action for People and Their Communities, 2009 Edition".

Restructure Medicare & Medicaid: Social Factors—Rising Obesity Pushes Up Healthcare Cost

- **An estimated 7% of $2.1 trillion healthcare costs (including those linked to diabetes, cancer, heart / respiratory / joint diseases) were related to obesity in 2008. By comparison, that's more than all corporate income tax revenue that year.**

Note: Nearly half of all people in the U.S. with European ancestry carry a variant of the fat mass and obesity associated (FTO) gene, vs. 25% of U.S. Hispanics, 15% of African Americans and 15% of Asian Americans, per UCLA.
Source: "Annual Medical Spending Attributable To Obesity: Payer- And Service-Specific Estimates." Eric A. Finkelstein, Justin G. Trogdon, Joel W. Cohen, and William Dietz. Health Affairs , July 27, 2009.

1) Growing and Aging Population

2) Unhealthy Lifestyles

3) Possible Solutions

Restructure Medicare & Medicaid: Social Factors—Possible Solutions Boost Healthcare Education & Incentives to Drive Better Choices

- **Emphasize on disease prevention and wellness.**
  - Education and information
  - Highlight health risk associated with certain behaviors and lifestyles
  - Financial incentives for healthy habits
  - Create social programs to champion healthy lifestyles and consumption
  - Subsidize healthy foods for lower income population
- **Discourage unhealthy behavior and consumption.**
  - Penalize poor health choices (create new incentives based upon lessons learned from higher life insurance fees for smokers and car insurance fees for speeders)
  - Consider additional / new taxes on cigarettes, non-diet sodas, etc.

Source: Morgan Stanley Healthcare Research.

Restructure Medicare & Medicaid: Economic Forces that Push Up Healthcare Spending

1) *Open access healthcare plans can increase access to care (via greater choices of care providers), but can also increase cost.*
2) *Consumers and providers are not always incentivized to constrain their healthcare costs.*
3) *Even when appropriate, poor information & lack of price transparency complicate comparison shopping for consumers.*
4) *Advances in medical technology drive demand and costs.*

Restructure Medicare & Medicaid: Economic Factors—Rise in Usage of "Open Access" Healthcare Plans Makes It Harder to Control Patient Choices…Subsequently, Cost of Care Increases

Societal demand for less restrictive health insurance has driven a gradual switch to open access plans. These plans offer consumers greater choices of medical providers, but at higher costs.

Share of Tightly Managed vs. Open Access Healthcare Plans in USA, 1988 - 2008

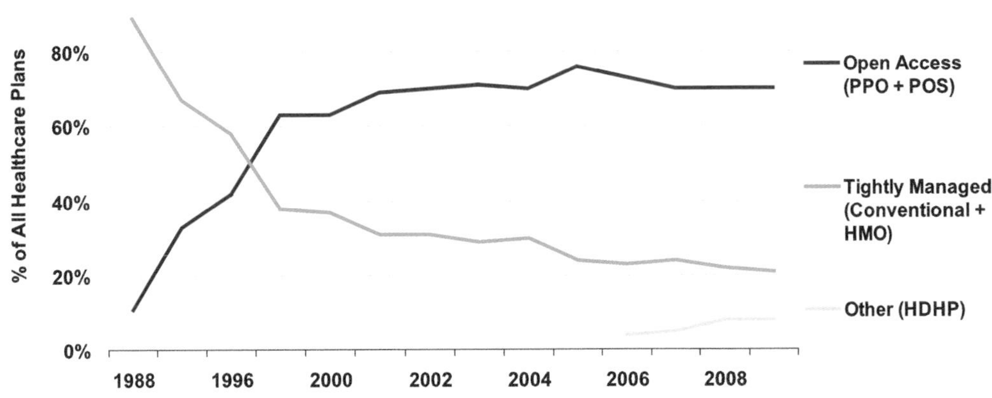

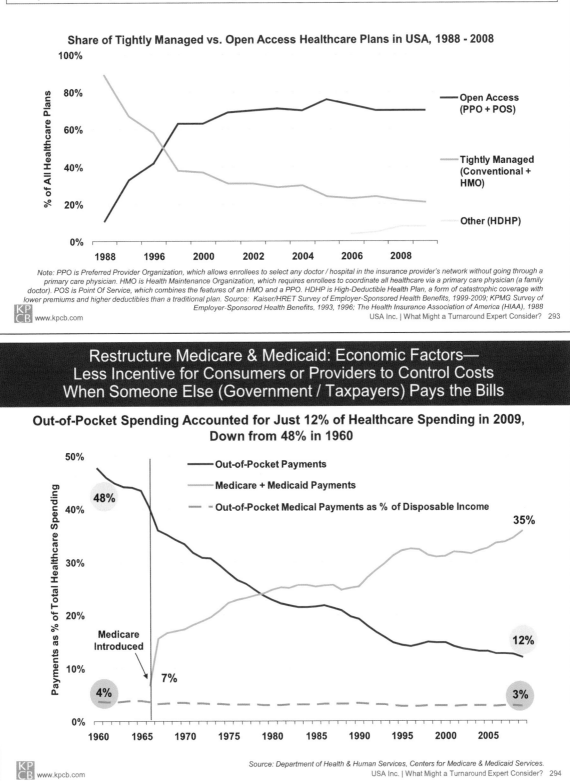

Note: PPO is Preferred Provider Organization, which allows enrollees to select any doctor / hospital in the insurance provider's network without going through a primary care physician. HMO is Health Maintenance Organization, which requires enrollees to coordinate all healthcare via a primary care physician (a family doctor). POS is Point Of Service, which combines the features of an HMO and a PPO. HDHP is High-Deductible Health Plan, a form of catastrophic coverage with lower premiums and higher deductibles than a traditional plan. Source: Kaiser/HRET Survey of Employer-Sponsored Health Benefits, 1999-2009; KPMG Survey of Employer-Sponsored Health Benefits, 1993, 1996; The Health Insurance Association of America (HIAA), 1988

Restructure Medicare & Medicaid: Economic Factors—Less Incentive for Consumers or Providers to Control Costs When Someone Else (Government / Taxpayers) Pays the Bills

Out-of-Pocket Spending Accounted for Just 12% of Healthcare Spending in 2009, Down from 48% in 1960

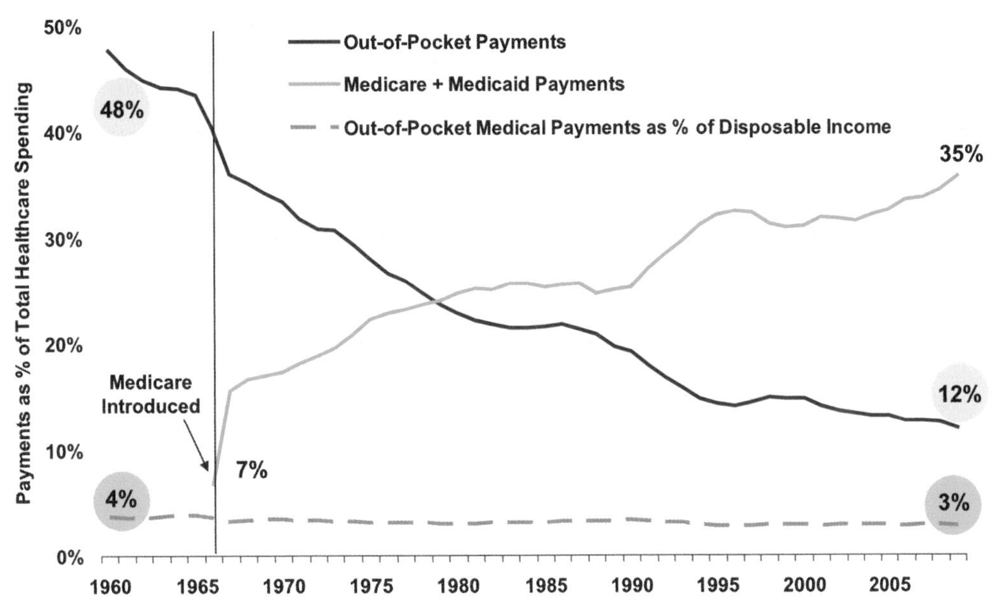

Source: Department of Health & Human Services, Centers for Medicare & Medicaid Services.

Restructure Medicare & Medicaid: Economic Factors – Employer and Government Funding System Separates Consumers from True Costs of Healthcare

- **When one doesn't pay directly and gets an expensive good / service for free (or well below cost), one tends to consume more – it's basic supply and demand economics.**
- **Count up the subsidies:**
  - **Medicaid:** 47 million (24MM children / 12MM low-income adults / 7MM disabled / 4MM elderly) Americans (15% of population) each received $6,872 in taxpayer funds, on average, for healthcare in 2008 through Medicaid. That $6,872 equals ~19% of annual per-capita income for Americans.
  - **Medicare:** 45 million elderly Americans (15% of population) averaged $7,991 per person for healthcare in 2008 ($4,875 for hospital care; $3,116 for medical insurance and prescription drugs). That equals ~23% of annual per capita income.
  - **Private Market:** 157mm Americans with private health coverage (subsidized by employers) in 2008 paid just 16% of the total premium cost themselves for single coverage and 27% for family coverage. In effect, that represented tax-free "earnings" of $3,951 for singles or $9,256 for families (not including the tax savings on their personal premium contributions).

Source: Department of Health & Human Services, Centers for Medicare & Medicaid Services.

Restructure Medicare & Medicaid: Economic Factors—Healthcare Providers Are Rewarded for Driving Revenue

- **While striving to provide the best care possible, healthcare providers tend to have financial / legal / societal incentives to provide more care, all else equal.**
- Reimbursement for providers is generally volume-based (e.g., more procedures generate more revenue for care providers), though there are efforts to increasingly focus on quality.
- Unlike car buyers, for example, who often disregard a dealer's maxed-out model and choose only the features that are important to them and what they can afford, healthcare buyers tend to buy all the "features" as: 1) buyers (patients in this case) are typically not medical experts, so they defer to doctors / care providers for decisions; and 2) buyers only bear a small portion of the costs as someone else (employer or government) is paying for the features.

Restructure Medicare & Medicaid: Economic Factors— Rising Healthcare Costs Disproportionately Borne by Employers and Individuals

Over the last few decades, private payors (employer-sponsored health insurance plans) have consistently paid more than government payors (Medicare / Medicaid) and have, in effect, subsidized government reimbursement.

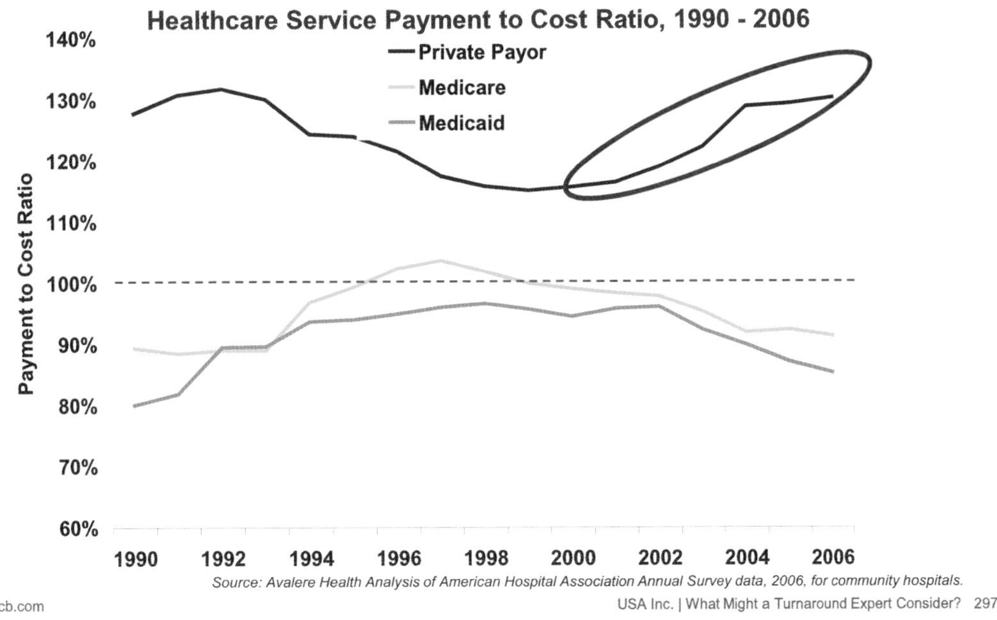

Source: Avalere Health Analysis of American Hospital Association Annual Survey data, 2006, for community hospitals.

Restructure Medicare & Medicaid: Differential Payment Rates Can Create a Negative Cycle Leading to Erosion of Private Healthcare Coverage and Higher Entitlement Spending

1. Providers Charge Higher Prices to Private Market than to Government Market

2. Cost Shifting onto the Private Market

3. Higher Private Market Cost Trend

4. Higher Health Insurance Premiums

5. Employers/ Consumers Drop Insurance Coverage

6. Increasing Number of Uninsured

7. Increasing Use of Medicaid / Medicare

8. Government Reimbursement Pressure Rises

9. Government Lowers Reimbursement Rate to Providers

Source: Doug Simpson, Morgan Stanley Healthcare Research.

Restructure Medicare & Medicaid: Economic Factors— Reimbursement Reform Is Easier Said than Done Owing to Political Sensitivity…

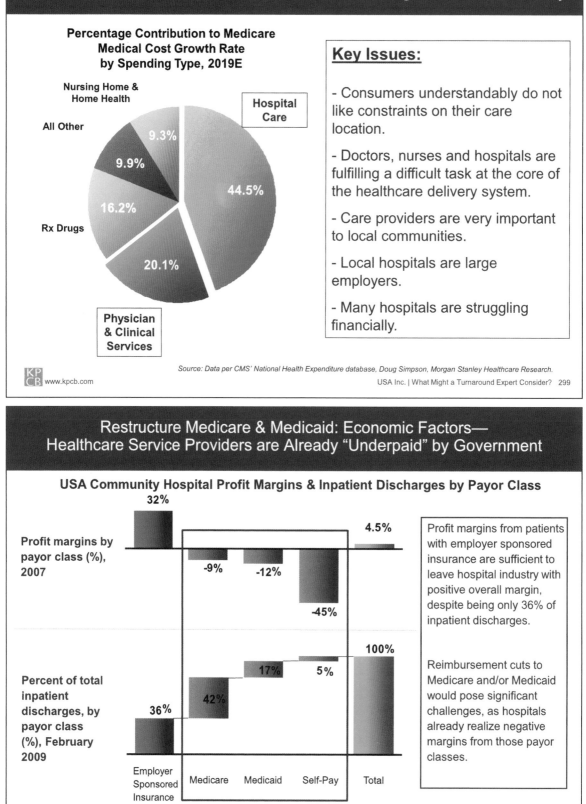

Percentage Contribution to Medicare Medical Cost Growth Rate by Spending Type, 2019E

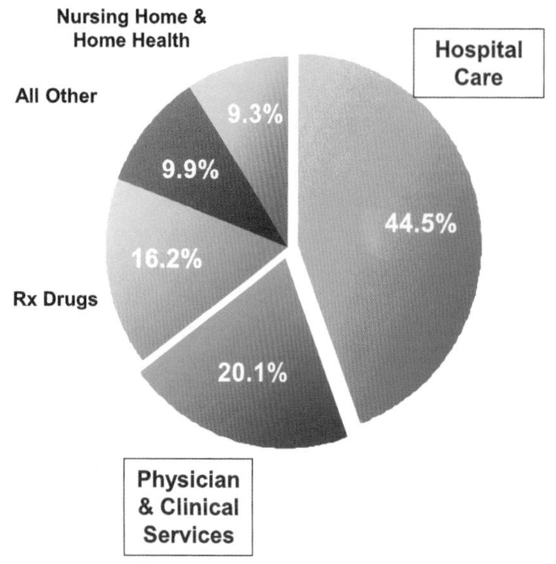

Key Issues:

- Consumers understandably do not like constraints on their care location.
- Doctors, nurses and hospitals are fulfilling a difficult task at the core of the healthcare delivery system.
- Care providers are very important to local communities.
- Local hospitals are large employers.
- Many hospitals are struggling financially.

Source: Data per CMS' National Health Expenditure database, Doug Simpson, Morgan Stanley Healthcare Research.

Restructure Medicare & Medicaid: Economic Factors— Healthcare Service Providers are Already "Underpaid" by Government

USA Community Hospital Profit Margins & Inpatient Discharges by Payor Class

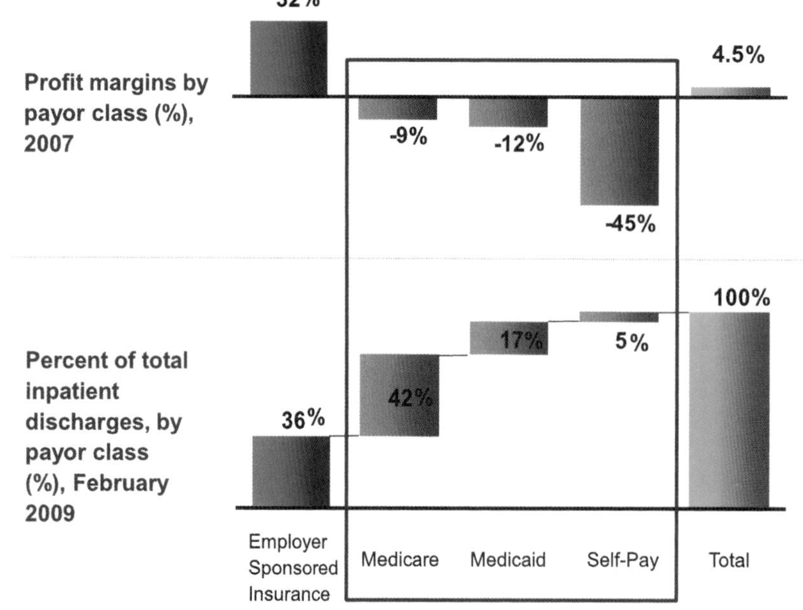

Profit margins from patients with employer sponsored insurance are sufficient to leave hospital industry with positive overall margin, despite being only 36% of inpatient discharges.

Reimbursement cuts to Medicare and/or Medicaid would pose significant challenges, as hospitals already realize negative margins from those payor classes.

Source: Avalere Health analysis of American Hospital Association Annual Survey data, 2007, for community hospitals. Morgan Stanley Healthcare Research.

Restructure Medicare & Medicaid: Economic Factors— Poor Information & Lack of Price Transparency Make it Harder for Consumers to "Comparison Shop"

Patients are at a healthcare information disadvantage in two respects[1]:

- **Lack of transparency:**
  - It's **harder for consumers to compare prices** of healthcare services from different healthcare providers than in other consumer markets given the complexity of healthcare market.
  - With employer- / government-subsidized insurance, many patients are **'locked in' with their insurance plans** that do not incentivize "shopping around."
- **Knowledge gap:**
  - Unlike other markets where consumers tend to use their own information and preferences, consumers **depend more on the advice and guidance of physicians** or other healthcare suppliers.
  - Unlike other "merchandise," **healthcare is literally of life-and-death importance to consumers, making risk aversion – and price insensitivity – higher**. This price insensitivity is exacerbated because the consumer, in effect, gets it at a discounted price anyway.

Source: 1) Accounting for the cost of US healthcare, McKinsey Global Institute

Restructure Medicare & Medicaid: Economic Factors— Consumers Increasingly Demand Expensive Treatment and Are Able to Pay for it With Government Subsidies

Total High-End Surgeries up <u>50x</u> from 1970-2004, Driven by Medical Advancements + Consumer Ability to Spend Assisted by Government Payments

	# of Patients (Aged 50+) Undergoing Advanced Procedures in USA		Typical Costs per Procedure ($)
	1970	**2004**	
Coronary Procedures			
Angioplasty / Stent Implantation	<20,000	1.1 million	$12,000
Pacemaker / ICD[1]	<10,000	350,000	$15-34,000
Bypass	<10,000	220,000	$28,000
Dialysis Procedures	<10,000	480,000	$24-72,000 per year
Joint Replacement Procedures			
Hip	<20,000	390,000	$12,500
Knee	--	440,000	$12,500

Note: 1) ICD is Implantable Cardioverter Defibrillator, which is similar to a pacemaker but for a heart rhythm that beats too fast. Cost of procedure approximated by Medicare reimbursement.

Restructure Medicare & Medicaid: Economic Factors— Unconstrained Access to Medical Technology Increases Cost of Care…

- **Researchers generally agree that advances in medical technology have contributed to rising US Health Spending**[1]
- Medical technology affects the costs of care through several "mechanisms of action"[2]
  - **New treatments** for previously untreatable terminal conditions
  - Major advances in clinical **ability to treat previously untreatable acute conditions**
  - **New procedures** for discovering and treating secondary diseases
  - **New indications** for a treatment over time
  - Ongoing, **incremental improvements** in existing capabilities
  - **Major advances** or the cumulative effect of incremental gains extending clinical practice to conditions once regarded beyond its boundaries
- **Very expensive, high-end medical procedures (such as dialysis and heart bypass) – which can easily cost as much as the average annual income of an American – are increasingly <u>60-70% subsidized by taxpayer dollars</u>.**

Source: 1) "How Changes in Medical Technology Affect Healthcare Costs," Kaiser Family Foundation, March 2007; 2) Richard A. Retting, "Medical Innovation Duels Cost Containment," Health Affairs (Summer 1994).

Opportunity for Two Mutually Reinforcing Cycles: <u>Information</u> + Incentives…

- More widespread adoption of healthcare information technology, in particular clinical decision support software, should yield better information and provider decisions.
  - Healthcare is at the cusp of leveraging decision-support technology after historically lagging other industries.
  - Opportunity to develop best practices to improve patient care and outcomes and reduce medical errors and costs.
  - More evidence-based care could help to narrow the variation in practice norms
  - The American Recovery and Reinvestment Act of 2009 provided approximately $19 billion for Medicare and Medicaid Health IT incentives.
- Medpac summarizes the opportunities and issues succinctly.
  - "Drivers of investment in IT include the promise of quality and efficiency gains. Barriers include the cost and complexity of IT implementation, which often necessitates significant work process and cultural changes. Certain characteristics of the health care market—including payment policies that reward volume rather than quality, and a fragmented delivery system—can also pose barriers to IT adoption."

Source: Morgan Stanley Healthcare Research.

…Opportunity for Two Mutually Reinforcing Cycles: Information + **Incentives**

- Improving incentives for providers and consumers is also critical.
  - Providers need appropriate incentives to improve quality of care and lower costs.
  - Drivers include more widespread adoption of bundled payments and accountable care organizations.
  - Tort reform could play an important role.
  - Consumers need to take more responsibility for their own health and to utilize the healthcare system appropriately.
  - Appropriate social and financial incentives are key.

Source: Morgan Stanley Healthcare Research.

Restructure Medicare & Medicaid: Economic Factors–Possible Solutions

1) Cost-Sharing and/or

2) Reimbursement Reform and/or

3) Improving Cost & Quality Transparency and/or

4) Deploy Cost-Benefit Analysis for Medical Technology Spending

Restructure Medicare & Medicaid: Economic Factors–Possible Solutions 1) Cost-Sharing

- **Cost-sharing can help control demand for a portion of healthcare by creating incentives for consumers to shop for most cost-effective treatments (although those benefits would be somewhat mitigated by the skew in health spending toward high users).**
- Once again, a Math Problem: Consider a routine physician office visit in which a provider suggests and / or patient requests various tests, procedures, etc.
  - Patient #1 covered by a plan with a $20 co-pay (i.e., a flat fee regardless of the level or intensity of care performed during the visit)
  - Patient #2 covered by a plan with a 10% co-insurance for in-network care (i.e., responsible for 10% of the aggregate billed charges)
  - Clearly, patient #2 will become more sensitive to necessity and cost of care beyond a level of $200 of total healthcare services
  - Note that deductibles drive similar dynamic as a co-pay: once the deductible is met, the member has little or no “skin in the game”
- Only 14-18% of employer-sponsored health insurance plans use pro-rata cost sharing (i.e. co-insurance in example #2 above). Most (77%) insurance plans only use a co-pay (in example #1), which gives consumers little incentive to shop the most cost-effective treatment path.

Source: Kaiser/HRET Survey of Employer-Sponsored Health Benefits, 2009

Restructure Medicare & Medicaid: Economic Factors–Possible Solutions 2) Reimbursement Reform

Reimbursement reform could help shift drivers of payment from quantity of care to quality of care. The following list provides a few options to consider.

- Bundled Payments: Providers get a fixed budget to treat an episode of care (i.e. a broken hip). Exceeding the budget means providers absorb additional costs; staying under it lets provider benefit from savings.
  - Examples: PROMETHEUS Payment System[1], Medicare Acute Care Episode Demonstration[2]
- Global payment system[3] (i.e., capitation): Providers are paid up-front to provide care that their patient receives over a period, incentivizing them to manage costs and quality. This global payment is adjusted periodically to reward accessible and high-quality care.
- Pay for performance[4]: Reimbursement for care providers varies, based on various quality and efficiency measures such as discharge rate and readmission rate.
- Accountable Care Organizations (ACOs): Provider groups accept responsibility for the cost and quality of care for a specific population of patients[5]
  - The recently enacted *Patient Protection and Affordable Care Act* includes regulations supporting the creation of Accountable Care Organizations
  - Other models often discussed to improve coordination / efficiency and reduce costs : 1) integrated delivery systems; 2) multispecialty group practices; 3) physician-hospital organizations; 4) independent practice associations; 5) virtual physician organizations

Source: 1) Cutting Healthcare Costs by Putting Doctors on a Budget, Time 1) Adopted in Rockford, IL in Jan 2010 2) Medicare Demonstration Project Overviews, www.cms.gov/demoprojects 3) Recommendations of the Special Commission on the Healthcare Payment, Commonwealth of Massachusetts 4) Pay for Performance Incentive Programs in Healthcare , Geoffrey Baker 5) How the Center for Medicare & Medicaid Innovation Should Test Accountable Care Organizations, Stephen Shortell, Lawrence P. Casalino and Elliott S. Fisher for Health Affairs, July 2010

Restructure Medicare & Medicaid: Economic Factors–Possible Solutions 3) Improving Cost & Quality Transparency

- **Improving cost and quality transparency of healthcare services could help doctors and patients make more informed decisions for each situation.**
- **Though enhancing competition and price transparency in healthcare is not easy,[1] new models for encouraging "comparison shopping" are emerging:**
  - Castlight Health, a start-up financed by venture capitalists and the Cleveland Clinic, is working to build a search engine for healthcare prices[2]
  - Other services beginning to publish price information: Thomson Reuters, Change: healthcare, and health insurers (e.g., the Aetna Navigator)[2]
- **A 2007 study by Deloitte proposes a "Price Transparency Checklist for States":**
  - provide prices for services that matter to consumers
  - make it easy to understand
  - keep care providers, insurance & pharmaceutical companies engaged and informed
  - provide price and quality measures
  - keep expanding price transparency initiatives
  - maintain methodological rigor
  - promote access and use of price information
  - evaluate impact and ROI

Source: 1) The Market for Medical Care: Why You Don't Know the Price; Why You Don't Know about Quality; And What Can Be Done About It, by Devon M. Herrick and John C. Goodman, March 12, 2007; 2) "Bringing Comparison Shopping to the Doctor's Office," The New York Times, June 10, 2010; 3) Healthcare Price Transparency: A Strategic Perspective for State Government Leaders, by Deloitte Center for Health Solutions, 2007

Restructure Medicare & Medicaid: Economic Factors–Possible Solutions 4) Deploy Cost-Benefit Analysis for Medical Technology Spending

- **Deploying cost-benefit analysis for medical technology spending can help ensure we are spending resources wisely.**
- **Directly measuring the impact of new technology on total healthcare spending – and its true value – is very difficult[1]**
- The Kaiser Foundation outlines some of the more common policy suggestions for dealing with this driver of costs:
  - Cost-effectiveness analysis (i.e., comparative effectiveness)
  - Rationing (unlikely to be adopted owing to political sensitivity), regulation, budget-driven constraints (used by other countries but generally not popular in the U.S.)
  - Market-based rationing (consumer-driven healthcare, pay-for-performance, information technology)

Source: 1) "How Changes in Medical Technology Affect Healthcare Costs," Kaiser Family Foundation, March 2007.

Restructure Medicare & Medicaid: Legal Forces that Push Up Healthcare Spending

1) Defensive Medicine

2) Possible Solutions

Restructure Medicare & Medicaid: Legal Factors— "Defensive Medicine" Drives up Healthcare Spending

- **Defensive Medicine consists of procedures or tests that a doctor orders to avoid possible future malpractice lawsuits.**
- **The practice is prevalent among US physicians and is contributing factor to healthcare spending. According to a survey of 824 physicians in 2005[1]:**
  - 93% said they had engaged in the practice of Defensive Medicine
  - 59% said they often ordered more diagnostic tests than medically necessary
  - 52% said they referred patients to other specialists in unnecessary circumstances
  - 33% said they often prescribed more medications than medically necessary

Source: 1) David Studdert, et al., American Medical Association, "Defensive Medicine Among High-Risk Specialist Physicians in a Volatile Malpractice Environment," 6/2005.

Restructure Medicare & Medicaid: Legal Factors—Possible Solution
Tort Reform Could Reduce Incentives of Defensive Medicine

Ways to control costs from tort litigation without jeopardizing patient health

The CBO listed a package of tort reform proposals (10/09):

- Cap of $250,000 on awards for noneconomic damages for malpractice
- Cap on awards for punitive damages of $500,000 or twice the award for economic damages, whichever is greater
- Modification of the "collateral source" rule to allow evidence of income from such sources as health and life insurance, workers' compensation, and automobile insurance and subtract it from jury awards
- A statute of limitations – one year for adults and three years for children – from the date of discovery of an injury
- Replacement of joint-and-several liability with fair-share rule: Defendants would be liable only for the percentage of a final award equal to their share of responsibility

Source: Congressional Budget Office, Letter to the Honorable Orrin G. Hatch dated October 9, 2009; Congressional Budget Office, Letter to the Honorable John D. Rockefeller IV dated December 10, 2009

Restructure Medicare & Medicaid: Legal Factors—Possible Solution
Tort Reform Could Save USA Inc. $54 Billion Over Next 10 Years

- **CBO estimates that a package of typical tort reform proposals could reduce total US health spending by 0.5% annually:**
  - Direct savings: Roughly 0.2% of this reduction stems from lower national premiums for medical malpractice insurance.
  - Indirect savings: Another 0.3% stems from slightly lower utilization of services related to defensive medicine.
- **Over 10 years, CBO estimated tort reform could reduce net healthcare spending by $54 billion:**
  - Spending for Medicare, Medicaid, Children's Health Insurance Program, and Federal Employees Health Benefits could fall ~$41 billion over the next decade (with the greatest savings in Medicare).
  - Federal tax revenues could rise by ~$13 billion as lower health insurance costs for employers could lead to higher take-home pay for employees and therefore higher income taxes for USA Inc.

Source: Congressional Budget Office, Letter to the Honorable Orrin G. Hatch dated October 9, 2009; Congressional Budget Office, Letter to the Honorable John D. Rockefeller IV dated December 10, 2009

Restructure Medicare & Medicaid: Policy Option #3

Improve Efficiency / Productivity of Healthcare System

Restructure Medicare & Medicaid: Most Businesses are Performance-Based, Many Components of Healthcare System are Not

USA Healthcare Outcome (based on Life Expectancy) Have Room For Improvement Relative to Other Countries

Healthcare Spending per capita vs. Average Life Expectancy Among OECD Countries, 2007

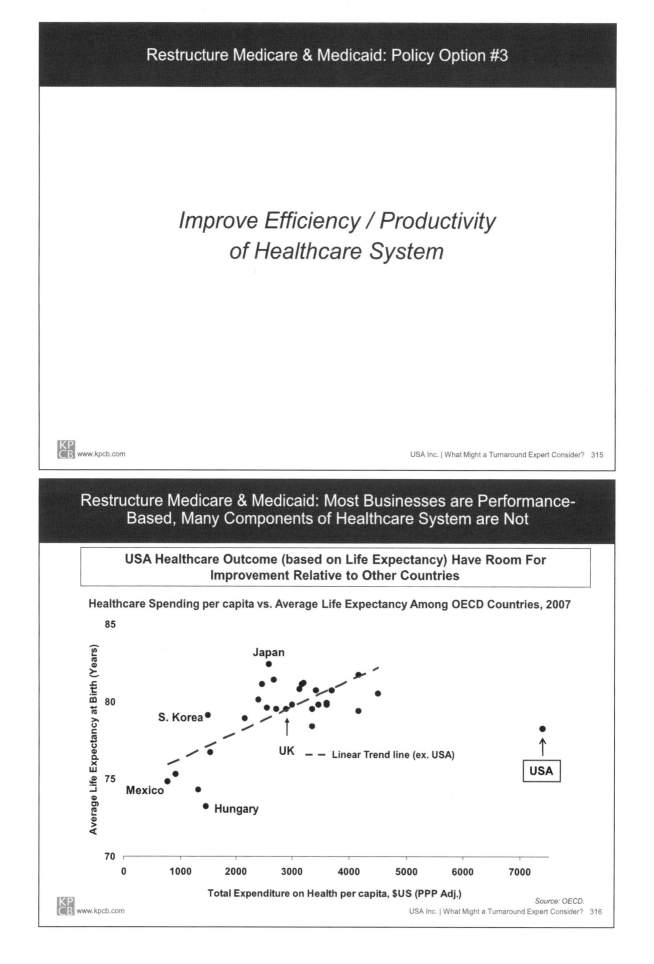

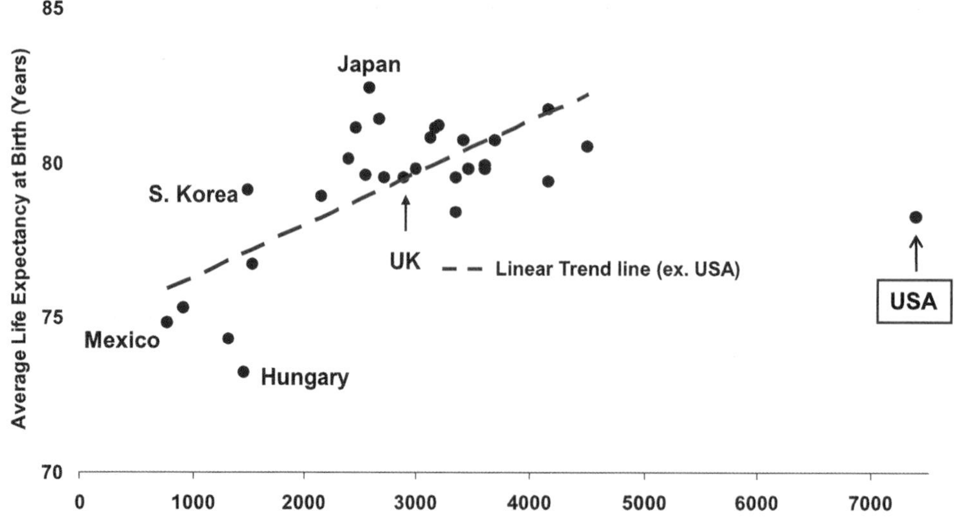

Source: OECD.

Restructure Medicare & Medicaid: In Addition to Life Expectancy, USA Falls Behind OECD Averages in Many Other Health Indicators

2007 Health Indicators	USA	OECD Median	USA Ranking (1 = Best, 30 = Worst) RED = Below Average
Obesity (% of total population)	**34**	**15**	30
Infant Mortality (per 1,000 live births)	**7**	**4**	27
Medical Resources Available (per 1,000 population)			
Total Hospital Beds	**3**	**6**	25
Practicing Physicians	**2**	**3**	22
Doctors' Consultations per Year	**4**	**6**	19
MRI Machines* (per million population)	**26**	**9**	1
Cause of Death (per 100,000 population)			
Heart Attack	**216**	**178**	22
Respiratory Diseases	**60**	**45**	21
Diabetes	**20**	**12**	20
Cancer	**158**	**159**	14
Stroke	**33**	**45**	8

*Note: *MRI is Magnetic Resonance Imaging. Source: OECD.*

Restructure Medicare & Medicaid: Effectiveness Research Could Improve Efficiency (i.e., Outputs Track Inputs)

- **Comparative Effectiveness** evaluates different options for treating a condition for a specific set of patients[1]
  - Either relative benefits and risks of various treatment options (technology assessment, evidence-based medicine), or
  - Both clinical effectiveness and relative cost (cost-benefit analysis).
- Without rigorous data about comparative effectiveness, according to the CBO:
  - Treatment decisions often depend on anecdotal evidence, conjecture, and the experience/judgment of involved physicians.
  - Treatments and types of care vary widely from one area of the country to another.
- To affect healthcare spending meaningfully, comparative effectiveness must alter doctor and patient behavior, potentially through reimbursement scheme changes, the CBO notes.
- Note that by law, Medicare is effectively precluded from considering costs when making coverage decisions.

Source: "Research on the Comparative Effectiveness of Medical Treatments", A CBO Paper, December 2007.

Restructure Medicare & Medicaid: Policy Option #4

Reducing Optional Services + Optional Beneficiary Groups[1] Could Save Up to ~60% of Annual Medicaid Cost, per Kaiser Family Foundation

Note: 1) Medicaid is a jointly financed federal and state program that provides health and long-term care services to 55 million low-income Americans. As a condition of participating in Medicaid, states are required to cover certain "mandatory" populations and to provide a specified set of benefits. States also have discretion to cover additional low-income individuals in each of these categories ("optional groups") and receive federal matching payments. Optional eligibility categories include children and parents, persons with disabilities and the elderly above mandatory coverage limits; persons residing in nursing facilities; and the medically needy. Source: Kaiser Family Foundation, 2005

Restructure Medicare & Medicaid: Policy Option # 4 – Reducing Optional Services + Beneficiary Groups[1] Could Save Up to 60% of Annual Medicaid Spending

Medicaid Expenditures by Eligibility Group and Type of Service, 2001

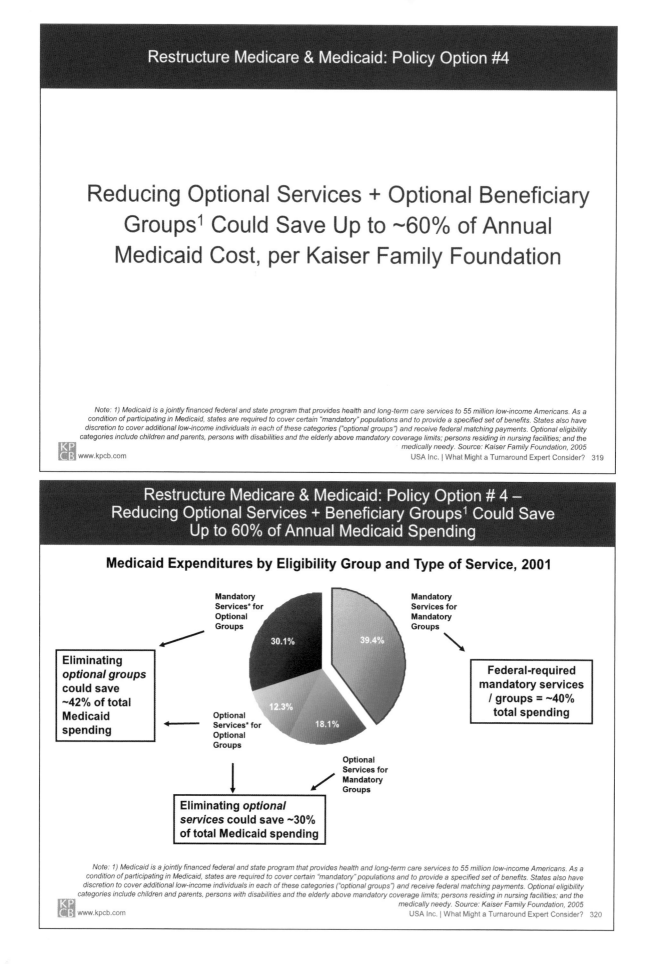

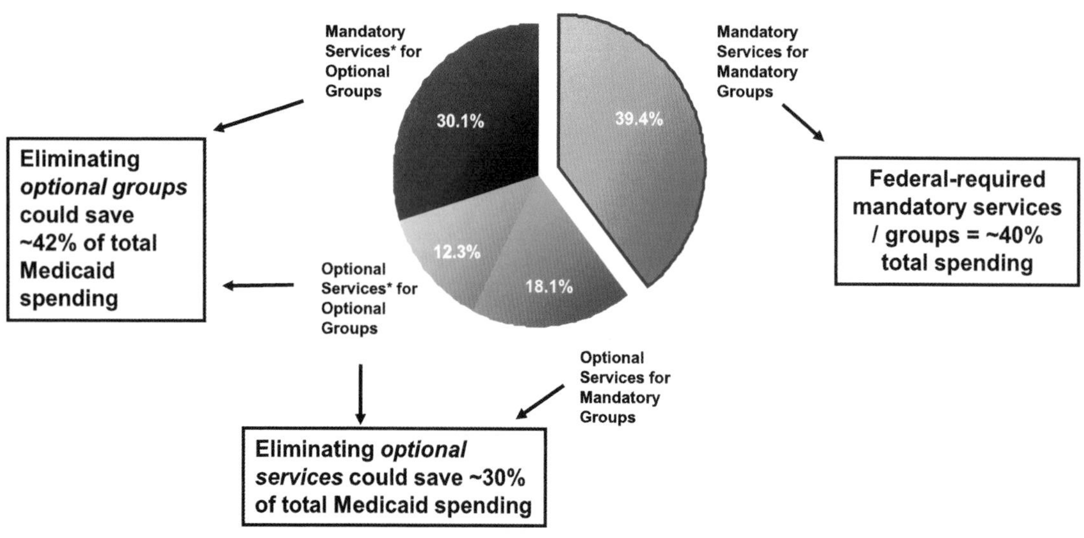

Note: 1) Medicaid is a jointly financed federal and state program that provides health and long-term care services to 55 million low-income Americans. As a condition of participating in Medicaid, states are required to cover certain "mandatory" populations and to provide a specified set of benefits. States also have discretion to cover additional low-income individuals in each of these categories ("optional groups") and receive federal matching payments. Optional eligibility categories include children and parents, persons with disabilities and the elderly above mandatory coverage limits; persons residing in nursing facilities; and the medically needy. Source: Kaiser Family Foundation, 2005

Restructure Medicare & Medicaid: Examples of Medicaid's **Mandatory** Beneficiaries & Services

Examples of Mandatory Beneficiaries

- Children under age 6 with family annual income below $20,841
- Children age 6 or older with family annual income below $15,670
- Pregnant women with annual income below $12,382
- Elderly and disabled with annual income between below $6,768 (for an individual)

Examples of Mandatory Services

- Physician services
- Laboratory & x-ray services
- Inpatient hospital services
- Outpatient hospital services
- Rural health clinic services
- Certified pediatric and family nurse practitioner services
- Early & periodic screening, diagnostic, and treatment (EPSDT) services for individuals under 21

Note: Supplementary Security Income and Federal Poverty Levels are 2005 levels. Source: Kaiser Family Foundation, 2005.

Restructure Medicare & Medicaid: Examples of Medicaid's **Optional** Beneficiaries & Services

Examples of Optional Beneficiaries

- Disabled and elderly with annual income between $7,082 (Supplementary Security Income, or SSI) and $9,310 (Federal Poverty Level, or FPL)
- Nursing home residents with annual income between $7,082 (SSI) and $21,000 (3x SSI)
- Pregnant women with annual income above $12,382 (>133% of FPL)
- Children under 6 with annual family income above $20,841

Examples of Optional Services

- Prescription drugs
- Dental services
- Rehabilitation and other therapies
- Prosthetic devices, eyeglasses, durable medical equipment
- Hospice services
- Inpatient psychiatric hospital services for individuals under age 21
- Other specialist medical or remedial care

Note: Supplementary Security Income and Federal Poverty Levels are 2005 levels. Source: Kaiser Family Foundation, 2005.

Restructure Medicare & Medicaid: Policy Option #5

Consider / Implement CBO's 26 policy options that could reduce annual budget deficit by up to 38% over the next 10 years

Restructure Medicare & Medicaid: CBO Policy Options— Regulate Private Health Insurance Market; Modify Tax Code; Modify Insurance Eligibility; Improve Efficiency

Policy Options	Gov. Future Deficit Reduction (%)[1]
Require large employers to either pay government for providing insurance or offer employees basic insurance coverage	0.7%
Replace the income tax and payroll tax exclusion with a refundable credit	8.8%
Replace the income tax exclusion for employment-based health insurance with a deduction	8.0%
Reduce the tax exclusion for employment-based health insurance and the health insurance deduction for self-employed individuals	6.6%
Raise the age of eligibility for Medicare to 67	1.2%
Convert Medicare and Medicaid "Disproportionate Share Hospital Payments" into a block grant	1.2%
Consolidate Medicare and Federal Medicaid payments for graduate medical education costs at teaching hospitals; set consolidated payment equal to:	
• Adjusted IME[3] payments using a 2.2% adjustment factor + DGME[4] and Medicaid GME[2] funding inflated by the CPI-U[5] minus 1 percentage point	0.8%
• 90% total mandatory GME[2] funding inflated by the CPI-U minus 1 percentage point	0.4%

Note: 1) As % of Cumulative Total Government Deficit from 2010 to 2019 2) Graduate Medical Education 3) Indirect Medical Education 4) Direct Graduate Medical Education 5) Consumer price index for all urban consumers Source: CBO

Restructure Medicare & Medicaid: CBO's Policy Options – Reduce Medicare / Medicaid Payments; Modify Premium and Cost-Sharing in Federal Health Programs

Policy Options	Gov. Future Deficit Reduction (%)[1]
Reduce Medicare's payment rates across the board in high-spending areas	**0.7%**
Remove or reduce the floor on Federal matching rates for Medicaid services	
• **Remove the floor on the federal medical assistance percentage**	**3.3%**
• **Reduce the floor on the federal medical assistance percentage to 45%**	**1.9%**
Reduce the taxes that states are allowed to levy on Medicaid providers	**0.7%**
Increase the basic premium for Medicare Part B to 35% of the program's costs	**3.2%**
Combine changes to Medicare's cost sharing with restrictions on Medigap policies[2]	**1.1%**
Require a copayment for home health episodes covered by Medicare	**0.7%**
Restrict Medigap coverage of Medicare's cost sharing	**0.6%**
Introduce minimum out-of-pocket requirements under TRICARE for life	**0.6%**

Note: 1) As % of Total Cumulative Government Deficit from 2010 to 2019 2) Individual insurance policies designed to cover most or all of Medicare's cost-sharing requirements. Source: CBO

Restructure Medicare & Medicaid: Policy Option #6

Consider / Implement National Commission on Fiscal Responsibility and Reform's medium- and long-term policy options

Restructure Medicare & Medicaid: **Medium-Term** Policy Options From the Report of the National Commission on Fiscal Responsibility and Reform

Medium-Term Policy Options	Deficit Reduction F2012-F2020E[1]
Convert the federal share of Medicaid payments for long-term care into a capped allotment	$89 billion
Reform Tricare for Life[2] to increase cost sharing for Military retirees	$55
Cut federal spending on graduate and indirect medical education	$54
Reduce taxes that States may levy on Medicaid providers	$49
Expand ACOs, payment bundling, and other payment reform	$38
Accelerate phase-in of DSH payment cuts[3], Medicare Advantage cuts and home health cuts in PPACA	$37
Other[4]	$73
Total Deficit Reduction F2012-F2020E	**$395 billion**

Note: 1) Cost reductions are Fiscal Commission staff estimates based on CBO and other available sources. Most numbers were generated pre-healthcare reform and may differ significantly. 2) Tricare for Life is a supplementary military health insurance designed to minimize Medicare-eligible military retirees' out-of-pocket medical expenses. 3) DSH is the Medicare and Medicaid disproportionate share hospital payments for hospitals that receive disproportionately large Medicare and Medicaid patients. 4) Other includes reduce Medicaid administrative costs, increase nominal Medicaid copays, cut Medicare payments for bad debt, increase cost sharing for federal civilian retirees and place dual-eligible individuals in Medicaid Managed Care. Source: National Commission on Fiscal Responsibility and Reform, "The Moment of Truth: Report of the National Commission on Fiscal Responsibility and Reform," 12/1/10.

Restructure Medicare & Medicaid: **Long-Term** Policy Options From the Report of the National Commission on Fiscal Responsibility and Reform

- Set global target for total federal health expenditures after 2020 (Medicare, Medicaid, CHIP, exchange subsidies, employer health exclusion), and review costs every two years. Keep federal health expenditure growth to one percentage points above GDP growth.
- If costs have grown faster than targets (on average of previous 5 years), require President to submit and Congress to consider reforms to lower spending, such as:
  - Increase premiums (or further increase cost-sharing)
  - Overhaul the fee-for-service system
  - Develop a premium support system for Medicare
  - Add a robust public option and/or all-payer system in the exchange
  - Further expand authority of the Independent Payment Advisory Board (IPAB)*

Note: IPAB is a 15-member Independent Payment Advisory Board established under PPACA with significant authority with respect to Medicare payment rates. Beginning in 2014, in any year in which the Medicare per capita growth rate exceeded a target growth rate, the IPAB would be required to recommend Medicare spending reductions. The recommendations would become law unless Congress passed an alternative proposal that achieved the same level of budgetary savings. Source: National Commission on Fiscal Responsibility and Reform, "The Moment of Truth: Report of the National Commission on Fiscal Responsibility and Reform," 12/1/10.

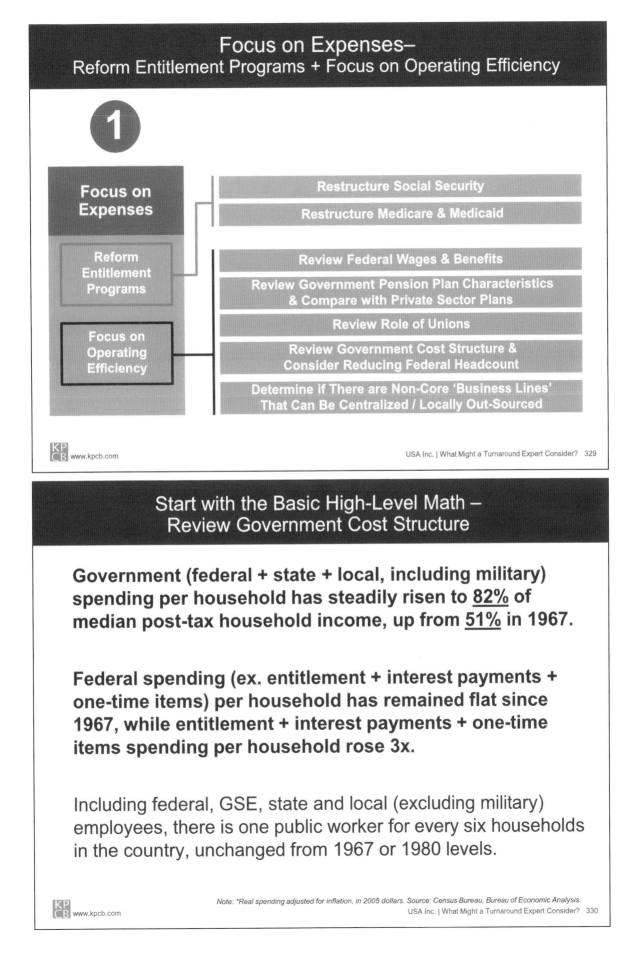

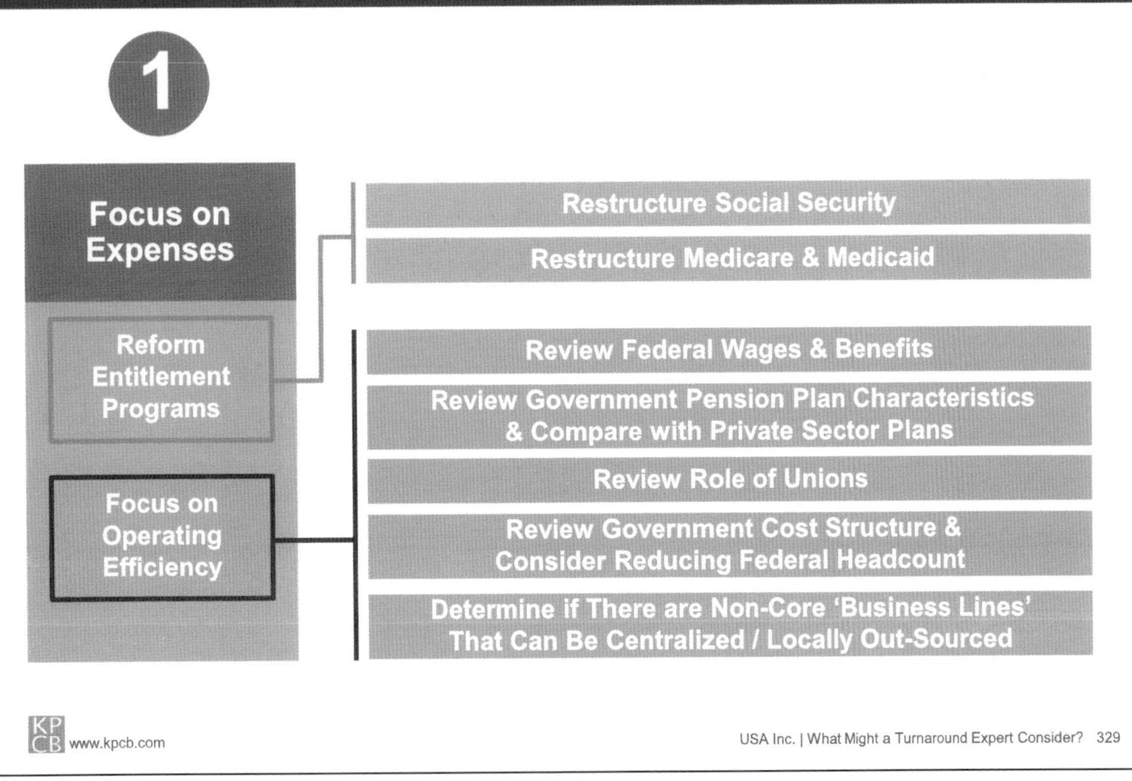

Start with the Basic High-Level Math – Review Government Cost Structure

Government (federal + state + local, including military) spending per household has steadily risen to 82% of median post-tax household income, up from 51% in 1967.

Federal spending (ex. entitlement + interest payments + one-time items) per household has remained flat since 1967, while entitlement + interest payments + one-time items spending per household rose 3x.

Including federal, GSE, state and local (excluding military) employees, there is one public worker for every six households in the country, unchanged from 1967 or 1980 levels.

*Note: *Real spending adjusted for inflation, in 2005 dollars. Source: Census Bureau, Bureau of Economic Analysis.*

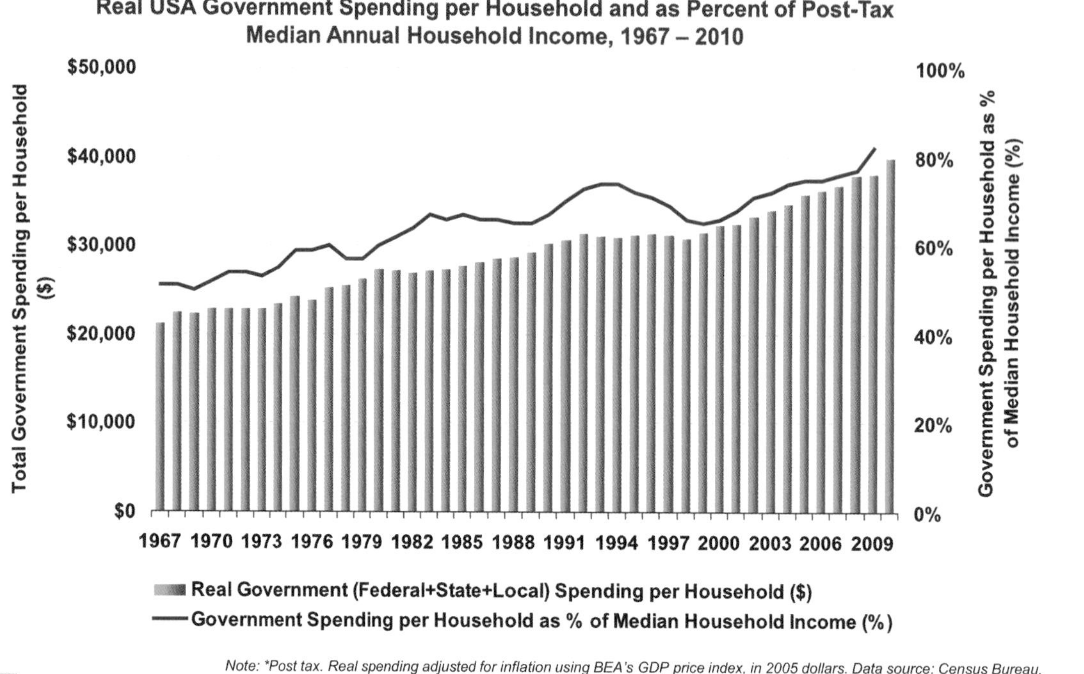
Total Government (Federal + State + Local, including Military) Spending Has Risen to 82% of Median Household Income*, Up from 51% in 1967
Real USA Government Spending per Household and as Percent of Post-Tax Median Annual Household Income, 1967 – 2010
$50,000
$40,000
$30,000
$20,000
$10,000
$0
100%
80%
60%
40%
20%
0%
Total Government Spending per Household ($)
Government Spending per Household as % of Median Household Income (%)
1967 1970 1973 1976 1979 1982 1985 1988 1991 1994 1997 2000 2003 2006 2009
Real Government (Federal+State+Local) Spending per Household ($)
Government Spending per Household as % of Median Household Income (%)
Note: *Post tax. Real spending adjusted for inflation using BEA's GDP price index, in 2005 dollars. Data source: Census Bureau, Bureau of Economic Analysis.
KPCB www.kpcb.com
USA Inc. | What Might a Turnaround Expert Consider? 331

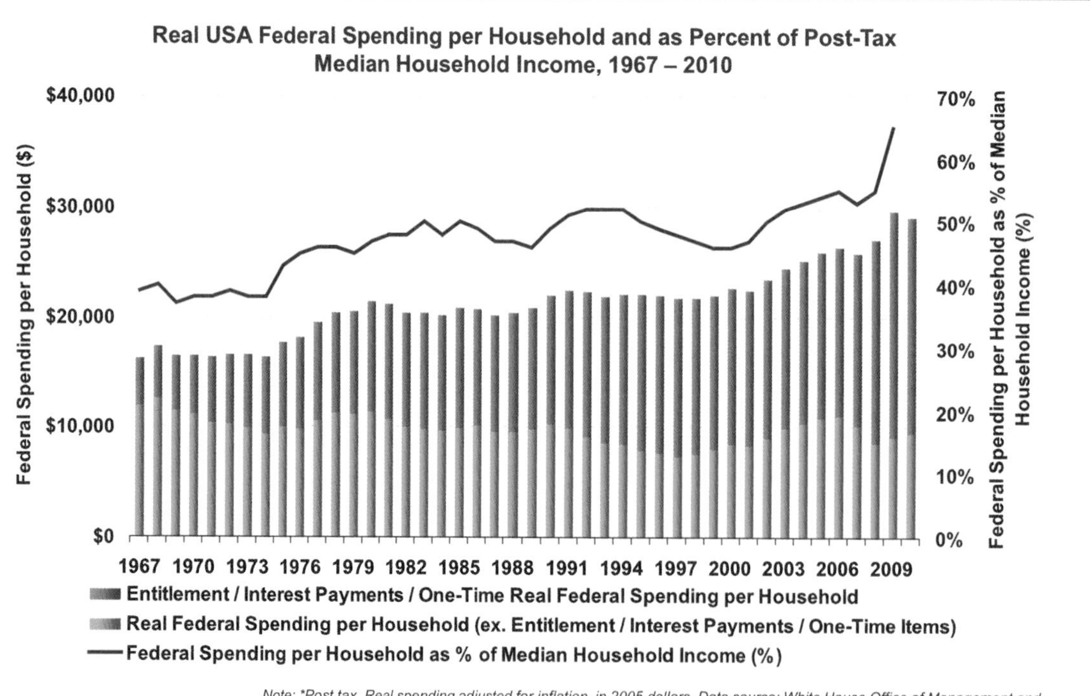
Federal (Including Military) Spending Has Risen to 65% of Median Household Income*, Up from 39% in 1967, Driven by Entitlement Spending + Interest Payments
Real USA Federal Spending per Household and as Percent of Post-Tax Median Household Income, 1967 – 2010
$40,000
$30,000
$20,000
$10,000
$0
70%
60%
50%
40%
30%
20%
10%
0%
Federal Spending per Household ($)
Federal Spending per Household as % of Median Household Income (%)
1967 1970 1973 1976 1979 1982 1985 1988 1991 1994 1997 2000 2003 2006 2009
Entitlement / Interest Payments / One-Time Real Federal Spending per Household
Real Federal Spending per Household (ex. Entitlement / Interest Payments / One-Time Items)
Federal Spending per Household as % of Median Household Income (%)
Note: *Post tax. Real spending adjusted for inflation, in 2005 dollars. Data source: White House Office of Management and Budget, Census Bureau, Bureau of Economic Analysis.
KPCB www.kpcb.com
USA Inc. | What Might a Turnaround Expert Consider? 332

Federal (Including Military) Spending Per Household = $29,043 in F2010 Federal Entitlement Spending Per Household = More Than Half ($16,670)

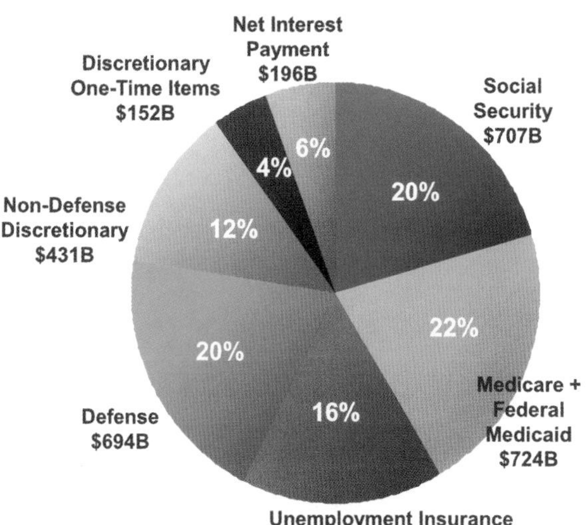

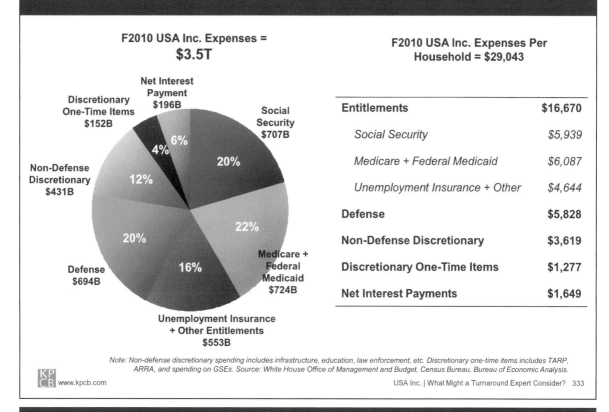

F2010 USA Inc. Expenses Per Household = $29,043

Entitlements	**$16,670**
Social Security	*$5,939*
Medicare + Federal Medicaid	*$6,087*
Unemployment Insurance + Other	*$4,644*
Defense	**$5,828**
Non-Defense Discretionary	**$3,619**
Discretionary One-Time Items	**$1,277**
Net Interest Payments	**$1,649**

Note: Non-defense discretionary spending includes infrastructure, education, law enforcement, etc. Discretionary one-time items includes TARP, ARRA, and spending on GSEs. Source: White House Office of Management and Budget, Census Bureau, Bureau of Economic Analysis.

At a High Level, With Focus on Improving Operating Efficiency, USA Inc. Might Consider Ways to Do Things Like…

- Consider empowering an independent / 3rd party auditor with expertise in government operations around the world / corporate turnarounds to conduct a broad-ranging audit of USA Inc.'s operations.
- Restore strong rules for budget process: Require annual budget resolutions and reconciliation; PAYGO* to limit spending, enforce annual appropriations process consider biennial budgeting.
- Consider giving the President 'line-item' veto / rescission authority.
- Empower commissions analogous to the military base closing panels to review and consolidate government functions and agencies, as well as aid to State and local governments.
- Seek flexibility to manage performance and terminate poor-performing Federal employees.
- Develop flexible / long-term compensation plans including bonus payments for Federal employees when annual budget deficit reduction goals are met.
- Privatize government real estate and other assets with little use, expanding on current efforts to trim $3 billion in government-owned real estate.
- Identify additional opportunities to increase public/private investment, management and operations to drive innovation and investment in infrastructure

Note: PAYGO is the practice of financing expenditures with funds that are currently available rather than borrowed.
Source: KPCB and Alvarez & Marsal Public Sector Services, LLC.

1

Focus on Expenses

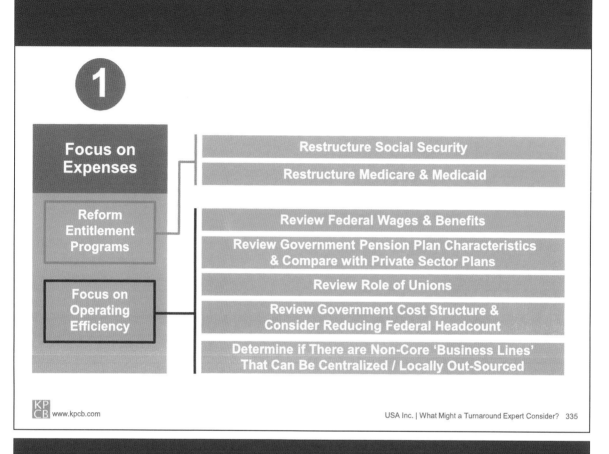

- **Reform Entitlement Programs**
  - Restructure Social Security
  - Restructure Medicare & Medicaid
- **Focus on Operating Efficiency**
  - Review Federal Wages & Benefits
  - Review Government Pension Plan Characteristics & Compare with Private Sector Plans
  - Review Role of Unions
  - Review Government Cost Structure & Consider Reducing Federal Headcount
  - Determine if There are Non-Core 'Business Lines' That Can Be Centralized / Locally Out-Sourced

Review Wages: A Comprehensive / Independent Review of Federal Wages & Benefits System May Be Worthwhile

- **Analysis of existing data on federal wages & benefits is controversial.**
- *USA Today* and the Cato Institute examined simple averages of federal (excluding military) wages & benefits vs. private sector using Bureau of Economic Analysis (BEA) data and concluded that federal wages & benefits are ~100% higher than private industry – wages are 58% higher while benefits are 3x higher.[1] (March 2010, updated in August 2010)
- The White House Office of Management and Budget (OMB) and the U.S. Office of Personnel Management (OPM) responded that gross average comparisons are 'unfair and untrue.' And when one holds education and age constant, federal employees earn slightly less than those in the private sector on average, although the difference is not statistically significant.[2] (March 2010)
- The Heritage Foundation, in response to OPM and OMB's comments, released a statistical analysis based on BEA data, and claimed that adjusting for variables such as age, education, marital status, race, gender, size of the metropolitan area, and several others, federal wages & benefits are 31% higher than private industry for occupations in both government and private sector.[3] (July 2010)

Source: 1) Dennis Cauchon, USA Today, "Federal Workers earning double their private counterparts," http://www.usatoday.com/money/economy/income/2010-08-10-1Afedpay10_ST_N.htm Tad DeHaven, "Federal Employees Continue to Prosper," http://www.cato-at-liberty.org/federal-employees-continue-to-prosper/; 2) John Berry, "OPM Statement on Federal Employee Pay – Recent Comparisons of Federal Pay to Private Sector are Unfair and Untrue," http://www.opm.gov/opm_federalemployeepay/ & Peter Orszag, "Salary Statistics," http://www.whitehouse.gov/omb/blog/10/03/10/Salary-Statistics; 3) James Sherk, "Comparing Pay in the Federal Government and the Private Sector," http://www.heritage.org/research/reports/2010/07/comparing-pay-in-the-federal-government-and-the-private-sector

Review Wages: A Turnaround Expert Would Drill Down on Compensation Differences Between Public & Private Sectors

- In the absence of reliable, generally accepted adjustment factors, USA Inc. needs a comprehensive 3rd-party review of its compensation practices.
- Most businesses constantly review their compensation practices; these reviews typically intensify when the financials of the core business erode.
- Considerations include compensation for comparable jobs, uniqueness of skill sets and education required for particular roles, productivity, hours worked, regional cost of living, job security, years of service, and financial health of the business unit.

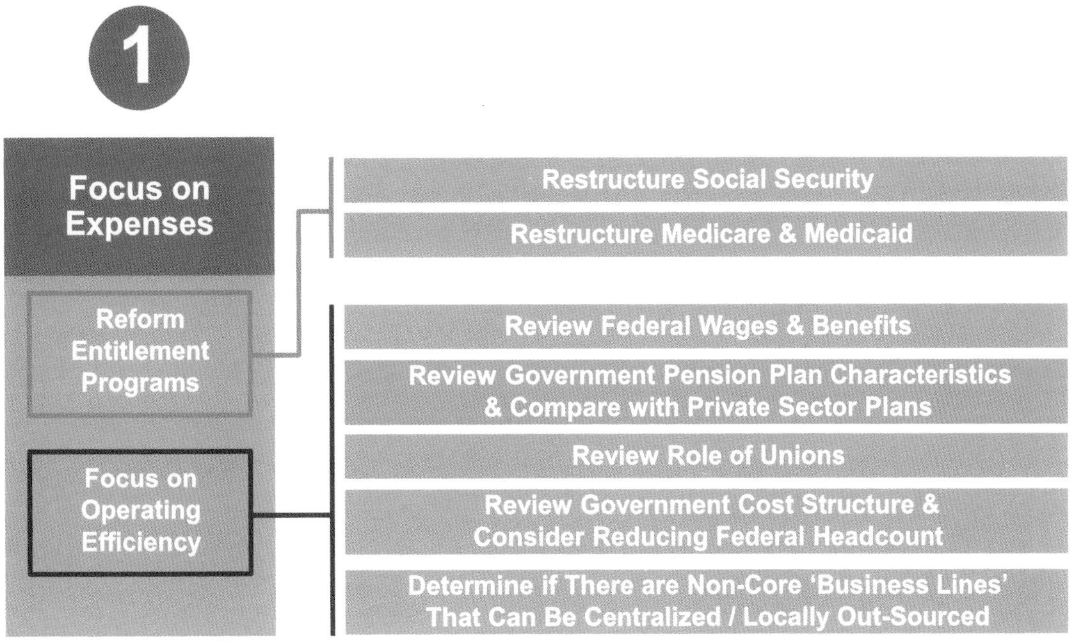

1

Focus on Expenses

- **Reform Entitlement Programs**
  - Restructure Social Security
  - Restructure Medicare & Medicaid
- **Focus on Operating Efficiency**
  - Review Federal Wages & Benefits
  - Review Government Pension Plan Characteristics & Compare with Private Sector Plans
  - Review Role of Unions
  - Review Government Cost Structure & Consider Reducing Federal Headcount
  - Determine if There are Non-Core 'Business Lines' That Can Be Centralized / Locally Out-Sourced

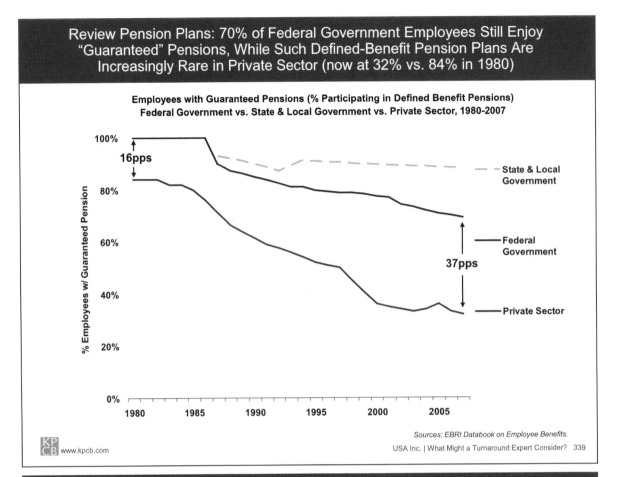

Review Pension Plans: 70% of Federal Government Employees Still Enjoy "Guaranteed" Pensions, While Such Defined-Benefit Pension Plans Are Increasingly Rare in Private Sector (now at 32% vs. 84% in 1980)

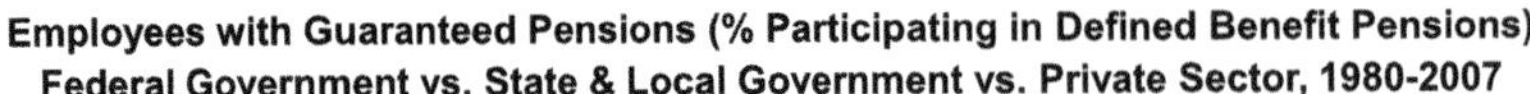

Employees with Guaranteed Pensions (% Participating in Defined Benefit Pensions)
Federal Government vs. State & Local Government vs. Private Sector, 1980-2007

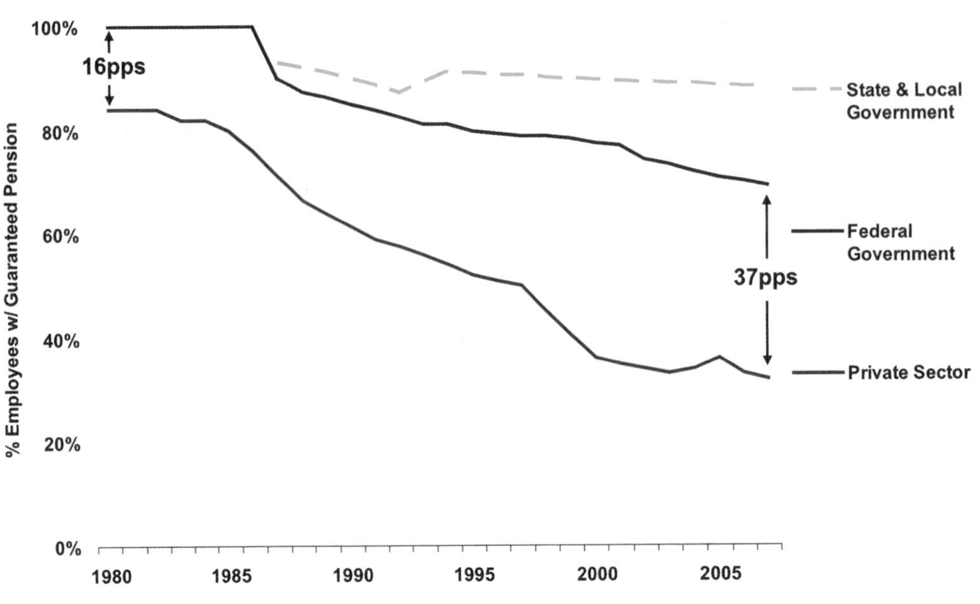

Sources: EBRI Databook on Employee Benefits.

Review Pension Plans: Private Sector Has Embraced "Defined Contribution" Pension Plans, While Federal + State & Local Governments Lag Behind

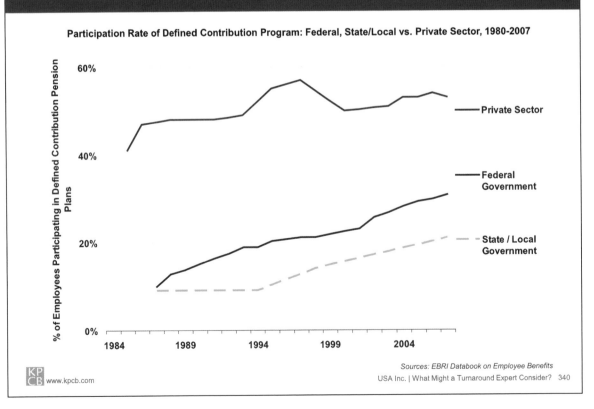

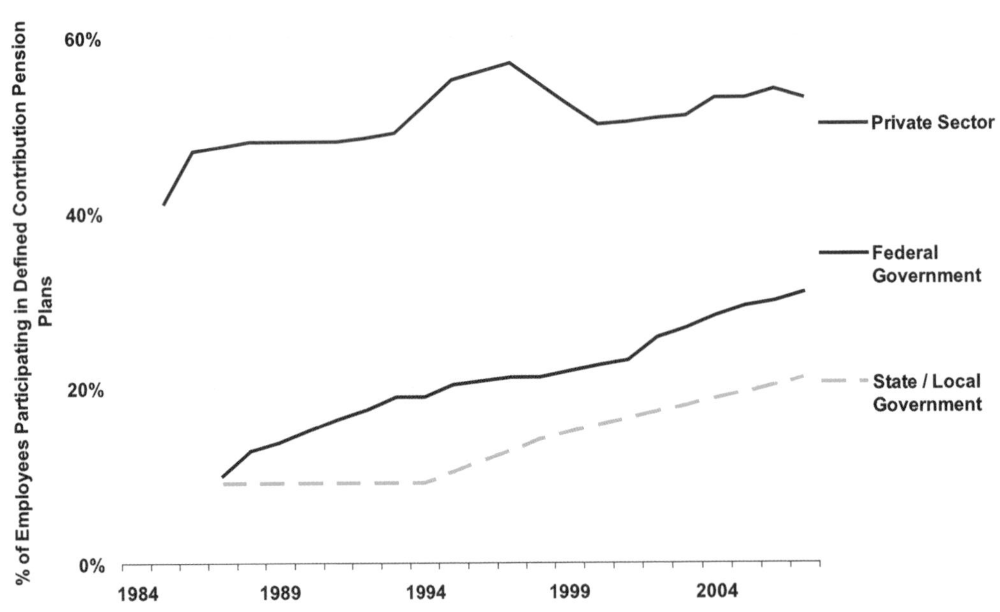

Sources: EBRI Databook on Employee Benefits

Review Pension: Pension Plan Definitions / Characteristics

- **"Guaranteed" Pension Plan** – Retirees receive predetermined monthly retirement benefits from employers despite the funding status / investment returns of their pension funds. Also known as defined benefit pension plan.

- **Defined Contribution Pension Plan** – Retirees contribute specified amounts to their pension funds and receive variable monthly retirement benefits depending on investment returns. Examples include Individual Retirement Accounts (IRAs) and 401(k) plans.

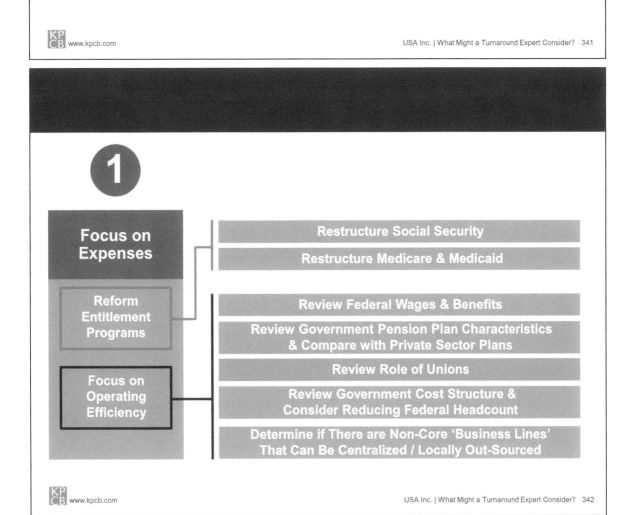

1

Focus on Expenses

- **Reform Entitlement Programs**
  - Restructure Social Security
  - Restructure Medicare & Medicaid
- **Focus on Operating Efficiency**
  - Review Federal Wages & Benefits
  - Review Government Pension Plan Characteristics & Compare with Private Sector Plans
  - Review Role of Unions
  - Review Government Cost Structure & Consider Reducing Federal Headcount
  - Determine if There are Non-Core 'Business Lines' That Can Be Centralized / Locally Out-Sourced

Review Unions: Government Employee Union Membership Rate = 5x of Private Sector Union Membership Rate & Rising

- **More government (federal / state / local) employees belong to unions (8 million) than did private sector employees (7 million) in 2009.**
- Government employee union membership rate of 37% is 5x higher than private sector employee union membership rate of 7% in 2009.
- Private sector union membership rate declined 180 basis points to 7% in 2009 from 9% in 2000, while government employee union membership rate rose 50 basis points 37.4% in 2009 from 36.9% in 2000.

Source: Bureau of Labor Statistics.

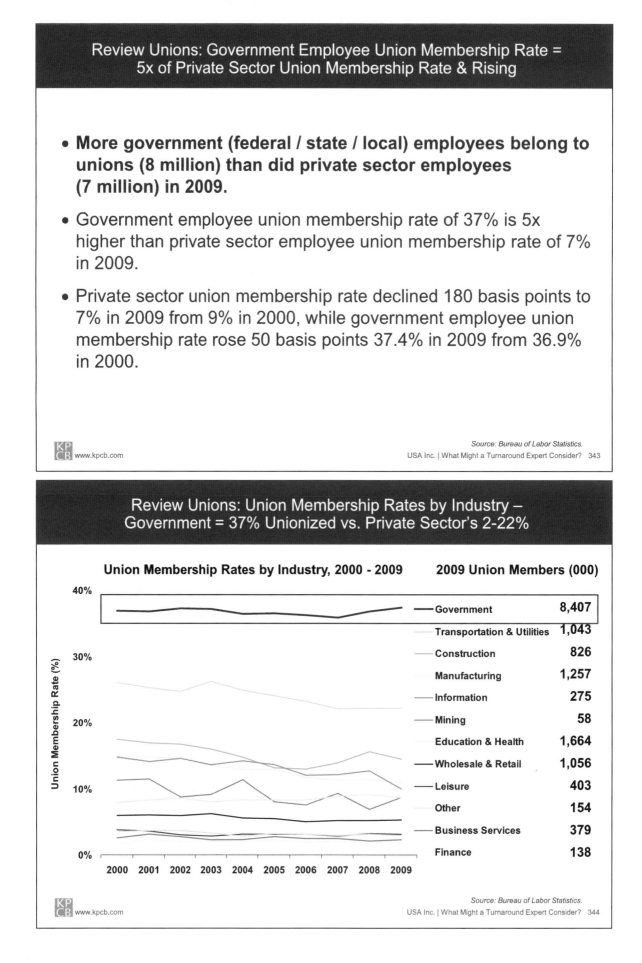

Review Unions: Union Membership Rates by Industry – Government = 37% Unionized vs. Private Sector's 2-22%

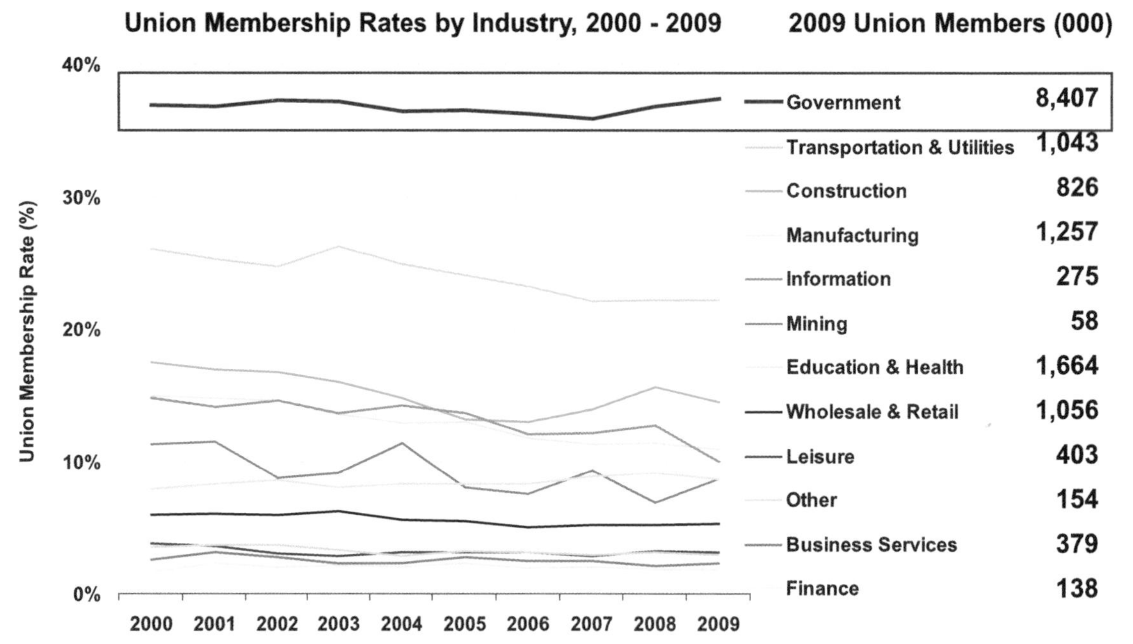

Source: Bureau of Labor Statistics.

1

Focus on Expenses

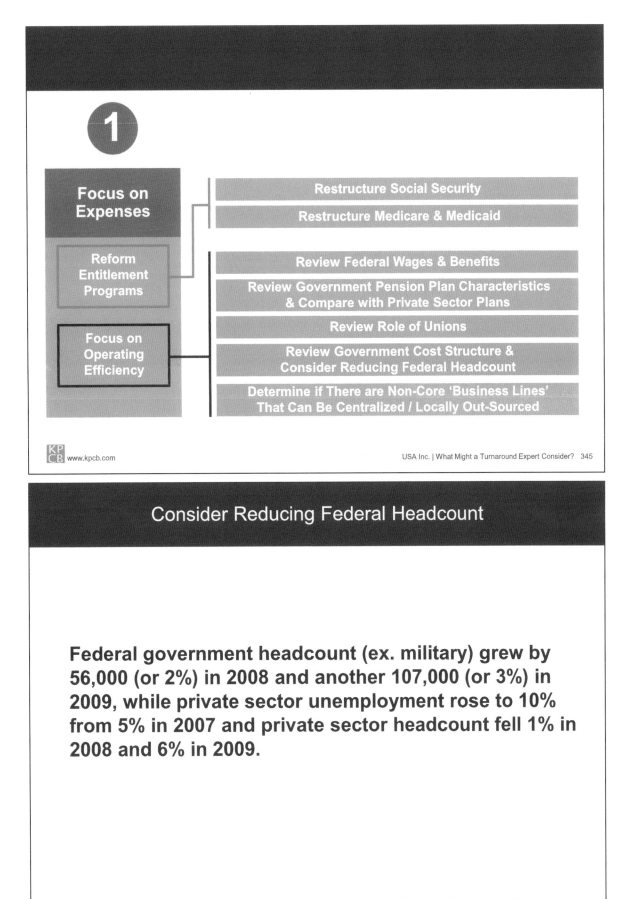

Reform Entitlement Programs

- Restructure Social Security
- Restructure Medicare & Medicaid

Focus on Operating Efficiency

- Review Federal Wages & Benefits
- Review Government Pension Plan Characteristics & Compare with Private Sector Plans
- Review Role of Unions
- Review Government Cost Structure & Consider Reducing Federal Headcount
- Determine if There are Non-Core 'Business Lines' That Can Be Centralized / Locally Out-Sourced

Consider Reducing Federal Headcount

Federal government headcount (ex. military) grew by 56,000 (or 2%) in 2008 and another 107,000 (or 3%) in 2009, while private sector unemployment rose to 10% from 5% in 2007 and private sector headcount fell 1% in 2008 and 6% in 2009.

Source: Census Bureau, Bureau of Economic Analysis.

Federal Headcount Has Risen Over Past Five Years and Is Above Trendline Level

Federal Civilian Headcount & Share of Total Employment, 1988 - 2009

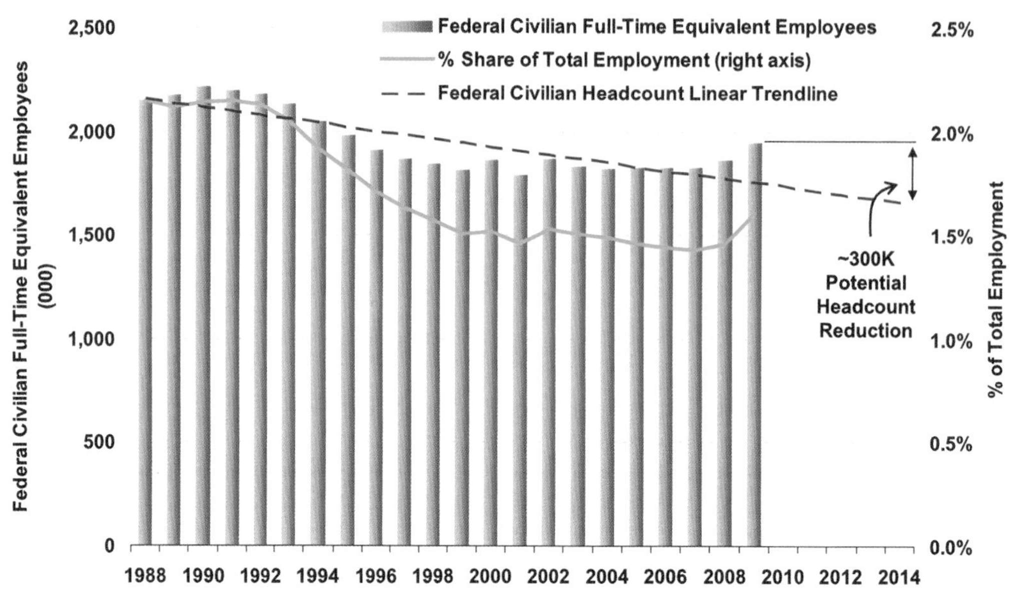

Data source: BEA (1988-2009).

Reduce Headcount: Mathematical Illustration on Reducing Federal Headcount – Could Save Up to $275 Billion Over Next 10 Years, or 4% of Total Deficit

Scenario Analysis on Potential Federal Headcount Reduction & Impact on Budget Deficits

	Savings ($B) For USA Inc. Over			Headcount Reduction
	F2009	**F2010-19E**	**F2010-85E**	**(000)**
Scenario 1				
-- Trim Headcount by 1%	$2	$17	$44	20
% of Budget Deficits	*0%*	*0%*	*0%*	
Scenario 2				
-- Trim Headcount by 5%	$11	$91	$219	98
% of Budget Deficits	*1%*	*1%*	*1%*	
Scenario 3				
-- Trim Headcount by 10%	$23	$183	$439	195
% of Budget Deficits	*2%*	*3%*	*3%*	
Scenario 4 - Trendline*				
-- Trim Headcount by 15%	$34	$274	$658	293
% of Budget Deficits	*2%*	*4%*	*4%*	

Note: Federal fiscal year ends in September. *Based on 20-year trend line, federal civilian headcount would have been 15% below actual levels.

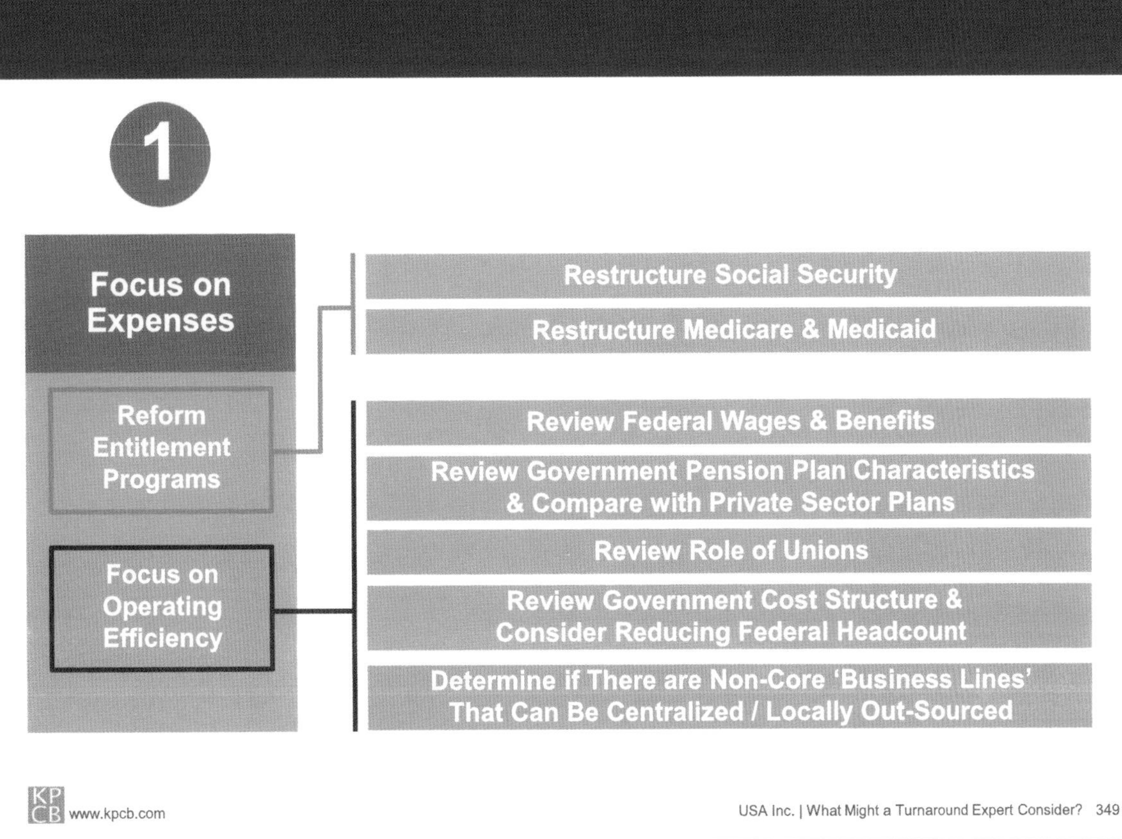
1
Focus on Expenses
Reform Entitlement Programs
Focus on Operating Efficiency
Restructure Social Security
Restructure Medicare & Medicaid
Review Federal Wages & Benefits
Review Government Pension Plan Characteristics & Compare with Private Sector Plans
Review Role of Unions
Review Government Cost Structure & Consider Reducing Federal Headcount
Determine if There are Non-Core 'Business Lines' That Can Be Centralized / Locally Out-Sourced
KP CB www.kpcb.com
USA Inc. | What Might a Turnaround Expert Consider? 349

Local Outsourcing/Consolidation: Improve Efficiency of Public Services Through Automation / Scale / Flexibility

1. **Automation** – Government agencies cannot afford to perform manual routine-based processes that can be replaced more efficiently by technology.

2. **Scale** – Consolidation of non-core processes across agencies or outsource non-core processes to local companies can deliver scale efficiencies.

3. **Flexibility** – Outsourced labor enables temporary employment in situations where hiring full-time workers would be costly and unnecessary.

Sources: Adam Frisch, Morgan Stanley Research.

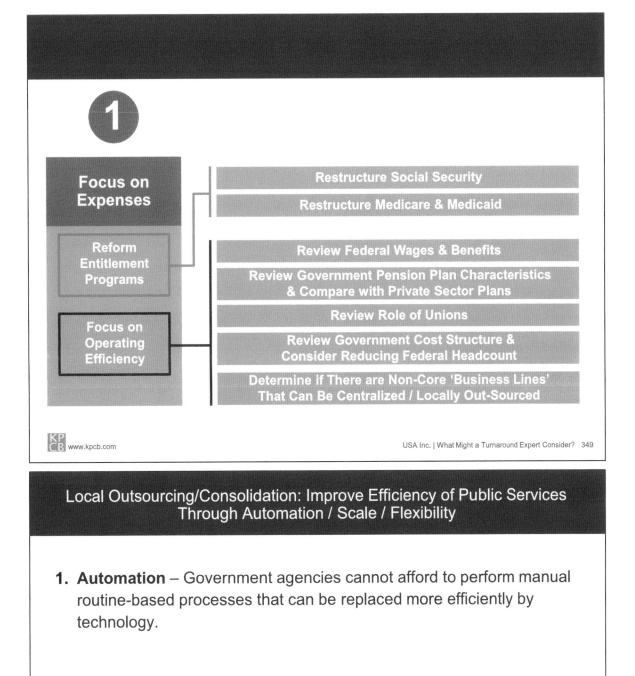

Local Outsourcing/Consolidation: Proven to Be Viable Cost-Cutting Measures for State / Local Governments

	Years	Public Sector	Details	Total Cost Saving ($)	As % of Total Budget[1]	As % of Program Budget[1]
Automation	2002-2010	Missouri State Government	Digitized State Medicaid health record	~87MM	--	--
Automation	1993-2010	Port Authority of New York and New Jersey	*E-ZPass* (electronic toll collection) can process 2.5x to 3x more vehicles per lane than toll attendants	--	--	--
Scale	2003	Pennsylvania State Government	Consolidated office supplies + computer procurement	~$30MM	--	--
Scale	2002-2004	Dept. Management Services, FL	Outsourced HR and supporting IT system to local contractors	~173MM	0.3%	11.5%
Scale	2004-2005	Health and Human Services Commission, TX	Outsourced HR, payroll and enterprise service center to private vendors	~1B	0.8%	5.0%
Scale	2010	Maywood, CA	Outsourced police force to county sheriff in an effort to avoid bankruptcy	~3.7MM	25%	50.7%
Flexibility	2005	American Red Cross	Set up a Family Assistance Hotline within 10 days via an outsourcer (vs. 3-6 months doing it in-house)	--	--	--

Note: 1) Annual Budget of the year when outsourcing program started. Sources: HR Outsourcing in Government Organizations, The Conference Board; Outsourcing Methods & Case Studies, 2009; Maywood, CA data per The Economist. PA state government data per Ed Rendell, Governor of Pennsylvania.) E-ZPass per E-Zpass New Jersey Customer Service Center; Missouri Medicaid case study per ACS; American Red Cross per Tholons, Government Sector Outsourcing.

Focus on Operating Efficiency –

Policy Options From National Commission on Fiscal Responsibility and Reform Co-Chairs' Proposal

Focus on Operating Efficiency: Illustrative Policy Options From the Report of the National Commission on Fiscal Responsibility and Reform

Illustrative Policy Options	Deficit Reduction in F2015E
Eliminate 250,000 non-defense service and staff augmentee contractors	$18 billion
Eliminate all earmarks[1]	$16
Freeze federal salaries, bonuses, and other compensation at non-Defense agencies for three years	$15
Cut the federal workforce by 10% (2-for-3 replacement rate)	$13
Create a Cut-and-Invest Committee charged with trimming waste and targeting investment	$11
Slow the growth of foreign aid	$5
Other[2]	$22
Total Deficit Reduction F2015E	**$100 billion**

Note: 1) an earmark is a legislative (especially congressional) provision that directs approved funds to be spent on specific projects, or that directs specific exemptions from taxes or mandated fees. 2) Other includes eliminate NASA funding for commercial spaceflight, terminate low-priority Army Corps of Engineers programs, sell excess federal property, reduce congressional & White House budgets by 15%, reduce unnecessary printing costs and more. Source: National Commission on Fiscal Responsibility and Reform, "The Moment of Truth: Report of the National Commission on Fiscal Responsibility and Reform," 12/1/10.

What Might a Turnaround Expert Consider?

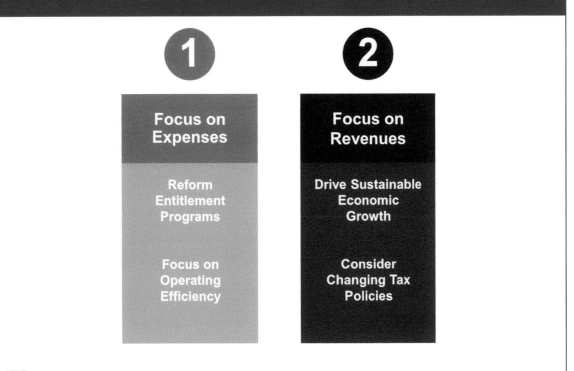

Focus on Expenses	Focus on Revenues
Reform Entitlement Programs	Drive Sustainable Economic Growth
Focus on Operating Efficiency	Consider Changing Tax Policies

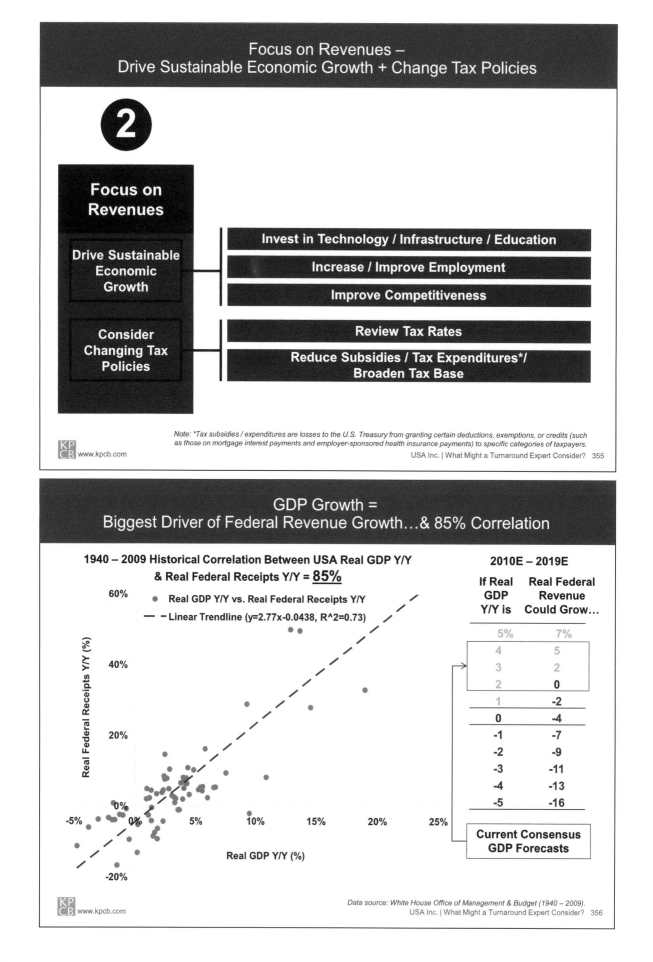

Focus on Revenues –
Drive Sustainable Economic Growth + Change Tax Policies

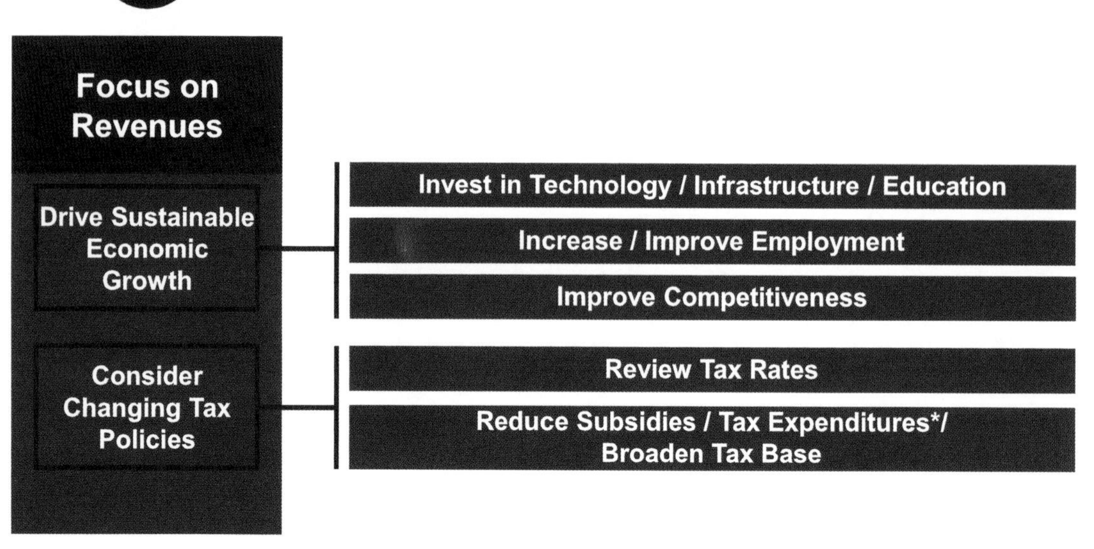

*Note: *Tax subsidies / expenditures are losses to the U.S. Treasury from granting certain deductions, exemptions, or credits (such as those on mortgage interest payments and employer-sponsored health insurance payments) to specific categories of taxpayers.*

GDP Growth =
Biggest Driver of Federal Revenue Growth…& 85% Correlation

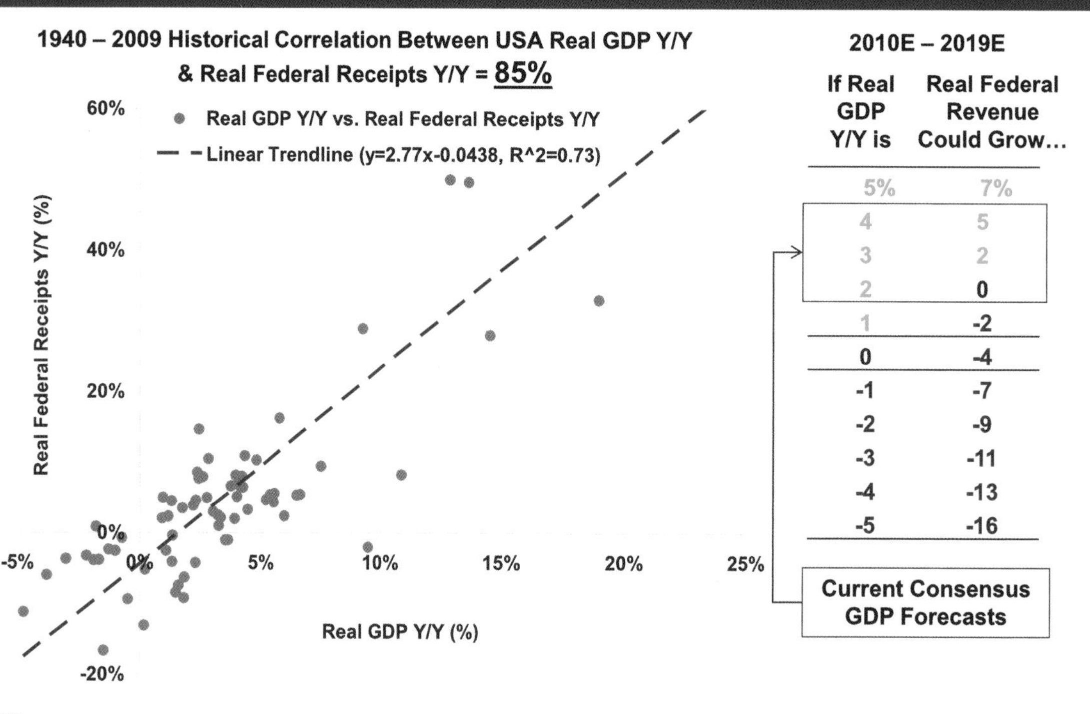

2010E – 2019E

If Real GDP Y/Y is	Real Federal Revenue Could Grow…
5%	7%
4	5
3	2
2	0
1	-2
0	-4
-1	-7
-2	-9
-3	-11
-4	-13
-5	-16

Data source: White House Office of Management & Budget (1940 – 2009).

It's Easy to Gripe About USA Inc.'s High Expense Levels... That Said, High Expenses Could be Covered by High Revenue

- **There are two primary drivers of USA Inc.'s revenue: 1) GDP growth and 2) related tax levies on consumers and businesses.**
- To bring its income statement mechanically to break-even for 2009 (excluding one-time charges), USA Inc. would have needed to raise individual income tax rates by ~2x across-the-board to an average of ~26-30% (from ~13%) of gross income.[1] This certainly seems draconian. And a tax increase of this nature would surely have a significant negative impact on USA's GDP growth as consumers would have far less disposable income to buy goods and services.
- This brings us to a key element of USA's financial challenges – the need to drive economic (GDP) AND related job growth. This is not easy. A material portion of GDP growth over the past few decades was driven by rising consumption aided by rising leverage and we have now entered a period of de-leveraging.
- Stronger economic growth would be hugely beneficial for USA Inc.'s revenues. But the legacy of the financial crisis – severe housing imbalances and the need to complete the long process of writing off private mortgage debt – means that the US recovery will probably remain slow for at least several years. The silver lining: A booming global economy should provide a modest lift to US growth.

Note: 1) USA Inc.'s F2009 revenue shortfall was $997B (excluding one-time discretionary spending items). F2009 total income tax receipts from individuals were $915B. As a result, if one were to raise individual income tax rates alone to achieve financial break-even, one would have to more than double individual income tax rates across-the-board.

Drive Growth: If Real GDP Grows 0.1 Percentage Point Faster Than Current CBO Projection For F2011-F2020E, the Budget Deficit Could Shrink by 5% Without Other Policy Changes

- CBO analysis shows that for every 0.1 percentage point (pps) increase in real GDP annual growth rate above CBO's baseline estimate for F2011-F2020E, USA Inc.'s revenue (driven by taxes) could be $247 billion higher, spending could be $41 billion lower (driven by reduced welfare spending) and the budget deficit could be reduced by $288 billion, or 5%.

		F2011-F2020E Impact on USA Inc.'s		
CBO's baseline assumption for annual real GDP growth	**What if real GDP grows faster than CBO's forecast by...**	**Revenue** ($B / %)	**Spending** ($B / %)	**Deficit Reduction** ($B / %)
2.1% F2011E **4.4% F2012-14E** **2.4% F2015-20E**	**0.1 pps**	**+$247** +1%	**-$41** --%	**-$288** -5%
	0.5 pps	**+$1,235** +3%	**-$205** --%	**-$1,440** -23%
	1 pps	**+$2,470** +6%	**-$410** -1%	**-$2,880** -46%
	2 pps	**+$4,940** +13%	**-$820** -2%	**-$5,760** -92%

Note: pps is percentage point(s). $ amount and % changes in revenue / spending / deficit are over the entire F2011-F2020E period. Source: CBO, "The Budget and Economic Outlook: Fiscal Years 2010 to 2020," 8/10.

How Much Would Real GDP Need to Grow to Drive USA Inc. to Break-Even Without Policy Changes? 6-7% in F2012E-F2014E & 4-5% in F2015-F2020E…Well Above 40-Year Average of 3%

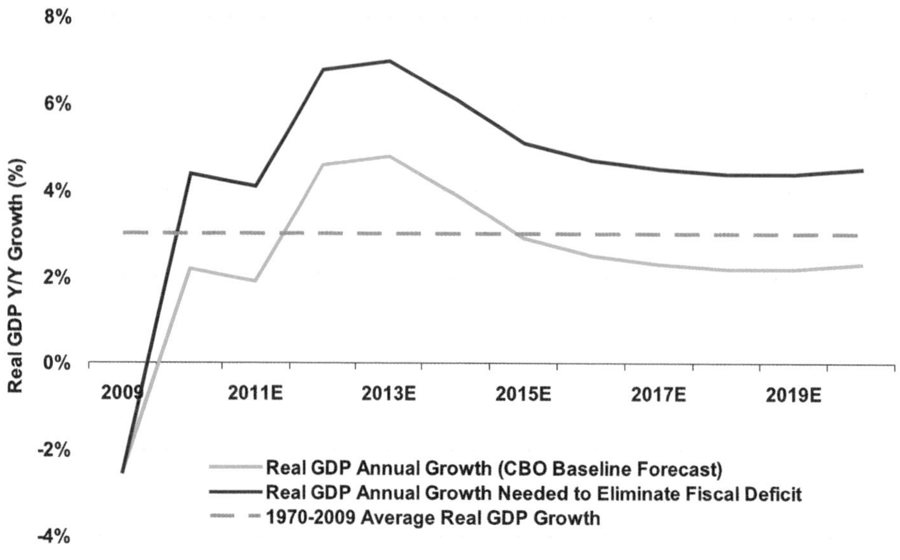

Source: CBO, "The Budget and Economic Outlook: Fiscal Years 2010 to 2020," 8/10.

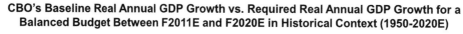

It's Highly Unlikely That Annual Real GDP Can Grow Faster Than 6%… It Happened Only 8 Times in Past 60 Years and Was Always Linked to a Cyclical Bounce Back

CBO's Baseline Real Annual GDP Growth vs. Required Real Annual GDP Growth for a Balanced Budget Between F2011E and F2020E in Historical Context (1950-2020E)

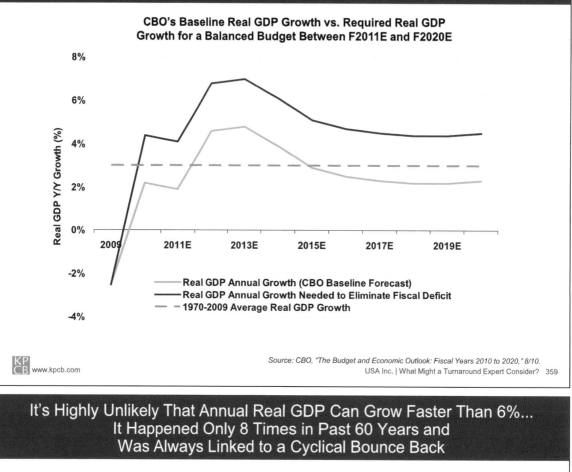

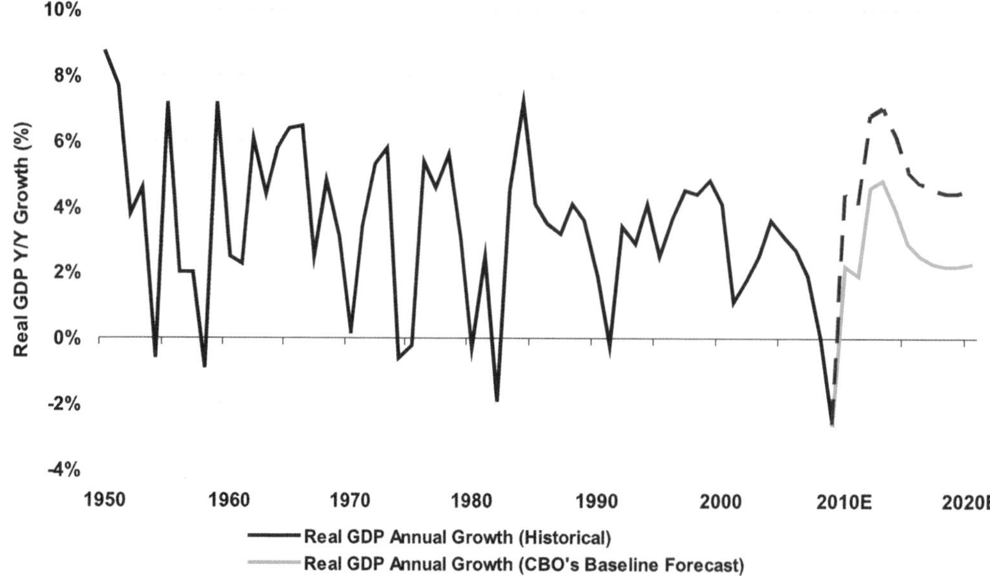

Source: CBO, "The Budget and Economic Outlook: Fiscal Years 2010 to 2020," 8/10.

USA Consumers = Biggest Demand Driver For GDP Growth, Until 2007

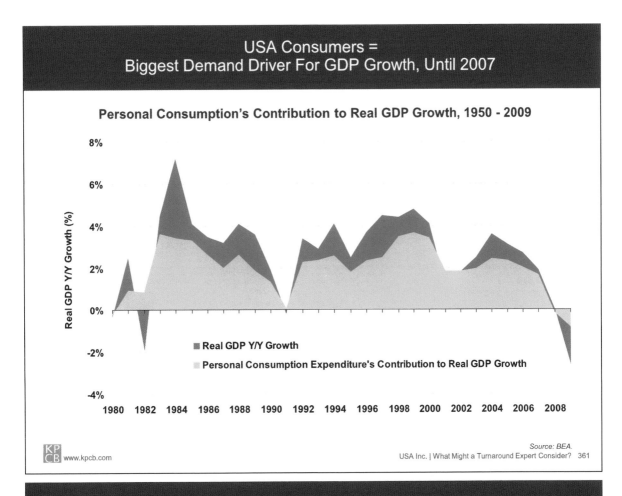

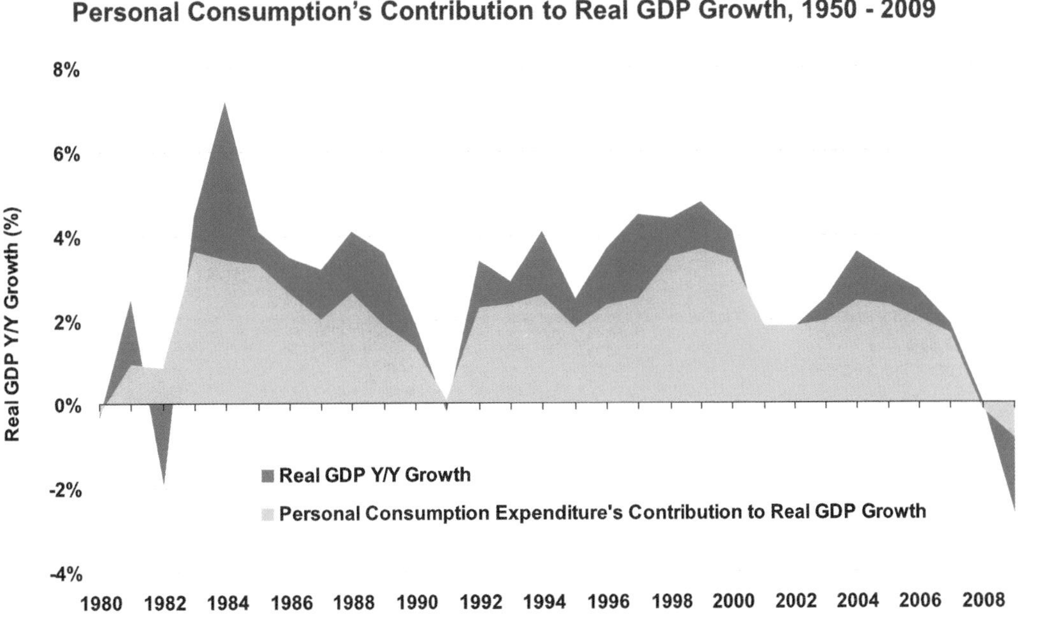

Source: BEA.

Beginning in 2007, Wealth Destruction + High Unemployment Forced Consumers to Save Again, Potentially Reducing Short-Term Demand for Goods & Services

3% average annual GDP growth (1981 - 2007) was helped as the average USA consumer:

1) Increased personal consumption as percent of GDP to 71% from 62%;

2) Decreased personal savings rate to 2% of disposable income from 11%;

Beginning in 2007, things changed as:

1) The average US consumer experienced a material decline in the value of his / her largest investment assets (real estate and equities) from 2007 to 2009 when peak-to-trough valuations for USA residential real estate declined 30% and the S&P 500 declined 56%;

2) Unemployment rose to 10% in 2009 / 2010 from 30-year trough of 4% in 1999, creating uncertainty regarding future personal income levels;

3) Personal savings rate increased to 6% in 2009 / 2010 of disposable income from 2% in 2007, as uncertainty grows and appetite for consumption ebbs;

All in, the key driver of US GDP growth – the US consumer's ability to spend – is severely constrained in the short term as he / she aims to rebuild savings and contain spending. This raises the question – 'How fast can US GDP grow annually over the next ten years?' Determining ways to drive GDP (and related job growth) is crucial…

Source: Residential real estate decline based on CQ1:07 to CQ1:09 changes in S&P Case-Shiller Home Price Index. GDP growth & composition / personal savings rate per BEA. Unemployment rate per BLS.

Economic Policy–Short-Term vs. Long-Term

- Economic theory + experience of the Great Depression suggest government can use fiscal policy (increase direct spending + investment) to offset near-term shortfalls in private demand.

- In the long term, USA Inc. cannot sustain higher levels of direct spending / investment without crowding out private consumption / investment.

- Therefore, USA Inc. should prioritize and allocate available resources to stimulate growth in productivity + employment, which drive long-term GDP growth.

 www.kpcb.com

Improving Employment, Productivity, & Hours Worked Are Source of Sustainable Long-Term GDP Growth

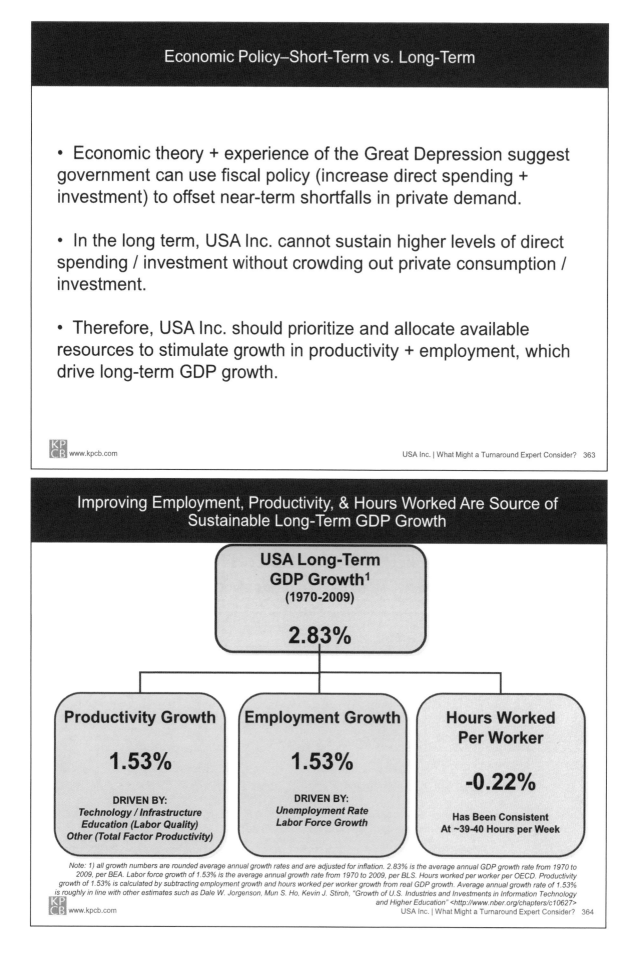

Note: 1) all growth numbers are rounded average annual growth rates and are adjusted for inflation. 2.83% is the average annual GDP growth rate from 1970 to 2009, per BEA. Labor force growth of 1.53% is the average annual growth rate from 1970 to 2009, per BLS. Hours worked per worker per OECD. Productivity growth of 1.53% is calculated by subtracting employment growth and hours worked per worker growth from real GDP growth. Average annual growth rate of 1.53% is roughly in line with other estimates such as Dale W. Jorgenson, Mun S. Ho, Kevin J. Stiroh, "Growth of U.S. Industries and Investments in Information Technology and Higher Education" <http://www.nber.org/chapters/c10627>

www.kpcb.com

Focus on **Productivity** & **Employment** Growth, Each of Which Accounts for ~50% of Long-Term Real GDP Growth

- **Investments in Technology / Infrastructure / Education Boost Productivity.**
  - Newer technology improves efficiency of communication and lowers costs of providing goods and services.
  - Better infrastructure reduces transportation costs for input and output materials
  - Better education improves general labor quality and enables specialization for more efficiency.
- **Removing Restrictions / Uncertainties in Various Regulations Can Stimulate Private Employment.**
  - Immigration does not reduce employment opportunities for US-born workers, per Federal Reserve study in 8/10.
  - Removing tax / regulatory uncertainty could help create hiring incentives for private industries.
- **Hours Worked per Worker Have Remained Steady at ~39-40 Hours per Week From 1970 to 2009 and Will Likely Remain Steady.**

Source: OECD, Dale W. Jorgenson, Mun S. Ho, Kevin J. Stiroh, "Growth of U.S. Industries and Investments in Information Technology and Higher Education" http://www.nber.org/chapters/c10627, Federal Reserve.

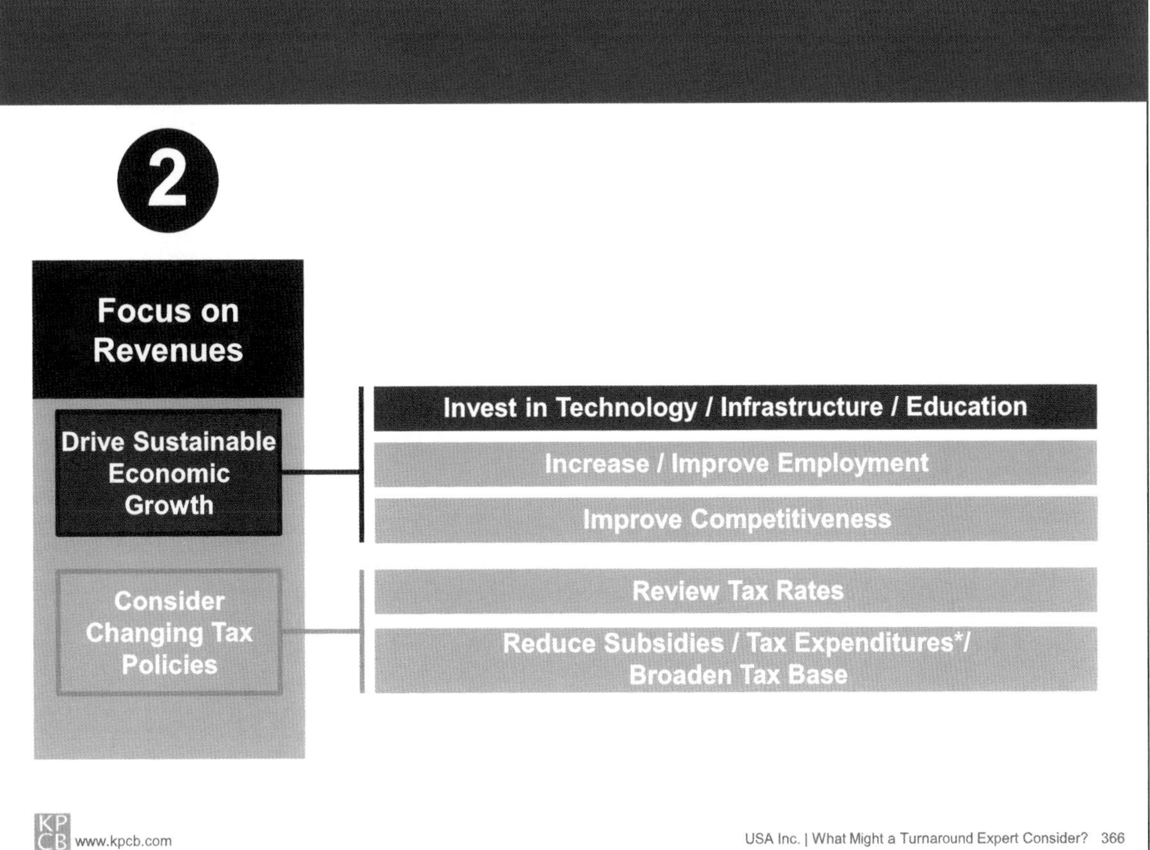
2
Focus on Revenues
Drive Sustainable Economic Growth
Consider Changing Tax Policies
Invest in Technology / Infrastructure / Education
Increase / Improve Employment
Improve Competitiveness
Review Tax Rates
Reduce Subsidies / Tax Expenditures*/ Broaden Tax Base

Technology + Infrastructure + Education Investments Drove ~90% of Labor Productivity Growth for Past ~30 Years

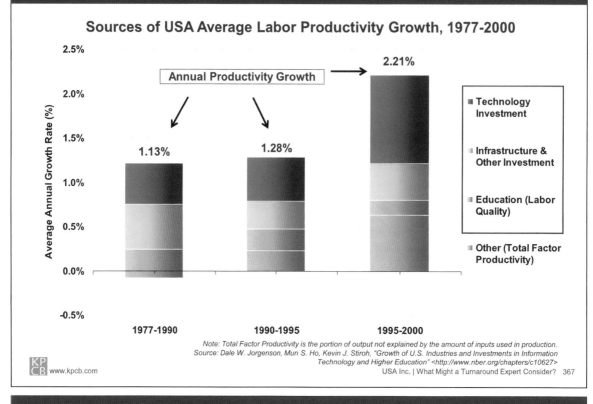

Sources of USA Average Labor Productivity Growth, 1977-2000

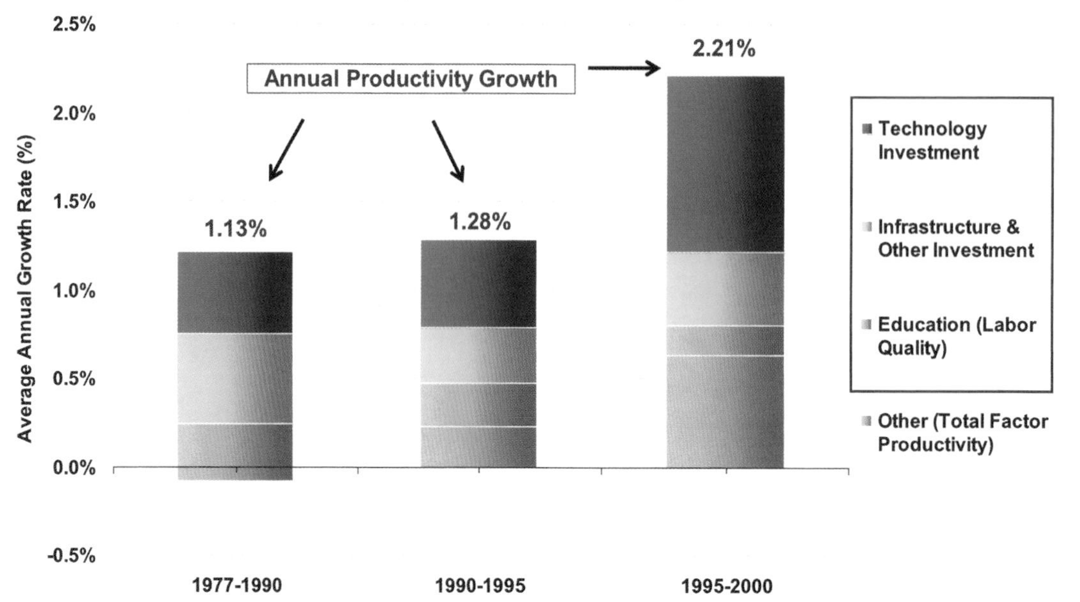

Note: Total Factor Productivity is the portion of output not explained by the amount of inputs used in production.
Source: Dale W. Jorgenson, Mun S. Ho, Kevin J. Stiroh, "Growth of U.S. Industries and Investments in Information Technology and Higher Education" <http://www.nber.org/chapters/c10627>

However, USA Inc. Has Increasingly Allocated Resources Away from Productive Technology + Infrastructure + Education *Investment / Spending* Toward Less-Productive Entitlement Program *Spending*

USA Real Federal Productive vs. Less-Productive Spending*, 1970-2009

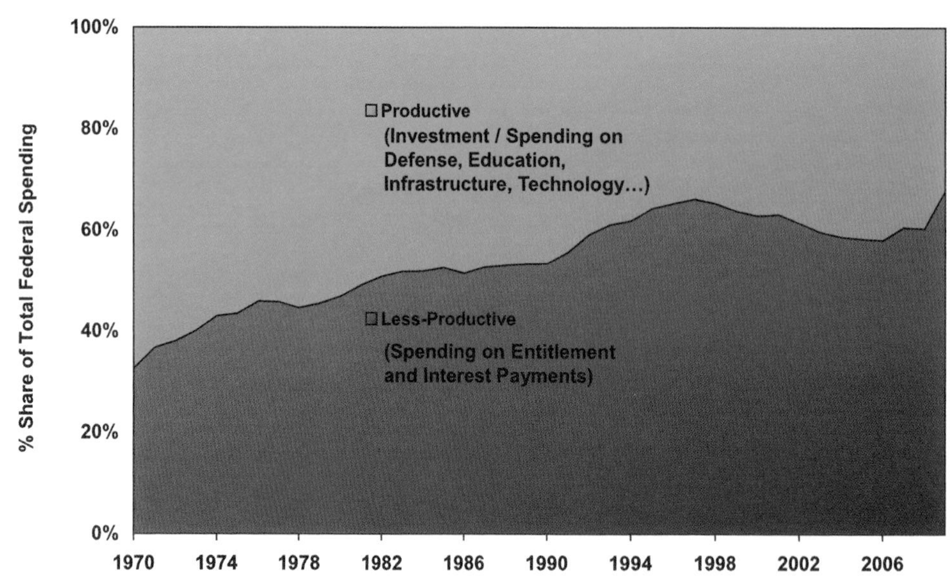

*Note: *Total spending excludes one-time items (such as TARP / GSE / ARRA) for F2008 / F2009 data.*
Data source: White House Office of Management & Budget (1970-2009).

Drive Growth: Technology

Technology Improves Efficiency of Communication and Lowers Costs of Providing Goods and Services

Technology Has Driven Significant Wealth & Job Creation

S&P 500 Sector Market Value Share, 1995 – 2010

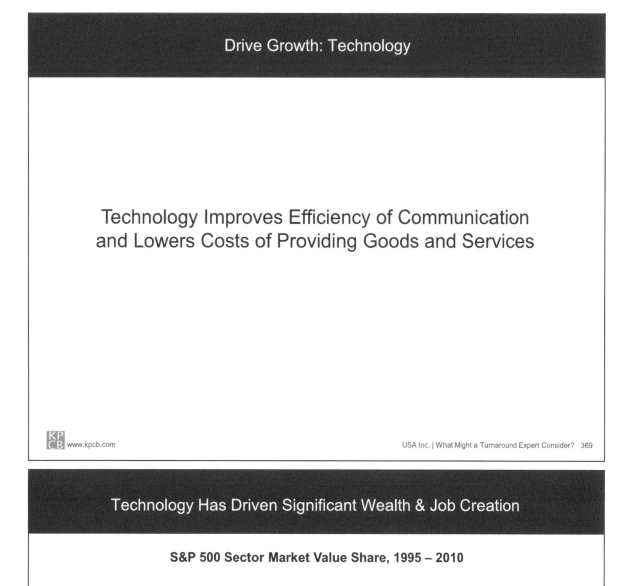

	1995	1996	1997	1998	1999	2000	2001	2002	2003	2004	2005	2006	2007	2008	2009	2010
Information Technology	**9%**	**12%**	**12%**	**18%**	**29%**	**21%**	**18%**	**14%**	**18%**	**16%**	**15%**	**15%**	**17%**	**15%**	**20%**	**19%**
Financials	13	15	17	15	13	17	18	20	21	21	21	22	18	13	15	16
Consumer Staples	13	13	12	11	7	8	8	9	11	10	9	9	10	13	12	12
Health Care	11	10	11	12	9	14	14	15	13	13	13	12	12	15	12	11
Energy	9	9	8	6	6	7	6	6	6	7	9	10	13	13	11	11
Industrials	13	13	12	10	10	11	11	12	11	12	11	11	12	11	10	10
Consumer Discretionary	13	12	12	13	13	10	13	13	11	12	11	11	8	8	10	10
Utilities	5	4	3	3	2	4	3	3	3	3	3	4	4	4	4	4
Materials	6	6	4	3	3	2	3	3	3	3	3	3	3	3	3	4
Telecom Services	9	7	7	8	8	5	5	4	3	3	3	4	4	4	3	3
S&P 500 Mkt Cap ($T)	**$5**	**$6**	**$8**	**$10**	**$12**	**$12**	**$10**	**$8**	**$10**	**$11**	**$11**	**$13**	**$13**	**$8**	**$10**	**$11**

Note: 2010 data as of 12/31/10. Source: FactSet, Bloomberg.

But USA Inc. Has Steadily Scaled Back Investment in Technology R&D Since the 1960s…the Good News is That Private Industry Has Picked Up Lots of Slack, So Far

Total USA Technology Research & Development Spending as % of GDP by Funding Source, 1953 – 2008

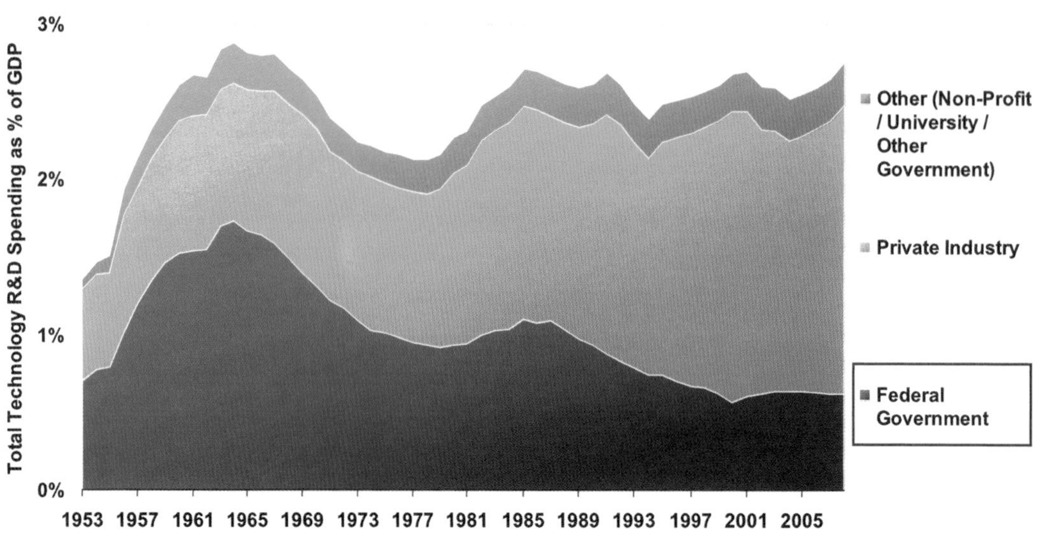

Source: National Science Foundation, Science and Engineering Indicators, 2008.

For GDP Growth & Job Creation, It's Key for Private Industry to Remain Incentivized to Invest in R&D

As we contemplate our future, we must accept the fact that many of the assumptions under which business operated for the past 50 years no longer hold true…If we are committed to investing in ideas to improve – not just maintain – what we have and what we know, the United States will do more than just recover from this recession. We will emerge, once again, as a competitive, global powerhouse…Innovation…accrues to countries in proportion to the quality and rigor of their educational systems…The future of every nation will be shaped by new ideas and creativity. These are the engines of future prosperity.

– Paul Otellini, CEO, Intel Corporation, 2/10/09

Government targeted and 'blue sky' investment in technology (and defense) has led to crucial technology inventions for America – such as ARPANET / Internet (1970s) and Global Positioning System (1980s)..., which, on a net basis, have created jobs, wealth and related tax revenue.

Government investment in technology remains important, but, perhaps more important, government must help incentivize private industry (via tax policies such as allowing companies to repatriate overseas cash at lower tax rates[1] and other tools) to invest in domestic research & development and to create jobs…and create a stable environment in which to operate.

Note: 1) See John Chambers and Safra Catz, "The Overseas Profits Elephant in the Room," The Wall Street Journal, 10/20/10.

Drive Growth: Infrastructure

Better Infrastructure Reduces Transportation Costs For Input and Output Materials

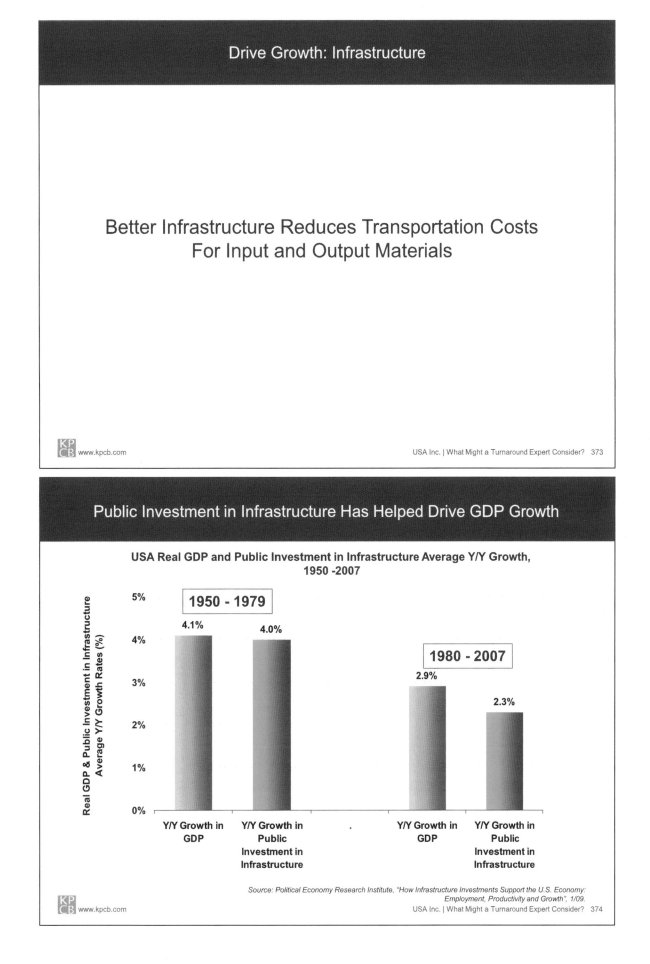

Public Investment in Infrastructure Has Helped Drive GDP Growth

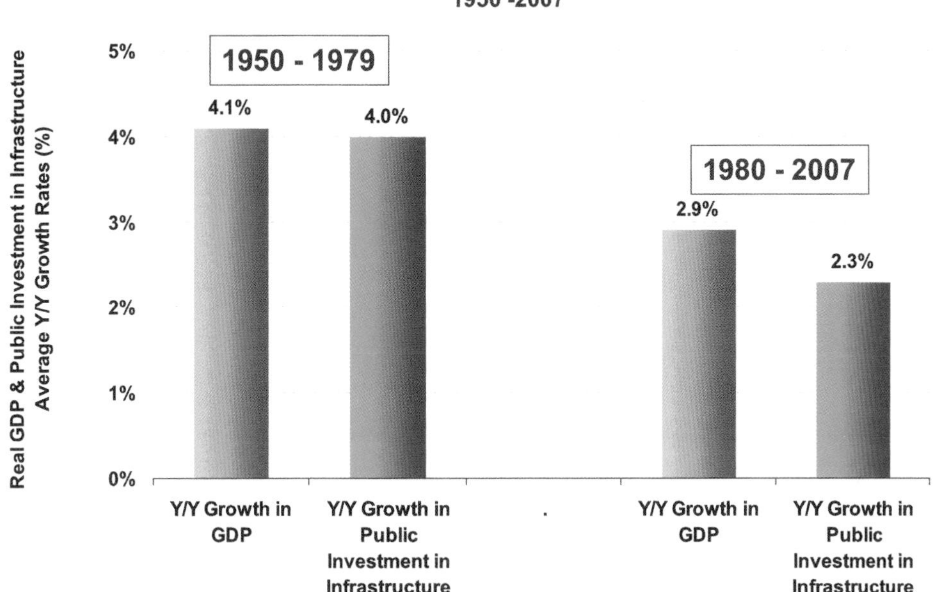

Source: Political Economy Research Institute, "How Infrastructure Investments Support the U.S. Economy: Employment, Productivity and Growth", 1/09.

But USA Inc.'s Investment in Infrastructure Has Been Steadily Declining for Five Decades…

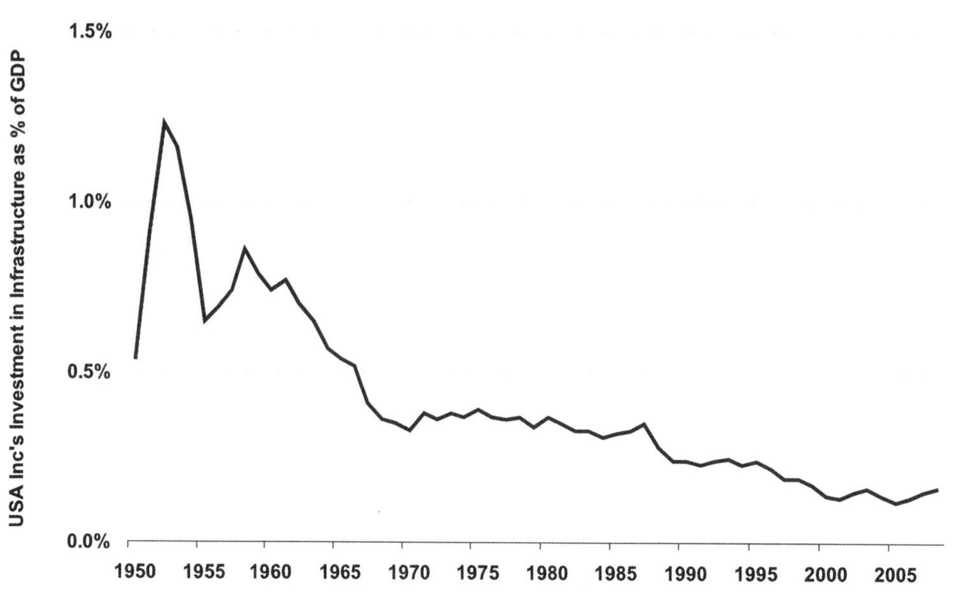

Source: BEA.

…Leading to Deteriorating Infrastructure in America and Pent-Up Demand for Investment

American Society of Civil Engineers' Report Card Grades for America's Infrastructure, 1988 vs. 2009

	1988	2009
Aviation	B-	D
Bridges	--	C
Dams	--	D
Drinking Water	B-	D-
Energy	--	D+
Hazardous Waste	D	D
Inland Waterways	B	D-
Levees	--	D-
Rail	--	C-
Roads	C+	D-
School Buildings	D	D
Solid Waste	C-	C+
Transit	C-	D
Wastewater	C	D-
Overall USA Infrastructure G.P.A.	**C**	**D**
Cost to Improve	**--**	**$2.2T**

Note: The first infrastructure grades were given by the National Council on Public Works Improvements in its report "Fragile Foundations: A Report on America's Public Works, released in February 1988." Source: American Society of Civil Engineers, "2009 Report Card for America's Infrastructure".

Drive Growth: Education

Better Education Improves General Labor Quality and Enables Specialization For More Efficiency

Education = High Long-Term ROI* Investment
Each $1 of Government Spending Could Generate Up to $3 of Incremental Tax Return

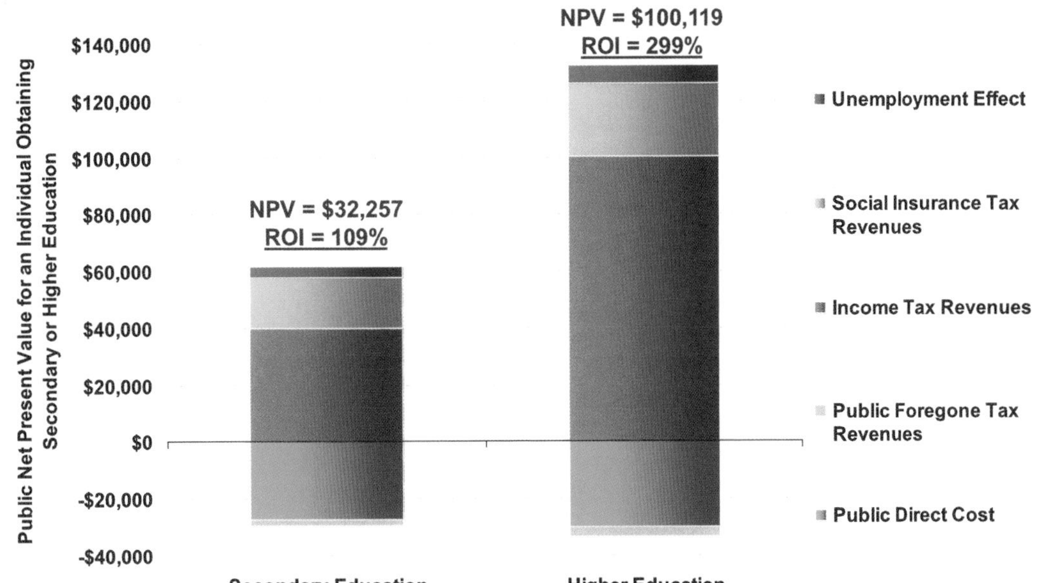

Note: * ROI (return on investment) calculated as NPV of future incremental tax revenues divided by cost for government to support an individual for education. **Limited to male samples, female samples tend to have a lower public NPV. Source: OECD.

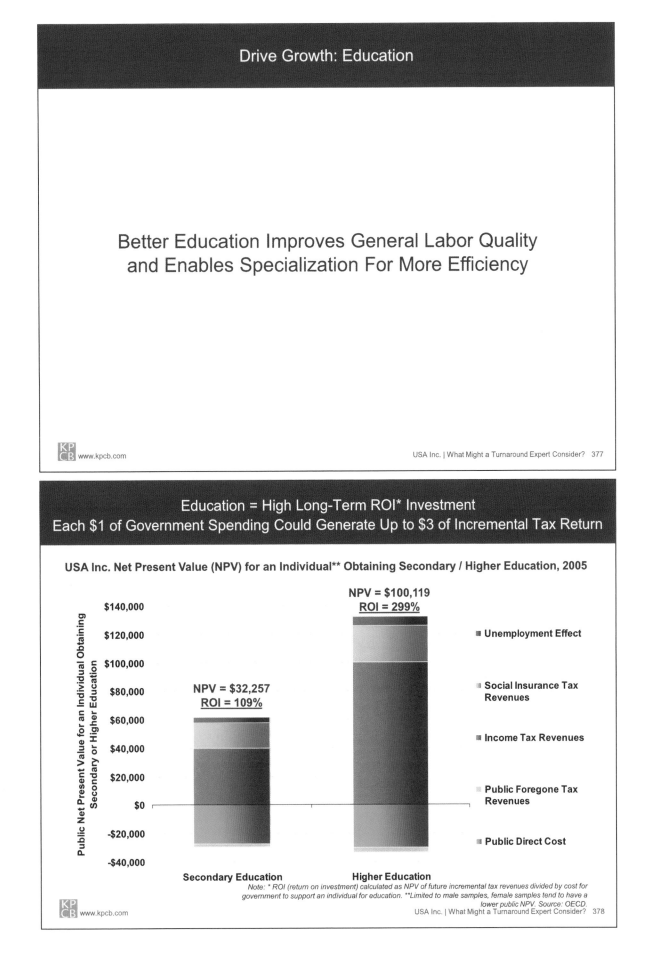

While Government Spending on Education Increased 60% Over Past 50 Years, At Margin, Government Spent More on Healthcare…

USA Total Government Healthcare vs. Education Spending as % of GDP, 1960 – 2008

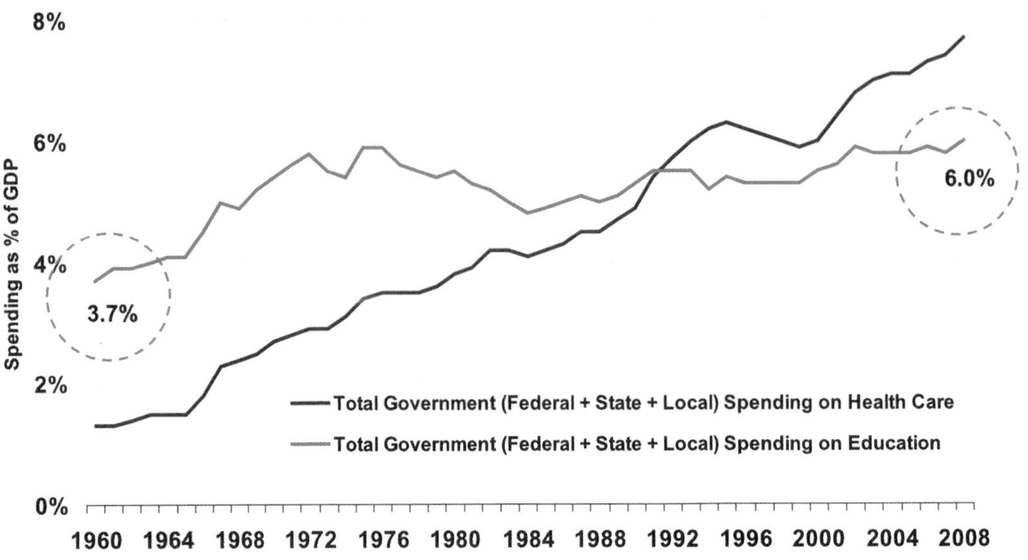

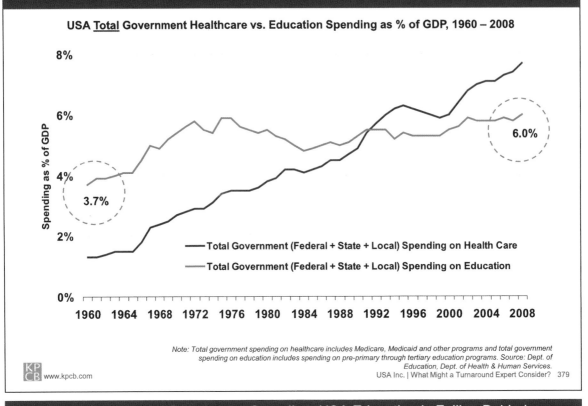

Note: Total government spending on healthcare includes Medicare, Medicaid and other programs and total government spending on education includes spending on pre-primary through tertiary education programs. Source: Dept. of Education, Dept. of Health & Human Services.

Despite Increased Government Spending, USA Education is Falling Behind – Math / Science Tests Scores Well Below OECD Average & Getting Worse Though Self Confidence Rising

USA Ranking Out of 30-34* OECD Countries

in PISA (Program for International Student Assessment for 15-Year Olds)
2000 / 2003 / 2006 / 2009

	2000	2003	2006	2009	2000-2009 Trend
Mathematics	18	23	25	25	↓↓
Science	14	19	21	17	↓
Reading	16	15	--**	14	↑
Self Confidence[1]	2	1	1	--	↑

*Note: *30 OECD countries participated in 2000 / 2003 PISA, 34 OECD countries participated in 2006 / 2009 PISA. 1) Confidence is the self-perceived efficacy in learning abilities (for year 2000); mathematical problem solving abilities (for year 2003) and scientific problem solving abilities (for year 2006). USA tied in confidence ranking with Canada, Hungary, Slovakia, Switzerland and Liechtenstein in 2003 and tied with Poland and Canada in 2006. **2006 reading scores for USA were rendered invalid because of a printing error in questionnaire instructions. Source: OECD.*

USA Student Achievement Rankings* in Mathematics / Science Have Fallen vs. Other OECD Countries

Mathematics Ranking*

	2000	2009
1	Japan	S. Korea
2	S. Korea	Finland
3	New Zealand	Switzerland
4	Finland	Japan
5	Australia	Canada
6	Canada	Netherlands
7	Switzerland	New Zealand
8	UK	Belgium
9	Belgium	Australia
10	France	Germany
11	Austria	Estonia
12	Denmark	Iceland
13	Iceland	Denmark
14	Sweden	Slovenia
15	Ireland	Norway
16	Norway	France
17	Czech Republic	Slovakia
18	**USA**	Austria
19	Germany	Poland
20	Hungary	Sweden
21	Spain	Czech Republic
22	Poland	UK
23	Italy	Hungary
24	Portugal	Luxembourg
25	Greece	**USA**
26	Luxembourg	Ireland
27	Mexico	Portugal
28		Spain
29		Italy
30		Greece
31		Israel
32		Turkey
33		Chile
34		Mexico

Science Ranking*

	2000	2009
1	Korea	Finland
2	Japan	Japan
3	Finland	S. Korea
4	UK	New Zealand
5	Canada	Canada
6	New Zealand	Estonia
7	Australia	Australia
8	Austria	Netherlands
9	Ireland	Germany
10	Sweden	Switzerland
11	Czech Republic	UK
12	France	Slovenia
13	Norway	Poland
14	**USA**	Ireland
15	Hungary	Belgium
16	Iceland	Hungary
17	Belgium	**USA**
18	Switzerland	Czech Republic
19	Spain	Norway
20	Germany	Denmark
21	Poland	France
22	Denmark	Iceland
23	Italy	Sweden
24	Greece	Austria
25	Portugal	Portugal
26	Luxembourg	Slovak Republic
27	Mexico	Italy
28		Spain
29		Luxembourg
30		Greece
31		Israel
32		Turkey
33		Chile
34		Mexico

*Note: *USA ranking out of OECD countries in PISA (Program for International Student Assessment for 15-Year Olds). Source: OECD.*

USA Young Adults' (25-34) Higher-Education* Penetration Significantly Lags Behind Canada / Korea / Russia / Japan

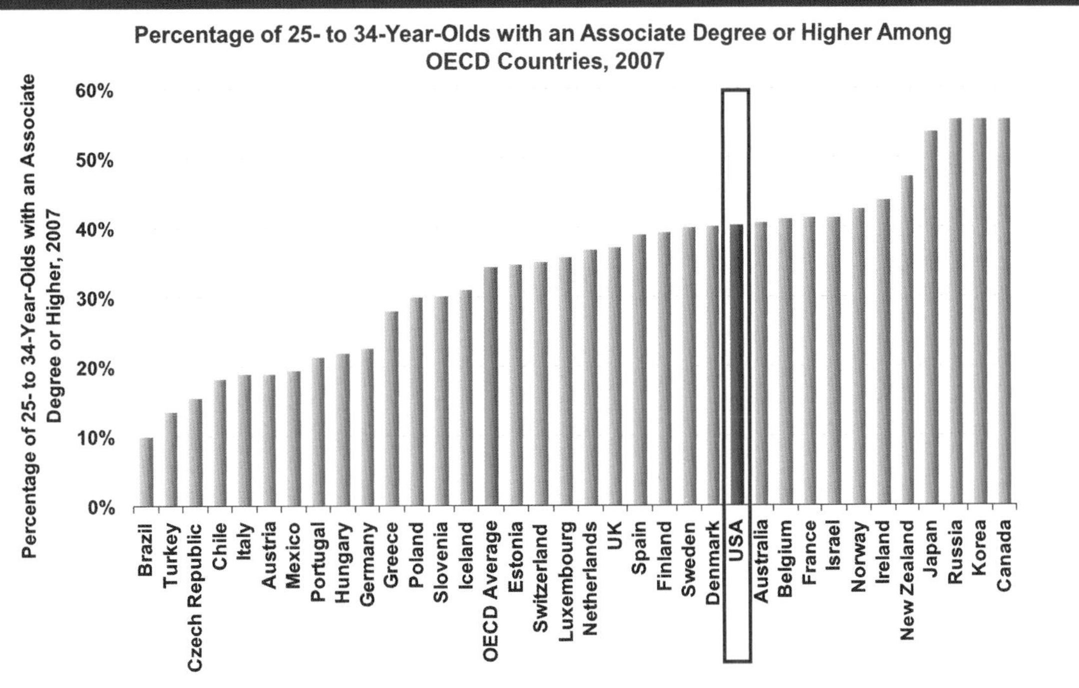

*Note: *Higher education defined as post-secondary (college / university) education. Source: OECD.*

2

Focus on Revenues

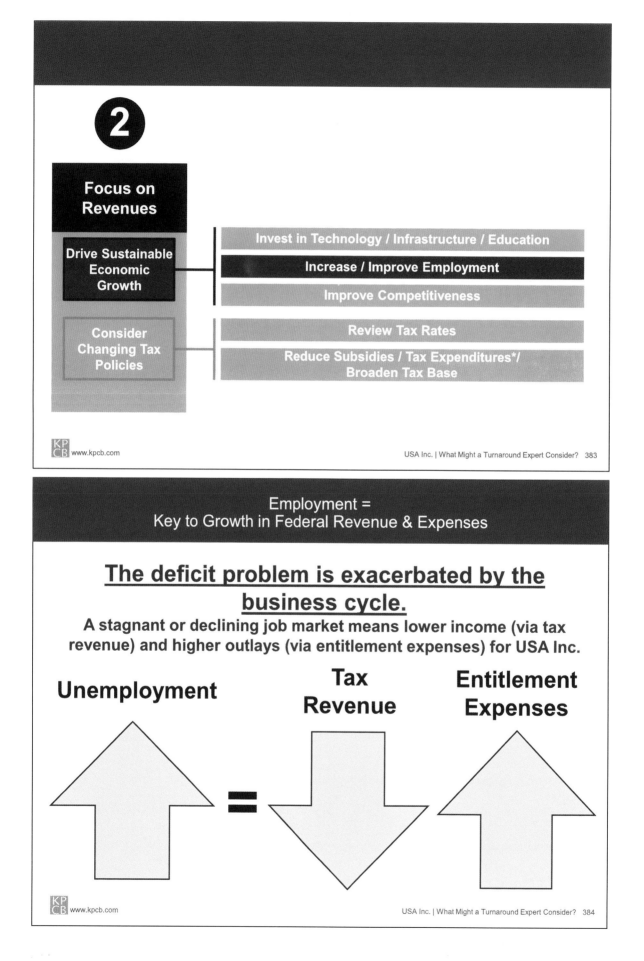

- **Drive Sustainable Economic Growth**
  - Invest in Technology / Infrastructure / Education
  - Increase / Improve Employment
  - Improve Competitiveness
- **Consider Changing Tax Policies**
  - Review Tax Rates
  - Reduce Subsidies / Tax Expenditures*/ Broaden Tax Base

Employment = Key to Growth in Federal Revenue & Expenses

The deficit problem is exacerbated by the business cycle.

A stagnant or declining job market means lower income (via tax revenue) and higher outlays (via entitlement expenses) for USA Inc.

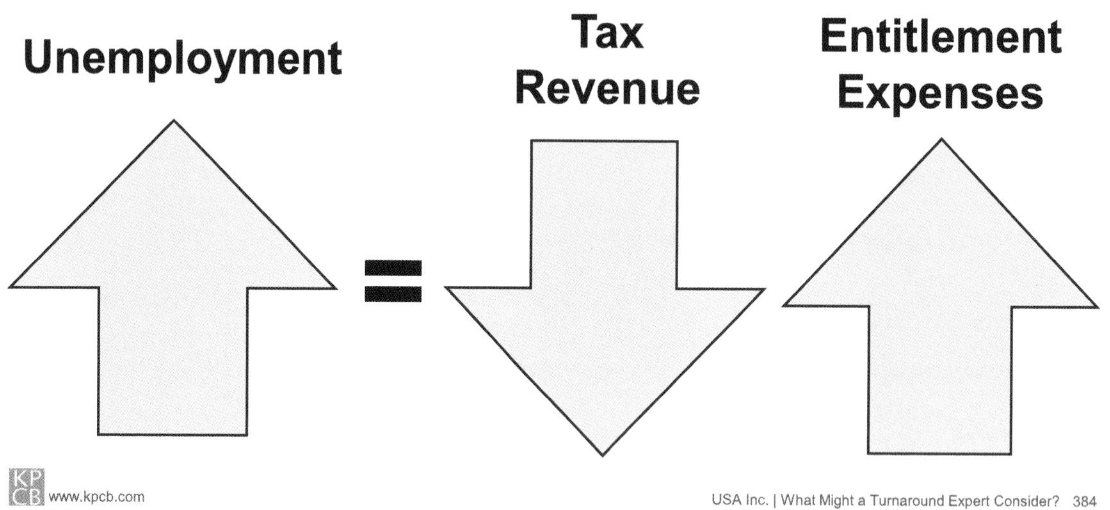

Though Entitlements Are Structural, Not a Cyclical Problem, Entitlement Outlays Go Up with High Unemployment

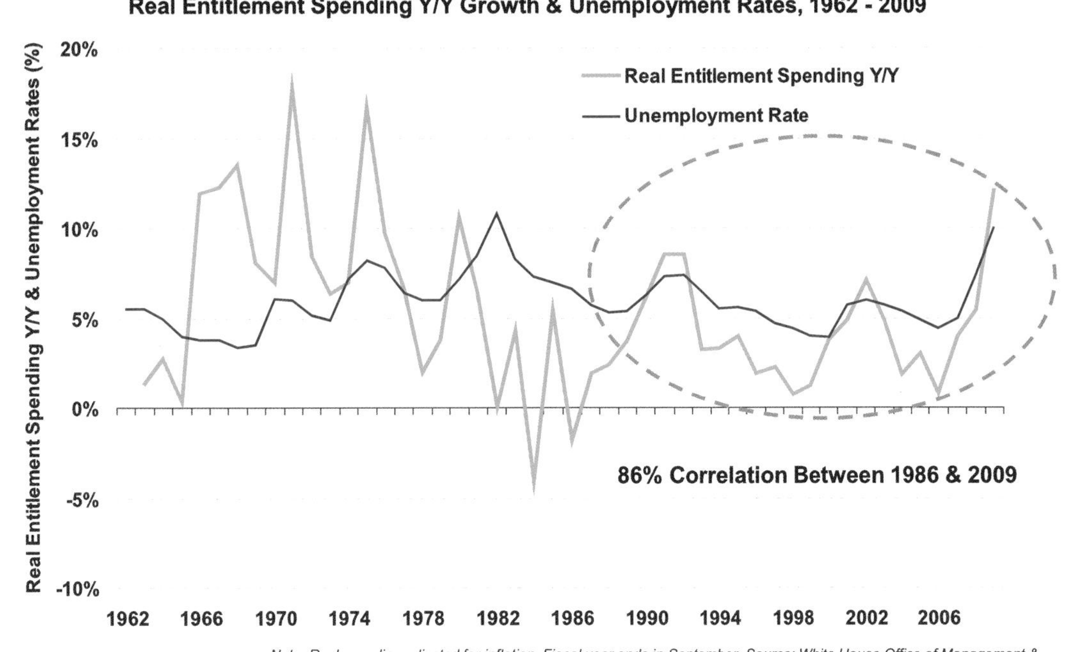

Note: Real spending adjusted for inflation. Fiscal year ends in September. Source: White House Office of Management & Budget, Bureau of Labor Statistics.

Increase Employment – High-Level Policy Options to Consider

Short-run options:

1) Payroll tax holiday ***and/or***
2) Employment tax credit ***and/or***
3) Job training ***and/or***
4) Restore labor mobility by reducing housing imbalances

Medium- to long-run options:

1) Reduce employer health care costs ***and/or***
2) Improve vocational training/education ***and/or***
3) Encourage inward foreign direct investment, "onshoring" which would increase domestic employment

Source: Richard Berner, "Employment Prospects and Policies to Improve Them" (2/26/10), Morgan Stanley Research.

Increase Employment: Structural Problems in USA Labor Force High Healthcare Costs + Skills Mismatch + Labor Immobility

- **Healthcare costs may be a barrier to hiring for employers**
  - Healthcare benefits = 8% of average total employee compensation; grew at 6.9% CAGR from 1998 to 2008 compared with 4.5% CAGR in salaries.
  - Healthcare benefits are fixed costs as they are paid on an annual per-worker basis and do not vary with hours worked.
  - As employers try to lower fixed costs to right-size to reduced revenue levels, layoffs are the only way to reduce fixed healthcare costs.

- **Skills mismatch may be a barrier to hiring for employers**
  - A large portion of the long-term unemployed may lack requisite skills.
  - 14% of firms reported difficulty filling positions due to the lack of suitable talent, per 5/10 Manpower Research survey.

- **Labor immobility resulting from the housing bust may be a barrier to hiring**
  - One in four homeowners are "trapped" because they owe more than their houses are worth, so they cannot move to take new jobs – until they sell or walk away.

Source: Richard Berner, "Why is US Employment So Weak" (7/23/10), Morgan Stanley Research.

Increase Employment: Immigration Does Not Take Away Jobs in USA; It Improves Productivity + Boosts Income per Worker

- **Immigration = Positive Impact on USA Productivity & Income per Worker**
- **Immigration = Neutral Impact on Employment for U.S.-Born Workers**

% Change in USA Productivity / Income per Worker / Employment for U.S.-Based Workers In Response to an Inflow of Immigrants Equal to 1% of Employment

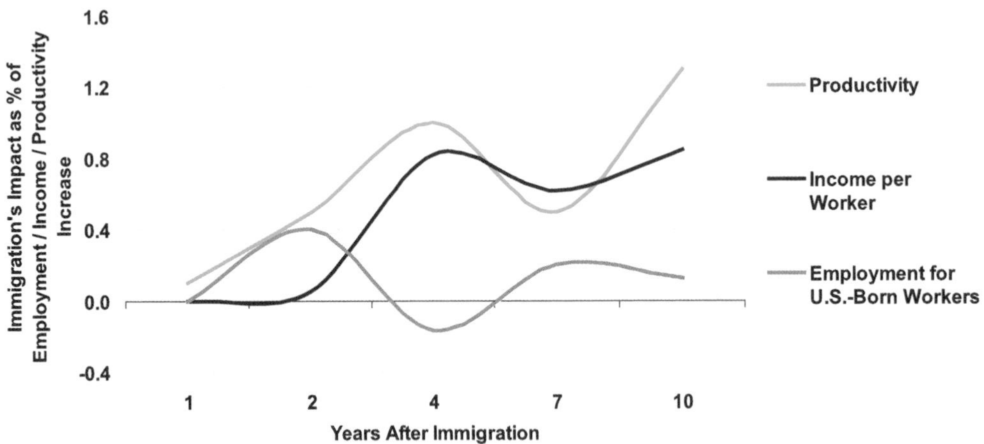

Source: Giovanni Peri, "The Effect of Immigrants on U.S. Employment and Productivity," 8/30/2010 Federal Reserve Board of San Francisco (FRBSF) Economic Letter 2010-26.

Focus on Revenues

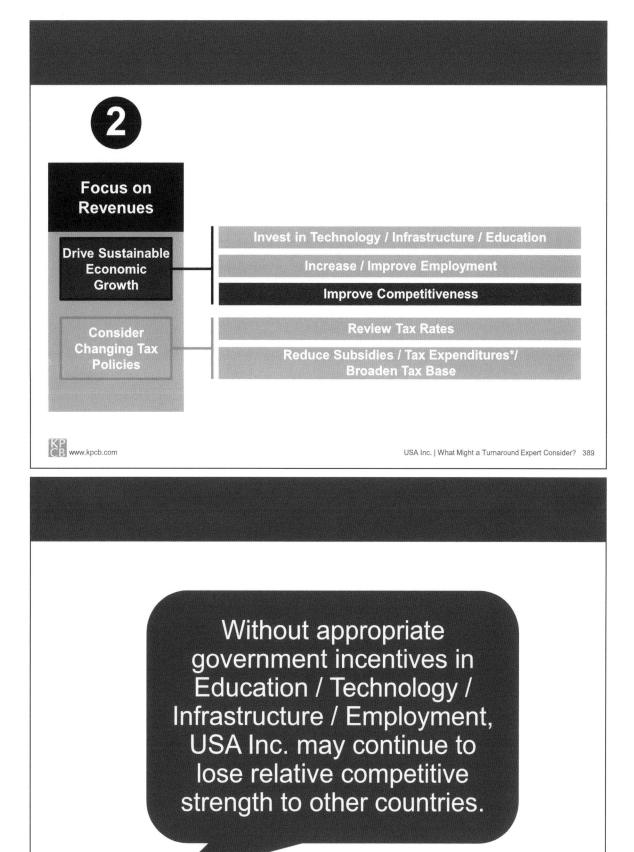

Drive Sustainable Economic Growth
- Invest in Technology / Infrastructure / Education
- Increase / Improve Employment
- **Improve Competitiveness**

Consider Changing Tax Policies
- Review Tax Rates
- Reduce Subsidies / Tax Expenditures*/ Broaden Tax Base

Without appropriate government incentives in Education / Technology / Infrastructure / Employment, USA Inc. may continue to lose relative competitive strength to other countries.

Compared to 10 Years Ago, USA is Losing Competitiveness at the Margin vs. Its Peers

- **McKinsey conducted a study in 2010 that compares the USA with other countries on 20 attributes related to economic fundamentals, business climate, human capital and infrastructure. McKinsey compared current status vs. status in 2000.**
- We augmented the McKinsey study with 9 additional attributes across those aforementioned areas as well as government spending metrics.
- Through this study, we found that **America**, relative to other countries, **improved on none of the 29 attributes**, **remained the same on 9 attributes** (including GDP per capita, public debt as % of GDP, public spending on healthcare, public spending on education, growth in local innovation clusters, population & demographic profile, retention of foreign-born talents, total healthcare spending and cost-adjusted labor productivity) and **deteriorated on 20** (including trade surplus, national spending on R&D, industrial production, corporate tax rate, business environment, FDI, tax incentives for R&D, number of patent applications, availability of high-quality labor, higher education penetration, telecom & transportation infrastructure, etc.).

USA Ranking High in Country Attractiveness Indicators But Losing Share at the Margin…

	Key metrics	US Relative Position: Ten Years Ago	US Relative Position: Today	Trend
Economic Fundamentals	Household consumption	Top Ranked	Top Ranked	▼
	Household consumption growth	Top Ranked	Top Quartile	▼
	GDP	Top Ranked	Top Ranked	▼
	GDP per capita[2]	Top Quartile	Top Quartile	—
	Stock market capitalization	Top Ranked	Top Ranked	▼
	Technology company market cap[2]	Top Ranked	Top Ranked	▼
	Industrial production	Top Ranked	Top Quartile	▼
	Trade as % of GDP	Average	Average	▼
	Trade surplus[2]	Bottom Quartile	Bottom Quartile	▼
	National spending on R&D	Average	Average	▼
Government Spending	Defense spending[2]	Top Ranked	Top Ranked	▼
	Government public debt as % GDP[2]	Average	Average	—
	Public healthcare spending as % of GDP[2]	Top Quartile	Top Quartile	—
	Government surplus as % of GDP[2]	Bottom Quartile	Bottom Quartile	▼
	Public expenditure on education	Top Ranked	Top Ranked	—

■ Top Ranked ■ Top Quartile ■ Average ■ Bottom Quartile

Source: 1) Growth and competitiveness in the United States: The role of its multinational companies, McKinsey & Company. 2) estimates based on data from IMF / OECD

…USA Ranking High in Country Attractiveness Indicators But Losing Share at the Margin

	Key metrics	US relative position: Ten Years Ago	US relative position: Today	Trend
Business climate	Statutory corporate tax rate	Average	Bottom Quartile	▼
	Business environment	Top Ranked	Top Quartile	▼
	FDI as % of GDP	Average	Average	▼
	Growth of local innovation clusters	Top Ranked	Top Ranked	—
	Tax incentives for R&D	Top Quartile	Average	▼
Human capital	Population and demographic profile	Top Quartile	Top Quartile	—
	Availability of high-quality labor	Top Ranked	Top Ranked	▼
	Retention of foreign-born talent	Top Ranked	Top Ranked	—
	Cost-adjusted labor productivity	Average	Average	—
	Total healthcare spending per Capita[2]	Top Ranked	Top Ranked	—
	Higher education penetration[2]	Top Ranked	Top Quartile	▼
	Number of patent applications	Top Ranked	Top Quartile	▼
Infrastructure	Transportation	Top Ranked	Top Quartile	▼
	Telecommunications	Top Ranked	Top Quartile	▼

Top Ranked · Top Quartile · Average · Bottom Quartile

Source: 1) Growth and competitiveness in the United States: The role of its multinational companies, McKinsey & Company. 2) estimates based on data from IMF / OECD

USA's Share of Global GDP Has Declined from 33% in 1985 to 24% in 2010, While China / Brazil / Korea's Shares Have Risen

Share of World GDP, USA vs. China / Brazil / India, 1985 – 2010E

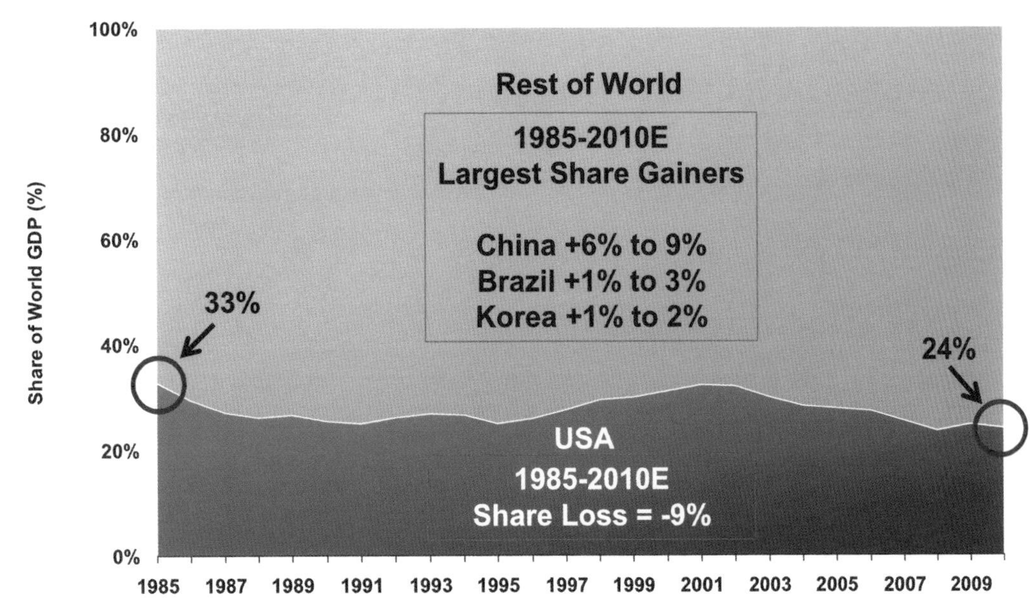

Note: Data are NOT adjusted for purchasing power parity. Source: IMF.

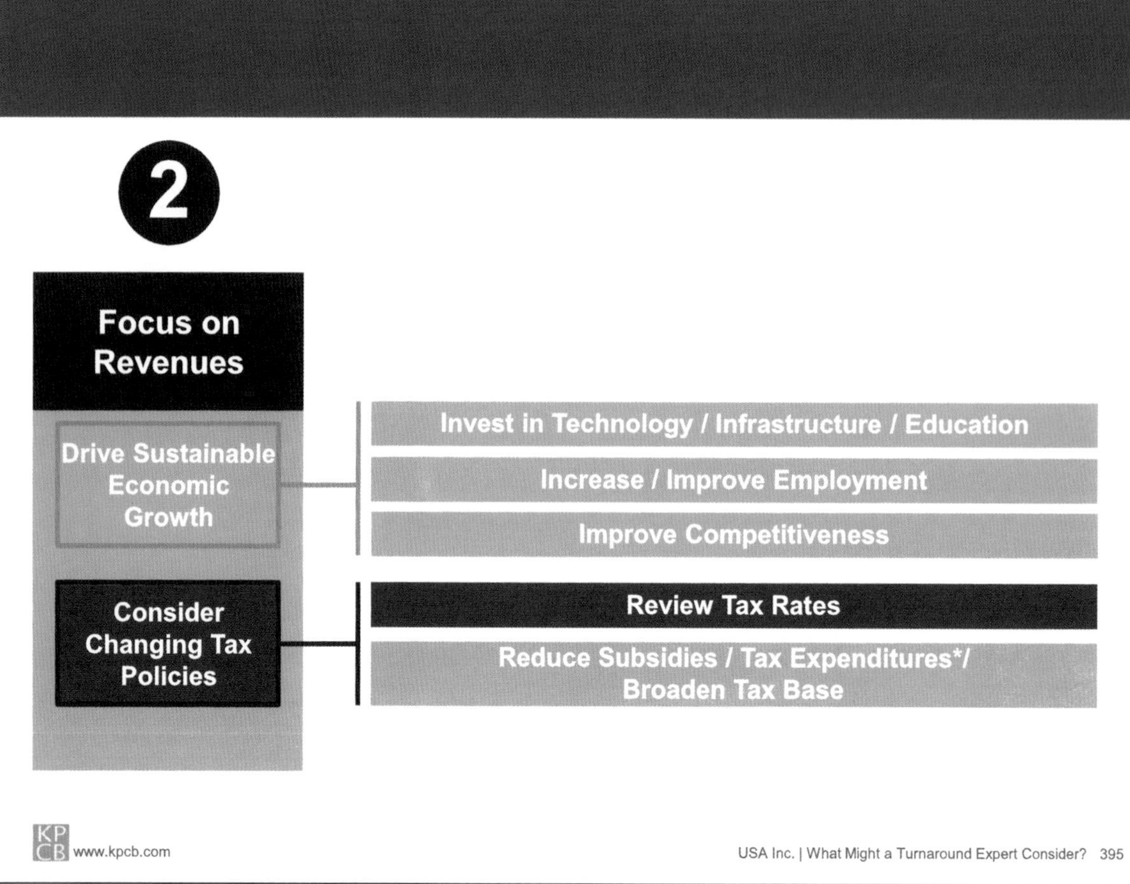
2
Focus on Revenues
Drive Sustainable Economic Growth
Invest in Technology / Infrastructure / Education
Increase / Improve Employment
Improve Competitiveness
Consider Changing Tax Policies
Review Tax Rates
Reduce Subsidies / Tax Expenditures*/ Broaden Tax Base

Simple Tax Math* – Big Across-the-Board Tax Rate Increases Would Be Needed to Potentially Generate Meaningful Revenue Improvements

Each one percentage point across-the-board tax rate increase would generate an incremental $127 billion revenue for USA Inc. in F2010E[1]...excluding any related negative impact on spending / GDP growth, which is difficult to do…

Across-the-Board Tax Rate Increase	Hypothetical Revenue Increase for USA Inc. in F2010E ($ billions)	…Which Would Reduce Estimated Losses in F2010E by
1 Percentage Point	$127	8%
2 Percentage Points (pps)	$254	16%
3 pps	$381	24%
4 pps	$508	33%
5 pps	$635	41%
10 pps	$1,270	82%

*Note: *The simple tax math presented here are pure mathematical illustrations – we simply calculated how big a broad-based tax rate increase (for individual and corporate income, as well as payroll) would have to be for USA Inc. to financial break-even. These calculations are merely mechanical illustrations and are not meant to portray realistic solutions. 1) Incremental dollar amount calculated as 1% of projected total personal & corporate income, which historically has been at ~87% of GDP. Source: F2010E revenue & deficit per White House OMB, GDP per CBO.*

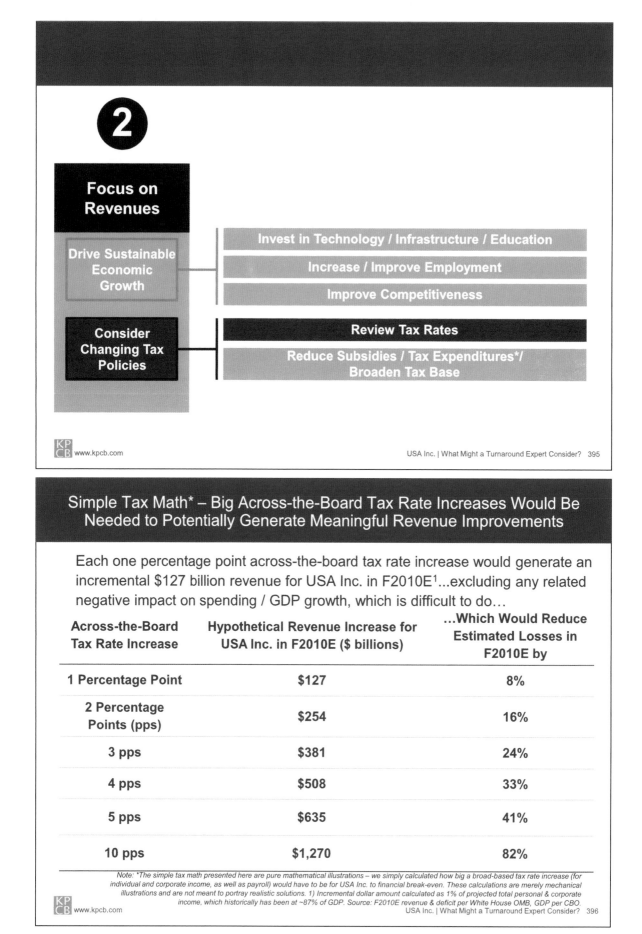

More Complex Tax Math: If Lower Brackets Excluded, Draconian Rate Hikes Required to Attempt to Bring USA Inc. Budget Into Financial Balance

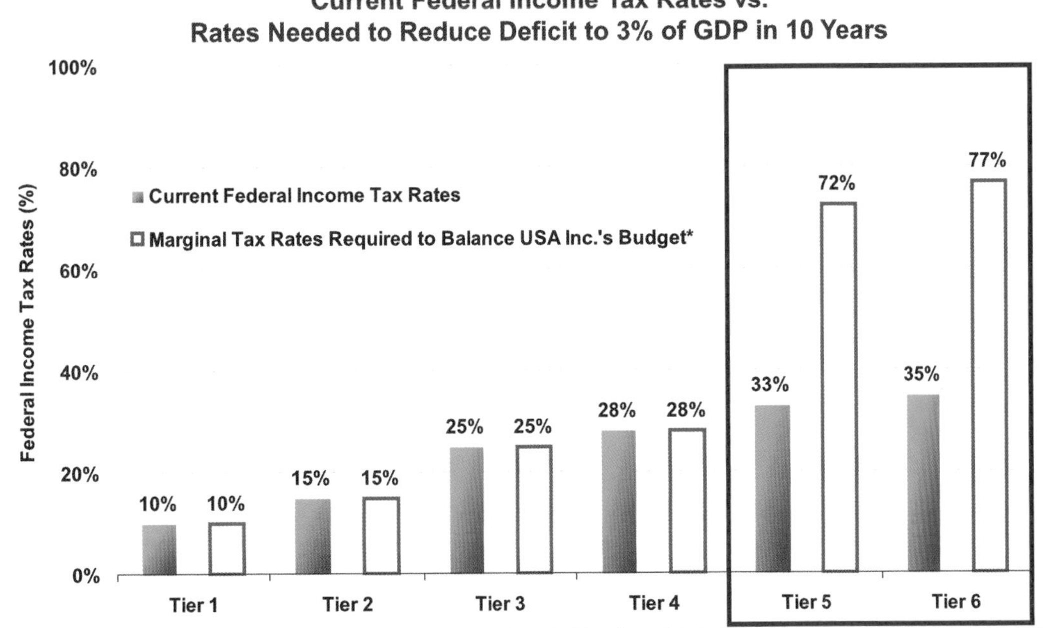

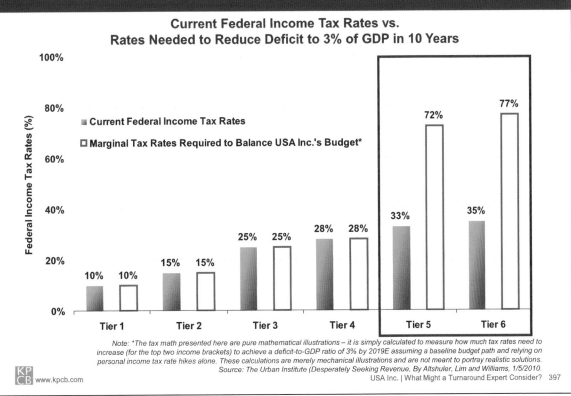

*Note: *The tax math presented here are pure mathematical illustrations – it is simply calculated to measure how much tax rates need to increase (for the top two income brackets) to achieve a deficit-to-GDP ratio of 3% by 2019E assuming a baseline budget path and relying on personal income tax rate hikes alone. These calculations are merely mechanical illustrations and are not meant to portray realistic solutions.*
Source: The Urban Institute (Desperately Seeking Revenue, By Altshuler, Lim and Williams, 1/5/2010.

Pros + Cons of Tax Rate Hikes

- A more progressive income tax system could lower tax burden from potential subsidy cuts and carbon taxes on the low-income population.
- Addressing income inequality may enhance perceived fairness – and political chances – of comprehensive deficit measures.
- Across-the-board tax rate increases would hurt nearly everyone, but especially lower-income taxpayers.
- Rate increases on upper brackets usually spur tax avoidance, and revenues often fall short of targets.
- Rate increases, which discourage savings, amplify distortions in the economy from tax subsidies, exclusions and tax expenditures, all of which encourage consumption.

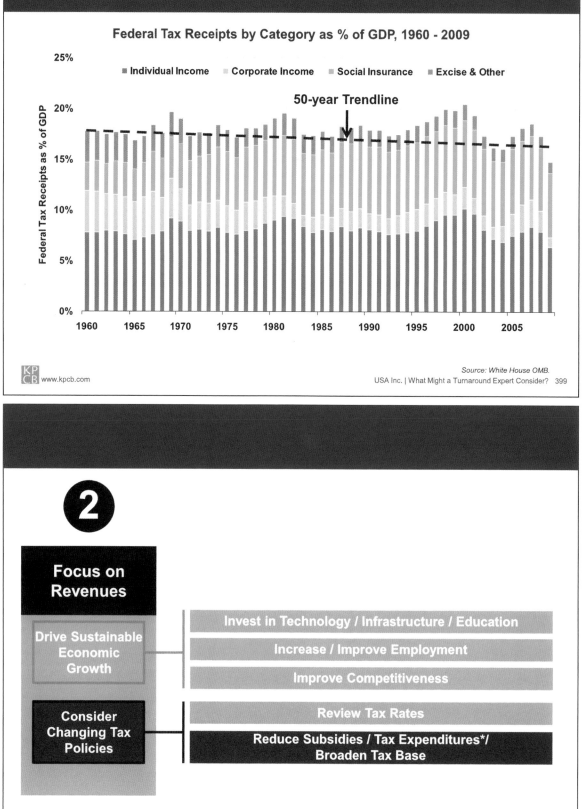

Despite Multitudes of Tax Rate Changes, USA Inc.'s Tax Revenue as Percent of GDP Remained Roughly Stable at 15-20% from 1960-2002

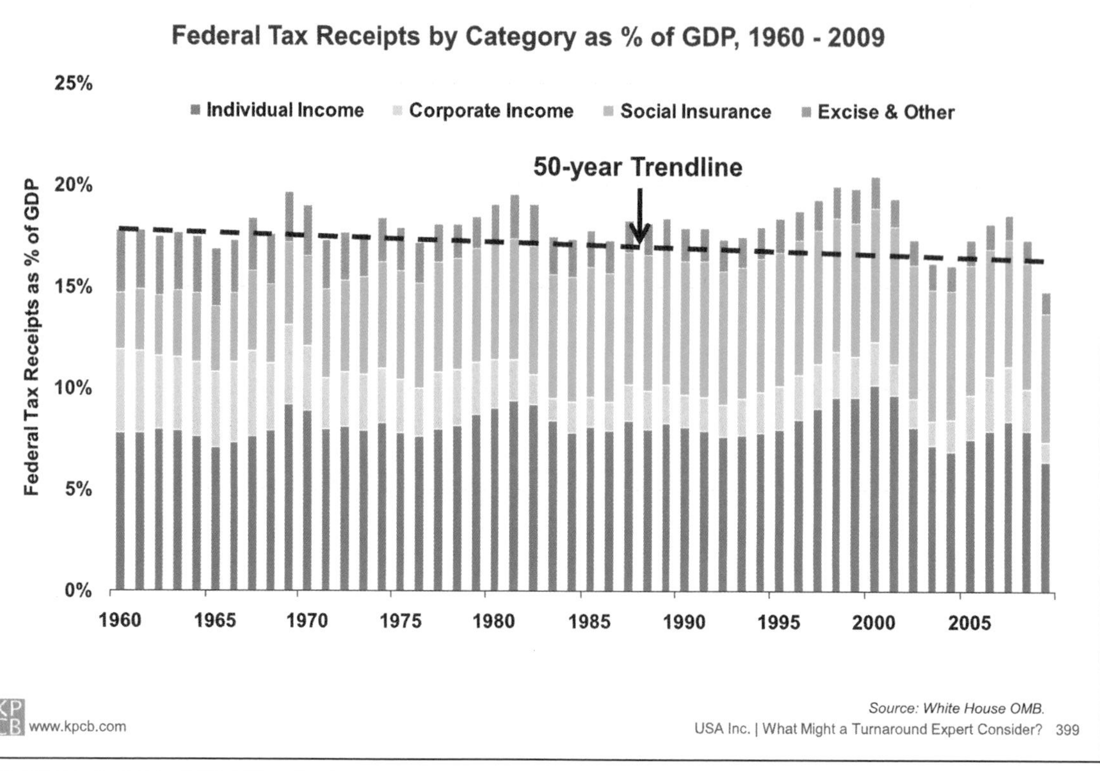

Source: White House OMB.

2

Focus on Revenues

- **Drive Sustainable Economic Growth**
  - Invest in Technology / Infrastructure / Education
  - Increase / Improve Employment
  - Improve Competitiveness
- **Consider Changing Tax Policies**
  - Review Tax Rates
  - Reduce Subsidies / Tax Expenditures*/ Broaden Tax Base

Illustrating the Revenue Tradeoffs – Changing Tax Rates vs. Broadening the Tax Base

Mathematical Illustrations*

1) To eliminate F2010 deficits by increasing individual / corporate / payroll tax rates across-the-board would require +12 percentage points of tax rate increase (raising $1.4 trillion) – and would likely damage economic growth? *or*

2) To eliminate primary budget deficit** by F2019E by increasing top two tiers of income tax rates would require moving marginal rates to 72% / 77% from 33% / 35% – also likely to damage growth and encourage tax avoidance? *or*

3) Broadening tax base could require reducing 'tax expenditures' and subsidies, e.g., limiting deductions and subsidies for housing & healthcare?

Policy Options

1) A combination of somewhat higher rates and a broader tax base? *and/or*

2) Changing taxation of individual income to encourage saving / investment rather than consumption (perhaps a value-added tax and/or carbon tax)? *and/or*

3) Changing taxation of corporate income to reflect global competition?

*Note: *The simple tax math presented here are pure mathematical illustrations – we simply calculated how big a broad-based tax rate increase (for individual and corporate income, as well as payroll) would have to be for USA Inc. to financial break-even. These calculations are merely mechanical illustrations and are not meant to portray realistic solutions. **Primary budget deficit is the budget deficit excluding net interest payments.*

Changing USA Inc.'s Tax System Could Help Rebalance the Economy & Reallocate Resources

- **Though there would be adjustment costs, reducing subsidies and 'tax expenditures' could broaden the tax base and collect more revenue, while allowing income tax rates to stay low or go lower.**
- The current system favors consumption, penalizes saving; a tax based on consumption (or "value added") could offset some of that penalty, though there are risks and drawbacks.
- Subsidies create incentives to consume more health insurance and housing – both account for 20% of GDP, vs. 11% in 1965[1] – and take resources from other sectors like education, technology, infrastructure.
- A worldwide corporate tax system with a lower tax rate could reduce incentives for companies to keep income offshore.
- A carbon tax could raise some additional revenue to reduce the deficit, while encouraging sustainable economic development.

Source: 1) per BEA and CMS.

Changing Tax Policy to Broaden Tax Base: Subsidies + Tax Expenditures = 70% of USA Inc.'s Cash Flow Deficit

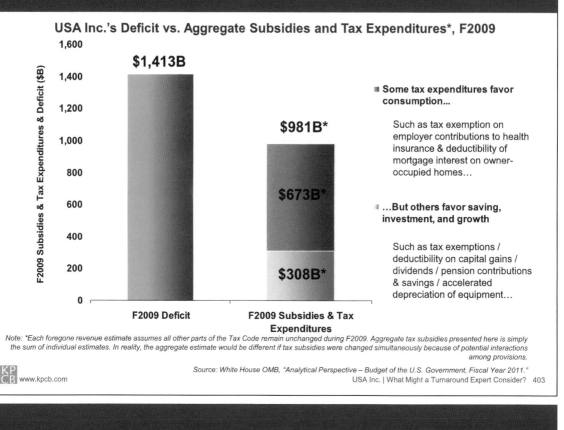

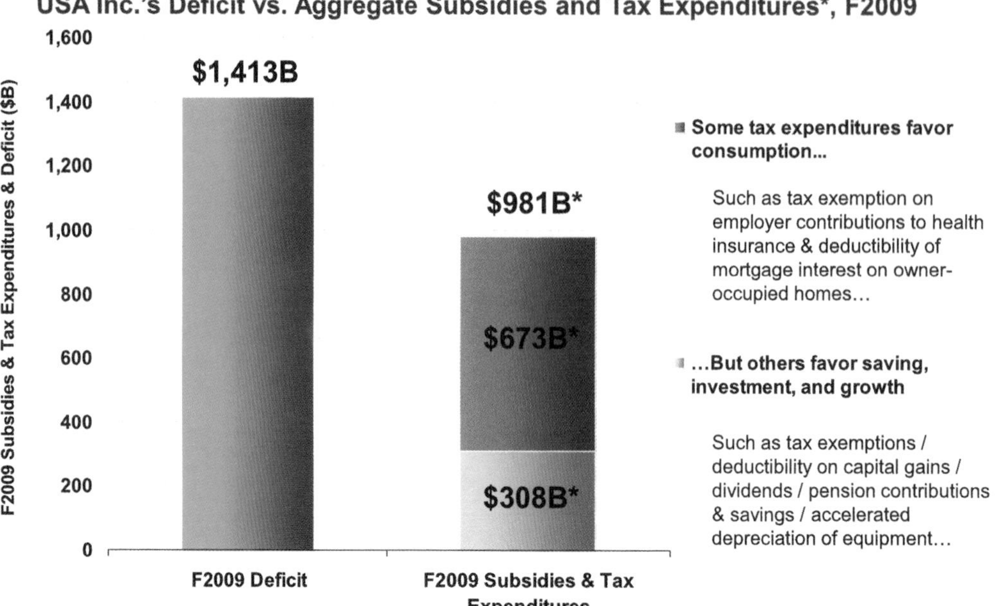

USA Inc.'s Deficit vs. Aggregate Subsidies and Tax Expenditures*, F2009
F2009 Subsidies & Tax Expenditures & Deficit ($B)
1,600
1,400
1,200
1,000
800
600
400
200
0
$1,413B
$981B*
$673B*
$308B*
F2009 Deficit
F2009 Subsidies & Tax Expenditures
Some tax expenditures favor consumption...
Such as tax exemption on employer contributions to health insurance & deductibility of mortgage interest on owner-occupied homes…
...But others favor saving, investment, and growth
Such as tax exemptions / deductibility on capital gains / dividends / pension contributions & savings / accelerated depreciation of equipment…

*Note: *Each foregone revenue estimate assumes all other parts of the Tax Code remain unchanged during F2009. Aggregate tax subsidies presented here is simply the sum of individual estimates. In reality, the aggregate estimate would be different if tax subsidies were changed simultaneously because of potential interactions among provisions.*

Source: White House OMB, "Analytical Perspective – Budget of the U.S. Government, Fiscal Year 2011."

Raising Revenue by Reducing Tax Expenditures & Subsidies: Examples

- **Reducing the biggest tax expenditures and subsidies could net $1.7 trillion in additional revenue over the next decade, per CBO and the Committee for a Responsible Federal Budget:**
  - **Reduce the tax exclusion for health insurance or replace with a credit**
  - **Cap the deduction for state and local taxes**
  - **Gradually reduce the mortgage interest deduction or change to a credit**
  - **Limit the tax benefit of other deductions, e.g., charitable contributions**
- **Some subsidies encourage saving or investment…and cutting them could mean short-term revenue gain but a net loss over time. Examples:**
  - **Favorable taxation of capital gains, dividends, and pension contributions**
  - **Exclude investment income from life insurance and annuities in taxable income**
  - **Accelerated depreciation or expensing of capital equipment outlays**

Source: Sources: Congressional Budget Office, Budget Options Volume 1: Health Care and Volume 2, 2009; Committee for a Responsible Federal Budget, Let's Get Specific: Tax Expenditures (October 2010)

USA's Unbalanced Economy – Personal Consumption (Driven in Part by Healthcare) = 71% of GDP vs. 62% From 1950 To 1980…

Personal Consumption as % of GDP, 1950 - 2009

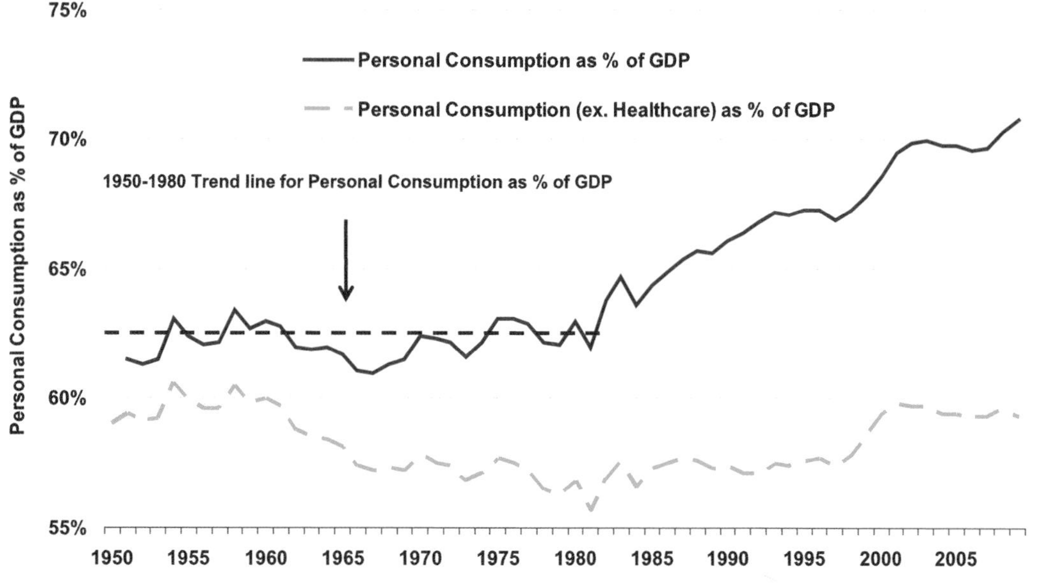

Note: Personal consumption includes household consumption of all goods and services. Source: BEA, Federal Reserve.

…USA's Unbalanced Economy – National Savings (Personal + Corporate + Government Savings) = -3% of GDP, vs. 10% From 1950 To 1980

USA Net Saving as % of GDP, 1950 - 2009

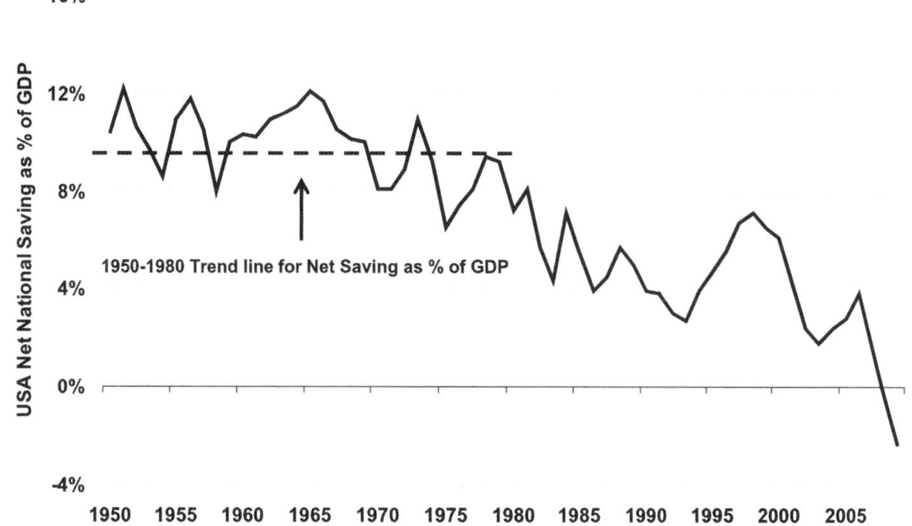

Note: National savings equal the aggregate savings by household, corporate and government sectors. Source: BEA, Federal Reserve.

Current Tax Policies Help Spur Consumption – USA's Taxes on Consumption of Goods & Services Lowest Among Peers

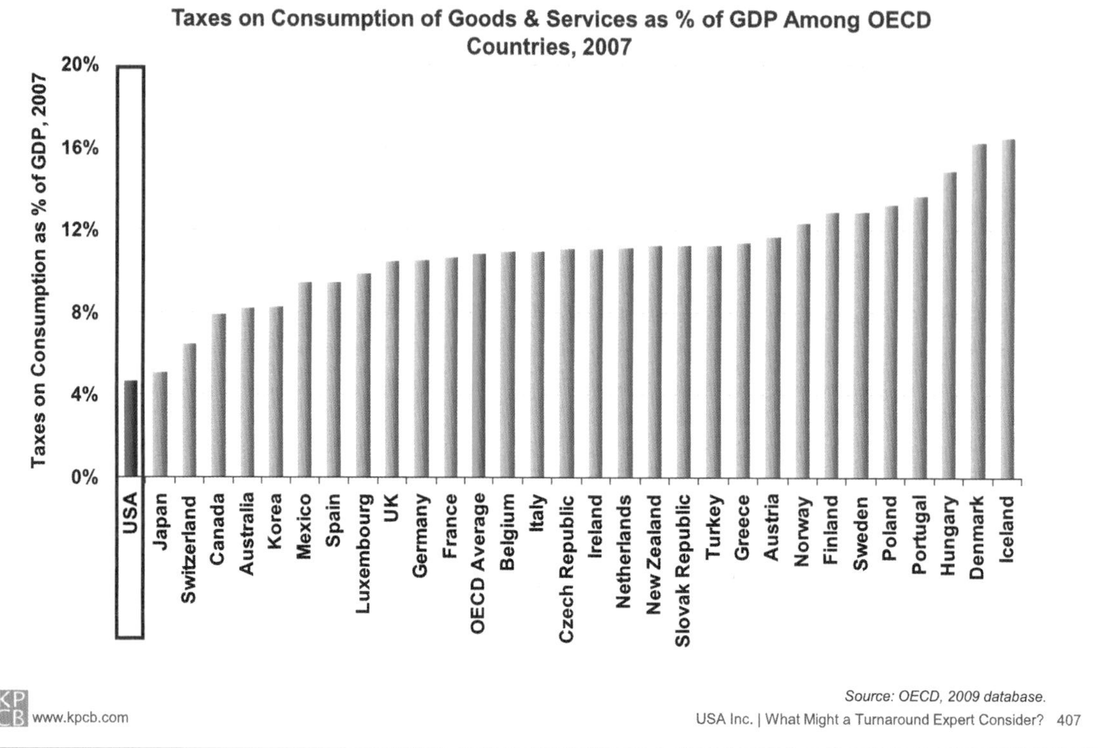

Source: OECD, 2009 database.

America's Resources Allocated to Housing + Healthcare Nearly Doubled as a Percent of GDP Since 1965, While Household and Government Savings Fell Dramatically

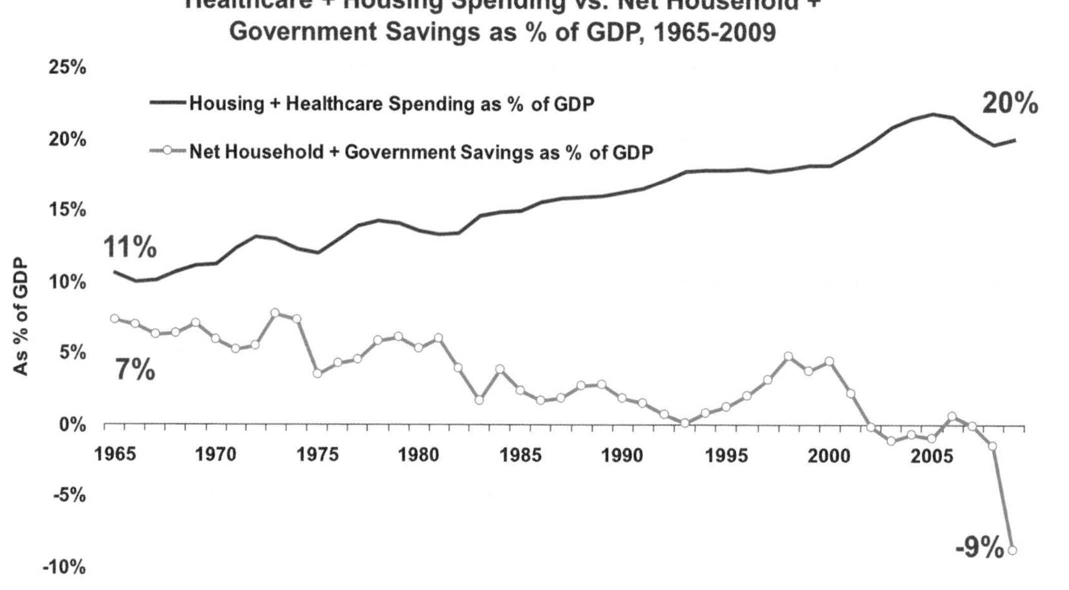

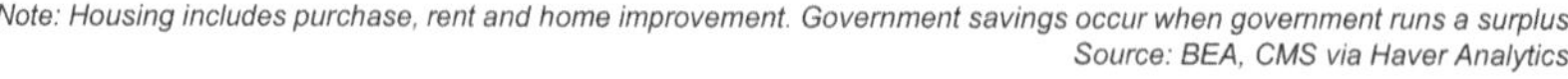
Note: Housing includes purchase, rent and home improvement. Government savings occur when government runs a surplus.

Source: BEA, CMS via Haver Analytics.

USA Income Taxes Higher, Consumption Taxes Lower Than OECD Peers

Government Tax Revenue as % of GDP, USA vs. OECD Average, 2007

Tax Type	USA	OECD Average	Variance (USA – OECD)
Individual Income Taxes	10.8%	9.4%	1.4%
Property Taxes	3.1	1.9	1.2
Other	4.7	5.0	-0.3
Corporate Income Taxes	3.1	3.9	-0.8
Social Security Taxes	6.6	9.1	-2.5
Value Added Taxes	--	6.5	-6.5
Total	**28.3%**	**35.8%**	**-7.5%**

Source: OECD Tax Database.

Tax Policy Options From Report of the National Commission on Fiscal Responsibility and Reform

- Consolidate the tax code into three individual income rates (15% / 25% / 35%) and one corporate income rate (26%)
- Eliminate the complex tax codes such as AMT[1], PEP[2], and Pease[3]
- Triple standard deduction to $30,000 ($15,000 for individuals)
- Repeal state & local tax deduction and miscellaneous itemized deductions
- Limit mortgage deduction to exclude 2nd residences, home equity loans, and mortgages over $500,000
- Limit charitable deduction with floor at 2% of Adjusted Gross Income
- Cap income tax exclusion for employer-provided healthcare at the amount of the actuarial value of Federal Employees Health Benefits Plan (FEHBP) standard option
- Permanently extend the research tax credit for businesses
- Eliminate and modify several business tax expenditures (domestic production deduction / LIFO[4] method of accounting / energy tax preferences for the oil and gas industry / depreciation rules)
- International tax reform including a territorial system[5]

Note: 1) AMT is the Alternative Minimum Tax; 2) PEP is Personal Exemption Phase-out designed to eliminate personal income exemptions for high earners; 3) Pease is a similar phase-out, but instead of applying to personal exemption, it applies to most of the itemized deductions of a taxpayer's claims (mortgage interest, charitable gifts, state & local taxes paid, etc.); Pease is named after Representative Donald Pease (D-OH) who pushed for its enactment in 1990. 4) LIFO is 'Last In, First Out' which tend to reduce corporations' income taxes in times of inflation. 5) A territorial tax system is a tax system that taxes only income that is created within the borders of a specific territory (usually a country). Source: National Commission on Fiscal Responsibility and Reform, "The Moment of Truth: Report of the National Commission on Fiscal Responsibility and Reform," 12/1/10. Note that the Report also identified two other scenarios called the 'The Zero Plan' which eliminates all tax expenditures and 'Tax Reform Trigger' which forces Congress to undertake comprehensive tax reform by 2012 by raising taxes for each year Congress fails to act.

This page is intentionally left blank.

This page is intentionally left blank.

Consequences of Inaction

To Take a Step Back…

- **We Asked the Question**
  - How would public shareholders view USA Inc.?
- **What Have We Found?**
  - USA Inc.'s finances – short-term and long-term, income statement and balance sheet – are challenged. Management's policies have created incentives to invest in healthcare, housing, and current consumption rather than in productive capital, education, and technology – the tools needed to compete in the global marketplace.

Consequences of Inaction – Investor Perspective

- **Short Term, No Problem Yet**
  - Global bond investors, in part, have looked past USA Inc.'s deteriorating financials because growth, inflation, and Fed purchases matter more, and because income statements and balance sheets of many other developed countries (such as Greece / Spain / Portugal / Ireland) are worse.
- **Long Term, Consequences of Inaction Could Be Severe**
  - If USA Inc.'s "managers" and "board" continue to ignore rising unfunded entitlement spending, investors could eventually demand a higher return to lend money to USA Inc. – leading to rising bond yields / higher borrowing costs for USA Inc. At some point, USA Inc.'s currency could also weaken significantly.

Source: Richard Berner, "America's Fiscal Train Wreck" (7/2/2009), Morgan Stanley Research.

For Perspective, USA Inc.'s 55% Public Debt as % of GDP (2009) is in Middle of Pack When Compared with 'Top 25' Global Peers, Though Rising to 90% 'Warning' Level*

Rank	Country	2009 Net Debt Outstanding ($B)	Y/Y	As % of World Total	Net Debt as % of GDP 2009	2005	05-09 Change	2009 GDP ($B)	Y/Y	As % of World Total	2009 Budget Surplus / Deficit ($B)	As % of World Gross Deficit	2009 Unemploy-ment Rate	Y/Y (pps)
1	Japan	$9,149	12%	26%	181%	162%	19%	$5,049	-5%	9%	-960	33%	5%	+1
2	Italy	2,434	0	7	116	106	11	2,090	-5	4	-0	--	8	+1
3	Greece	374	8	1	111	99	12	338	-2	1	-27	1	9	+2
4	Belgium	454	0	1	98	92	6	461	-3	1	-1	0	8	+1
5	France	2,028	5	6	77	66	11	2,635	-2	5	-105	4	9	+2
6	Germany	2,423	1	7	75	68	7	3,235	-5	6	-16	1	7	+0
7	Austria	263	2	1	70	64	6	374	-4	1	-5	0	5	+1
8	India	854	-3	2	69	80	-12	1,243	6	2	31	--	--	--
9	UK	1,444	3	4	66	42	24	2,198	-5	4	-49	2	7	+2
10	Canada	870	-5	3	66	70	-4	1,319	-3	2	44	--	8	+2
11	Netherlands	503	-1	1	64	52	12	790	-4	1	4	--	4	+1
12	Argentina	178	-7	1	59	59	0	301	1	1	14	--	--	--
13	USA	7,811	23	23	55	37	17	14,266	-2	25	-1,438	50	9	+3
14	Poland	223	-11	1	53	47	6	423	2	1	26	--	--	--
15	Spain	757	20	2	53	43	10	1,438	-4	2	-125	4	18	+7
16	Norway	187	-17	1	51	45	6	369	-2	1	38	--	3	+1
17	Sweden	175	-5	1	44	51	-7	398	-4	1	9	--	8	+2
18	Brazil	650	-6	2	44	44	0	1,482	0	3	40	--	--	--
19	Switzerland	212	5	1	44	53	-9	484	-1	1	-10	0	4	+1
20	Denmark	125	7	0	40	38	3	308	-5	1	-8	0	3	+2
21	Turkey	219	-14	1	37	52	-15	594	-5	1	36	--	--	--
22	Australia	309	-3	1	34	36	-3	920	1	2	8	--	6	+1
23	Venezuela	95	11	0	27	27	0	353	-3	1	-9	0	--	--
24	China	609	7	2	13	18	-5	4,758	9	8	-38	1	--	--
25	Russia	92	-15	0	7	14	-7	1,255	-8	2	17	--	--	--
	Top 1-25	$32,438	0%	94%	55%	52%	3%	$47,081	-3%	81%	$2,790	97%	7%	+1
	Global	34,632	8	100	68	66	2	57,937	-2	100	2,885	100	7	+2

*Note: *Carmen Reinhart and Kenneth Rogoff observed from 3,700 historical annual data points from 44 countries that the relationship between government debt and real GDP growth is weak for debt/GDP ratios below a threshold of 90 percent of GDP. Above 90 percent, median growth rates fall by one percent, and average growth falls considerably more. . We note that while Reinhart and Rogoff's observations are based on 'gross debt' data, in the U.S., debt held by the public is closer to the European countries' definition of government gross debt. For more information, see Reinhart and Rogoff, "Growth in a Time of Debt," 1/10. Pps is percentage points. Source: IMF, Business Intelligence Monitor .*

On a Net Worth Basis, USA Inc. Also Sits in Middle of Pack vs. Western European Peer Governments

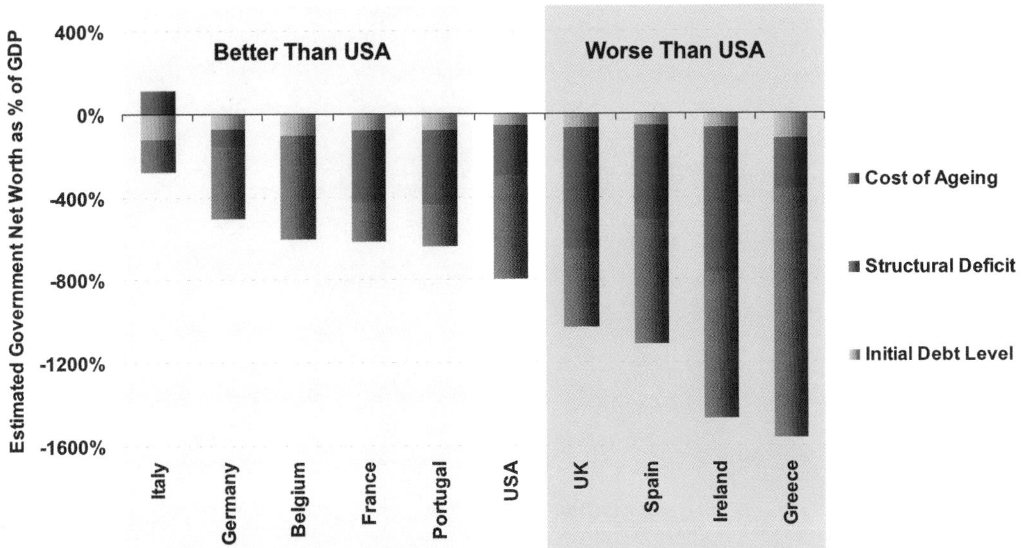

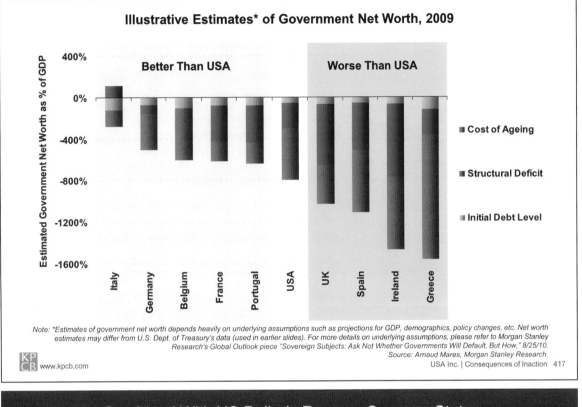

*Note: *Estimates of government net worth depends heavily on underlying assumptions such as projections for GDP, demographics, policy changes, etc. Net worth estimates may differ from U.S. Dept. of Treasury's data (used in earlier slides). For more details on underlying assumptions, please refer to Morgan Stanley Research's Global Outlook piece "Sovereign Subjects: Ask Not Whether Governments Will Default, But How," 8/25/10.*
Source: Arnaud Mares, Morgan Stanley Research.

Combined With US Dollar's Reserve Currency Status, Investors Still Prefer USA Inc.'s Debt, For Now

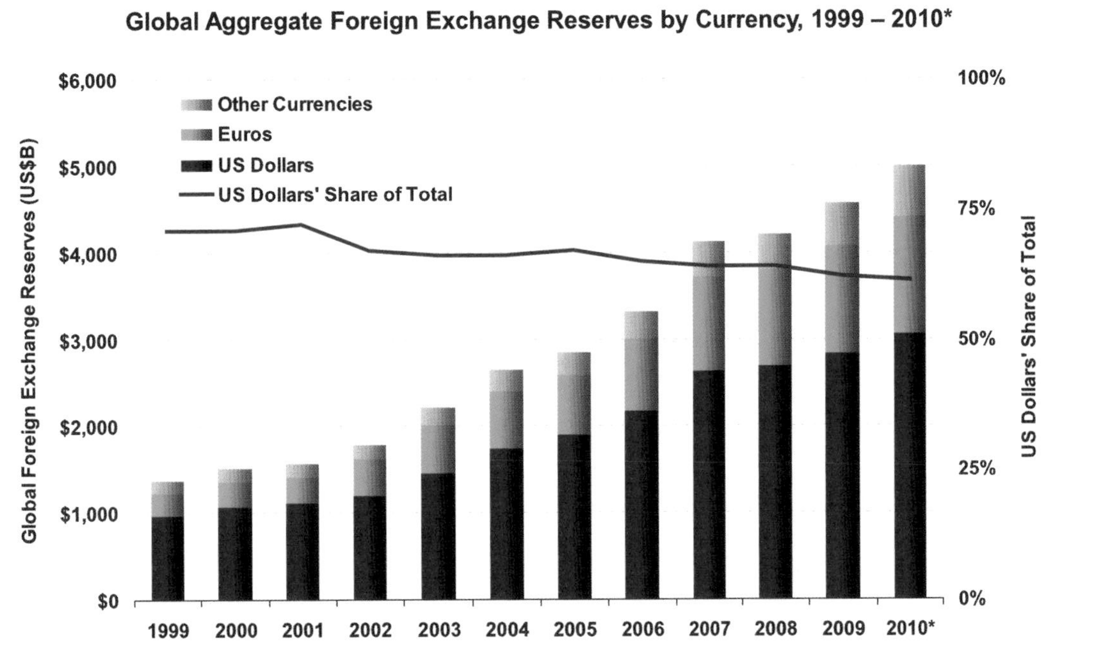

Note: 2010 data are preliminary and as of CQ3. Source: IMF.

However, in Longer Term, Credit Rating Agencies Have Begun to Worry About USA Inc.'s Debt Affordability

*On balance, we believe that the ratings of all large Aaa governments [including USA Inc.] remain well positioned, although their '**distance-to-downgrade' has in all cases substantially diminished**…Growth alone will not resolve an increasingly complicated debt equation…Preserving debt affordability at levels consistent with Aaa ratings will invariably require fiscal adjustments of a magnitude that, in some cases, will test social cohesion.* [1]

- Pierre Cailleteau

Managing Director of Sovereign Risk at Moody's, 3/16/2010

…if there are not offsetting measures to reverse the deterioration in negative fundamentals in the U.S., the likelihood of a negative outlook over the next two years will increase. [2]

Sarah Carlson,

Senior Analyst at Moody's, 1/14/2011

Sources: 1) Bloomberg, The New York Times; 2) The Wall Street Journal

Treasury Swap Spread[1] Turned Negative For First Time in History[2] – Now Cheaper for Some Private Companies to Borrow than USA Government

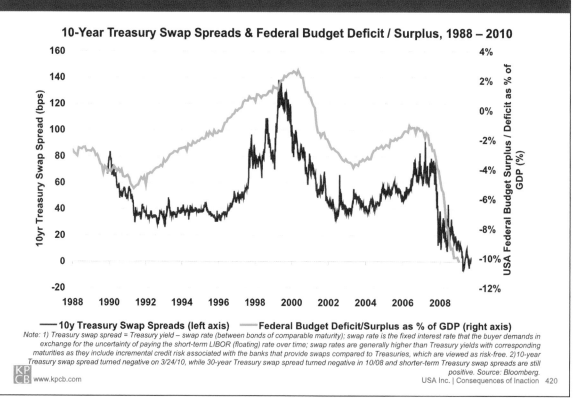

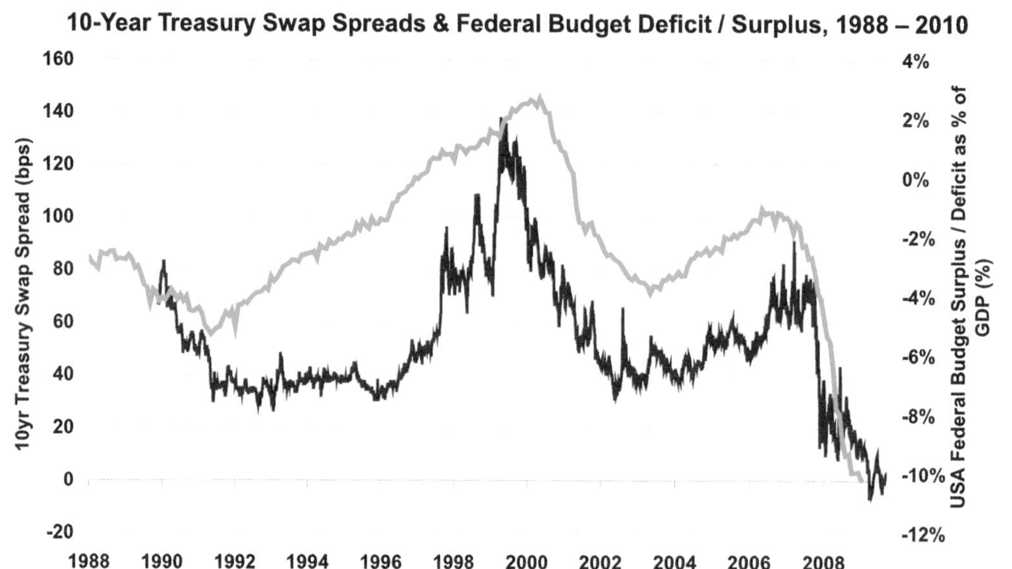

10y Treasury Swap Spreads (left axis) Federal Budget Deficit/Surplus as % of GDP (right axis)

Note: 1) Treasury swap spread = Treasury yield – swap rate (between bonds of comparable maturity); swap rate is the fixed interest rate that the buyer demands in exchange for the uncertainty of paying the short-term LIBOR (floating) rate over time; swap rates are generally higher than Treasury yields with corresponding maturities as they include incremental credit risk associated with the banks that provide swaps compared to Treasuries, which are viewed as risk-free. 2) 10-year Treasury swap spread turned negative on 3/24/10, while 30-year Treasury swap spread turned negative in 10/08 and shorter-term Treasury swap spreads are still positive. Source: Bloomberg.

Financial Challenges for Countries are Not Uncommon

Of course, there are no exact precedents for the financial challenges faced by America and many other countries in the world today.

Yet a quick overview of a few government and corporate financial crises may illustrate how managements have addressed – or failed to address – the problems of their day.

History Doesn't Repeat Itself, But It Often Rhymes[1] – What Can We Learn From These Credit Crises?

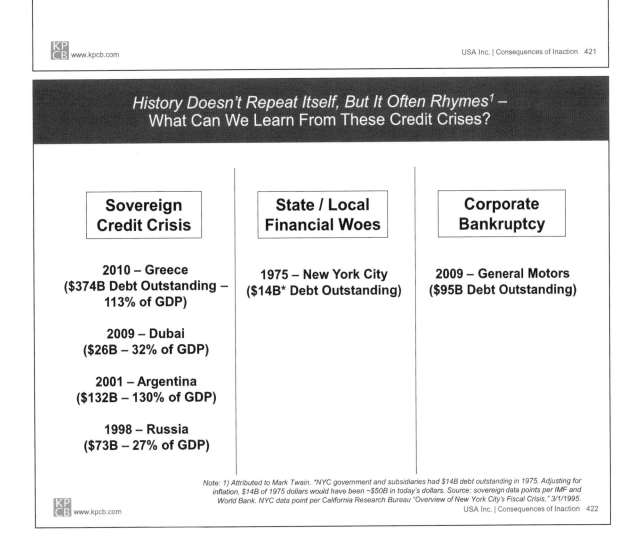

Sovereign Credit Crisis

2010 – Greece ($374B Debt Outstanding – 113% of GDP)

2009 – Dubai ($26B – 32% of GDP)

2001 – Argentina ($132B – 130% of GDP)

1998 – Russia ($73B – 27% of GDP)

State / Local Financial Woes

1975 – New York City ($14B* Debt Outstanding)

Corporate Bankruptcy

2009 – General Motors ($95B Debt Outstanding)

*Note: 1) Attributed to Mark Twain. *NYC government and subsidiaries had $14B debt outstanding in 1975. Adjusting for inflation, $14B of 1975 dollars would have been ~$50B in today's dollars. Source: sovereign data points per IMF and World Bank. NYC data point per California Research Bureau "Overview of New York City's Fiscal Crisis," 3/1/1995.*

Simple Pattern Recognition From Historical Debt Crisis Reveal Common Drivers (Leverage & Entitlements) + Triggers

	Year of Crisis	Debt Restructured		Long-Term Drivers	Short-Term Triggers	Key Stakeholders
		Amount	% of GDP			
Greece	2010	$374B	113%	Rising Underfunded Entitlement Spending	Financial Crisis	International Bond Investors
Dubai	2009	26B	32	Leveraged Construction / Real Estate Bubble	Financial Crisis	International Bond Investors
Argentina	2001	132B	130	Rising Underfunded Entitlement Spending + Currency Peg	Financial Crisis	International Bond Investors
Russia	1998	73B	27	Declining Productivity + Currency Peg	Financial Crisis	International Bond Investors
New York City	1975	14B[1]	--	Rising Underfunded Entitlement Spending	Recession	Bond Investors + Federal Government

Note: 1) NYC government and subsidiaries had $14B debt outstanding in 1975. Adjusting for inflation, $14B of 1975 dollars would have been ~$50B in today's dollars. Source: sovereign data points per IMF and World Bank. NYC data point per California Research Bureau "Overview of New York City's Fiscal Crisis," 3/1/1995.

Lessons Learned: Historical Debt Crisis

- **Rising Unfunded Entitlement Spending = Often a Long-Term Driver of Debt Crisis**
  - Countries such as Greece / Argentina and cities such as New York all nearly brought down by unfunded entitlement spending.
- **Financial Crisis / Economic Downturn = Often the Short-Term Trigger of Debt Crisis**
  - All cases had similar short-term triggers.
- **External Forces = Often Key Stakeholders in Crisis & Driving Ensuing Changes**
  - Most sovereign credit crises + ensuing reforms were driven by loss of confidence of international bond investors.
  - New York City's near default was driven by demands from bond holders + refusal of bailout from federal government.

While High Government Debt Levels Could Hasten Economic Recovery Post Recession, There Are Many Long-Term Negative Consequences

- **Crowding Out Investment ➔ Lower Output & Income**
  - A growing portion of people's savings would be diverted to purchase government debt rather than toward investment in productive capital goods.
- **Higher Interest Payments ➔ Higher Tax Rates & Lower Output & Income**
  - Government may be forced to raise marginal tax rates and / or reduce spending on other programs to meet interest payments.
- **Reduced Ability to Borrow ➔ Less Policy Flexibility**
  - In case of economic downturns or international crises, government may not be able to raise substantially more debt.
- **Increased Chance of Sudden Fiscal Crisis ➔ Social / Economic Disruption**
  - Investors may lose confidence in government's ability to repay debt & interest without causing inflation.

Source: Congressional Budget Office, "Federal Debt and the Risk of a Fiscal Crisis." 7/10.

Lessons Learned: For Countries Burdened by High Debt Levels, Austerity Measures are Necessary

	2009 Deficit as % of GDP	Gross Debt as % of GDP	2009-2010 Austerity Measures	New Revenue Streams
Greece	14%	113%	• Wage freeze & bonus cut of 14% on all public sector employees • Reduction in government contract workers • 11% reduction in pensions & Increase in retirement age to 65 from 58	• Joint IMF–EU bailout of $146B • Tax increases for VAT (+2%) / fuel / alcohol / cigarette (+10%) • Clamp down on tax evasion
Ireland	11%	66%	• 5-15% pay cut & 4% benefit reduction for all public sector employees • $1.5B+ broad spending cuts in healthcare & infrastructure	• Carbon tax on fuel • 1% tax rise on personal income about 120K euros
Spain	11%	54%	• Hiring freeze for public sectors • Increase of retirement age to 67 from 60 • Total budget cut of $70B 10-13E	• Sold $7B in new bonds
Portugal	9%	78%	• Wage freeze on all public sector employees • Reduce state payroll via attrition	• 50% bonus tax on top bank executives • Privatize state-owned industries

Source: Eurostat, European Commission, IMF, New York Times, Financial Times, BBC, Wall Street Journal.

European Countries (including Greece, Portugal, Ireland and Spain) Have Committed A Rising Share of GDP to 'Social Benefits' Over Past Decade

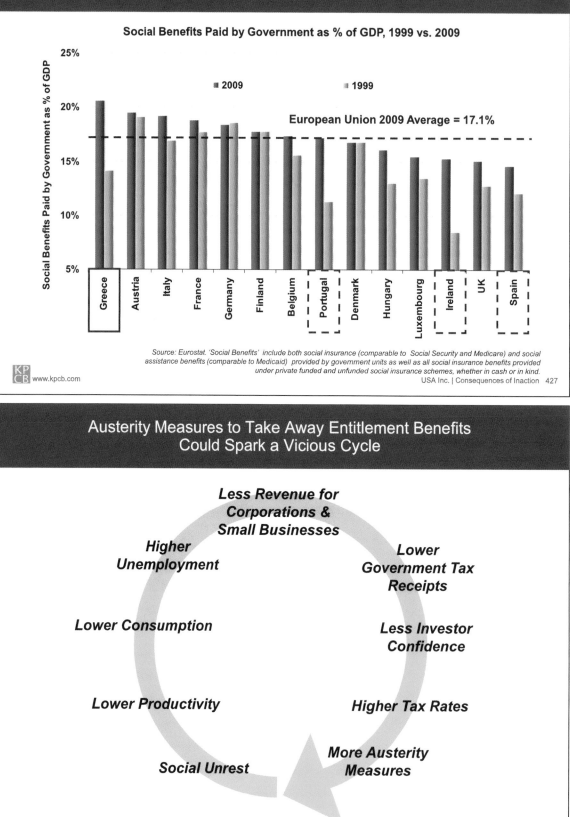

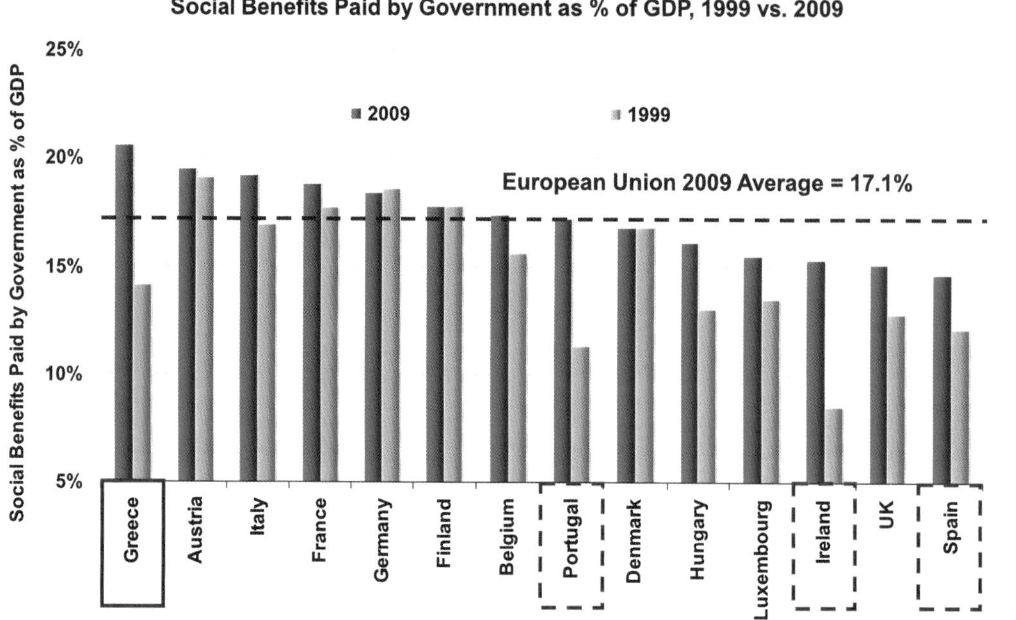

Source: Eurostat. 'Social Benefits' include both social insurance (comparable to Social Security and Medicare) and social assistance benefits (comparable to Medicaid) provided by government units as well as all social insurance benefits provided under private funded and unfunded social insurance schemes, whether in cash or in kind.

Austerity Measures to Take Away Entitlement Benefits Could Spark a Vicious Cycle

Less Revenue for Corporations & Small Businesses

Lower Government Tax Receipts

Less Investor Confidence

Higher Tax Rates

More Austerity Measures

Social Unrest

Lower Productivity

Lower Consumption

Higher Unemployment

Social Unrest Can Shake Investor Confidence And Contagion Can Spread

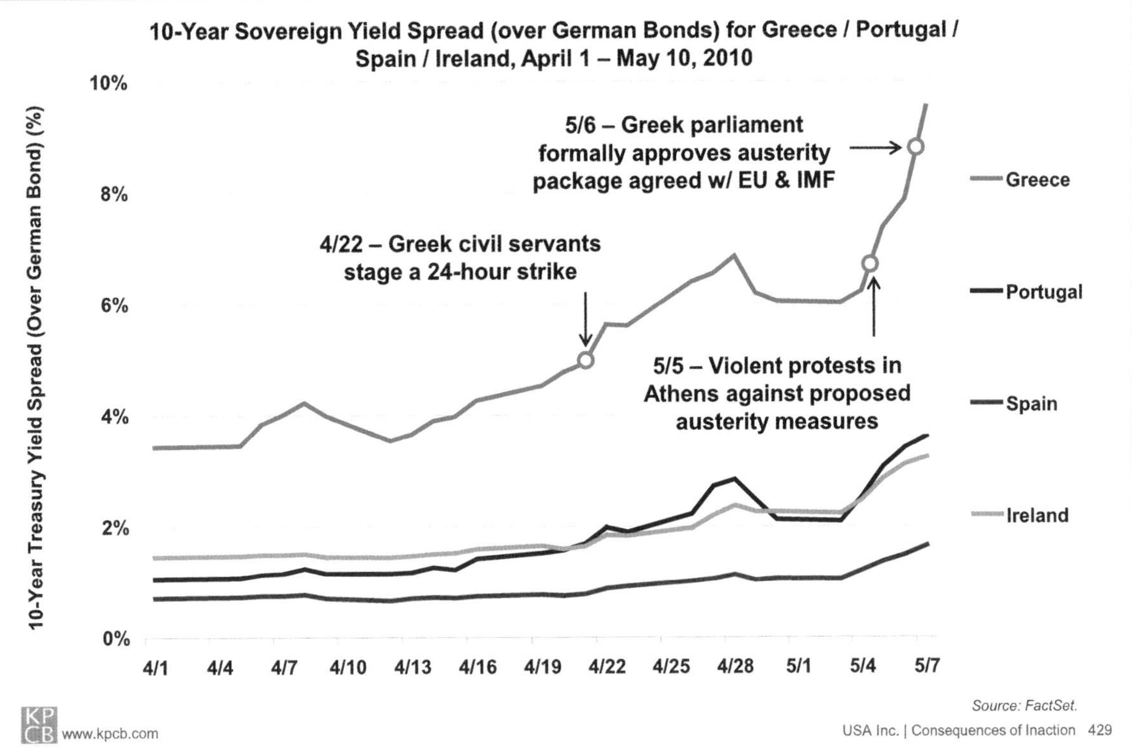

Source: *FactSet.*

Government Deficits and Changes in Sovereign Credit Default Swap Rates = Positively Correlated

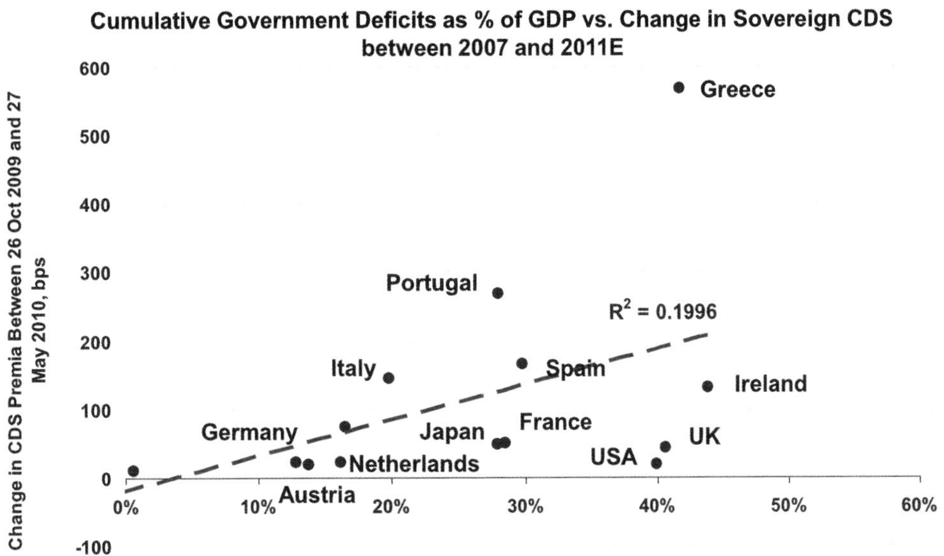

Cumulative Government Deficits as % of GDP for 2007-2011 (10-11 Projections)

Sources: *OECD; Markit; National Data*

When Corporations Like General Motors Run Out of Cash, Eventually They File for Bankruptcy

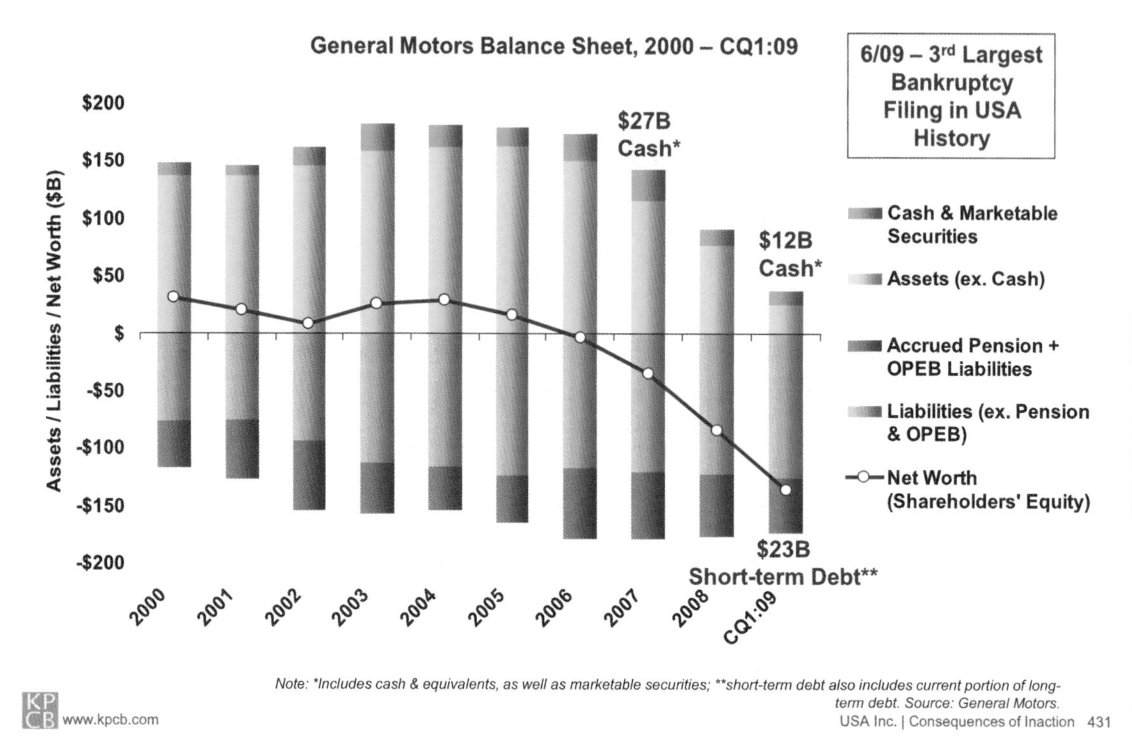

General Motors –
Entitlement Spending Became Too Onerous for this Great American Company

1908 – Founded in Flint, Michigan to manufacture automobiles

1954 – Shipped 50 millionth automobile

1988 – Free cash flow peaked at $6.3B

1999 – Reached a peak market capitalization of $61B

2006 – Revenue peaked at $207B

2009 – Filed for bankruptcy

Why did GM file for bankruptcy?

Products became increasingly uncompetitive. In addition, pension plans to support 650,000 retirees and their dependents (compared with 80,000 active employees in N. America as of 2010) rose to 4.8% of GM's annual expenses and $4,679 in annual pension payments per worker to former workers.

Source: General Motors, FactSet, DataStream, History News Network.

Comparing GM & USA, Inc…

	USA 2010	General Motors 2008	
Gross Debt as % of GDP	93%	82%	Gross Debt as % of Revenue[1]
Federal Spending as % of GDP	24	114	Total Cost as % of Revenue
Federal Budget Surplus as % of GDP	-9	-21	Net Income as % of Revenue
Interest Payments as % of GDP	1	2	Interest Payments as % of Revenue
% of Citizens Receiving Government Subsidy or on Government Payroll	36	75	% of Total GM Population[2] Dependent on the company

Note: 1) Gross debt of GM calculated as total liabilities – future OPEB & pension liabilities, as these liabilities are not reflected in USA gross debt. 2) % of total GM population dependent on the company = all living retirees / (living retirees + current workers). Source: White House Office of Management and Budget, OECD, Heritage Foundation, General Motors.

…Good News for GM Is It Has 'Taken Its Medicine' and Has Begun to Implement a Successful Turnaround

Basic Framework of GM Turnaround:

- **Focus on Expenses**
  - Eliminated some of the legacy entitlements - swapped employee healthcare for equity ownership.
  - Significantly changed operating efficiency - took out costs so that GM was able to operate at breakeven at bottom of the cycle and turn cash flow positive during other parts of its business cycle.
- **Focus on Revenue**
  - Changed business model to move away from lowering cost to improving vehicle quality, engineering and styling.

This page is intentionally left blank.

This page is intentionally left blank.

Summary

Highlights from F2010 USA Inc. Financials

- **Summary** – USA Inc. has challenges.
- **Cash Flow** – While recession depressed F2008-F2010 results, cash flow has been negative for 9 consecutive years ($4.8 trillion, cumulative), with no end to losses in sight. Negative cash flow implies that USA Inc. can't afford the services it is providing to 'customers,' many of whom are people with few alternatives.
- **Balance Sheet** – Net worth is negative and deteriorating.
- **Off-Balance Sheet Liabilities** – Off-balance sheet liabilities of at least $31 trillion (primarily unfunded Medicare and Social Security obligations) amount to nearly $3 for every $1 of debt on the books. Just as unfunded corporate pensions and other post-employment benefits (OPEB) weigh on public corporations, unfunded entitlements, over time, may increase USA Inc.'s cost of capital. And today's off-balance sheet liabilities will be tomorrow's on-balance sheet debt.
- **Conclusion** – Publicly traded companies with similar financial trends would be pressed by shareholders to pursue a turnaround. The good news: USA Inc.'s underlying asset base and entrepreneurial culture are strong. The financial trends can shift toward a positive direction, but both 'management' and 'shareholders' will need collective focus, willpower, commitment, and sacrifice.

Note: USA federal fiscal year ends in September; Cash flow = total revenue – total spending on a cash basis; net worth includes unfunded future liabilities from Social Security and Medicare on an accrual basis over the next 75 years. Source: cash flow per White House Office of Management and Budget; net worth per Dept. of Treasury, "2010 Financial Report of the U.S. Government," adjusted to include unfunded liabilities of Social Security and Medicare.

Drilldown on USA Inc. Financials...

- **To analysts looking at USA Inc. as a public corporation, the financials are challenged**
  - Excluding Medicare / Medicaid spending and one-time charges, USA Inc. has supported a 4% average net margin[1] over 15 years, but cash flow is deep in the red by negative $1.3 trillion last year (or -$11,000 per household), and net worth[2] is negative $44 trillion (or -$371,000 per household).
- **The main culprits: entitlement programs, mounting debt, and one-time charges**
  - Since the Great Depression, USA Inc. has steadily added "business lines" and, with the best of intentions, created various entitlement programs. Some of these serve the nation's poorest, whose struggles have been made worse by the financial crisis. Apart from Social Security and unemployment insurance, however, funding for these programs has been woefully inadequate – and getting worse.
  - Entitlement expenses (adjusted for inflation) rose 70% over the last 15 years, and USA Inc. entitlement spending now equals $16,600 per household per year; annual spending exceeds dedicated funding by more than $1 trillion (and rising). Net debt levels are approaching warning levels, and one-time charges only compound the problem.
  - Some consider defense spending a major cause of USA Inc.'s financial dilemma. Re-setting priorities and streamlining could yield savings – $788 billion by 2018, according to one recent study[3] – perhaps without damaging security. But entitlement spending has a bigger impact on USA Inc. financials. Although defense nearly doubled in the last decade, to 5% of GDP, it is still below its 7% share of GDP from 1948 to 2000. It accounted for 20% of the budget in 2010, but 41% of all government spending between 1789 and 1930.

Note: 1) Net margin defined as net income divided by total revenue; 2) net worth defined as assets (ex. stewardship assets like national parks and heritage assets like the Washington Monument) minus liabilities minus the net present value of unfunded entitlements (such as Social Security and Medicare), data per Treasury Dept.'s "2010 Annual Report on the U.S. Government"; 3) Gordon Adams and Matthew Leatherman, "A Leaner and Meaner National Defense," Foreign Affairs, Jan/Feb 2011)

...Drilldown on USA Inc. Financials...

- **Medicare and Medicaid, largely underfunded (based on 'dedicated' revenue) and growing rapidly, accounted for 21% (or $724B) of USA Inc.'s total expenses in F2010, up from 5% forty years ago**
  - Together, these two programs represent 35% of all (annual) US healthcare spending; Federal Medicaid spending has doubled in real terms over the last decade, to $273 billion annually.
- **Total government healthcare spending consumes 8.2% of GDP compared with just 1.3% fifty years ago; the new health reform law could increase USA Inc.'s budget deficit**
  - As government healthcare spending expands, USA Inc.'s red ink will get much worse if healthcare costs continue growing 2 percentage points faster than per capita income (as they have for 40 years).
- **Unemployment Insurance and Social Security are adequately funded...for now. The future, not so bright**
  - Demographic trends have exacerbated the funding problems for Medicare and Social Security – of the 102 million increased enrollment between 1965 and 2009, 42 million (or 41%) is due to an aging population. With a 26% longer life expectancy but a 3% increase in retirement age (since Social Security was created in 1935), deficits from Social Security could add $11.6 trillion (or 140%) to the public debt by 2037E, per Congressional Budget Office (CBO).

…Drilldown on USA Inc. Financials

- **If entitlement programs are not reformed, USA Inc.'s balance sheet will go from bad to worse**
  - Public debt has doubled over the last 30 years, to 62% of GDP. This ratio is expected to surpass the 90% threshold* – above which real GDP growth could slow considerably – in 10 years and could near 150% of GDP in 20 years if entitlement expenses continue to soar, per CBO.
  - As government healthcare spending expands, USA Inc.'s red ink will get much worse if healthcare costs continue growing 2 percentage points faster than per capita income (as they have for 40 years).
- **The turning point: Within 15 years (by 2025), entitlements plus net interest expenses will absorb all – yes, all – of USA Inc.'s annual revenue, per CBO**
  - That would require USA Inc. to borrow funds for defense, education, infrastructure, and R&D spending, which today account for 32% of USA Inc. spending (excluding one-time items), down dramatically from 69% forty years ago.
  - It's notable that CBO's projection from 10 years ago (in 1999) showed Federal revenue sufficient to support entitlement spending + interest payments until 2060E – 35 years later than current projection.

*Note: *Carmen Reinhart and Kenneth Rogoff observed from 3,700 historical annual data points from 44 countries that the relationship between government debt and real GDP growth is weak for debt/GDP ratios below a threshold of 90 percent of GDP. Above 90 percent, median growth rates fall by one percent, and average growth falls considerably more. We note that while Reinhart and Rogoff's observations are based on 'gross debt' data, in the U.S., debt held by the public is closer to the European countries' definition of government gross debt. For more information, see Reinhart and Rogoff, "Growth in a Time of Debt," 1/10.*

How Might One Think About Turning Around USA Inc.?...

- **Key focus areas would likely be reducing USA Inc.'s budget deficit and improving / restructuring the 'business model'…**
  - One would likely drill down on USA Inc.'s key revenue and expense drivers, then develop a basic analytical framework for 'normal' revenue / expenses, then compare options.

  Looking at history…
  - Annual growth in revenue of 3% has been roughly in line with GDP for 40 years* while corporate income taxes grew at 2%. Social insurance taxes (for Social Security / Medicare) grew 5% annually and now represent 37% of USA Inc. revenue, compared with 19% in 1965.
  - Annual growth in expenses of 3% has been roughly in line with revenue, but entitlements are up 5% per annum - and now absorb 51% of all USA Inc.'s expense - more than twice their share in 1965; defense and other discretionary spending growth has been just 1-2%.

  One might ask…
  - Should expense and revenue levels be re-thought and re-set so USA Inc. operates near break-even and expense growth (with needed puts and takes) matches GDP growth, thus adopting a 'don't spend more than you earn' approach to managing USA Inc.'s financials?

*Note: *We chose a 40-year period from 1965 to 2005 to examine 'normal' levels of revenue and expenses. We did not choose the most recent 40-year period (1969 to 2009) as USA was in deep recession in 2008 / 2009 and underwent significant tax policy fluctuations in 1968 /1969, so many metrics (like individual income and corporate profit) varied significantly from 'normal' levels.*

…How Might One Think About Turning Around USA Inc.?

One might consider…

- **Options for reducing expenses by focusing on entitlement reform and operating efficiency**
  - Formula changes could help Social Security's underfunding, but look too draconian for Medicare/Medicaid; the underlying healthcare cost dilemma requires business process restructuring and realigned incentives.
  - Resuming the 20-year trend line for lower Federal civilian employment, plus more flexible compensation systems and selective local outsourcing, could help streamline USA Inc.'s operations.
- **Options for increasing revenue by focusing on driving long-term GDP growth and changing tax policies**
  - USA Inc. should examine ways to invest in growth that provides a high return (ROI) via new investment in technology, education, and infrastructure and could stimulate productivity gains and employment growth.
  - Reducing tax subsidies (like exemptions on mortgage interest payments or healthcare benefits) and changing the tax system in other ways could increase USA Inc.'s revenue without raising income taxes to punitive – and self-defeating – levels. Such tax policy changes could help re-balance USA's economy between consumption and savings and re-orient business lines towards investment-led growth, though there are potential risks and drawbacks.
- **History suggests the long-term consequences of inaction could be severe**
  - USA Inc. has many assets, but it must start addressing its spending/debt challenges now.

Sizing Costs Related to USA Inc.'s Key Financial Challenges & Potential AND / OR Solutions

- **To create frameworks for discussion, the next slide summarizes USA Inc.'s various financial challenges and the projected future cost of each main expense driver.**
  - The estimated future cost is calculated as the net present value of expected 'dedicated' future income (such as payroll taxes) minus expected future expenses (such as benefits paid) over the next 75 years.
- **Then we ask the question: 'What can we do to solve these financial challenges?'**
  - The potential solutions include a range of simple *mathematical illustrations* (such as changing program characteristics or increasing tax rates) and/or *program-specific policy solutions* proposed or considered by lawmakers and agencies like the CBO (such as indexing Social Security initial benefits to growth in cost of living).
- **These mathematical illustrations are only a mechanical answer to key financial challenges and not realistic solutions. In reality, a combination of detailed policy changes will likely be required to bridge the future funding gap.**

Overview of USA Inc.'s Key Financial Challenges & Potential and/or Solutions

Rank	Financial Challenge	Net Present Cost[1] ($T / % of 2010 GDP)	Mathematical Illustrations and/or Potential Policy Solutions[2]
1	Medicaid	$35 Trillion[3] / 239%	• Isolate and address the drivers of medical cost inflation • Improve efficiency / productivity of healthcare system • Reduce coverage for optional benefits & optional enrollees
2	Medicare	$23 Trillion / 156%	• Reduce benefits • Increase Medicare tax rate • Isolate and address the drivers of medical cost inflation • Improve efficiency / productivity of healthcare system
3	Social Security	$8 Trillion / 54%	• Raise retirement age • Reduce benefits • Increase Social Security tax rate • Reduce future initial benefits by indexing to cost of living growth rather than wage growth • Subject benefits to means test to determine eligibility
4	Slow GDP / USA Revenue Growth	--	• Invest in technology / infrastructure / education • Remove tax & regulatory uncertainties to stimulate employment growth • Reduce subsidies and tax expenditures & broaden tax base
5	Government Inefficiencies	--	• Resume the 20-year trend line for lower Federal civilian employment • Implement more flexible compensation systems • Consolidate / selectively local outsource certain functions

Note: 1) Net Present Cost is calculated as the present value of expected future net liabilities (expected revenue minus expected costs) for each program / issue over the next 75 years, Medicare estimate per Dept. of Treasury, "2010 Financial Report of the U.S. Government," Social Security estimate per Social Security Trustees' Report (8/10). 2) For more details on potential solutions, see slides 252-410 or full USA Inc. presentation. 3) Medicaid does not have dedicated revenue source and its $35T net present cost excludes funding from general tax revenue, NPV analysis based on 3% discount rate applied to CBO's projection for annual inflation-adjusted expenses.

The Essence of America's Financial Conundrum & Math Problem?

While a hefty 80% of Americans indicate balancing the budget should be one of the country's top priorities, per a Peter G. Peterson Foundation survey in 11/09…

…only 12% of Americans support cutting spending on Medicare or Social Security, per a Pew Research Center survey, 2/11.

Some might call this 'having your cake and eating it too…'

The Challenge Before Us

Policymakers, businesses and citizens need to share responsibility for past failures and develop a plan for future successes.

Past generations of Americans have responded to major challenges with collective sacrifice and hard work.

Will ours also rise to the occasion?

Current Observations About America…

- **On many fronts, USA Inc. is in great shape, but it has one big problem – USA Inc. spends too much and, in effect, is maxing out its credit card. USA Inc. must address the problem.**
- In 2009, 64% of America's revenue went to Social Security, Medicare & Medicaid, compared with 31% in 1980 and 20% in 1970.
- Using current projections, 100% of America's revenue in 2025 will go to Social Security, Medicare, Medicaid and Net Interest Expense.
- This raises the question, 'How will America pay for the likes of education, national defense, homeland security, infrastructure improvement, R&D, law enforcement, postal service, etc.?'
- **USA Inc.'s fundamental tradeoff is that it must balance its FUTURE (education) with its PRESENT (national defense & homeland security) and its PAST (Social Security & Medicare & Medicaid).**

Source: 2009 data per White House OMB, 2025 forecast per CBO's Alternative Fiscal Scenario.

...Current Observations About America

- **It's Time to Rise to the Occasion, It's America's Tradition...**

- The essence of the 'American dream' is about the underdog succeeding / the turnaround story...every generation or so has an opportunity to rise to an occasion (and sacrifice) and show why America (and its democratic form of government) are great. For this generation, the biggest challenge may be staving off financial hardship.

- **Collective Sacrifice and Hard Work are the Two Inter-Related Ways out of USA Inc.'s Problems...**

This page is intentionally left blank.

This page is intentionally left blank.

This page is intentionally left blank.

Appendix

Appendix

Additional Datapoints on Federal Debt

Federal Debt Held by the Public vs. Gross Debt

- **Federal Debt Held by the Public ($9 Trillion Outstanding, 62% of GDP in 2010)**
  - Value of all federal securities sold to the public that are still outstanding.
  - Represents the cumulative effect of past federal borrowing on **today**'s economy and on the **current** federal budget.
  - Net interest payments represent a burden on **current** taxpayers.
- **Gross Debt ($14 Trillion Outstanding, 94% of GDP in 2010)**
  - Public debt + intragovernmental debt (related to entities including the Social Security Trust Fund and federal employee / veterans' pension fund) + net liability of GSEs (related to likes of Fannie Mae and Freddie Mac).
  - Represents a claim on both **current** and **future** resources.
- **We Focus on Public Debt Levels**
  - Public debt is the base for calculating net interest payments.
  - Gross debt level could be misleading (to take an extreme example, simply eliminating all trust funds without changing promised benefits for the associated programs would dramatically reduce gross debt from 94% of GDP to 62% of GDP without improving long-term fiscal outlook at all*).
  - In the future, when intragovernmental debt + net liability of GSEs begin demanding repayments, it is likely financed via material increases in public debt levels.

*Note: *for more details, see James R. Horney, "Recommendation That President's Fiscal Commission Focus on Gross Debt is Misguided," 5/27/10. Data source: White House OMB, CBO.*

Public Debt = Gross Debt – Intra-Governmental Holdings – Net Liabilities of Government-Sponsored Enterprises (GSEs)

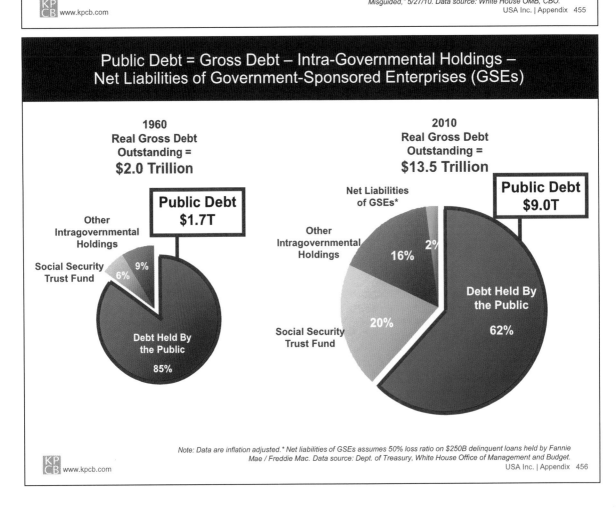

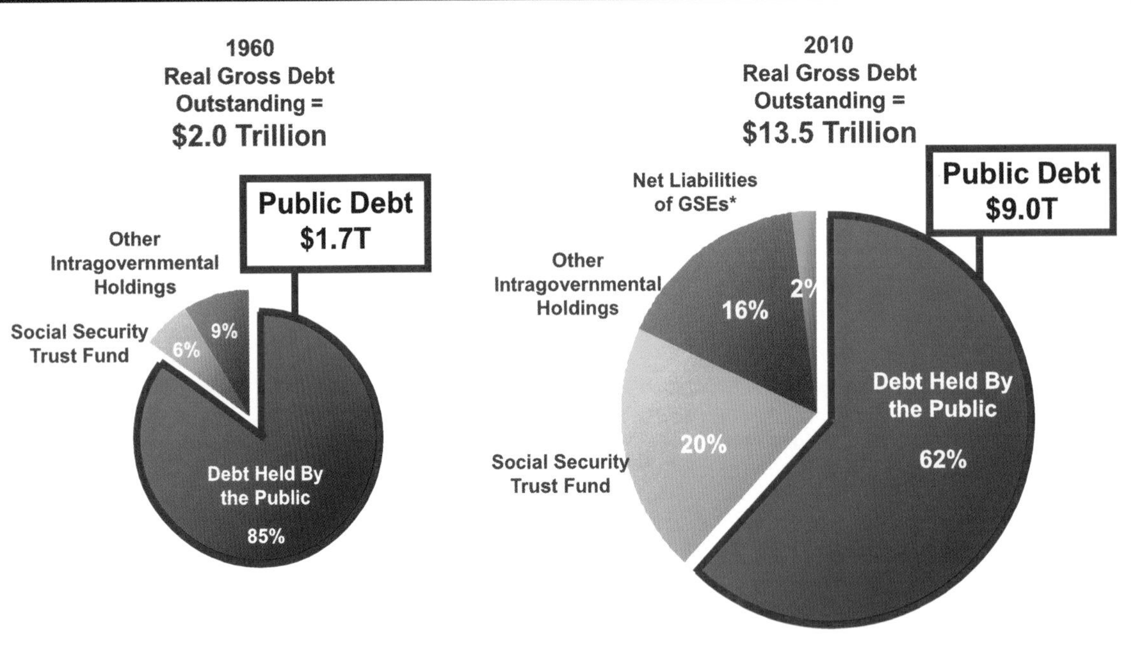

Note: Data are inflation adjusted. Net liabilities of GSEs assumes 50% loss ratio on $250B delinquent loans held by Fannie Mae / Freddie Mac. Data source: Dept. of Treasury, White House Office of Management and Budget.*

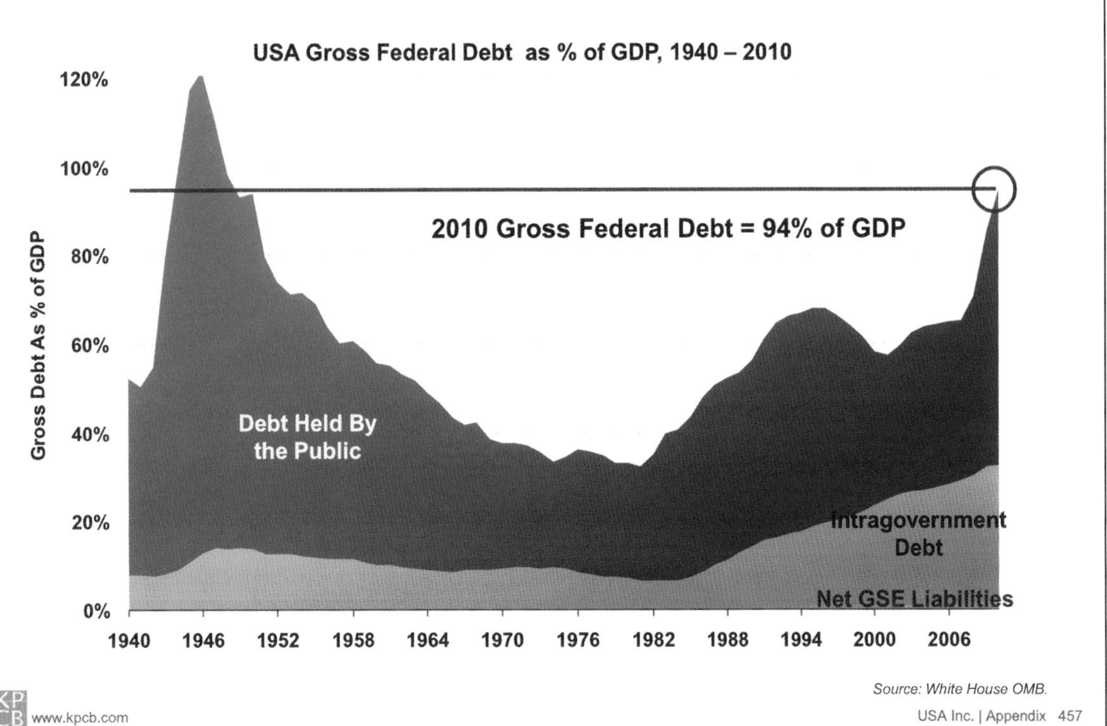
Gross Debt Level =
Approaching 100% of GDP
USA Gross Federal Debt as % of GDP, 1940 – 2010
2010 Gross Federal Debt = 94% of GDP
Gross Debt As % of GDP
120%
100%
80%
60%
40%
20%
0%
Debt Held By
the Public
Intragovernment
Debt
Net GSE Liabilities
1940
1946
1952
1958
1964
1970
1976
1982
1988
1994
2000
2006
Source: White House OMB.
www.kpcb.com
USA Inc. | Appendix 457

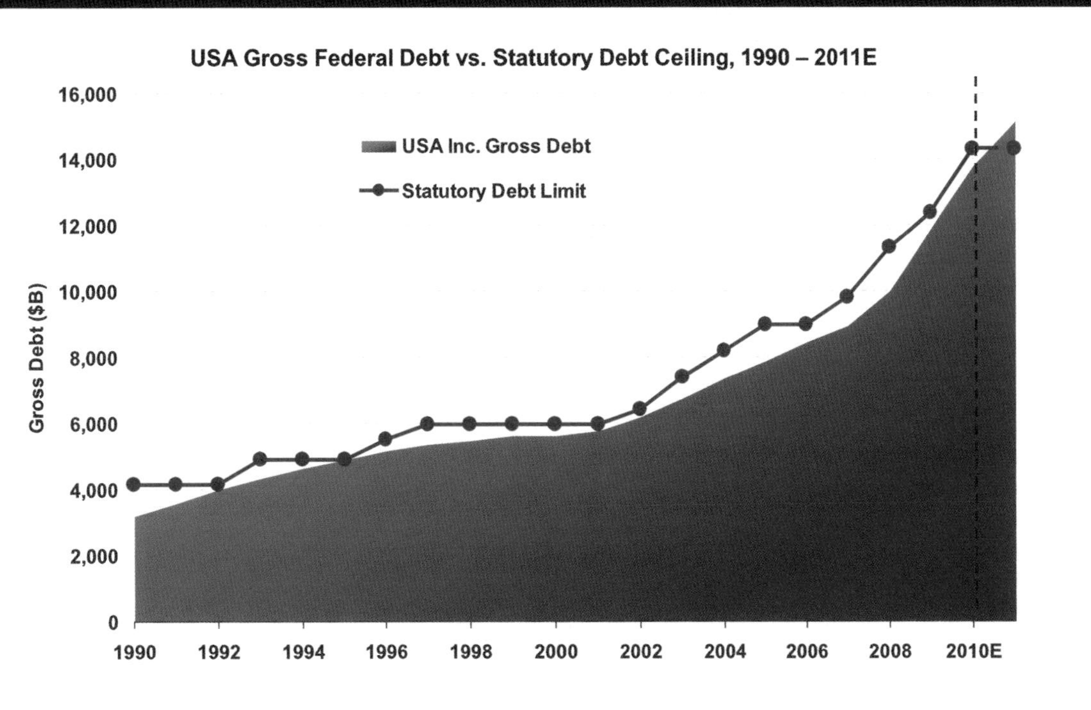
Gross Debt Level =
Would Exceed Current Statutory Limit of $1.43T* Within One Year
USA Gross Federal Debt vs. Statutory Debt Ceiling, 1990 – 2011E
USA Inc. Gross Debt
Statutory Debt Limit
Gross Debt ($B)
16,000
14,000
12,000
10,000
8,000
6,000
4,000
2,000
0
1990
1992
1994
1996
1998
2000
2002
2004
2006
2008
2010E
Note: * As of 1/11. Source: White House OMB.
www.kpcb.com
USA Inc. | Appendix 458

'Top 75' Countries Ranked by **Net Debt as % of GDP**...

Rank	Country	2009 Net Debt Outstanding ($B)	Y/Y	As % of World Total	Net Debt as % of GDP			2009 GDP ($B)	Y/Y	As % of World Total	2009 Budget Surplus / Deficit ($B)	As % of World Gross Deficit	2009 Unemploy-ment Rate	Y/Y (pps)
					2009	2005	05-09 Change							
1	Zimbabwe	$7	13%	0%	190%	--	--	$4	4%	0%	-$1	0%	--	--
2	Japan	9,149	12	26	181	162	19	5,049	-5	9	-960	33	5%	+1
3	Italy	2,434	0	7	116	106	11	2,090	-5	4	-0	--	8	+1
4	Singapore	186	3	1	114	99	15	163	-2	0	-5	0	3	+1
5	Greece	374	8	1	111	99	12	338	-2	1	-27	1	9	+2
6	Egypt	198	16	1	105	--	--	188	5	0	-27	1	--	--
7	Belgium	454	0	1	98	92	6	461	-3	1	-1	0	8	+1
8	Sudan	53	-6	0	97	--	--	54	5	0	4	--	--	--
9	Hungary	104	-8	0	84	62	22	124	-6	0	9	--	--	--
10	Cote d'Ivoire	19	-3	0	81	--	--	23	--	0	0	--	--	--
11	France	2,028	5	6	77	66	11	2,635	-2	5	-105	4	9	+2
12	Portugal	167	3	0	76	63	13	220	-3	0	-6	0	9	+2
13	Germany	2,423	1	7	75	68	7	3,235	-5	6	-16	1	7	0
14	Austria	263	2	1	70	64	6	374	-4	1	-5	0	5	+1
15	India	854	-3	2	69	80	-12	1,243	6	2	31	--	--	--
16	Uruguay	21	-2	0	67	67	0	32	3	0	0	--	--	--
17	UK	1,444	3	4	66	42	24	2,198	-5	4	-49	2	7	+2
18	Canada	870	-5	3	66	70	-4	1,319	-3	2	44	--	8	+2
19	Netherlands	503	-1	1	64	52	12	790	-4	1	4	--	4	+1
20	Morocco	58	2	0	64	--	--	91	5	0	-1	0	--	--
21	Ireland	140	19	0	62	27	34	227	-7	0	-23	1	12	+6
22	Albania	7	-3	0	60	57	3	12	3	0	0	--	--	--
23	Argentina	178	-7	1	59	59	0	301	1	1	14	--	--	--
24	Philippines	93	-2	0	59	71	-13	159	1	0	2	--	--	--
25	USA	7,811	23	23	55	37	17	14,266	-2	25	-1,438	50	9	+3
	Top 1-25	$29,836	1%	86%	75%	67%	8%	$35,595	-2%	61%	$2,662	92%	8%	1
	Global	34,632	8	100	68	66	2	57,937	-2	100	2,886	100	7	2

Source: IMF, Business Intelligence Monitor .

...'Top 75' Countries Ranked by **Net Debt as % of GDP**...

Rank	Country	2009 Net Debt Outstanding ($B)	Y/Y	As % of World Total	Net Debt as % of GDP			2009 GDP ($B)	Y/Y	As % of World Total	2009 Budget Surplus / Deficit ($B)	As % of World Gross Deficit	2009 Unemploy-ment Rate	Y/Y (pps)
					2009	2005	05-09 Change							
26	Tunisia	$22	-3%	0%	55%	55	0	$40	3%	0%	1	0	--	--
27	Ethiopia	18	29	0	55	--	--	34	10	0	-4	0	--	--
28	Colombia	123	-5	0	54	54	0	229	0	0	7	--	--	--
29	Cyprus	12	2	0	54	68	-14	23	-2	0	-0	--	5	+2
30	Poland	223	-11	1	53	47	6	423	2	1	26	--	--	--
31	Spain	757	20	2	53	43	10	1,438	-4	2	-125	4	18	+7
32	Kenya	15	2	0	51	--	--	30	2	0	-0	0	--	--
33	Norway	187	-17	1	51	45	6	369	-2	1	38	--	3	+1
34	Ghana	7	-11	0	48	--	--	15	4	0	1	--	--	--
35	Bolivia	8	6	0	46	46	0	18	3	0	-0	--	--	--
36	Sweden	175	-5	1	44	51	-7	398	-4	1	9	--	8	+2
37	Brazil	650	-6	2	44	44	0	1,482	0	3	40	--	--	--
38	Switzerland	212	5	1	44	53	-9	484	-1	1	-10	0	4	+1
39	Latvia	10	56	0	43	12	30	24	-18	0	-4	0	--	--
40	Malawi	2	15	0	42	--	--	5	8	0	-0	0	--	--
41	Malaysia	84	0	0	41	44	-3	207	-2	0	0	--	--	--
42	Denmark	125	7	0	40	38	3	308	-5	1	-8	0	3	+2
43	Gabon	4	-25	0	38	--	--	11	-1	0	1	--	--	--
44	Finland	91	-2	0	37	42	-4	242	-8	0	2	--	8	+2
45	Turkey	219	-14	1	37	52	-15	594	-5	1	36	--	--	--
46	Czech Republic	68	6	0	36	30	6	190	-4	0	-4	0	7	+2
47	Slovenia	17	43	0	35	27	8	50	-7	0	-5	0	6	+2
48	Slovakia	30	10	0	34	44	-10	88	-5	0	-3	0	--	--
49	Croatia	21	-5	0	34	38	-5	62	-6	0	1	--	--	--
50	Australia	309	-3	1	34	36	-3	920	1	2	8	--	6	+1
	Top 26-50	$3,392	0%	10%	44%	44%	0%	$7,682	-2%	13%	$164	6%	6%	2
	Global	34,632	8	100	68	66	2	57,937	-2	100	2,886	100	7	2

Source: IMF, Business Intelligence Monitor.

…'Top 75' Countries Ranked by **Net Debt as % of GDP**

Rank	Country	2009 Net Debt Outstanding ($B)	Y/Y	As % of World Total	Net Debt as % of GDP 2009	2005	05-09 Change	2009 GDP ($B)	Y/Y	As % of World Total	2009 Budget Surplus / Deficit ($B)	As % of World Gross Deficit	2009 Unemployment Rate	Y/Y (pps)
51	Zambia	$4	-16%	0%	32%	32	--	$12	6%	0%	1	--	--	--
52	Macedonia	3	1	0	31	47	-16	9	--	0	-0	0	--	--
53	Ecuador	17	2	0	30	30	0	56	0	0	-0	0	--	--
54	Lithuania	11	45	0	30	18	11	36	-15	0	-3	0	--	--
55	Peru	37	0	0	29	29	0	127	1	0	0	--	--	--
56	South Africa	78	0	0	28	--	--	277	-2	0	-0	0	--	--
57	Paraguay	4	-15	0	27	27	0	14	-5	0	1	--	--	--
58	**Venezuela**	**95**	**11**	**0**	**27**	**27**	**0**	**353**	**-3**	**1**	**-9**	**0**	**--**	**--**
59	New Zealand	29	-10	0	26	27	-1	110	-2	0	3	--	6	+2
60	Thailand	64	1	0	24	26	-2	266	-2	0	-0	0	--	--
61	Namibia	2	2	0	24	--	--	9	-1	0	-0	--	--	--
62	Tanzania	5	7	0	24	--	--	22	5	0	-0	0	--	--
63	Senegal	3	-6	0	23	--	--	13	2	0	0	--	--	--
64	Mozambique	2	-2	0	22	--	--	10	6	0	0	--	--	--
65	Romania	35	29	0	22	16	6	161	-7	0	-8	0	--	--
66	Uganda	3	8	0	21	--	--	16	7	0	-0	0	--	--
67	Bulgaria	7	-4	0	15	29	-14	45	-5	0	0	--	--	--
68	Nigeria	24	-20	0	15	--	--	165	6	0	6	--	--	--
69	Angola	10	-18	0	15	--	--	70	0	0	2	--	--	--
70	Cameroon	3	-8	0	14	--	--	22	2	0	0	--	--	--
71	**China**	**609**	**7**	**2**	**13**	**18**	**-5**	**4,758**	**9**	**8**	**-38**	**1**	**--**	**--**
72	Kazakhstan	11	3	0	11	--	--	107	1	0	-0	0	--	--
73	Algeria	13	-16	0	10	--	--	135	2	0	2	--	--	--
74	**Russia**	**92**	**-15**	**0**	**7**	**14**	**-7**	**1,255**	**-8**	**2**	**17**	**--**	**--**	**--**
75	Estonia	1	15	0	7	5	2	18	-14	0	-0	0	--	--
	Top 51-75	**$1,163**	**0%**	**3%**	**23%**	**27%**	**-4%**	**$8,064**	**0%**	**14%**	**$60**	**2%**	**6%**	**2**
	Global	**34,632**	**8**	**100**	**68**	**66**	**2**	**57,937**	**-2**	**100**	**2,886**	**100**	**7**	**2**

Note: China's net debt may be under-reported as it excludes potential liabilities from bad loans of state-owned banks.
Source: IMF, Business Intelligence Monitor.

OECD Countries Ranked by **Gross Debt as % of GDP**

Rank	Country	2009 Gross Debt Outstanding ($B)	Y/Y	As % of OECD Total	Gross Debt as % of GDP 2009	2005	05-09 Change	2009 GDP ($B)	Y/Y	As % of OECD Total
1	Japan	$974	14%	27%	193%	175%	18%	$5,049	-5%	13%
2	Italy	269	1	7	129	120	9	2,090	-5	5
3	Iceland	1	-8	0	123	53	70	12	-28	0
4	Greece	40	8	1	119	114	5	338	-2	1
5	Belgium	47	-1	1	101	96	5	461	-3	1
6	Portugal	19	4	1	87	74	13	220	-3	1
7	France	227	5	6	86	76	11	2,635	-2	7
8	Hungary	10	-13	0	84	69	16	124	-6	0
9	USA	1,184	17	32	83	61	22	14,266	-2	36
10	Canada	109	4	3	82	72	11	1,319	-3	3
11	Germany	247	-2	7	76	71	5	3,235	-5	8
12	UK	159	4	4	72	46	26	2,198	-5	6
13	Austria	26	-4	1	70	71	-1	374	-4	1
14	Ireland	16	23	0	70	33	38	227	-7	1
15	Netherlands	54	-6	1	69	61	7	790	-4	2
16	Spain	90	18	2	63	51	12	1,438	-4	4
17	Poland	25	-14	1	58	55	4	423	2	1
18	Finland	13	15	0	53	48	4	242	-8	1
19	Denmark	16	11	0	52	46	6	308	-5	1
20	Sweden	21	-8	1	52	60	-8	398	-4	1
21	Norway	18	-28	0	49	49	0	369	-2	1
22	Czech Republic	8	2	0	42	34	8	190	-4	0
23	Switzerland	20	-5	1	42	56	-15	484	-1	1
24	Slovakia	3	17	0	39	38	1	88	-5	0
25	New Zealand	4	3	0	35	27	8	110	-2	0
26	Korea	29	-3	1	35	27	8	833	-11	2
27	Australia	18	28	0	19	16	3	920	1	2
28	Luxembourg	1	-5	0	18	8	11	52	-11	0
	OECD Total	**$3,648**	**9%**	**100%**	**90%**	**76%**	**14%**	**$39,261**	**-4%**	**100%**

Note: Data for Slovenia and Estonia not available. Data may differ from Eurostat / national government figures. Gross debt data are not always comparable across countries due to different definitions or treatment of debt components. Notably, USA and Australia gross debt include the funded portion of government employee pension liabilities, which overstates their debt levels relative to other countries. Source: OECD.

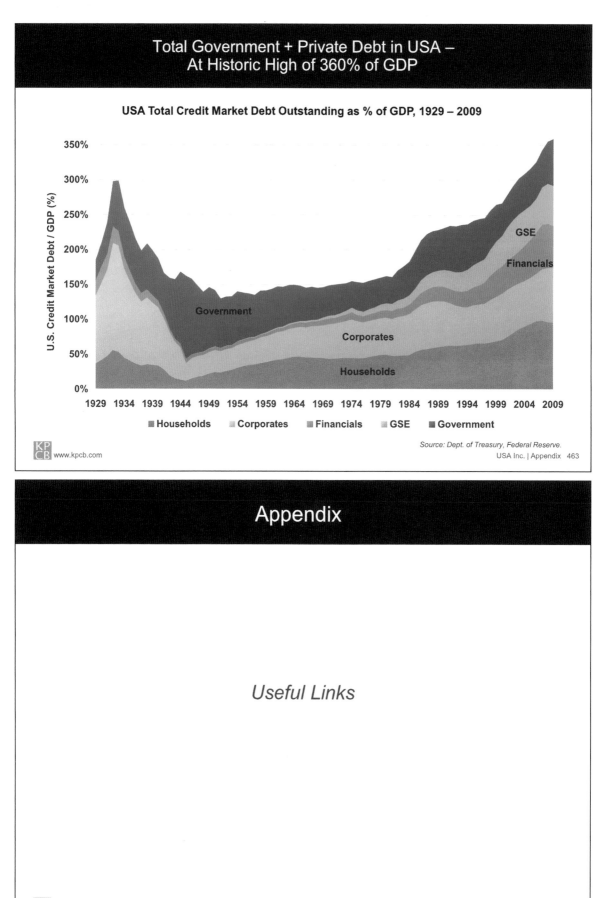

Total Government + Private Debt in USA – At Historic High of 360% of GDP

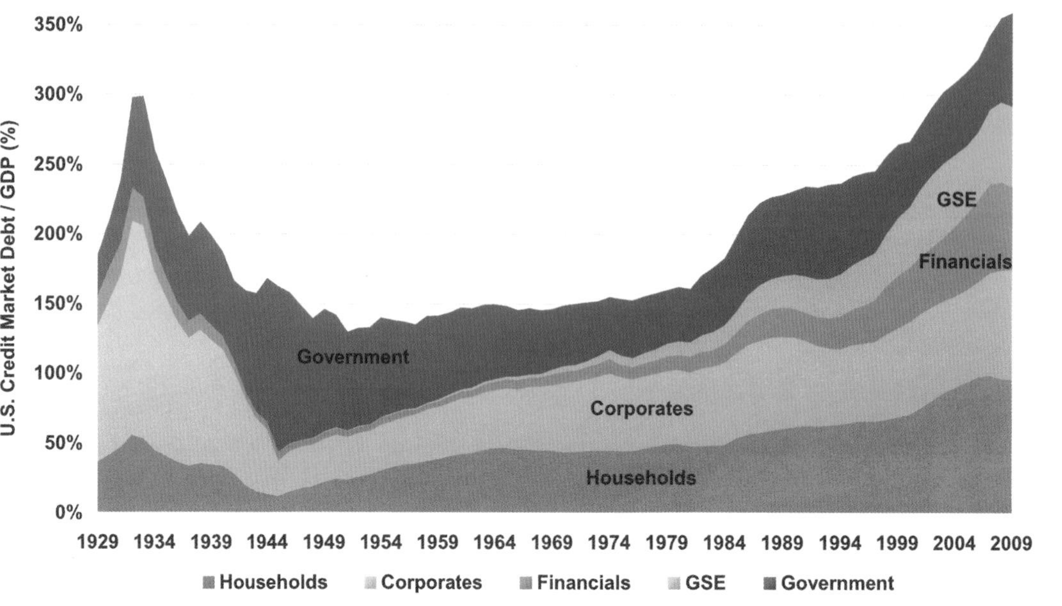

Source: Dept. of Treasury, Federal Reserve.

Appendix

Useful Links

Appendix – Useful Links

- Congressional Budget Office, "The Long-Term Budget Outlook," 6/2010 http://cbo.gov/doc.cfm?index=11579
- Congressional Budget Office, "Budget and Economic Outlook, Fiscal Years 2011 Through 2021," 1/2011 http://cbo.gov/doc.cfm?index=12039
- Department of Health & Human Services, Centers for Medicare & Medicaid Services, "The 2010 Annual Report of the Board of Trustees of the Federal Hospital Insurance and Federal Supplementary Medical Insurance Trust Funds," 8/5/2010 https://www.cms.gov/ReportsTrustFunds/downloads/tr2010.pdf
- Department of the Treasury, "2010 Financial Report of the United States Government," 12/2010 http://www.fms.treas.gov/fr/10frusg/10frusg.pdf
- National Commission on Fiscal Responsibility and Reform, "The Moment of Truth: Report of the National Commission on Fiscal Responsibility and Reform," 12/1/2010 http://www.fiscalcommission.gov/sites/fiscalcommission.gov/files/documents/TheMomentofTruth12_1_2010.pdf
- Social Security Administration, "The 2010 Annual Report of the Board of Trustees of the Federal Old-Age and Survivors Insurance and Federal Disability Insurance Trust Funds," 8/9/2010 http://www.ssa.gov/oact/tr/2010/tr2010.pdf
- White House Office of Management and Budget, "Budget of the United States Government, Fiscal Year 2012," 2/2011 http://www.whitehouse.gov/omb/budget/Overview/

Disclaimer

This report has been compiled by Mary Meeker and her co-contributors (collectively referred to below as the "Contributors") for informational purposes only. It is not intended to serve as the basis for investment, legal, political, tax or any other advice. Furthermore, this report is not to be construed as a solicitation or an offer to buy or sell securities in any entity, including any entity that is associated with the Contributors.

The information contained in this report has been compiled from public sources that the Contributors believe to be reliable. While the Contributors find no reason to believe that the data relied upon and presented in this report are factually incorrect, they have made no separate investigation or otherwise independently verified the accuracy of such data. As such, the Contributors cannot guarantee the accuracy of any of the data (raw or interpreted) and accordingly the Contributors make no warranties (express, implied or statutory) as to the information in this report.

This report summarizes a significant amount of publicly available data, and is not intended to be all-inclusive. The Contributors have complied this report based on selected sources that they believe to be most pertinent to the presented subject matter. Furthermore, the graphic illustrations are based on generalized calculations and are provided for illustrative purposes. Readers are encouraged to conduct their own analysis of the data underlying this report, as well as data from other sources, so as to come to their own conclusions.

The information presented in this report represents the view of the Contributors, and does not necessarily reflect the views of Kleiner Perkins Caufield & Byers or any of its associated management personnel, investment vehicles, investors, portfolio companies or any affiliates or associates of the foregoing.

This page is intentionally left blank.

This page is intentionally left blank.

Accountable Care Organization (ACO) - A health system model with the ability to provide, and manage with patients, the continuum of care across different institutional settings, including at least ambulatory (outpatient) and inpatient hospital care and possibly post acute care. ACOs have the capability of planning budgets and resources and are of sufficient size to support comprehensive, valid, and reliable performance measurement. The ACO model is one of the latest designs for managing healthcare costs and especially Medicare costs, and is gaining traction among policymakers desperate to control costs and boost quality in healthcare.

Accrual accounting - A system of accounting in which revenues are recorded when they are earned and outlays are recorded when goods are received or services are performed, even though the actual receipt of revenues and payment for goods or services may occur, in whole or in part, at a different time. Compare with cash accounting.

Adjusted Gross Income (AGI) - All income that is subject to taxation under the individual income tax after "above-the-line" deductions for such things as alimony payments and certain contributions to individual retirement accounts. Personal exemptions and the standard or itemized deductions are subtracted from AGI to determine taxable income

Alternative Minimum Tax (AMT) - A tax intended to limit the extent to which higher-income people can reduce their tax liability (the amount they owe) through the use of preferences in the tax code. Taxpayers subject to the AMT are required to recalculate their tax liability on the basis of a more limited set of exemptions, deductions, and tax credits than would normally apply. The amount by which a taxpayer's AMT calculation exceeds his or her regular tax calculation is that person's AMT liability.

American Recovery and Reinvestment Act of 2009 (ARRA) - This act provided appropriations for several federal programs and increased or extended some benefits payable under Medicaid, unemployment compensation, and nutrition assistance, among others. ARRA also reduced individual and corporate income taxes and made other changes to tax laws.

Asset-Backed Security - Security backed by real estate or another type of asset; a claim on an income flow, such as expected interest payments on loans, payments on leases, royalty payments, or receivables; a claim on the principal of a loan; or a claim on the expected appreciation of an asset.

Automatic Stabilizers - Taxes that decrease and expenditures that increase when the economy goes into a recession (and vice-versa when the economy booms) without requiring any action on the part of the government. Stabilizers tend to reduce the depth of recessions and dampen booms.

Bundled Payment (Healthcare) - Also known as episode-based payment, defined as the reimbursement of health care providers (such as hospitals and physicians) on the basis of expected costs for clinically-defined episodes of care. It has been described as "a middle ground" between fee-for-service reimbursement (in which providers are paid for each service rendered to a patient) and capitation (in which providers are paid a "lump sum" per patient regardless of how many services the patient receives).

Business Cycle - Fluctuations in overall business activity accompanied by swings in the unemployment rate, interest rates, and corporate profits. Over a business cycle, real (inflation-adjusted) activity rises to a peak (its highest level during the cycle) and then falls until it reaches a trough (its lowest level following the peak), whereupon it starts to rise again, defining a new cycle. Business cycles are irregular, varying in frequency, magnitude, and duration. (NBER) See real and unemployment rate.

Cash Accounting - A system of accounting in which revenues are recorded when they are actually received and outlays are recorded when payment is made. Compare with accrual accounting.

Centers for Medicare & Medicaid Services (CMS) – US federal agency which administers Medicare, Medicaid, and the Children's Health Insurance Program.

Copayment – A flat amount paid out of pocket per medical service, e.g., $5 per office visit.

Congressional Budget Office (CBO) – A non-partisan federal agency within the legislative branch of the U.S. government, charged with reviewing congressional budgets and other legislative initiatives with budgetary implications.

Conservatorship - The legal process by which an external entity (in the case of Fannie Mae and Freddie Mac, the federal government) establishes control and oversight of a company to put it in a sound and solvent condition.

Consumption - In principle, the value of goods and services purchased and used up during a given period by households and governments. In practice, the Bureau of Economic Analysis counts purchases of many long-lasting goods (such as cars and clothes) as consumption even though the goods are not used up. Consumption by households alone is also called consumer spending. See national income and product accounts.

Cost-of-Living Adjustment (COLA) - An annual increase in Social Security and other entitlement payments to reflect price inflation.

Current-Account Balance - A summary measure of a country's current transactions with the rest of the world, including net exports, net unilateral transfers, and net factor income (primarily the capital income from foreign property received by residents of a country offset by the capital income from property in that country flowing to residents of foreign countries).

Cyclical Deficit or Surplus - The part of the federal budget deficit or surplus that results from the business cycle. The cyclical component reflects the way in which the deficit or surplus automatically increases or decreases during economic expansions or recessions.

Cyclically Adjusted Budget Deficit or Surplus - The federal budget deficit or surplus that would occur under current law if the influence of the business cycle was removed—that is, if the economy operated at potential gross domestic product.

Debt - In the case of the federal government, the total value of outstanding bills, notes, bonds, and other debt instruments issued by the Treasury and other federal agencies. That debt is referred to as federal debt or gross debt. It has two components - debt held by the public (federal debt held by nonfederal investors, including the Federal Reserve System) and debt held by government accounts (federal debt held by federal government trust funds, deposit insurance funds, and other federal accounts). Debt subject to limit is federal debt that is subject to a statutory limit on the total amount issued. The limit applies to gross federal debt except for a small portion of the debt issued by the Treasury and the small amount of debt issued by other federal agencies (primarily the Tennessee Valley Authority and the Postal Service).

Deductible (Medical Insurance) - A fixed amount, usually expressed in dollars in the form of an annual fee, that the beneficiary of a health insurance plan must pay directly to the health care provider before a health insurance plan begins to pay for any costs associated with the insured medical service.

Deficit - The amount by which the federal government's total outlays exceed its total revenues in a given period, typically a fiscal year. The primary deficit is that total deficit excluding net interest.

Defined Benefit Pension Plan – Retirees receive predetermined monthly retirement benefits from employers despite the funding status / investment returns of their pension funds.

Defined Contribution Pension Plan – Retirees contribute specified amount to their pension funds and receive variable monthly retirement benefits depending on investment returns. Examples include Individual Retirement Accounts (IRAs) and 401(k) plans.

Disposable Personal Income - Personal income—the income that people receive, including transfer payments—minus the taxes and fees that people pay to governments.

Economic Stimulus - Federal fiscal or monetary policies aimed at promoting economic activity, used primarily during recessions. Such policies include reductions in taxes, increases in federal spending, reductions in interest rates, and other support for financial markets and institutions.

Entitlement - A legal obligation of the federal government to make payments to a person, group of people, business, unit of government, or similar entity that meets the eligibility criteria set in law and for which the budget authority is not provided in advance in an appropriation act. Spending for entitlement programs is controlled through those programs' eligibility criteria and benefit or payment rules. The best-known entitlements are the government's major benefit programs, such as Social Security and Medicare.

Excise Tax - A tax levied on the purchase of a specific type of good or service, such as tobacco products or air transportation services.

Federal Poverty Level (FPL) - Income amounts set each February by the U.S. Department of Health and Human Services used to determine an individual's or family's eligibility for various public programs, including Medicaid and the State Children's Health Insurance Program.

Federal Reserve System - The central bank of the United States. The Federal Reserve is responsible for setting the nation's monetary policy and overseeing credit conditions. See central bank and monetary policy.

Fiscal Policy - The government's tax and spending policies, which influence the amount and maturity of government debt as well as the level, composition, and distribution of national output and income. See debt.

Fiscal Year - A yearly accounting period. The federal government's fiscal year begins October 1 and ends September 30. Fiscal years are designated by the calendar years in which they end—for example, fiscal year 2011 will begin on October 1, 2010, and end on September 30, 2011.

GDP price index - A summary measure of the prices of all goods and services that make up gross domestic product. The change in the GDP price index is used as a measure of inflation in the overall economy.

General Fund - One category of federal funds in the government's accounting structure. The general fund records all revenues and offsetting receipts not earmarked by law for a specific purpose and all spending financed by those revenues and receipts.

Government-Sponsored Enterprise (GSE) - A financial institution created by federal law, generally though a federal charter, to carry out activities such as increasing credit availability for borrowers, reducing borrowing costs, or enhancing liquidity in particular sectors of the economy, notably agriculture and housing. Two housing GSEs (Fannie Mae and Freddie Mac) were taken into federal conservatorship in 2008.

Health Maintenance Organization (HMO) - A managed care plan that combines the function of insurer and provider to give members comprehensive health care from a network of affiliated providers. Enrollees typically pay limited copayments and are usually required to select a primary care physician through whom all care must be coordinated. HMOs generally will not reimburse all costs for services obtained from a non-network provider or without a primary care physician's referral. HMOs often emphasize prevention and careful assessment of medical necessity.

Independent Payment Advisory Board (IPAB) - A 15-member Independent Payment Advisory Board created under PPACA with significant authority with respect to Medicare payment rates. Beginning in 2014, in any year in which the Medicare per capita growth rate exceeded a target growth rate, the IPAB would be required to recommend Medicare spending reductions. The recommendations would become law unless Congress passed an alternative proposal that achieved the same level of budgetary savings. Subject to some limitations—hospitals, for example, would be exempt until 2020—the IPAB could recommend spending reductions affecting Medicare providers and suppliers, as well as Medicare Advantage and Prescription Drug Plans.

Labor Force - The number of people age 16 or older in the civilian non-institutional population who have jobs or who are available for work and are actively seeking jobs. (The civilian non-institutional population excludes members of the armed forces on active duty and people in penal or mental institutions or in homes for the elderly or infirm.) The labor force participation rate is the labor force as a percentage of the civilian non-institutional population age 16 or older.

Marginal Tax Rate - The tax rate that would apply to an additional dollar of a taxpayer's income. Compare with effective tax rate and statutory tax rate.

Medicaid - Public health insurance program that provides coverage for low-income persons for acute and long-term care. It is financed jointly by state and federal funds (the federal government pays at least 50 percent of the total cost in each state) and is administered by states within broad federal guidelines.

Medicare - Federal health insurance program for virtually all persons age 65 and older, and permanently disabled persons under age 65, who qualify by receiving Social Security Disability Insurance.

Mortgage-Backed Securities (MBSs) - Securities issued by financial institutions to investors with the payments of interest and principal backed by the payments on a package of mortgages. MBSs are structured by their sponsors to create multiple classes of claims, or tranches, of different seniority, based on the cash flows from the underlying mortgages. Investors holding securities in the safest, or most senior, tranche stand first in line to receive payments from borrowers and require the lowest contractual interest rate of all the tranches. Investors holding the least senior securities stand last in line to receive payments, after all more senior claims have been paid. Hence, they are first in line to absorb losses on the underlying mortgages. In return for assuming that risk, holders of the least senior tranche require the highest contractual interest rate of all the tranches.

National Commission on Fiscal Responsibility and Reform - A bipartisan commission created by President Obama to address the nation's fiscal challenges. The Commission is charged with identifying policies to improve the fiscal situation in the medium term and to achieve fiscal sustainability over the long run. Specifically, the Commission shall propose recommendations designed to balance the budget, excluding interest payments on the debt, by 2015. In addition, the Commission shall propose recommendations that meaningfully improve the long-run fiscal outlook, including changes to address the growth of entitlement spending and the gap between the projected revenues and expenditures of the Federal Government.

Net Interest - In the federal budget, net interest comprises the government's interest payments on debt held by the public (as recorded in budget function 900), offset by interest income that the government receives on loans and cash balances and by earnings of the National Railroad Retirement Investment Trust. See budget function and debt.

Office of Management and Budget (OMB) – White House office responsible for devising and submitting the president's annual budget proposal to Congress.

Organization for Economic Co-operation and Development (OECD) – An international organization of 31 developed and emerging countries (see list on slide 354) with a shared commitment to democracy and the market economy.

Other Post-Employment Benefits (OPEB) – An accounting concept created by the Governmental Accounting Standards Board (GASB) by pronouncements designed to address expenses that entities may or may not be legally bound to pay, but pay as a moral obligation (such as retirees' healthcare costs).

Pay-As-You-Go (PAYGO) - Procedures established in House and Senate rules that are intended to ensure that laws that affect direct spending or revenues are budget neutral. The Senate and the House have had such rules in place since 1993 and 2007, respectively.

PEP / Pease (Tax Policy) - PEP is Personal Exemption Phase-out designed to eliminate personal income exemptions for high earners; 3) Pease is a similar phase-out, but instead of applying to personal exemption, it applies to most of the itemized deductions of a taxpayer's claims (mortgage interest, charitable gifts, state & local taxes paid, etc.); Pease is named after Representative Donald Pease (D-OH) who pushed for its enactment in 1990.

Present Value - A single number that expresses a flow of current and future income (or payments) in terms of an equivalent lump sum received (or paid) today. The present value depends on the rate of interest used (the discount rate). For example, if $100 is invested on January 1 at an annual interest rate of 5 percent, it will grow to $105 by January 1 of the next year. Hence, at an annual 5 percent interest rate, the present value of $105 payable a year from today is $100.

Patient Protection and Affordable Care Act (PPACA) – A federal statute as the result of the healthcare reform. Signed into law on 3/23/10, the PPACA aims to expand Medicaid eligibility, incentivize businesses to provide health care benefits, prohibit denial of coverage/claims based on pre-existing conditions, establish health insurance exchanges, and support for medical research. The costs of these provisions are offset by a variety of taxes, fees, and cost-saving measures, such as new Medicare taxes for high-income brackets, taxes on indoor tanning, improved fairness in the Medicare Advantage program relative to traditional Medicare, and fees on medical devices and pharmaceutical companies.

Productivity - Average real output per unit of input. Labor productivity is average real output per hour of labor. The growth of labor productivity is defined as the growth of real output that is not explained by the growth of labor input alone. Total factor productivity is average real output per unit of combined labor and capital services. The growth of total factor productivity is defined as the growth of real output that is not explained by the growth of labor and capital. Labor productivity and total factor productivity differ in that increases in capital per worker raise labor productivity but not total factor productivity.

Tax Expenditures - Losses to the U.S. treasury from granting certain deductions, exemptions, or credits to specific categories of taxpayers. Tax breaks are one method Congress uses to promote certain policy objectives. For example, deductions for mortgages encourage home ownership, while credits for childcare expenses allow single parents to work. Tax expenditures are an alternative to direct government spending on policy programs.

Troubled Asset Relief Program (TARP) - A program that permits the Secretary of the Treasury to purchase or insure troubled financial assets. Authority for the program was initially set by the Emergency Economic Stabilization Act of 2008 at $700 billion in assets outstanding at any one time and remains in effect until October 3, 2010. The TARP's activities have included the purchase of preferred stock from financial institutions, support to automakers and related businesses, a program to avert housing foreclosures, and partnerships with the private sector.

Trust Funds - In the federal accounting structure, accounts designated by law as trust funds (regardless of any other meaning of that term). Trust funds record the revenues, offsetting receipts, or offsetting collections earmarked for the purpose of the fund, as well as budget authority and outlays of the fund that are financed by those revenues or receipts. The federal government has more than 200 trust funds. The largest and best known finance major benefit programs (including Social Security and Medicare) and infrastructure spending (such as the Highway Trust Fund and the Airport and Airway Trust Fund).

Made in the USA
Lexington, KY
17 March 2011